New York Times bestselling author Rebecca Zanetti has worked as an art curator, Senate aide, lawyer, college professor, and a hearing examiner – only to culminate it all in stories about Alpha males and the women who claim them. She writes dark paranormals, romantic suspense, and sexy contemporary romances.

Growing up amid the glorious backdrops and winter wonderlands of the Pacific Northwest has given Rebecca fantastic scenery and adventures to weave into her stories. She resides in the wild north with her husband, children, and extended family who inspire her every day – or at the very least give her plenty of characters to write about.

Find Rebecca at www.rebeccazanetti.com,
on Facebook at www.facebook.com/RebeccaZanetti.books
or on Twitter @RebeccaZanetti.

Just some of the reasons to fall for Rebecca Zanetti's powerful romances:

'Action packed, thrilling, and heart-stopping romantic suspense at its best'
Harlequin Junkie

'Zanetti pulls together a heady mix of sexy sizzle, emotional punch and high-stakes danger in this truly outstanding tale' *Romantic Times*

'A fast-paced, action-packed thriller that will have you on the edge of your seat the whole time' *Fresh Fiction*

'Rebecca Zanetti had me from the moment I read the description . . . I could barely breathe, let alone set down the book . . . you'll want to add Rebecca Zanetti to your must-read list too!' *The Best Reviews*

'Plenty of action, lots of steamy romance and even a few moments of laughter and tears . . . I was on the edge of my seat until the very last chapter' *K&T Book Reviews*

By Rebecca Zanetti

The Blood Brothers Series
Deadly Silence
Lethal Lies
Twisted Truths

The Sin Brothers Series
Forgotten Sins
Sweet Revenge
Blind Faith
Total Surrender

The Scorpius Syndrome Series
Mercury Striking
Shadow Falling
Justice Ascending

TWISTED TRUTHS
REBECCA ZANETTI

HEADLINE
ETERNAL

Published by arrangement with Forever,
an imprint of Grand Central Publishing.

First published in Great Britain in 2017
by HEADLINE ETERNAL
An imprint of HEADLINE PUBLISHING GROUP

1

Cataloguing in Publication Data is available from the British Library

ISBN 978 1 4722 4468 0

Typeset in 10.91/15.27 pt Granjon LT Std by Jouve (UK), Milton Keynes

Printed and bound in Great Britain by CPI Group (UK) Ltd, Croydon, CR0 4YY

Headline's policy is to use papers that are natural, renewable and
recyclable products and made from wood grown in well-managed forests
and other controlled sources. The logging and manufacturing processes
are expected to conform to the environmental regulations
of the country of origin.

HEADLINE PUBLISHING GROUP
An Hachette UK Company
Carmelite House
50 Victoria Embankment
London EC4Y 0DZ

www.headlineeternal.com
www.headline.co.uk
www.hachette.co.uk

This one is for Jillian Stein, who has saved my sanity throughout the last year. You're an amazing social media director and an even better friend. No matter what happens in this crazy life, we'll always have Michigan.

Acknowledgments

I'm thrilled to bring the third and final book of the Blood Brothers to readers, and I have many people to thank. This series and its predecessor, the Sin Brothers, found a wonderful home with Grand Central Forever, and I'm thankful to be able to work with such amazing people.

Thank you to my wonderful family, Big Tone, Karlina, and Gabe. I appreciate you telling people that I'm working out dialogue instead of honestly telling them I just talk to myself. Thank you for the support and understanding when I forget which day it is because I'm in the middle of a book. I love you immensely.

Thanks to my editor, Michele Bidelspach, who is so very insightful and hardworking. She puts incredible thought into every book, and I appreciate it so much. These Blood Brothers books have gotten RT Top Pick reviews and have won awards because of the editing, without question.

Thanks to Jodi Rosoff and Michelle Cashman for the brilliant and outside-the-box marketing. More specifically, thank you for getting me full-week speaker passes to Emerald City Comicon and San Diego Comic-Con. I kind of love you guys for that.

Thanks to Brian Lemus for the awesome covers, and thanks to Kallie Shimek, Yasmin Mathew, Dianna Stirpe, and Jessica Pierce from Grand Central Forever for their hard work.

Thank you to my agent, Caitlin Blasdell, who gives fantastic ad-

ACKNOWLEDGMENTS

vice across the board and who has been with me through six series. Thanks also to Liza Dawson and the entire Dawson gang for their hard work and support.

Thanks to Jillian Stein, Minga Portillo, Rebecca's Rebels, Writerspace, and Fresh Fiction for getting the word out about the books.

Thanks to my constant support system: Jim and Gail English, Travis and Debbie Smith, Donald and Stephanie West, Jonah and Jessica Namson, and Herb and Kathy Zanetti.

TWISTED TRUTHS

PROLOGUE

Twenty years ago

Denver sat in the front seat of the fancy car while the pretty lady drove through the small town, her nails a bright red against the white steering wheel. She'd said her name was Dr. Sylvia Daniels, she'd arrived at the boys home yesterday to meet him, and today she'd told him he had to go to get a physical. At least she hadn't come in the room with him when the doctor had checked him out.

The front seat was too big for him. He was small enough he was supposed to sit in the backseat, but he didn't want to argue with her.

"You're turning into such a big boy at only eight years old." She glanced at him, her eyes bluer than the ocean on television. "I know after speaking with you yesterday that you don't have selective mutism. You can talk if you want, correct?"

He nodded. But he rarely wanted to talk. Why bother?

She smiled. "I didn't get a chance to tell you yesterday that I'm sorry it took me so long to find you."

It had been his first day at the boys home. He bit his lip. She sounded super smart, and she knew he could talk, so it'd be rude not to try. "You were lookin' for me?"

She turned back to the road. "Yes." Her grip tightened until her knuckles were as white as the leather. "From the second you disappeared."

His stomach felt funny. Was that his fault? "I'm sorry." Sometimes if he said he was sorry, even if he didn't know why, he didn't get hit. Though a lady like her wouldn't hit as hard as his uncle, probably. "Really sorry."

Her chin lifted, and her dark hair bounced down her shoulders. "None of this is your fault."

Denver glanced out at the small stores on the quiet street. When the authorities had taken him out of school and driven him to the boys home, nobody had explained anything to him. "Um, where's my uncle?"

The lady turned toward him. "Do you care?"

Denver lifted one shoulder. He didn't like getting hit, but he needed family. That was an odd way for a grown-up to answer the question, too. He plucked at a string next to the hole in his jeans. Why was life so scary?

She sighed. "Landrey Mishna is not your uncle, and you don't have to worry about him any longer. He kidnapped you. From me."

Denver wiggled on the smooth seat, his heart leaping. "He's not my uncle?" A heavy weight lifted from his shoulders. If the guy hadn't been his uncle, then Denver wasn't related to a total asshole. Denver had thought it was his fault his uncle always hit him, but maybe Landrey was just a bad guy. Maybe Denver didn't have to turn out to be a bad guy, too, since they didn't share blood. "He lied?"

"Yes." The lady sniffed. "He was a soldier who worked for me, and he took you away when I had other plans for you. Apparently I made him angry when I stopped seeing him."

Denver turned to face her. Who was she? What did she want from him? God, he wished he were bigger and could just get out of the car and run. Did that mean he wasn't alone? His chest got heavy. "You know my family?"

She stiffened but didn't turn. "I know everything about you."

He swallowed and leaned toward her. His heart beat faster. "Do I have a dad?"

Now she turned, her face not telling him anything. "No."

He crossed his arms. "Do I have a mom?" Maybe his mom needed him. She had to be lost, or she'd be with him.

Dr. Daniels stopped at a crosswalk. "You don't have a mom. You're quite alone, Denver."

He didn't have a mom? His shoulders fell. Yeah, figured. His eyes stung. If he had a mom, then he wouldn't be alone. "Okay."

Then Dr. Daniels turned and watched him as if they had all day. "Yesterday when I arrived, you were talking with Ryker and Heath. I figured the three of you would bond quickly. At least I hoped."

The older boys had protected him from a bully, although he'd been giving it a good fight. "Um, Doctor? What should I call you, and what do you want with me?" She hadn't explained anything the day before.

She swallowed and pressed her high heel on the gas pedal. "You may call me Sylvia. I'm a doctor who studies smart kids like you."

He tilted his head to the side. Being quiet helped him to study people, and he somehow knew when they were lying. This lady was lying. She was a doctor, and she studied people, but that wasn't her name. He'd noticed the hitch in her voice yesterday when he'd first met her. Why would she give him a fake name? If he called her on it, she might hit him. "You gonna study me?" he asked quietly.

Her mouth lost its firm line and she looked softer. She turned the car down a long dirt road toward a big white building. "Yes, I am. You, Ryker, and Heath are special." Suddenly she reached over and grabbed his hand, enclosing it with her soft skin. "You are the most special of all, Denver. Someday I'll tell you why."

He blinked and looked around as she stopped the car. None of this made sense, but he didn't have a choice in anything. He never had. Not really. "We're back at the home."

"Yes," she said, squeezing his hand before releasing him. "It's time to get started, my sweet boy."

* * *

Four years later

Ned Cobb was dead.

A bruised and battered Denver huddled in the corner and stared wide-eyed at the dead adult on the ground. Ned's brown eyes, so often filled with pure mean, now stared blindly from his smashed head. He had been the owner of the boys home, and he had liked to punch kids. The man had just killed another child, one who'd shown up only yesterday. Ralph's small body was in the corner, and Denver couldn't look at him.

Death made the room feel heavy. It even smelled funny. Like old cut grass that had been under wet wood for an entire spring.

Ryker and Heath, Denver's brothers, stood with bloody baseball bats in their hands, staring at Ned's body. Like Denver, they both had special senses, including abnormal strength. Right now they were pale, and Heath looked like he was gonna throw up.

"We had to do it," Ryker said, his voice shaking. He was the oldest of them at around sixteen, and his voice *never* shook. "Ned killed that kid and was going to kill us."

Heath nodded, his long brown hair pulled back and his greenish brown eyes filled with terror.

They'd both swung only once.

Denver grabbed the wall and climbed up it to stand. His hands hurt from trying to defend himself from Ned's belt, but he didn't think any fingers were broken this time. Though his pinkie was numb.

Ryker dropped the bat and ran over to the kid on the ground. "Ralph?" His voice really trembled now.

"He's dead," Denver whispered. His stomach hurt so bad he needed to go to the bathroom.

Ryker checked the kid's neck anyway. His hands looked like they were shaking, but he touched Ralph carefully, pressing on the jugular. Then Ry leaned over to listen for breathing. He slowly straightened up. "Yeah." He turned around.

Heath threw his bat over into a corner. "The sheriff is coming back soon. We have to run and get out of here."

The sheriff was Ned's brother, and he liked to hit them with his baton. A lot. Denver straightened his shoulders. He might be younger than Ryker and Heath, but this was his fault. They wouldn't have come down into the basement of the crappy boys home unless it was to save him. Now he had to save them. Even if it made him bad and he'd have to go to hell. Right now he had to protect them. "Burn it. The whole place."

Ryker looked up at him, surprise in his greenish blue eyes.

Denver flushed. He didn't talk much, mainly because talking just got kids hit. Also, speaking was hard to do, so he didn't do it. But this was too important. "We'll burn the evidence." Plus, the boys home sucked and it should burn to the ground.

Heath paused and looked wildly around. His shoulders settled, and he breathed out. "Run. We have to run." He started moving for the door. "I know where the fuel is. We'll just burn this main building and leave the barracks alone."

Denver nodded. They didn't want to kill anybody else. It was after midnight, so they were alone in the main building.

The fire was surprisingly easy to start, and since they spilled lighter fluid and gasoline in almost every room, the building went up in flames fast. Crackling wood had a nice smell, and Denver tried not to think about the burning bodies.

"Let's go," Ryker said, turning, his voice sounding older than it had earlier. "Now."

Denver followed him, with Heath taking up the rear. They hustled across the scrub field into the forest and kept running. Ryker had hidden packs for them nearly a month ago that contained food, knives, and additional clothes. They'd known either they would have to escape, or Ned would kill one of them.

They ran all night, finally stopping to rest at the far edge of the forest, miles away from hell.

Denver leaned against a tree, his chest heaving, tears in his heart. His hands shook. And his legs ached. What had they just done? "We're just kids."

"That's okay. It was him or us." Ryker slid an arm around his shoulders, his voice cracking and then strengthening. "We're smart, and we'll figure out a way to survive until we're not kids anymore."

"She'll find us," Denver whispered, his stomach rolling over. The woman who studied the three of them, the one dating the sheriff—*she'd* find them. The doctor lady. There was something *wrong* about her. She showed up every once in a while to make them take written and physical tests like they were lab rats. She took notes and then went away. And she looked at him funny. Different from the way she looked at Ryker and Heath. Denver bit his lip to keep from crying. Even if the lady didn't find them, the lawman would never stop looking for them. "The sheriff is gonna want to murder us for killing his brother."

Heath coughed. "Yeah, but they're alone, and we're family. You can't take down an entire family."

Denver scratched his chin, his chest aching. "We're family." He looked at the scar on his hand. It was four years old, and it meant everything.

"Family," Ryker affirmed, stepping away to grab cereal bars out of his pack. He stared at the crushed food but didn't open the wrapper. His body swayed, and he sat down. "Let's take a minute."

"Yeah." Denver's knees wobbled as he looked at his scar line. Four years ago. He'd felt like a dork, but he'd asked Heath and Ryker for blood. They'd been behind the main building after a day of being tested, and he'd wondered if he was making a mistake. What if they had laughed at him?

He went instantly back to that day that had changed so much.

Denver took a deep breath. "Let's become blood brothers. There's one thing that will bind us." What if he was wrong? Was this stupid? He reached for a knife he'd stolen from the kitchen earlier, wanting only one thing in life. Even if he died tomorrow, he didn't want to be alone anymore. Maybe they had a chance together in the next life, wherever that was. "Blood."

Ryker straightened.

Heath moved away from a tree he'd been leaning against, his jaw hard. "I get it."

"Blood brothers," Ryker said, grabbing a knife from his back pocket. One Ned didn't know he had. "This one is sharper. Let's use this one."

Denver's chest exploded. They were gonna do it. Create a brotherhood like he'd dreamed about when they became friends four years ago. It was important that they each cut their own hand—make the choice.

The slice hurt, but somehow it healed what ached so badly inside him. When he pressed his hand to Ryker's and Heath's, when they all pressed together, it got kind of messy. Bloody. But it meant something. It meant everything. If he died now, it was okay. He had brothers. Maybe they'd all meet again in heaven. He kind of believed in the place. Tears clogged his eyes.

His hand hurt when everyone let go.

Heath looked down at his bloody palm. "Should we put on bandages?"

Denver shook his head, letting the tears fall. It was okay to cry. They were family. "Let the scars get bigger."

"Yeah," Ryker said, his eyes glassy. "We're brothers now."

Denver jerked back to the present, and tears filled his eyes, but he didn't care. They were on the run, and they were just kids. If the sheriff caught them, he'd kill them with a lot of pain. But he could never take away who they were. What they'd formed.

They were family.

CHAPTER
1

Present day

Noni tossed her laptop and stack of maps on the faded patchwork bedspread, her eyes gritty and her temples aching. The battered electric heater rattled from the corner of the motel room, providing a surprising amount of heat. Her fingers tingled as they started to warm up.

Winter blew snow around outside, and ice scattered against the window. She shivered and knelt one knee on the bed as she spread out the closest map. Where was her pen? Scrambling for her bag on the floor, she drew out a black marker and made several notations across the mountainous Pacific Northwest. Her heart raced, and her lungs compressed. She had to be closing in. Then she crossed out several towns, including Seattle, before pulling her phone from her pocket and hitting speed dial for number one.

Static crackled and then an expletive echoed as it sounded like the phone was dropped. Something shuffled. "Eagle? This is Sparrow" finally came over the line.

Noni rubbed her aching head. "Hi, Aunt Franny. I thought we agreed to forget the nicknames."

"So did I, dear, but Verna likes being called Hawk Two."

Why would they have a Hawk Two when there wasn't a Hawk One? Noni swallowed down a sharp retort. "We have to get serious, Fran. This is dangerous." Though she'd done everything possible to make sure the two older women were out of the line of fire. "Where are you?"

"I just set up camp and am staying in the Motel Burnside just north of Portland. Verna should be pulling into Salt Lake City any second now," Franny said. "My meeting with our private detective is tomorrow morning—he has already left Seattle and is heading here."

"Good. I'm going to scout around here in Greenville before back-tracking to Snowville in a day or so." Greenville was near the Washington-Idaho border, fifty miles out from Snowville. People back home familiar with the street gang had told her of its affiliations in Greenville. Now all she had to do was find them. Somehow.

She was leading a team—an untrained, totally vulnerable team—in a chase after a dangerous gang member. She was a lotion and candle maker, for God's sakes. What the hell had she been thinking?

"What about the FBI office in Snowville?" Franny asked.

Noni swallowed, trying to shove away self-doubt. "The FBI is a last resort." If she contacted them, the agents would immediately send out an AMBER Alert for a missing child. If that happened, Richie might kill the baby. She couldn't let that happen. Plus, the law wasn't exactly on her side right now since she was working outside it because of time constraints. God, she hoped she wasn't making the hugest mistake of her life by handling this herself.

"Any news from Denver?" Franny asked, sounding weary.

"No." Noni lifted her chin, her heart cracking at the mere mention of his name. He had given her a fake last name, so all she had was his picture and some basic information she knew about him. "But I've posted a search for him all over the Internet, even on dating sites. He has to see something." Her chest hurt to even think about the asshole who'd broken her heart so easily, but she needed his help, and she'd take the pain to save the missing baby. "I'll find him."

"Honey." Fran cleared her throat. "He's probably no better than that first private detective we hired, the one who stole half of our savings."

Noni's shoulders slumped. "Denver has to be better, and I'll get our money back from that other detective. I promise." How, she had no clue. The first detective she'd found had been a fraud. He'd taken everything he could—twenty thousand dollars. But they'd been desperate. Sharon's baby had been kidnapped two weeks ago, and the baby was only three months old.

Poor Sharon. The question of what exactly had caused her death would have to be answered later—after Noni made sure her baby, Talia, was safe from her dick of a father. Noni would bet her life that Richie had given Sharon the drugs she'd overdosed on.

Was Talia safe? Was anybody reading her stories at night? She liked to cuddle with her special blanket and listen, even at only three months old. Did she miss her blanket? Noni glanced at the light pink edging peeking out of her pack. Her hand shook, and her heart felt like somebody had punched her in the chest. What if Talia wasn't safe?

She couldn't think like that. She had to focus on what to do to get the baby back.

The second detective Noni had hired had at least traced Richie and the baby to somewhere in the Pacific Northwest. The PI was heading to Portland, but Noni's gut and a source back home had told her to head to Greenville. "Get some sleep, Franny."

"I mean it. Let's forget Denver What's-His-Real-Name-Who-the-Hell-Knows-Because-He's-a-Damn-Liar and just do this ourselves."

"Let's go back to calling him 'dickhead,'" Noni said, even her arms feeling heavy. She'd met Denver, a private detective, while he was on a case in her town of Anchorage about a year ago, and he had seemed like a bloodhound who'd always find the guy he was looking for. She'd fallen for him and hard. Then he'd left, and her world was a darker place without him. A colder place. But she needed his help now, and she'd do whatever it took to get it. "We might be taking on an entire gang, Auntie. Denver is tough enough to do it."

"I don't know," Franny said, drawing out the words. "I guess, worst-case scenario, we can just stand behind him if bullets start flying."

"Absolutely," Noni agreed, pushing the map out of the way. In fact, she wanted to shoot Denver herself. How could he just leave her? Her skin heated, and she took a deep breath to calm her emotions. "Get some sleep. I'll call in tomorrow."

"Honey, this has to be about finding the baby and not, ah, meeting up with Denver again."

"I know." The words felt hollow, just like her chest.

Fran sighed. "I know you know, but you've never given up on anything in your life, and you really had feelings for that man. You didn't get any closure."

Because the dickhead had left her without a word. Noni swallowed a lump in her throat. "Yeah, I want closure. But I want that baby back and safe more. She's all that matters right now." Noni had made a promise to both Sharon and her baby, right after Talia's birth, that she'd be there for them. That she'd protect them. She'd helped take care of Talia for three months, and her arms already felt empty. "I'm focused. Get some sleep, Auntie."

"All right. Night, sweetie," Franny said before disconnecting the call.

Noni set the phone on the nightstand and stretched out on the bed. She should get out her notes and keep working. Her eyelids fluttered shut, and she relaxed into the worn mattress as her mind wandered.

Would she find Denver? Of course she needed him to save the baby. But that wasn't all. She needed answers, and if she was honest with herself, she wanted to see him. Wanted at least a chance to seek that connection again. She was too tired to feel pathetic about that.

She drifted, trying to just relax.

A whisper of sound jerked her back to the motel room. She tensed and looked toward the door, partially sitting up out of instinct.

Oh God. Denver. In the flesh.

He stood inside the room, quietly shutting the door against the freezing cold. The entire atmosphere electrified. Holy crap on a mutinous cracker. Denver was *there*. Really there. After a year of having no clue whether or not he was alive, the sight of him seemed surreal. Was she dreaming about him? Again? How could he really be there?

"Noni," he breathed, his gaze settling on her.

"I locked that door," she mumbled, sitting all the way up, her mind blanking to avoid the rush of emotion pouring through her.

"What are you *doing*?" he snarled, his eyes turning a furious blue.

Her temper rolled from banked to a slow burn. She blinked. So much for her secret little fantasy of him finding her, begging forgiveness, and professing that his heart and soul belonged to her. Not that she'd take him back. But still. "Excuse me?" Her voice had risen.

"Pack. Now." He edged to the motel room window and moved the heavy curtain out of the way to peer out.

She shook her head, trying to grasp reality. It had been so long since she'd seen him, and within seconds, her entire body had flared to life. Her heart thundered. How could he still affect her like this?

He turned his head slowly back to her, as he must've realized she hadn't jumped into action. Stress cut lines around his mouth. "Noni. Now."

That dangerously deep and dark voice. She still heard that low tenor in the time between sleep and wakefulness…when dreams took her under. Like *he'd* taken her under.

Somehow he looked tougher than before. Even more remote and distant. So large and so…male.

His black hair brushed the collar of his battered leather jacket, and his ripped jeans led to snow-covered leather boots. A shadow covered his square jaw, showcasing each hard angle. His dark brows were arched, his eyes were a sizzling blue, and his full lips were set into a thin line. Tension choked the air around them, rolling through the room with a discernible heat.

She couldn't stop looking at him, watching him like a starving woman would a cheesecake.

There was something unreal about him—an elusive, too-male, predatory quality she'd never been able to define. Yet she felt it. She felt *him*—the danger and the kindness, the complexity and the simplicity. All characteristics he'd probably deny…if he bothered to talk at all.

"Noni," he snapped.

She jumped to her feet.

He was pissed?

Hurt rocketed through her, and she shoved most of it away, leaving a lump of coal in her gut. "Sorry to bother you and whatever woman you're lying your ass off to right now, but I need your help." Her knees wobbled, but she held herself upright.

He breathed out, and his nostrils flared. "Later." Angling around her, he shoved the maps and manila files off the bed and into her bag.

She'd forgotten. How had she forgotten his terseness? "I'm not going anywhere," she snapped.

He turned, and she instantly found herself up against the wall, his hand flat against her upper chest. How had she also forgotten how quickly he could move? He was almost supernatural that way. Fear shocked her, while desire pissed her off. She hated being in this position, where she *needed* him. His face lowered toward hers. Flecks of different shades of blue made up his spectacular eyes, which glittered with an emotion she couldn't quite read.

She was pinned easily—too easily—in place. This close, she could smell him. Male and forest and leather and something that was all Denver.

He didn't speak. No order, no sarcasm, no words. He just stared as if he could compel her into obedience with his intensity.

There was a time she'd responded to his looks. She'd read him—almost *felt* him. He wasn't much for talking, and she'd learned to interpret his movements and expressions. Because he had mattered to her.

Apparently she hadn't mattered a whit to him. Hurt exploded inside her again.

At the reminder, her head snapped back. Her stomach clenched. He had finally bothered to show up and now was giving her orders? Oh, hell no. She tried to struggle, and he kept her still and against the wall with one hand spread across her sternum.

His strength was unreal. Once she'd marveled at it. Not now.

His days of touching her were over. Hurt and anger mixed until she had to act. She pivoted and shot her knee toward his groin, fully intending to connect.

She failed.

His free hand grasped the back of her thigh, shoving her leg to the side and stepping into the vee of her legs. The full length of him, heated and hard, trapped her in place.

She gasped at the contact, sparks shooting through her. Her body warmed and then flashed to a boil, all from one simple touch. All from his nearness—something she'd so desperately missed. There were times she'd wished she hadn't met him, that she didn't know what it felt like to be loved by him. To feel as if she were the only thing in the world for him. "Damn it, Denver."

His nose nearly touched hers. "Are you crazy?"

Maybe. Probably. She'd been out of her mind since he'd shattered her heart. "Let me go."

"Can't. You have no idea what you've done." A muscle ticked in his jaw; the fierce anger on his face making him look like a stranger. Not the man she thought she'd known.

Her mind spun. "What *I've* done?" Wait a minute. All the thoughts, all the fears of the last year, bombarded her. How many precious moments had she wasted wondering about him? Asking herself why he'd left without a word. Why would posting about him on the Internet cause problems? Her breath stopped. "Oh God. You *are* married."

His gaze narrowed even further. "That's ridiculous."

All right. She scrambled. "Then wanted. You're wanted by the law."

He didn't answer.

That was an answer, wasn't it? Oh man. What had she done? Adrenaline flooded through her, and she fought for calmness. How dangerous was he? Really? Maybe she'd been wrong about trusting him to help her. "Leave now. Leave, and I'll take down all the posts about you." She clearly didn't know him. Maybe she never had. For the first time fear—the real kind—shivered down her spine. He was certainly more dangerous than anything else out there.

"Too late," he gritted out.

"I-I'm...sorry." The words breathed out of her as self-preservation took over. The man was one long line of coiled strength, and she didn't stand a chance in a fight, even on her best day. They were alone in her motel room, and she had no friends near. He'd left town without any loose ends. The photograph she had of them he hadn't known about. Was she a loose end? Just what would he do to her? Could she scream?

He blinked. His eyes darkened, and his jaw hardened visibly. "Don't be afraid of me."

"I'm not," she shot back, lying instantly. Free—she had to get free of him. "This was a mistake. I know that now." It wasn't her first time trying to survive danger, and it wouldn't be her last. She'd find the baby on her own. "Just leave. Please."

"Too late." His lip twisted. Was that regret or determination?

Oh God. What did that mean—*Too late*? What would he do? Even more awareness jolted through her veins. Panic shook her control. She opened her mouth to scream and had barely sucked in air when his mouth crashed down on hers.

She instantly groaned from a bombardment of way too many feelings. Shock, awareness, warmth, need.

His touch was too carnal to be called a kiss. She fragmented, splintering into pieces. Fire swept her, igniting her body even as her mind rebelled. Her nipples sharpened and her knees weakened, but alarm bells clanged throughout her head. The disconnect between her feelings and her thoughts nearly dropped her to the ground.

He held her upright and in place.

His touch, his taste, his smell were so familiar that her mouth moved beneath his, and her hands rose to his chest. Instead of pushing him away, her fingers curled into the leather jacket. It had been *so long*. Her body separated from her brain as she kissed him back, tilting her head to take more of him.

Afraid, lonely, stripped…She stopped thinking and just felt.

He growled low, and the sound reverberated in her mouth and down her body.

Her abdomen rolled and clenched, need flaring through her so quickly she gasped. What was she doing? No. God. She had to end this. With a muffled sob, she wrenched her head to the side. "Stop," she breathed.

He stiffened, his head lifting very slightly. Grasping her chin with a firm grip, he turned her to face him again, almost too easily controlling her. "No screaming."

She gulped, and a tremble shook her.

"I won't hurt you." His eyes had darkened to the hue of a night sky right before the moon softened the darkness. Now lust glimmered there along with the anger.

She swallowed, trapped. Her lungs completely gave up the fight and stopped working. She couldn't breathe. God, she couldn't breathe. "Okay." Tears filled her eyes.

"Noni." His voice gentled to the tone she remembered. "I promise. You'll be safe."

Her mouth had gone dry, so she just nodded. Didn't the devil have an angel's face? Confusion numbed her.

"We have to go. Now. Tell me you get me." His hoarse growl rumbled between them, his breath brushing her lips.

Go. That was good. He wanted to go, so at least he wasn't going to hurt her and leave her. But what then?

A shiver took her, head to toe, while all the areas in between heated. "Where?" she breathed, not nearly as forcefully as she would've liked. He brought out a vulnerability in her that she had explored while in the safety of his touch, and then he'd left. The vulnerability had remained, and she tried to hide it. Had he just become the thing to fear? What did he mean that it was too late for him to leave? Her chin lifted. There was strength in survival, and, oh, she knew how to survive.

He jerked his head to the side, his attention focused on the door.

His body stiffened, and he released her suddenly, moving back toward the window. "Get your bag."

What had he heard?

The urgency in his voice propelled her toward the laptop and bag. Getting out of that room and finding some space was crucial. Her stomach cramping and her breath quickening, she grabbed her possessions and moved toward him. If she got outside, could she get away from him?

The window blasted apart with a loud shatter, spraying glass.

Denver turned and leaped for her, tackling her to the floor. She hit with a hard thump, struggling against him. Pain flashed from her hip.

He covered her, and the entire room exploded.

CHAPTER
2

Denver covered Noni's head while levering up onto his knees, preparing to strike. A second projectile smashed through the broken window, and it took him nearly a second to realize it wasn't a flash grenade. Two more bottles flew into the room, shattering on impact. Fire flicked up and engulfed the bedspread. "What the hell?" He jumped to his feet and pulled Noni along. "You okay?"

She blinked, her black hair falling in a wild mass down her back. Shock filled her dark eyes, and she retreated from the burning bedspread. "Yes."

He lifted her chin to make sure he had her attention. She'd never know the importance she held in his life, in his heart, but he did. And he'd never let anybody hurt her. No matter what he had to do. "Trust me."

She nodded quickly.

A simple act but one that dug right in and took hold inside him. Her trust meant everything. She was in his hands again, and there was so much he needed to say. But he had to take care of the threat and focus. Now. "It'll be okay," he said, releasing her. Pivoting, he stomped out the fire from the third bottle.

The second slowly spread fire near the bathroom.

Who would send in three Molotov cocktails? Smoke started to cloud the room. "Stay behind me." Turning, he moved toward the window and yanked down the drape before it could catch fire. He reached for Noni's arm and made sure she was hidden behind him before angling himself to look outside.

Three men stood in the snow, legs braced, automatic weapons in their hands. They wore dark hoodies, but he could make out tattoos along two of the guys' necks and on their hands. A huge, lifted black truck was parked sideways behind them. Members of a street gang?

Denver shook his head. This made no sense.

Noni peeked around him. "Damn it. They found me."

The words took a moment to sink in. Gang members were looking for her? At the thought, his body settled into battle mode and his focus narrowed. "You can explain later." And she would. Hell yeah, she would. For now, he had to get them out of there.

She swallowed audibly. "My gun is in my pack."

He grabbed her hand before she could open the bag. The woman had brought a fucking gun? "I've got this one." Three gang members wouldn't take much of his time. The fire alarm started to blare throughout the motel. "Shit. Let's go. Now." He slid his gun from beneath his jacket. "We have to get out of here before they start shooting or backup arrives." God knew how many people would start running from the motel.

Noni clutched the back of his jacket. "Okay. Go."

"Stay behind me and keep your head down. My truck is black and to the right." He slowly slid open the door. Bullets instantly hit the top of the door.

A woman screamed from down the way, and people scrambled into the snowy night before running for cover.

Denver bit back a snarl. "New plan." He shoved Noni farther back, dropped, and leaned out to fire, aiming for their legs. Killing them would just cause more problems. One. Two. Three. As if choreographed, the three men dropped one by one. What kind of idiots just stood in front of their truck? There was no way they had been hired by his enemies. He reached back and grabbed Noni's hand, pulling her out into the cold. "Run, honey."

Down the front of the motel, a man wearing only his underwear ran out of a room, saw the fallen gang members, and started yelling as he ran back inside and slammed his door.

Damn it. He'd definitely call 911.

Noni fought Denver, pulling back. "My car."

He glanced toward a nondescript compact. "Rental?"

"Yes." Good. Without pausing, he dragged her through the snow and hefted her into his truck. "Seat belt." Slamming the door, he ran around the front and jumped in, then quickly tore out of the lot. Gunfire echoed behind them, at least one bullet hitting the tailgate. The truck fishtailed on the ice, and he corrected, heading for I-90.

She clutched the dash, her bag dropping to the floor. "Where are we going?" she gasped.

"Seat. Belt." He didn't like repeating himself—especially with people shooting at them. "Now."

She turned to stare at him, her mouth slack. "What the heck, Denver?"

His very deep well of patience went dry as he drove onto I-90. "Put on your fuckin' belt," he snarled, punching the gas even though black ice covered the road. Anger filled him. At the men shooting at them, at the circumstances, maybe even at Noni. He'd fought hard to get over her and hadn't even come close. He'd never be free of her.

She jerked back, her dark eyes widening. Finally showing some sense, she quickly fastened the seat belt around herself almost clumsily. "You've never sworn at me before."

His anger deepened. "You've never put yourself in the crosshairs and used me to do it before." Oh, he'd been the gentlest part of himself with her, and look what had happened. "Where did you hide the picture of us you put all over the Internet?" He thought he'd destroyed them all when he'd left her.

She clutched the dash. "My aunt had it."

The picture was of the two of them at Portage Glacier, and the blue of the ice had reflected the sun, making the entire day look almost magical. In it, he had his arm over her shoulder and they looked happy. How had he forgotten that picture? Was there a part of him that had wanted to leave her something to remember him by? Even so, he never would've thought she'd post it all over the Internet and put them both in danger.

He'd left to keep her safe, damn it. Yet here she was, being shot at by gang members. Anger pricked up his back like hot needles, and he pushed it away, searching for the cold.

He focused on the road and took the next exit. "We'll have to take back roads toward Snowville." His plates were covered, so nobody could've gotten the numbers, but the truck was easy to spot since it was fairly new and lifted. He'd have to secure it somewhere for a while and drive something else. For now, he had to concentrate. "Are you all right?" He'd tackled her pretty hard in the motel.

"I'm fine." She hunched her shoulders.

Oh, hell no. "Noni." He let his voice harden. There was no time to coddle her. "Are you hurt?"

"No." She kept her gaze out the front window and drew her legs up. Her slim arms wrapped around her knees.

His chest heated, and he wanted nothing more than to pull over and offer comfort. But keeping her alive was more important. He turned onto a road that passed through a residential area, and the cheerful Christmas lights strung on every house seemed foreign. As if they twinkled with lives he couldn't even imagine…which was probably true. "I left you safe," he muttered.

Her head swung toward him, and that glorious hair flew. "I can keep myself safe, you dick."

He barked out a laugh, unable to help himself. God, she had absolutely no clue what was out there. Who was out there. What form evil could take. But he had to explain it to her, even if he scared her. "Noni."

"What?" she snapped.

"Why did you put our picture on dating sites, missing persons sites, and some blog called *Find My Man*, and why are there gang members trying to shoot you?" He'd kept his voice as calm as possible while he wanted to snap. He couldn't help her unless he knew all the facts, so he'd stay factual and clear. This was just another case, and he could treat her like another client.

Yeah, right. Her scent of wild orchids, amplified in the cozy truck cab, was sending his system into overdrive. In a million years, he'd never forget the spicy way she smelled.

"I've changed my mind," she said softly, sadly. "Just let me off at the nearest motel, and you can go. I'll take the picture and posts down."

He glanced her way, his fingers itching to run through her thick hair again. "They're down already." He'd set his brother to it the second he'd rushed out to catch Noni at the motel where she'd all but advertised she'd be staying.

She straightened. "How? I put the posts up. Only I can take them down."

Jesus. "You want to tangle with gang members, you're gonna need to lose the naïveté." Sad but true. "The pictures and any trace of us together on the Internet, on both the light and the dark web, have been scrubbed."

Her mouth softened into a little O. "Who are you?"

If he knew, he'd probably tell her. "Doesn't matter. Time to fess up, Noni. I want all of it." So he could plan. That's what he did. He planned every op and then executed it. So he'd treat this the same way. "Why did you want my help?" After the way he'd left her, she had to have been desperate to reach out. The idea of her in danger flashed fury down him, through him, and he quashed it. For this, he needed to banish the emotions attacking him and just think. Clearly. "Well?"

She shook her head, turning back to the snowy world outside. "Doesn't matter. Drop me off, Denver. If that's your real name," she muttered, bitterness in the tone.

He barely kept from wincing. He'd hurt her, and that was a punch to the gut. "It is."

"But your last name isn't Peterson," she said.

"No. Jones is the closest thing I have to a real last name." Peterson was an alias he used on cases. One of many. His mouth still burned from the kiss in the motel room. For months he'd dreamed of her mouth. Of kissing her. Of losing himself in her softness. Yet the reality blew every dream away. He had to concentrate when all he wanted to do was kiss her again and make promises he could never keep. So he kept his words clipped. "Story. Now."

"No," she replied just as shortly.

He sighed. "Listen, Noni."

"Why? You actually going to talk?" she snapped.

The hair on the back of his neck rose. His chest heated. In his entire life she'd been the only woman who could shake his self-control. Slowly he swallowed down his temper until his anger banked low and hard in his gut. Where it belonged. "Yes," he said calmly.

She snorted.

Oh man, he wasn't going to be able to hold on to his temper. "You don't know me," he warned.

"I'm fully aware of that fact," she said evenly.

"If you did, you'd stop pushing. Right now." He drove down another road, heading west.

She turned again, facing him. "Is that a threat?"

"Yes," he said easily. There. They were on the same page. Good.

"Screw you, Denver."

His head snapped back. So *not* on the same page. "Noni."

"What are you going to do? Pull this truck right on over?" she taunted, a smugness in her voice.

He reacted instantly, slamming the brakes and spinning the truck around and into the edge of a deserted auto parts parking lot. They came to a lurching stop, and he shoved the gearshift into PARK. Silence and snow descended instantly upon them. If he was going to keep her safe, she had to understand he'd destroy any challenge, even if it came from her.

Her mouth was wide open this time, and she watched him warily, turning her back to her door as much as the seat belt would allow.

He scouted the silent area outside before turning his focus back on her. "You done challenging me?"

She swallowed. "Probably not."

His lips twitched. Her sense of humor, the honesty in it, had intrigued him from the very beginning. "I assume you called for my help because I get things done." It made his heart speed up to just sit in danger and talk, but he could take a moment if necessary. "Right?"

She nodded.

"Do you know how I do that?" he asked softly.

Her eyes widened very slightly. "How?"

"By any means necessary." He hadn't allowed her to know him fully when they were together because he had wanted her to *like* him. She was good and strong and sweet and somebody he shouldn't touch. But he'd wanted so badly to touch her, so he'd played a part he thought she'd like. For the briefest of time, he'd pretended he was a normal guy courting an amazing woman. But he wasn't normal, and he'd get her killed if she stayed in his life. "Do you understand that I'll stop at nothing to reach an objective?"

She studied him for several seconds. "I don't think so."

Fair enough. He'd have to show her with how he handled the current problem. First, he needed information. A lot of it. "Why did you track me down? Why is there a gang after you?"

A myriad of expressions crossed her face, including anger and regret. "It was a mistake to track you down. I realize that now, and I apologize." Her polite voice, the one she used when truly irritated, filled the cab. "It won't happen again."

"It's too late." That tone made him want to muss her up—kiss her until she was breathless and needy. "I'm in this now. Tell me what it is." He could see the struggle inside her. The one full of pride and self-preservation that told her to run from him. The other full of need and desperation, who knew she needed his help. He let her work it out without his interference.

Her stunning dark eyes were full of concern, and her paleness alarmed him. Finally, her shoulders slumped. "My foster sister, Sharon, gave birth to a baby three months ago and then died from what the authorities *thought* was an accidental overdose."

Denver's focus narrowed. There was a huge drug pipeline into Alaska through the gangs. He started to put pieces together. "All right."

Tears glimmered in Noni's eyes. "Sharon was one of the foster kids who'd passed through our home more than once, and we told everybody we were sisters. We have been good friends for ten years. We felt like family, you know? I liked her, but she fought a drug habit." Noni wiped the moisture off her face. "She had just graduated college, and she got pregnant by a real loser named Richie, who belongs to a local gang. A really bad guy."

Denver put his hands on the steering wheel to keep from reaching for her. "You don't think it was an accidental overdose?"

"No," she whispered, her voice tortured. "Sharon had kicked the drugs during the pregnancy, and she loved that baby so much. My aunt and I helped her to get an apartment, and she was going to make it. She wouldn't have risked her baby." Noni cleared her throat. "She had cut off all ties with Richie, and he was threatening her. I think he killed her."

Denver breathed out. If the guy was evil enough to kill the mother of his child, he needed to be put down. Now. "The baby?"

"Richie is a Kingdom Boys member, and he took her and left town. Since he's listed on the birth certificate, I guess he has the right to do that. Even if not, I'm afraid to call the police. If they come after him, he'll hurt the baby. He threatened to do just that if I didn't leave him alone. I've been chasing him ever since."

Denver leaned back. The woman was chasing a fucking gang member? Was she crazy? "So you have no legal claim to that baby?" Denver had connections who could create necessary papers if needed. He'd fix this. "Noni?"

"Sharon named me Talia's legal guardian in her will. If Richie is found to be a danger, then the will trumps a father's rights. But we have to go through the court system, and I don't think there's time." Noni handed over a picture of a new baby with tons of dark hair held back in a little pink clip.

The image kicked Denver square in the gut. So innocent and vulnerable. He knew firsthand what monsters could do to a helpless child. Even if Noni hadn't been involved, Denver would've stepped in. "What if Richie is found by the authorities to not be a danger to the baby?" he asked quietly, curious. Oh, he had no problem killing

Richie to protect a baby. But what about Noni? Did she really understand what might have to happen here?

Noni met his gaze directly, her eyes harder than he'd ever seen them. "Then I'm taking the baby anyway. No matter what I have to do."

CHAPTER
3

Noni stretched her aching back while walking into Denver's safe house in Snowville. They moved through an antiquated kitchen, complete with an avocado green stove, into a small living area with an empty fireplace in one corner. "It's weird you have a safe house," she murmured, taking in the scarred wooden tables and computer equipment set throughout the room. No couch, pictures, decorations. Just a working room with equipment. Drapes covered the windows and kept the storm hidden.

Denver set her bag on a ripped orange office chair. "This is just a temporary safe house we rented, but we have it for the rest of the month, so I figured it'd be a good place to form a plan and hide the truck." He looked around. "I haven't gotten a chance to transfer all the equipment to a new place, so this will work for now."

"Transfer? Meaning you've been living here?" How many nights had she wondered where he was and what he was doing? If he'd found somebody else?

"No. We had an op here." He looked around. "The other places we used are blown, but this one is safe for the moment."

Blown? Must've been some op. Man, when he started talking, he really kept the words rolling. "You've been working on your communication skills," she said, stretching her aching shoulders and trying to grab on to reality.

He gave a short nod. "I have. I've found people do what I say if I actually say something."

"I figured you were just the strong and silent type," she said, taking a couple of steps away from him. This near, he was just too much. His size, his intensity, his strength. She needed space.

"I am. Watching is more beneficial than talking." He ruffled his dark hair as he made his way to one of the computers and pushed a button on its keyboard, still facing her. "I need some information. Richie's last name, his gang affiliations, and any friends of his you can identify."

"Wait a minute." She hovered, eyeing the front door as well as the entry to the kitchen. "I need to know."

"What?" He paused in typing and looked at her, his focus digging right into her head.

She swallowed. "How—I mean, how dangerous are you?" It was probably stupid to ask him that question, considering she truly didn't know the answer.

He cocked his head to the side. "I'm a killer, Noni. Have been for most of my life. I'll take care of Richie if I have to."

Her stomach dropped. All the way. Her lungs seized, but she couldn't move. She couldn't run.

His gaze narrowed. "Isn't that why you tracked me down?"

Slowly, numbly, she shrugged. "I knew you were dangerous and relentless in pursuing somebody." But a killer? Her search for him had held a romantic element, and she knew it. This guy was all edge—no romance. "Am I in danger?" Her voice quivered, but she had to know.

"Yes." He didn't move. Didn't even seem to breathe.

She blinked. Rapidly. "From you?"

His eyes darkened. "No. With you, the only thing I'm capable of breaking is your heart."

Cold swam through her. The arrogance. "You think you broke my heart?"

His lip twisted. "I know I did." His tone was low with what seemed like self-hatred. Dark and raw. "I'm sorry."

Those words. She'd needed those words and hadn't realized how badly. "Thank you," she said, going on instinct. "Then how am I in danger?"

"I'm in danger, and anybody close to me is fair game for an enemy who will keep coming until I'm dead. Until everything I care about, everything I dream about, is taken away and I want death." He looked back down at the computer, intensity pouring from him.

Whoa. Okay. Denver didn't have one bit of hysteria in him. His words scared her, but curiosity still rose up. "Who's after you?"

"Irrelevant. As soon as we get Talia back, you have to forget me. Now. Back to Richie."

She could live forever, and she'd never forget him. Not for one second had she been able to pretend he didn't exist. He still needed to explain more. She had a right to know everything. But he was correct. They had to find Talia. "I have files on everything." She threw her pack at Denver, and he easily caught it before it smashed him in the face.

He didn't so much as frown. "Thank you."

She swallowed. They were in the same room. After a year of hurting for him, he was right here in solid form. More than solid. She hadn't imagined his hard body or intense charisma. He owned every room he walked into with no effort. She'd never met anybody like him, and here he was. Her body tingled, her heart ached, and her mind spun. Yeah. Denver was definitely here. "What now?" she asked, her eyes gritty and her throat scratchy.

"I'll do some research." He pulled out a chair and sat down to start typing almost absently. "There's one bedroom, and you can have it. The sheets are clean. None of my, ah, team slept here."

Everything inside her stilled. "Are you kidding me?" How surprising that her voice stayed soft when every nerve in her body had just flared into full anger.

He paused and looked up from the screen, his brows drawing down. "No. It's past midnight, and you should try to sleep. We might have to get on the road early."

She blinked. Once and then twice. Heat flared down her throat to explode in her lungs. How could he be so calm? So clueless? "You're not done explaining." Her voice shook, but she'd forced the words out.

He lifted his head, and awareness smoothed out his expression. "I'm done. Period."

Pain. Yep. Definite sharp knives ripped right on through her chest, and she had to fight to keep from blanching. "You said you cared about me." Pride could screw itself. She wanted answers.

He rose to his feet, his gaze alert on her. "I did. I do."

"Bullshit," she snapped, having felt much tougher when he'd been sitting. "Why are you lying about that? Even if you have some dangerous enemy, you used me." She wasn't completely buying the left-for-your-own-safety crap.

"I did not use you." He kept her gaze but leaned over and resumed typing.

Impressive. Now, wasn't he talented. "Why did you scurry away under the darkness of night like a rat with its tail tucked between its legs?" He could've at least said good-bye.

His upper lip twitched, but he wasn't stupid enough to grin. He abandoned the keyboard and straightened again to his full and rather impressive height. "That's quite an image. Been working on that long?"

Yeah, and sometimes it had involved her sobbing into tissues. Okay. She'd keep that to herself. Maybe pride did matter after all. "Explain, Denver. You left without a word. Not even a note."

"I left because it was over, Noni," he said evenly.

Ouch. Fucking ouch and double ouch. Well. She'd asked. "Why did you just leave without a word?" Her mind never stopped. She had to solve every puzzle. It was why she worked with ingredients and lotions. Carefully set out recipes. There was always an answer. "If you cared for me, why was it over? The sex was good, and your big enemy, if that's the truth, had no clue where you were."

"The sex was fuckin' amazing." His eyes darkened to a midnight blue. "We don't have to do this now."

"Chicken," she snapped.

He nodded. "Definitely."

Oh, he wasn't going to be cute. Nothing he could say or do would make her see him as cute tonight. No way. "Explain." She put her hands on her hips.

He sighed. "The *why* of it really doesn't matter. The end result does."

"You're wrong. The *why* matters a whole lot, Denver." Nothing in her would give him an inch on this. "I deserve the truth. One night you're there, with me, and then you're just gone, with no warning."

"Not true," he said gently. "I told you the job was temporary and then I'd have to leave."

Yeah, but she'd thought things had changed after they'd made love. And that's what it had been. The real kind. At the very least, she'd expected a good-bye, although a small part of her had thought they'd started something that would last. That they would figure it out together. "Then why not say good-bye?"

"I thought it'd be easier if you hated me." His deep blue eyes held nothing but earnest light. "And I couldn't say good-bye."

"You're a coward," she whispered. She'd suspected that was the truth. Was there more?

"Sure. If that helps you, believe it. But if I had tried to say good-bye, I wouldn't have been able to leave. Or I would've done something really stupid and tried to take you with me, and then you'd be in danger." He glanced around the dismal room. "Though you clearly ended up in danger anyway." He drew out the chair to sit again. "Done talking." Sweat dotted his brow, and a vein bulged in his neck.

Just a few words from him wasn't enough. She didn't care that he was done. "Too bad. I am not finished talking." Maybe if she had forced him to talk to her before, he wouldn't have just left her alone and with so many questions.

His head jerked back, and he focused again on her, his eyebrows drawing up.

Yeah. She'd never challenged him, had she? No, she'd been so perfectly understanding and accepting of his unwillingness to talk much because it just wasn't him. Or rather, he wasn't comfortable talking a lot. Instead, she'd acted like a housewife from the fifties and let him have his way. She'd wanted him to feel accepted and comfortable around her, and she'd tamped down her inclination to get to the bottom of things. Mistake. Definitely a mistake. "I see I have your attention."

"You do." There was a low warning in his tone. A dangerous glint in his eye.

Man, she'd missed out on this. Just how much of Denver did she not know? Oh, she'd thought she knew him physically. Even emotionally. But maybe not. Maybe in her unwillingness to push him, she'd missed out of the real man beneath the surface. Was that how he'd been able to leave so easily? "We both seem to have put our best foot forward when we dated."

"Meaning?" he asked silkily.

A shiver ticked down her back, and she ignored it. "You were sweet, I was patient, and we both wanted to make a good impression."

He slowly nodded. "Makes sense. We were just starting to date."

"Right." Her chin lowered, as did the intensity of her tone. "Now we're not dating. We're not in love, we're not sleeping together, and I don't give two fucks if you don't like to talk."

He didn't blink, but his gaze changed. Had his pupils narrowed? "Watch it."

"No." Her chest filled, and she faced him squarely. "I don't care if you like me. I certainly don't like you. But you're a private *dick*, a good one, and I'm hiring you." The flare in his eyes at her emphasis on *dick* sped up her heartbeat, but she didn't back down. She had to regain some control here and stay in a position of strength. "If I ask questions, then you answer them. Think of yourself as a really smart trained dolphin. Bark on command, buddy." Her mouth just wouldn't stop.

His head tilted just slightly to the side. "What are you doing?"

"I'm telling you how it's going to be." Her voice went breathy on the last because he started moving toward her. She stiffened. He kept coming. Straight at her. "Wh-what are *you* doing?" she stammered, taking several unwilling steps backward.

He kept moving inexorably toward her over the ugly shag carpet, taking his time, keeping her in his sights like any hunter stalking prey. Her stomach fluttered, and her hands clenched. She stumbled backward, instinct taking over. There wasn't time to turn and run. His long stride easily caught up to her lurching one.

And then the wall was at her back.

Nowhere to go. She held her hands up to ward him off, and he stepped in, gracefully flattening his palms against the paneling on either side of her head. Caging her. The heat of his body rushed over her as if in a physical touch, and her body sprang wide awake. Her nipples hardened. Her breath quickened.

She curled her fingers into her palms, her hands still up but not touching him. Not yet.

The look in his eyes stole every thought from her head. Lust and anger. Need and determination. Pride and warning. "Trained dolphin?" he asked slowly. Clearly. Softly.

She swallowed. All right. That might've been a bit much. "Denver."

He wasn't touching her, but he was all around her. His warmth and his strength. She was at his mercy, and instead of feeling frightened or even angry, she felt alive with an edge of sharp awareness. Who was this man? The Denver she'd known had been sweet and gentle. She'd just pushed this guy—on purpose—way past sweet. "Back off," she hissed.

"Make me," he rumbled.

Tingles blew through her abdomen to slam right to her core. She inhaled the scent of him—male and forest, wild and untamable. Like something she could lick and taste but never quite define. That was Denver. Her knees wobbled. If she put her hands on him, if she tried to fight him, what would he do? She truly didn't know. But her body—her entire damn body—clenched with anticipation. Any fear she'd felt disappeared, and a very welcome anger tried to shove through her haze of scary arousal. "Last chance," she snapped.

He smiled then, giving him a feral look.

A tremble shook her. She uncurled her fingers and pushed his chest as hard as she could.

He didn't move. Not only didn't he move, he didn't resist. Fully relaxed, caging her in place, he didn't need to do a thing to defend himself from her. The hard plane of his chest mocked her palms. Her temper flew, and she aimed her knee up.

He easily stepped into her, forcing her leg down. "You already tried that. Remember?"

God, she had. Never in her life had she tried to knee a guy in the nuts, and now she'd attempted it twice in a matter of hours. Both times she'd failed. "What do you want?" she gasped.

His eyes deepened. All of those blue flecks commingled into something dark. "Baby, if I answered that, I really would scare you." His heated breath brushed her face.

Oh, she wanted to know. What did that *mean*? What did he really want? Her chest started to rise and fall quickly, giving away her state of mind, but she couldn't stop it. There was too much, he was too much. Anger filled her, finally pushing away the intrigue. "We agreed we didn't know each other, so whatever you have in mind would probably bore me." Why in the hell had she said that? Her mouth seemed to want to push Denver as far as possible.

Even half out of it, she knew pushing him was a bad idea.

"Bore you?" he whispered.

The threat in that tone forced a whimper from her. She barely bit it down, so it came out as a sigh instead. "Enough of this." Her voice shook.

"Oh, baby. You started this." He leaned in, his lips nuzzling her earlobe. "I'd hate to bring you to my nice safe house and bore you."

Her breath caught. Panic rippled through her on the heels of a desire so sharp it hurt. "Stop playing."

His hand slid across the paneling with a rough sound and then tangled in her hair. He drew back her head so she met his gaze directly above her. "Listen good."

She gulped.

"I understand you're mad, and you have a right." His firm hold tightened, sending sparks of erotic pain across her scalp. "But enough for tonight. You have a choice. Think before you answer."

She couldn't look away from the heat in his eyes. Her mouth dried up. He was so close, she couldn't move her hands from his chest. Every inch of her was caught by him. Unable to move. The hard line of his erection dug into her stomach, and she could feel him pulse with need.

"We can continue this, and I can show you exactly why it was better I left. Or you can nicely turn and go get some sleep while I work." He slowly released her and took a very small step back. "I'm done right now, Noni. It's your call."

He wanted her. That much she knew. If she pushed him, they'd be in bed again for the night. A part of her—the physical, lonely, needy part—wanted to grab and kiss him. But the smart part of her—the one that had learned self-preservation at way too young of an age—urged her to get away from him. He'd given her the choice. She'd barely survived her heart breaking from the nice and easygoing Denver. This guy? This guy would eat her up, consume her, and take everything she had.

For good measure, she shoved him again.

This time he took several steps away.

Not trusting herself to speak, she slid to the side, turned, and headed toward the bedroom with her head up high.

And her body aching with a pain so real it nearly brought her to her knees.

CHAPTER
4

Denver sat typing commands into the PC, his dick still trying to punch through his jeans. Noni had left the room over an hour before, and the idea of her in the big bed wouldn't leave his mind. He'd done the right thing in letting her go, when all he'd wanted to do was kiss her, and hard. Maybe for hours.

He was off balance and out of control—two things he never was. He'd tried to control himself, and when that didn't work, he'd tried to control Noni. He'd failed miserably, but if he let her get to him, they'd both end up dead.

He wanted a drink. Bad.

Yeah, he'd lost himself in a bottle for a little while getting over her, and now he could almost taste the first sip. But no more. He had a job to do—two, actually. Drinking would just get in the way.

The search for Talia had to take precedence over his other mission, the one to hunt down his past. But the past was also coming after him. Quickly. The laptop to his right dinged, and he pressed a button to accept a video chat. "Why are you up so late?" he asked his older brother grumpily.

Ryker shoved his black hair away from his face. His eyes were bloodshot, and a shadow covered his angled jaw. "Update me. Are you safe?"

"Yes. I'm just on the computers working on this case," Denver said, eyeing the searches running on the other two monitors. "What's up, Ry?"

Ryker's bluish green eyes narrowed. "Seriously? Spill."

Denver sighed. "Can we be gossipy old women later? I have work to do."

Ryker growled low. "I see. All right. Heath and I will be there in about fifteen hours. We'll have to drive because I don't want to go through airport security. Just hang tight." As a threat, it was absolute. If Ryker made up his mind about something, it was a done deal.

"Knock it off," Denver said wearily, hiding the fact that he wished his brothers could be there. He needed them. "You're in place and have to stay there."

"Then fucking talk," Ryker said, scrubbing a hand across his eyes.

Why did everyone want him to talk all of a sudden? He really wasn't that interesting of a guy. "Fine. I have Noni, and we're at the safe house in Snowville."

Ryker leaned back, his eyebrows drawing down. "I thought you found her in Greenville."

"I did. Then a couple of gangbangers threw Molotov cocktails into her motel room, and we're here at the Snowville safe house now." He leaned over to the far keyboard to punch in a series of commands.

Ryker paused. "Gangbangers?"

Denver nodded. "Yeah. Apparently Noni is hunting for a gang member who stole a baby. The Kingdom Boys is the name of the gang." Man. When he put the words together like that, the whole thing sounded crazy. A quick look at his brother confirmed that fact.

Ryker's chin lowered. "Um. A baby?"

"Yeah."

Quiet. Then more quiet. "Your baby?"

Denver blinked. "Oh. No. The kid was Noni's foster sister's, who died from an overdose. So Noni is going after the baby." The idea of Denver having a kid was crazy. He could barely keep himself alive right now.

"Okay," Ryker said slowly. "What the hell am I supposed to do with that?"

"I don't know yet," Denver said, watching search results listing on the second monitor. "I'm researching the gang now, and I'll have an update by morning. If nothing else, we have to get that baby back."

"I think we'd better head your way."

Denver settled. He owed his brothers—more than he'd ever be able to repay. They'd saved his life, and they'd endangered theirs the second they'd killed Ned. "I wish you could be here," he said honestly. Lying to Ryker wasn't an option.

"Then we're there." Ryker made to stand up.

Denver swallowed. Yeah. That was family. His chest warmed. "But I *need* you to stay in South Dakota."

Ryker paused. "Den? What's going on?"

"I feel the past coming," Denver whispered, knowing his brother would understand. "It's climbing down my neck, you know?"

Ryker settled back into his chair. "Yeah." His chin lowered. "I sense it, too. They're so close I can feel them breathing."

Sheriff Cobb had been hunting them for years, and he'd come close to finding them a week ago. Denver cleared his throat. "My focus is split, so yours can't be. You have to keep with trying to find Cobb and Madison before they find us."

Isobel Madison was the real name of the lady doctor who'd studied them, the woman they'd known as Sylvia Daniels when they were in the boys home together, and Denver would give anything to never see her again. But his gut told him he'd see her and soon.

Ryker studied him quietly. "I think you need backup."

Hell, Denver needed more than backup. But they had to keep

their flanks covered. "Remain on our primary objective while I work this case. As soon as I need anything, I'll call you." He looked at his brother. "Are we any closer to finding them?"

"No. Pacific Northwest is all we've got—and we're guessing on that," Ryker said. "My gut says they're somewhere between us right now. We'll find them."

The determination flowing through Denver even felt dark. Like an ending of sorts. "Agreed." When they found Cobb and Madison, Denver was going to put them in the ground. He needed to end the threat hanging over his brothers' heads, and he'd do it bloody and fast. But first he needed to protect Noni. "Why don't you get some—"

A large hand shoved Ryker away from the camera, and Heath ducked into view. His brown hair was mussed, and his greenish brown eyes were unfocused. "You see Noni and tell her to stop posting your picture on the Internet?"

"Yes. I found her. She won't put up any more pictures." Denver relaxed more at seeing both of his brothers safe and in one place. Then he bit back another sigh. Of course neither of his brothers was sleeping. Why would they be? It was only two in the morning. "You okay?"

"Definitely," Heath said.

Denver took in his older brother. "Love looks good on you." Heath had just put down a serial killer while saving the woman he loved, whom he was now preparing to marry. "You're glowing."

Heath snorted. "I think the bride is supposed to glow."

Denver forced a smile. Heath was a badass who couldn't glow if he tried. Even so, it felt good to mess with him a little. "In your eyes there are stars filled with little hearts."

Ryker grinned, only half of his face visible now. "You're getting poetic, Den."

Yeah, that was him. A poet. "If it don't rhyme, it's not a poem," he murmured.

Heath stretched his neck. "I'm not sure that's true."

Denver shrugged. Like they'd know a poem, a real one, if it bit them on the ass. "Speaking of which, are you writing your own vows?"

Heath shook his head. "Hell no. But I think Ryker and Zara are."

Ryker's visible eye widened. "Why do you think that?"

Heath smiled a little smugly. "Zara said so."

The horror on Ryker's face finally pushed Denver to completely relax. "Just make it rhyme."

"Really?" Ryker asked, his expression clearing.

"No," Denver said, shaking his head. "God."

Heath's gaze narrowed. "Where are you, anyway?"

Denver sobered. He'd almost convinced Ryker to stay in place, and now he needed to do the same with Heath. "Noni and I are at the Snowville safe house, and I'm researching her case."

"Why did she try to find you?" Heath asked, his eyebrows rising.

Ryker shoved him aside, half taking over the view. "She's chasing a baby kidnapped by a gang and they've turned on her."

The sleep completely deserted Heath's eyes, and he snapped awake. "We can be there in twelve hours if I drive."

Ryker rolled his eyes. "I drive faster than you do."

"Do not." Heath grabbed a chair and dropped into it, setting himself shoulder to shoulder with Ryker. They each took up half the screen, morphing their faces into a parody of a clown mirror. "How is she?"

"Fine." Denver shook his head. "Would you guys back away from the camera a little so I don't go blind?"

They did so, both looking disgruntled. "Better, Whiney Butt?" Heath muttered.

"Noni is fine. Now go back to your warm beds and keep dreaming about chocolate fountains and place settings," Denver said, wanting to discuss anything in the world besides Noni. "Have either of you set a date to get hitched?"

"No." Ryker's jaw firmed. "Not until we're done with the past. With all of it."

Yet another reason Denver had to get Noni and the baby settled and safe. He had one last job to do afterward that would guarantee his brothers made it to their weddings. "Agreed."

Heath craned his neck, trying to see behind Denver. "Where is she?"

Denver held on to his patience with both hands. "In bed."

Amusement filled Ryker's eyes. "Ohhhhhhh," he said, grinning.

Heath clapped him on the back. "Yeah. In bed, huh? In that house all by yourselves with no chaperones? Hmmm. Yet you're *not* in bed."

"Maybe she kicked him out," Ryker mock-whispered.

Heath glanced at Ry. "Didn't you buy him that book about how to please a woman?"

Ryker frowned. "I thought you bought him that?"

"Well, shit," Heath said slowly, his lips tipping up. "Nobody gave him a book. He probably sucks in bed. No wonder she won't let him in."

Ryker rubbed his jaw and focused back on Denver. "Don't worry—I can draw you a couple of diagrams. You know. With the important places circled."

Denver couldn't help but snort. Sometimes his brothers were twelve years old again. Not that they'd had a normal childhood, but still. "Would you guys grow up?" He reached for the button to disconnect the camera.

"Cut us off, and we'll fly there in three hours, airport security be damned," Ryker said easily, losing his smile.

Denver paused. "Considering I don't know where the baby is, it's better if you stay there. For now."

"He just wants the place to himself," Heath mock-whispered to Ryker. "He has a girl there."

Ryker snorted. "Seriously, Denver. We're not done yet. Talk."

Denver wanted to snap his brother's head off for asking, but there was basis for the question. His brothers cared about him or they wouldn't push so hard. A lot of people didn't have that in life. He thanked God he did. "I'm fine. Haven't had a drink in two days and don't miss it." Not completely true, but he wasn't jonesing or trembling, so all was good. Maybe he'd spent too much time in a bottle since leaving Noni, but he refused to use alcohol any longer. It was the woman sleeping down the hallway that had his full attention. He needed to end the threats hanging over everyone he cared about, and to do that he had to be at full throttle. "Don't worry. I'm good."

Ryker studied him and then stood. "Fair enough. Send me the address for the motel where you were attacked and I'll get surveillance in place—I'll call in a favor or two. There's a good chance Cobb and Madison have sent forces to track you down. They had to have seen the postings Noni put up on the web."

Denver's gut roiled. "I know." Sheriff Cobb and Dr. Madison had soldiers and mercenaries on the payroll. "I'll e-mail you the info on Noni's rental car. It's still in the parking lot of the motel and needs to be returned. Have somebody do it. Keep me informed."

Ryker nodded. "Call me when you have a plan. I'm going to check our security." He turned and strode away.

Heath moved closer to the camera. "E-mail me the searches you're running. I'll do some from here."

Denver looked at him. Lines had cut into the sides of Heath's mouth, and his eyes were on full alert. "Can't sleep?"

"No. They're coming, man. Our enemies are getting close. I can feel it," Heath said. "Just send me something to do."

Denver leaned to the side and e-mailed the information he'd gathered. There was no way to sleep when a threat breathed, so he didn't bother arguing with Heath. If Heath was feeling it, so was Ryker. But Ry would prowl their property while Heath helped with the search. "Thanks."

"No problem. If you need me, call me." Heath pursed his lips, obviously searching for words.

Denver shook his head. "I can't talk about her. Not right now." It was too fresh, and she was too close. He couldn't think straight.

Heath, true to the brother he was, nodded. "Okay. I get that, I really do." He just stared at him as if looking for words.

Denver's chest heated. "You're a good brother, H," he said softly.

Heath grinned. "I'm a great brother. So are you." He glanced over his shoulder and then back. "We're all in this together. Please don't forget that."

Denver relaxed. Yeah. They were family, and that's what mattered. "I won't. Try to get some sleep."

"You too." Heath wiggled his eyebrows up and down. "With Noni…"

"Dork." Denver chuckled.

"I know. Later." Heath clicked off.

Denver took a deep breath and went back to work. An hour later, he had more information, but his head hurt. He glanced around the room. Nowhere to sleep. He headed down the hall and nudged open the door to the bedroom. The dim hall light spilled inside to illuminate the woman on the bed.

Noni slept quietly on her side, her silky hair spread over the pillow. She took up barely a quarter of the bed. Something welled up in his chest, and he let his throat fill. She was so damn close.

Every night when he closed his eyes and tried to sleep, he saw her face. Smelled her scent. Not once had he let himself hope that he'd see her again. Touch her again. He'd figured his short time with her would have to sustain him for the rest of his life. The time when he'd almost had a life—a real one with her. He'd whispered "Good-bye" as he'd left town, and he'd meant it, even though his chest had felt like somebody had sliced into him with a blade.

Yet now she was within his reach. Somehow it hurt worse knowing that he would have to let her go again.

He was so fucking tired. She was so fucking close. Without allowing himself to think about it, he snapped off the hall light and moved into the bedroom, gingerly lying down next to her.

She didn't move. Her breathing was even and her sleep seemingly peaceful.

He reached out and rubbed some of her smooth hair between his fingers. Soft and silky. Her scent of orchids wafted around him, settling him. It had amused him from day one that a woman from one of the coldest areas in the world would have such a warm smell. Like every day was a peaceful vacation.

He fell asleep surrounded by her, and for once the nightmares stayed away.

* * *

Noni slowly came awake with a heater at her back. The smell of male and forest filled her senses.

Denver.

She stilled and listened to his even breathing. He was asleep. Good. She took a moment to feel his presence in bed again. Some of the happiest times in her entire life had been with him in bed. Man, she'd fallen for him fast and hard. They'd dated for only about three months, but she could remember each and every detail as if it were yesterday. The feeling of him in bed was right.

Yet it wasn't. It couldn't be. For months after he'd left, she hadn't slept in her bed. She'd watched television until falling asleep on the sofa in her living room.

She couldn't do this. Be with him like this. Everything feminine in her wanted to turn around and snuggle into his arms. But he'd be gone soon, and she knew it. Why torture herself? The room was still dark, so dawn hadn't yet arrived. She slid from the bed as quietly as she could, turned, and backtracked to the doorway.

He slept on his back on top of the covers, his huge body taking up most of the bed. His movements were nil, but his breathing even. How tired had he been? A lock of his black hair had fallen onto his forehead, and her fingers itched to push it away. To caress down his hard jaw and muscled neck to that wide chest. She'd once spent an entire morning kissing that chest.

Man, she missed him. Even now, with him near and her so pissed, she missed those moments. When he had been hers to touch.

Enough wallowing. It was beneath her, and she was stronger than this. There was no choice. She swallowed and gathered her courage, stepping out of the room and quietly shutting the door. After a quick trip to the one bathroom, she tiptoed into the living room and surveyed the computers. The materials from her backpack were spread over a table, and other manila files and yellow notepads were scattered around.

Forgoing her notes for his, she flipped through them. A small— very small—part of her felt guilty to be going through Denver's things. The other part, the one he'd abandoned alone in a bed in Alaska, didn't give a hoot. The man would never level with her, so she'd be the detective on this case.

The file held a bunch of notes and pictures of redheaded women.

Something about the Copper Killer murderer. She pushed it aside and opened another file labeled DR. MADISON. A picture of a beautiful woman with black hair and cold blue eyes was taped to the inside cover.

"See anything that interests you?" Denver asked from hallway entry.

Noni jumped, her lungs compressing. "I'm just getting started." She would not feel bad. "I read about the Copper Killer case in the newspaper. He was a serial killer who focused on redheads. They caught the guy here in Snowville, right?"

"*We* caught the guy," Denver said, not moving. He leaned against the door frame, his hair mussed up, whiskers covering his square jaw. His ragged T-shirt was wrinkled and his jeans ripped, and nothing in the world had ever looked so delicious. Sexy, tousled, and dangerous.

Noni cleared her throat. A pulse set up between her legs. So that's why he had been in town. To catch a serial killer. "That wasn't in the news."

"It wouldn't be." He pushed away from the door frame and moved toward her, holding out his hand. "My records."

She clutched them to her chest. "I'm not done snooping."

"Yes, you are." He grasped the manila folders with two fingers and pulled.

She could fight him, but in a tug of war, she'd probably lose. Or at least get a paper cut, and those sucked. "Who is Dr. Madison?"

At the question, his lazy indulgence disappeared. A flash of heat hit his eyes, and for the moment, he looked every bit as deadly as he'd warned her that he could be. Barely leashed violence poured off him in a heat she could actually feel. "Nobody," he said, his voice guttural.

Noni gaped at him. At the change in him—in a second. "Right. I, ah, I can see that."

Then the gates closed. A veil fell over his expressive eyes, effectively shutting her out.

She exhaled. "I'd forgotten that look." When they'd dated, every time she'd asked about his life, about his childhood, he'd shut her out. And she'd let him. Oh, she'd sensed the pain in his past, and she'd just accepted him, knowing someday he'd open up to her. Someday he'd feel free enough, safe enough, to confide in her. "I was such a clueless idiot," she muttered, finally letting the truth in. Even when they'd been together, he hadn't let her know him.

"No, you weren't," he said gently. "I'm good at playing a part. Really good."

Fury lashed her. She jumped up, sending the chair flying back. He had fooled her, and he had done a good job of it. But there had been moments...real moments. She had to trust herself and what she felt. Could she shake him? Get him to admit it was more than just a part? "Oh, *baby*. You're not that good."

"No?" he asked silkily.

"No." She levered up right into his face, finally trusting her instincts. "I may not know the details of your life, of your big secrets, but I know you a little bit, asshole." She slapped a hand on his chest. Hard. "Whether you like it or not, you revealed some of your true self." While she didn't know the facts, she knew his heart. Whether he liked it or not. Since he'd shown up in her motel room, she hadn't had time to really think. No way would he hurt her. He might be dangerous, but she was safe. Well, probably. "You're not such a mystery."

"Maybe," he said, pressing his hand over hers. "It doesn't change anything. We're gonna find this baby and get you safe. Then I have another job to do."

"Jobs," she sputtered as his heart beat so steadily against her palm. "Tons of jobs, right?"

"No. Just one." His hand completely covered hers, and she couldn't move it. The way he'd said the words gave her pause. Such finality in each syllable.

Her gaze dropped to the files in his other hand. "Dr. Madison?"

He slowly nodded.

"You're trying to find her?" That's what he did, right? He found people or things. His detective agency found the lost. That's what he'd always said.

"Yes."

She swallowed. "Then what?" Instinct chilled her, but she didn't know why. Tension choked around them. "What happens to Dr. Madison?"

"I'm going to kill her." With that, Denver released Noni's hand and moved around her to the computers. "Now. Let's find that baby."

CHAPTER
5

Denver finished the dry cereal, his gaze on the computer. Ah shit. The Kingdom Boys had sources on the dark web, where they sold drugs. Anything and everything, including kids, could be sold there. He kept his expression stoic since Noni was in the room, but a fire burned in his chest. They had to save that baby.

She watched another monitor from the ripped orange chair.

The office chair he sat in barely held his weight, protesting every time he moved. "Store. Today."

"You're back to talking in incomplete sentences," she muttered.

So long as he got his point across, who cared? "Okay."

"Whatever." Noni sat on one leg. She wore light jeans with a pretty green sweater, looking sweet and tempting.

He pushed his bowl away. He'd rather have his mouth on her than a spoon. Then his search from the hacked traffic cams dinged, and he found pictures of Richie that he quickly printed out. Good. The gang member wasn't alone.

"I don't understand what we're doing," Noni said softly.

Denver searched for the right words. "Why would a known gang member, one who has been convicted twice for drug-related offenses, want a baby?" The complete profile on Richie Romano had been easy to compile. The man was hooked on meth and liked robbing people. The psychological profile by the prison shrink said Richie was a narcissist and probably a sadist. The bad kind.

Noni finished her Cheerios. "Talia is his kid."

Denver's heart warmed. How naive she still was. He had to explain things to her better. "That doesn't matter to a lot of folks, sweetheart. He doesn't want to take care of a baby. He has no family, no mama who might want to raise the girl. So why take her and run?"

Noni's eyes widened. "I don't know."

Denver pointed to the third monitor. "I'm on a site called Cashmere Street, and it's a place where everything can be bartered for."

Noni squinted at the relatively quiet screen. "Like eBay?"

He grimaced. "Yeah, if eBay was on the dark web and you could buy drugs, illegal porn, and hit men there."

She coughed and leaned away from the screen. "I've heard about the dark web on television, but I've never understood what it is."

"It's part of the web you can't reach from the surface. No search engine or spider can get to it." Denver pointed to the numbers at the top of the screen. "To get there, you use specific software that anonymizes your network. And you spend special coins—virtual coins—to buy what you want."

She paled and frowned as the truth obviously hit her. Hard. "You think Richie wants to sell the baby."

Denver kept a close eye on her. He had to tell her the truth, but maybe he could soften it somehow. "I spent half the night tracking his specific gang and what they do. They're actually pretty sophisticated, using the dark web to transport and distribute drugs as well as illicit porn. I haven't found a track to the baby angle."

Noni shook her head. "You're telling me there's a gang in Greenville that does this?"

"No. The gang pipeline, this one, goes from Alaska down the coast to Mexico and back up. Greenville is probably a gang hold. I think you were directed there for the hit." The woman was too pale. He had to get some protein in her so she could keep her strength. "We need to go to the store."

Noni held her stomach as if trying to keep from puking. "Who would want to buy a baby on the dark web? Who could even find the dark web?"

"It's not that tough to find." Denver hoped to leave the other question alone.

She lifted her eyes, those dark pools full of fear. "Who'd buy a baby?"

"Hopefully some desperate couple who wants a baby," he said evenly. It could happen.

She looked down, her body tensing. "There are a lot of bad people out there who want kids for bad things, Denver."

There wasn't anything to say to that. It sucked, and it was true. "We'll find Talia, Noni." He was a hunter, and he found the lost. He could save that baby for her. "Trust me."

She lifted her head again, and tears glimmered in her eyes. "Richie's a bad guy. What if he gets tired of a crying baby?"

Denver reached over his shoulder and grabbed a couple of photos off the printer. "First, if he's trying to sell the baby, then he'll keep her in good shape. Second, he's not traveling alone." He had to fight to keep his voice calm and express confidence to her. This was a bad fucking situation, and he wasn't sure how to protect her.

She took the photos of Richie driving a battered truck with a young blonde next to him. Denver had hacked into the surveillance cameras of a gas station to get them. The woman was probably eighteen or nineteen. "He has a friend," Noni murmured.

"Yep." Denver did a quick search for the woman using facial

recognition that he shouldn't be able to access. Leaning over, he studied a mug shot and then scrolled down. "Her name is Hailey Smithers, she's twenty, and she was convicted of hooking and possession a year ago. Pled no contest and was given probation." He pointed to the bottom of the screen. "Has been running with the Kingdom Boys since she was fifteen, and I have no doubt she's along to help take care of the baby."

"The fact that a drug-snorting hooker is helping care for Talia doesn't ease my mind." Noni looked away from the picture. "Any news on the three guys you shot last night at the motel?"

"They're all recuperating at the local hospital. When the police searched them, they were in possession of illegal firearms and crystal meth. They're known to deal drugs, so it wasn't a huge surprise." Denver forced a smile for her. There had to be a way to shield her from what he was about to do to one of them. As soon as he got her settled in the house for the day. "Sometimes things work out just fine."

Noni breathed out, her gaze direct. "All right. I need to see your contract before we go any further. What kind of a deposit does your company take?"

He went still. Fire unbanked in his gut at the offense. "You're fuckin' with me, right?"

She blinked. "What does that mean? I assume it's a retainer plus expenses and fees."

"Are you trying to piss me off?" He cocked his head to the side, wanting to delve into her brain. Was she insulting him on purpose? That didn't seem like her. He held on to his temper with both hands, almost not recognizing the accompanying hurt in his gut. Sure, he was an ass, but she had to know he'd save a baby because it was the right thing to do and not for money. "Noni?"

She straightened in her chair. "No."

"Right." He shook his head. Boy, did she have it wrong. Have him wrong. Heat rushed through his head, making his ears ring. "I'm not takin' money from you."

Her shoulders rose, her chin lowered, and she glared at him. "The hell you aren't."

* * *

Noni kept his gaze. She had to win this argument in order to stay in control of the situation. There was no backing down. "I will pay you."

His eyes darkened to what could only be interpreted as a warning. "No payment. Don't mention it again."

Had he been this bossy when they dated? Sure, he'd been rather commanding in bed, and she'd liked that. But she didn't remember him being overtly so in everyday life. "Oh, I'm mentioning it and right now. There will be a contract, there will be payment, and I'm the client." That meant she was in charge. Yeah.

He crossed his muscled arms. "No."

She bit the inside of her lip to keep from screaming at him. Calm. She needed to stay in control of herself to win this argument. "Yes. You might want to check with your partners about this. I'm sure they'd like to get paid."

"Brothers," he drawled. "My partners are my two brothers, and I'm sure they know we're not charging you."

He had brothers. Hurt blanketed her for a second, and she shoved it away. Yet another thing she hadn't known about him. "It's my way or no way, Denver. This will be a business relationship."

"Not a chance, baby. Let it go." The last was said rather clipped.

"Because we slept together?" She rolled her eyes so hard her entire head hurt. "It was just sex, and frankly I've forgotten about it." If lightning struck people who lied, she'd be deader than dead at that one. "If you haven't, that's your problem."

"I think about it every day and dream about it every night. Sometimes I still feel wrapped up in you when I wake up." His eyes burned, and his body had gone tense, even sitting down.

She couldn't think. What did that mean? Okay. Deep breath. One. Two. Then another one. Head clear. Her body tingled. Why did he say things like that? Especially when he usually kept silent. Yet an unrealistic hope, one she didn't want to feel, warmed her. He'd missed her. She'd needed to know that. But there was no chance for them—he wouldn't take the chance. That hurt, that reality, pissed her right off. "Aren't you the talkative fellow these days?" Her sarcastic tone made her wince.

"I try," he said evenly.

"That's nice. Considering you have family I didn't know about. Brothers?" She'd sounded hurt on the last, so she cleared her throat.

"Ryker and Heath," Denver said, holding up his right hand to show a long scar along his palm. "When I told you it was from a hunting accident, I lied. We cut our hands and became brothers a long time ago. For years they've been all I had." He breathed out at the end as if telling the entire story was difficult. The man had that look he used to get when he needed a moment of quiet. Of silence.

Too damn bad. "I see." She crossed her arms.

"Ry and Heath are both engaged." Denver stiffened, and his expression smoothed out.

What the heck? "What thought just grabbed you?" she whispered.

He breathed out, his muscled chest moving. "Just remembering I have a job to do after we get you safe."

Safe. After they found Talia and got her away from Richie. Oh, Denver might be finally opening up about his life, about his past, but it was too late. Only the present mattered. Only Talia mattered. "It sounds like your brothers will have weddings to pay for. So let's get our fee agreement set now, shall we?"

He shook his head. "Stop it."

Absolutely not. Her aunt was the negotiator in the family in their lotion and candle making business, while Noni was the creative one. When she mixed ingredients to create the perfect feel and smell of lotions or perfumes, she was in control. When she argued with other people, her anxiety level rose. Even now, spirals uncoiled in her chest. But she had no choice. "I'm not backing down on this, Denver. Quote me a deal."

"All right." He stood suddenly, a large man with surprising grace. A quick pivot, and he plucked her right out of her chair before dropping back down with her cradled on his lap.

She didn't have time to protest before he'd already settled her against his chest. The well-worn black T-shirt molded hard-cut muscles. "What are you doing?" she whispered.

"Quoting and dealing," he said wryly. His strong frame surrounded her, offering safety and protection she'd missed so much. The torn jeans encasing his muscled thighs let out warmth, but it was like sitting on a boulder. It took every ounce of her self-control to keep from snuggling right into him and letting him shield her from the world. "You need to listen, Noni."

She tilted her head to meet his gaze. "So do you."

His eyebrow lifted, and those stunning eyes studied her. "I'm sorry I hurt you." His voice rumbled low, sounding pained.

Her mouth gaped. Not what she'd been expecting. She wanted to matter to him badly. How pathetic was that? Even so, he was sorry he'd caused harm. Not sorry he'd left. She needed to remember that very important distinction—because nowhere in it was a promise of a future. A promise of anything. "I don't have an answer to that."

He brushed hair back from her face gently, sending her system into overdrive again. "But that has to remain in the past, at least for now. We're in danger. Serious danger."

His touch felt so right while his words cut deep. His honesty hurt her. She tried to follow his words and not hit him in the face. Because he was right about the danger. It was time to stop thinking about herself, about her heart, and put Talia first. The thought hit her then: she was going to be a mother. Oh God. She didn't know how to do that. Not really. She'd helped for three months, and she loved that baby. It was a start. "There's a gang after us."

He nodded. "Not just them. There are enemies from my past, ones far more dangerous than that gang, whom you've alerted with your posts of my picture. These people are ruthless and well trained."

Goose bumps rose on her arms. Not once had she thought she might be putting him in danger. "Who are they?" Her gaze caught on the manila file near the computer. The one he hadn't let her read. "Is that Dr. Madison one of them?"

"She is, and she's a psychopath," Denver said, his jaw hardening. "She's ruthless and doesn't understand the concept of mercy."

Icy fingers tracked down Noni's spine, and she shivered. Oh, she wanted the whole story and needed to know more about him. "I'm sorry I've exposed you."

"It's okay. The baby comes first." Denver tightened his hold. "But the personal stuff, the hurt and anger and sarcasm. That needs to go away and right now so we can get this job done."

Heat filled her cheeks. He was right. Their only priority right now had to be Talia. While she had no clue how to be a mother, she at least knew that the baby had to be her number-one priority. She could learn the rest. "I understand."

"Good. This is an op, and there's no arguing. I'm in charge, Non. You obey. I can't say it any clearer than that." His voice remained gentle, but his hold was unbreakable.

That so did not sit well. Not even a little. She opened her mouth to argue, and he bit her lip. Shock ripped through her, and she went rigid. Lightning speared her, making her ache. Making her need…more.

He licked the small wound and leaned back. "I don't play fair. In fact, I don't play. Learn that now."

She had no words. His mouth had seared her, imprinting hard. She could still feel the nip. Who the hell was this guy? Worse yet, why was she even more intrigued than before? She'd never been the type to go for a bad boy. Yet here she was.

But she needed him. Needed his strength and edge…even the darkness. To save Talia. If anybody could save her from a dangerous gang, it'd be him. That's why Noni had hunted him down.

She dropped her gaze to his chest, fighting to moderate her breath. Her heart beat wildly, and a terrifying ache set up between her thighs. "Your point?" she managed to force out without whimpering.

He twisted one hand in her hair and pulled back, forcing a helpless, choked sound from her. "No more arguing about payment. No more digs about the past. No more defiance." He drew her face closer, stealing her breath. "I'll keep you safe. I'll get that baby back. I'll do it my way."

Her gaze dropped to his lips. He was absolute, and he wasn't backing down. Could she fight him? Even if she wanted to? It didn't matter. Not really. She needed him to save Talia. "Denver."

"Tell me you get me. That's all I want to hear from you. Now." His breath brushed her lips.

What if she argued? What would he do? A part of her really

wanted to find out. The other part, the sane and rational part, knew she needed his help to find Talia. Even if she had to agree to his terms. There truly wasn't a better choice. "I get you," she said, her body stiffening as she gave in.

For now.

CHAPTER
6

Three hours after his heart to heart with Noni, Denver conducted another search on the Internet. Noni worked through her papers across the room from him, having avoided talking to him the rest of the morning. He couldn't really blame her. Playing the heavy had never sit well with him, but if he was going to keep her alive, he had no choice. He stood. "I have to run an errand." That sounded better than telling her he was going to steal a car, right?

She didn't look up. "Whatever."

He paused. His fingers itched to pick her up again and sit for a while, but he'd already made his point. "Okay." Footsteps outside caught his attention. He stiffened and moved instantly to the drapes, tugging his gun out from the back of his jeans. "Get down."

The sound of her moving reassured him.

One guy in thick boots strode easily up the snow-filled walk with two oversized boxes balanced in his hands. He had cropped dark hair and wore a dark brown uniform. His movements were graceful and steady.

Denver tensed. "Get ready to go out the back door." He could cover her. "If I yell to run, you run through the backyard, scale the fence to the west, and keep running. Get to the police station and ask for Detective Malloy. He's a friend."

Noni gasped. "What about you?"

"I'll be right behind you."

The delivery guy knocked on the door. "Delivery for Denver Gray," he said quietly.

Gray? Seriously? This might be really good or really, really, really bad. Denver stiffened. "Kitchen, Noni. Now." He waited until he heard her move before stepping to the door and opening it, pointing his gun instantly in the guy's face. "There's no Denver Gray here."

The guy didn't blink. If anything, his brown eyes appeared bored. "Wait for it," he muttered.

Denver's phone buzzed, and he pulled it from his pocket, keeping his gun level. A quick look down confirmed his suspicions, and he clicked to answer. "This is a bad time, Jory," he muttered into the phone.

Jory Dean sighed loudly over the line. "Don't shoot my guy. The packages are from me."

Damn it. Denver slid the phone back into his pocket and took the packages, waiting until the guy had returned to his running truck on the road and driven away. Then he locked the door and put the boxes down.

Noni walked in from the kitchen, her steps slow and unsure. "Denver?"

"We're okay." He tugged open the first box and whistled. Guns, knives, two bulletproof vests, and several stacks of cash were piled inside.

Noni leaned over to stare into the box and then gasped. She took several steps back. "Um."

Yeah, *um*. Denver opened the second box to find milk, butter, bread, and a bunch of other staples, including steak and fresh salads. "From a friend." Denver yanked his phone out of his pocket again.

"You have interesting friends," Noni murmured, her eyes wide and her face pale.

"Another long story. His name is Jory, he lives in Montana, and I just recently found out about him." Denver pressed a speed dial button.

Noni gulped. "You just found out about a friend?"

Denver paused. "It's a *really* long story. But Jory is a distant relative, somehow. Okay. He might be my brother. We don't know yet." Their jawlines were similar.

"Huh? You might have another brother out there?"

"Another brother from the same mother," Denver quipped before sobering. "Sorry. Inappropriate humor." He glanced at her.

Her chin dropped, her eyes wide. "This is weird. Right?"

He nodded. "My whole life is a little weird."

She shook her head. "Your friend—maybe brother—sends you weapons and money. Is he a drug kingpin or something?" She swallowed and eyed the steaks. "Or a grocer?"

Denver snorted. "He's one of the good guys." As if on cue, Jory's square face took up the screen of his phone. "It's not my birthday," Denver said quietly, clicking on the video chat.

Jory rolled his very gray eyes. "Like any of us know our birthdays." As always, he appeared cheerful. Like a cuddly guard dog that could instantly switch from wagging its tail to attacking with razor-sharp teeth. "You're broke, you're on mission, and you need this stuff. I can be there in two hours for backup."

Denver didn't know what to say. All of his family wanted to help, and right now he couldn't direct anybody anywhere. At some point, if he lived through taking out Cobb and Madison, he wanted to get to know Jory and his three brothers. "Any news?"

Jory shook his head. "The results aren't back yet."

That wasn't a surprise. Denver and Jory had taken a DNA test to see if they were genetically related. "Did you tell your brothers?"

"No."

"Me either." Denver sighed. "We could just go on faith like everyone else has, but I'd rather know the truth."

"Me too." Jory focused. "Though I consider us family no matter what."

Yeah. Denver studied him. He considered Ry and Heath his brothers, and that would never change. But it'd be nice to have a genetic connection to Jory and his family. "We should have the results soon." Okay. He didn't want to hope, so he didn't.

"You find the baby yet?" Jory asked.

Denver blinked. "You know about the current mission?"

"Of course. You're crazy if you think we're not monitoring everything you do. Might as well come to Montana," Jory said cheerfully.

"After I get the baby."

"After that?" Jory asked, his eyes glittering.

Denver settled. Of course Jory Dean could read him. It's what they all did. He knew Denver was going after Madison and Cobb on his own at some point soon. "You know it's gonna be me, right?" he whispered.

Jory's eyes darkened. "Yeah. I know." He didn't even try to pretend not to know what Denver was talking about. "You know it *was* me, right?"

Denver nodded. "Yeah." An evil man in Jory's past had chased Jory and his three older brothers, and it had been Jory who'd taken him down for good. Jory's brothers were all from the same father. "When it happens, I'll call."

Jory's expression darkened. "You need me, us, now?"

"Not yet. Stay there. I'll call when needed." Jory and his brothers had relocated to Montana, where they were safe and building normal lives. Well, pretty normal, anyway. "Thanks, Jory."

"You got it. There will be a car outside within ten minutes. Your truck is blown for now. Keep it in the garage, and I'll have it fetched when it's safe to do so." The screen went black.

Noni blew out air. "Your life is sure…interesting."

"You don't know the half of it," Denver muttered, reaching for the money. At least twenty thousand dollars. What exactly did Jory think he was going to do with this much cash?

"But I'd like to," she whispered, pain in her voice.

He jerked and looked at her. "The less you know, the safer you are. Don't you get that?"

Her eyebrows—both of them—lifted. "Think so? It's a little late, right? I mean, I posted the picture of us together, and there doesn't seem to be a doubt that it's been seen. Those enemies from your past know we were together. My not knowing about them puts me in more danger. At the very least, I need to recognize who's coming."

Damn if she didn't have a point. Denver gave a short nod. "You're right. I'll tell you everything later tonight." He drew out two knives and a gun.

She took a step back. "Why not now?"

If the woman wanted to be in the know, she could be. "Because I'm heading back to Greenville, to the hospital, to torture one of those gang members into telling me everything he knows."

She paled but remained in place. "Oh," she whispered. "I don't think—"

"It's a done deal." He grabbed another sheathed knife to place in his boot. "You don't have to be part of this, and I can definitely keep info like this from you." He'd prefer she didn't know what he was capable of doing. "But you can't stop me."

"I'm not trying to stop you," she whispered. "I just wanted to apologize for putting you in a place where you have to do this."

He stiffened and then rose. She was worried about *him*? Even more so, she understood and accepted that he would do what he needed to do. Maybe he'd underestimated her before. Could she handle his darkness? Really? "You're okay with me doing this?"

"No," she said softly. "I wish you didn't have to, and I'm so sorry. I'd offer to do it, but…"

But there was no way in hell a person as sweet as her could torture somebody. Thank God. He finished suiting up and handed her a gun. "This one fits your hand better than the one you have in your pack. Point and shoot at anybody who's not me. When I get back, we'll talk." Then he'd tell her everything.

* * *

Noni finished stirring the chicken in the large pot as the kitchen filled with the aroma of homemade chicken soup. She'd found a satellite radio station on one of the computers, and it blared Christmas music throughout the quiet house. No matter how hard she tried, she couldn't banish thoughts of Denver confronting the gang-bangers in the hospital. What if they had friends there? Would he try to take them all on?

Oh, she'd known he was a good private detective, but she hadn't realized he was so comfortable with the darker and illegal side of life. There was so much she didn't know about him.

Yet that just intrigued her more.

Her phone rang and she quickly grabbed it to see her aunt's face on the screen. "Hi, Franny," she answered the video chat.

"Sparrow here, Eagle," her aunt responded, her dark eyes sparkling. Light gray sprinkled her dark hair, which was piled high on her head. "I'm in Portland and have met with a cop on the local force. Pretended I was writing an article about gangs in the area. I'll e-mail you the information."

Noni nodded. Her aunt was pretty good at this. "The gang contact in Greenville was a bust. Nothing there. I've moved into Snowville," she said. There was no need to let Franny know about the hit squad. She would just worry.

"Okay. Hawk Two checked in and there doesn't seem to be any activity in Salt Lake City. She tried the same tactic as I did but didn't get as much information about the gangs. I've never thought Salt Lake was where Richie was headed."

"Did you meet with our PI?" Noni asked.

"Yes, and he has no new information. In fact, he wants another five-thousand-dollar retainer to keep working." Franny worried her lower lip with her teeth. "I still have some jewelry I could pawn."

"No. I'll call him and let him know we're finished with his services." Noni struggled to keep her expression light and factual. "Denver is here, and we're coming up with a plan. I think you and Verna should head back to Anchorage for the time being." While Franny was only in her early fifties, Verna was pushing sixty, and the women who'd raised and loved Noni since she was four years old needed to be kept safe. "Or you could go on that honeymoon you keep promising her."

Franny snorted. "We've been married for three years, and we live in a prime honeymoon spot."

Alaska? Noni tried again to help soothe her aunt's fear of flying. "Maybe somewhere warm. It's safe to travel." In fact, returning to Anchorage and facing members of Richie's gang there was probably a bad idea. "We have intel that Richie and other Kingdom Boys might be headed toward Oregon. How about you have Verna meet you in Portland and investigate?" She made the lie with a straight face.

Franny rolled her eyes. "You don't think he's coming here, but you don't know that he isn't. So I'll have Hawk Two head this direction come morning."

Okay. If Noni could keep them out of Alaska and away from Snowville, they'd be safe. "Good plan."

"How's dickhead?" Franny asked, her lips forming a white line.

"Sexy as ever." Noni sighed. "His chest seems even broader."

Franny tsked. "I told you to date the forest ranger who asked you out last year. At least you would've gotten some."

Sex every night with somebody else wouldn't have diminished her reaction to Denver, and Noni knew it. "He said he was sorry," she said quietly.

Franny's dark eyes narrowed. "For hurting you or for leaving you?"

Darn it. Franny was way too smart. "Hurting me." Noni stirred the soup again. "Now I've cooked for him," she muttered.

"Oh, honey," Franny said, her eyebrows lifting. "Something delicious or just okay?"

Noni bit her lip. "My soup. Chicken noodle."

"The good stuff," Franny breathed. "What are you thinking?"

"I was hungry," Noni said, hunching her shoulders. Plus, Denver was off torturing people for her, so the least she could do was cook something for him to eat afterward. She couldn't tell Franny that, however.

"At least tell me you hired him properly as a detective. That keeps us in the driver's seat," Franny said, leaning close to the camera.

Noni grimaced. "I did tell him that, but he disagreed, and I'm pretty sure he won the argument."

Franny shook her head. "Don't let him take control."

Denver was all control. "I won't," Noni said, afraid she was lying yet again. A car stopped outside, and she heard boots coming up the walk. "I think he's back. I'll call you tomorrow. Love you." She waited for the "Love you" response and then hung up.

The front door opened, and Denver came inside. Dried blood matted his neck and down his dark T-shirt. Noni swallowed. Her knees trembled, and she almost backed away. His eyes were dark and unfathomable, and his jaw looked harder than rock. "How did it go?" she asked, her voice breaking.

"Not great. The idiots were just wanna-be gang members. They had no clue who you were or why anybody wanted you shot." He kicked off his boots, and a sheathed knife fell out. The shiny handle glinted in the soft light while Christmas carols played from the nearest computer. He looked at the speaker briefly but didn't comment.

"Shot?" she asked, eyeing the knife, her breath cooling.

He nodded. "Yeah. They were told whoever made the kill shot would complete their initiation into the Kingdom Boys. They're all just hopeful members at the moment."

Kill shot. There had been three men with kill-shot orders on her. She gulped down complete panic. If Denver hadn't shown up at the motel, she would've been killed. The grim look on his face confirmed that. "But they failed."

He wiped blood off his chin. "They did, which means they're not done. There are also three other new wanna-be members who want a literal shot at you."

Chills clacked down her back.

"I won't let them hurt you," Denver said, his voice raw gravel. "After I questioned them, I made it clear what would happen if they tried. They promised nicely to let their friends know."

What would scare someone who wanted to be in a gang? She took a step back. "What did you do to them?" Her voice shook, but she couldn't help it.

The look in his eyes was stark. Haunted. "They're still alive, but that's all I'm telling you. They'll be put into the system, and since they'll probably be charged with organized crime, they won't get out for a long time. If ever." He glanced down at the blood on his hands. "I need to take a quick shower. Something smells really good." He strode through the living room and disappeared down the hall.

Blood. That had definitely been blood. Her stomach rolled, and a rock dropped to the bottom. Just who was that man?

CHAPTER
7

Denver smoothed back his wet hair after having dressed in a clean pair of faded jeans and a T-shirt, this one a dark blue. He loped into the kitchen, where Noni had already set the table with fuzzy yellow placemats and chipped ceramic bowls. Candles flickered in the middle of the table. He'd forgotten how much she liked to entertain. She'd been the first woman ever to cook for him and care if he enjoyed the meal or not. God, he'd missed her. "Smells good," he mumbled.

"Sit." She turned from the stove and dished up bowls of soup that smelled like heaven. Sourdough bread and butter came next, along with a bottle of white wine with a very fancy label. "Your brother has expensive taste in wine." She poured them both glasses and then took a seat. "I indulged a little while I was cooking, and it's excellent."

He kept himself from fidgeting in his chair and took a taste of the soup. Delicious spices exploded on his tongue, and he hummed in appreciation. "I've missed your cooking." Wrong thing to say, considering he'd abandoned her.

She let him off the hook and broke off a piece of bread. "It's cold outside and soup seemed a good choice." In her deep green sweater with her miles of dark hair pulled back, she looked like the perfect present to unwrap. He'd never seen a woman with eyes as dark as hers, and making them glow with pleasure was one of the few happy memories he kept. He remembered how to touch her, how to please her. Soft and sweet. His Noni.

His jeans felt too tight as his cock woke up. Her scent was just under the smell of the delicious dinner, making him want. He shook his head to regain control. The Christmas music still jingled in the background. "I'm sorry you're not home preparing for the holidays," he said. She probably loved it, right?

She took a drink of her wine. "Me too. Franny and Verna have always gone all out."

He ate more of the soup, wanting to keep the conversation relaxed. "Where are they?"

"They'll both be safely in Portland by tomorrow night," Noni said, her voice a mite high as she obviously tried to engage in normal conversation after seeing him covered in blood. "I think that's better than home, don't you?"

He thought about it while he chewed bread. Even that somehow tasted better than normal because she'd heated it. "Yeah. Let's keep them there." Besides, if he faced either one of them, he was pretty sure he'd get kicked in the balls for hurting their girl. He got that. In fact, he appreciated it. "Sorry I couldn't get any information from the gang members." Hearing them squeal in pain had made his day, however. To think that they might've gotten to Noni if he hadn't hit town in time. His hand tightened on his wineglass, and he forced himself to relax his hold.

She cleared her throat. "Did you, ah, hurt them badly?"

He wasn't going there with her. "Yes, and they deserved pain. Topic closed."

Her lips thinned, but she didn't argue. "Fine. You promised me your life story."

Man, he wasn't ready for that. "You talk first. How's the business?" She'd started her own lotion, candle, and perfume shop, and it had impressed the hell out of him. The place smelled like he assumed heaven would.

Her eyes lit. "Great. We're doing a lot more Internet sales these days, which is pretty normal. Franny does the business side, I create, and Verna has been doing the Internet stuff. She's getting swamped, though, so I think we might have to hire some help." Noni took another drink of the wine and gave a soft moan. "So good."

That sound shot right down his chest and landed in his balls. If she was still his, he'd reach for her and make her dessert. But he'd given her up, and he had no right to touch her, no matter how badly it hurt. But maybe he could know her better. He'd give anything to know all of her—to be the one person in life who did. "When we, ah, dated, you never told me how you ended up with them."

"That's because you never asked." Old hurts flared in her eyes and then quickly disappeared.

He winced, his breath hitching in his chest. The fact that he'd hurt her would torture him throughout his life. "I thought we should keep things casual since I had to leave at the end of the job." He'd been looking for an embezzler who had relocated to Anchorage, and he'd ultimately found the guy. "I did want to know, though." He'd wanted to know everything about her and had to appease himself with just knowing her scent and touch. He'd tried not to love her, and he'd tried to protect her by being honest about his plans to leave. Apparently he'd screwed that one up seriously. "I'm sorry I hurt you."

"So you've said," she snapped, sparks shooting from her eyes.

His cock hardened even more. "Tell me your story, and I'll tell mine." If he listened to her, he'd relax, and then he could stop mentally kicking himself for screwing up. He took a drink of the wine.

Tasted like wine. How she knew it was good, he had no clue. He was a straight whiskey man.

She sighed. "My parents, as you know, died."

Yeah, but he'd never asked how. He felt for the lost little girl she must've been. He could relate. "When you were young."

"Yeah. I was four years old, and they were snowmobiling and got caught in an avalanche." She shrugged, her eyes downcast. "I remember them only from pictures, to be honest. But I look like my mom, who also looked like Aunt Franny, so there's that."

It still hurt her. Not knowing the people who'd created her. That he could understand, and he wished he could ease her pain somehow. "Franny took you in?"

"Yes. She was working as a bookkeeper at that time and was around thirty years old."

So Franny had taken her in right away, providing love and security. "Was Verna with her yet?" he asked, taking another chunk of bread, needing to know more. The domesticity of the moment dug into him and grabbed hold with warmth. With comfort.

Noting his bowl was empty, Noni stood and ladled another bowl for him. "Yes. They've been together since college. So I got them both right away." She sat back down and smiled. "For years I couldn't understand why they couldn't get married like other parents. But now they can, and they did." She snorted. "But Franny won't go on a honeymoon, and Verna is driving her crazy about it."

"Why won't she go?" The woman had seemed like a pistol to him.

Noni smiled, her expression so full of love it hurt something in his chest. "She's terrified to fly, and Verna wants to go somewhere warm. Like on an island."

"They make drugs for people who are afraid to fly," Denver said dryly. He admired the women for taking Noni in and giving her a home. That secured his loyalty, for sure.

"That's what I told her," Noni exclaimed. "It'll happen. Verna is tough when she needs to be." She cleared her throat. "There's a chance we might meet up with them, right?"

He chewed thoughtfully. Not if he could help it. "Maybe."

"I should warn you. They call you 'dickhead.'"

He barked out a laugh. Two senior citizens called him 'dickhead.' "They're not wrong." He'd been called a helluva lot worse in his life. They loved Noni, and that's what mattered. "I won't get mad at them. I promise."

She sipped her wine. "I didn't think you would. Just didn't want your feelings hurt if they show up."

The statement hit him in the solar plexus. She was worried about his feelings? After what he'd done? Who he was? He swallowed and looked into his second empty bowl. He'd dreamed of meals like this with a woman like her years ago. It was too good to last. "Thank you for dinner. It was excellent."

"Not a problem." She waited until he looked up at her before speaking again. "It's your turn, Denver. You promised to tell me everything."

He hated to leave the comfort of talking about her family. But he'd promised. His chest hurt for a moment. What would she think if he told her everything? It was bizarre, and he was a wanted criminal. Kind of. "I know." He'd never break a promise to her.

She breathed out. "Would you like me to sit on your lap while you talk?"

His head jerked up, and his dick throbbed. "What?"

She flushed. "Before, when we dated. If I sat on your lap, you relaxed."

He hadn't known she'd figured that out. But of course she had. The woman was highly intelligent and paid attention to him. "You're right." He leaned back from the table. He was about to respond when his phone dinged. "Excuse me." He looked down to see Ryker's ID, and he answered the call. "I'm a little busy, Ryker."

"Open your e-mail and click on a link I just sent to you," Ryker said without preamble.

Denver jumped up, hustled into the living room, and sat at one of the computers, following instructions. A website came up with Sheriff Elton Cobb giving a press conference. Denver's heart slammed against his ribs.

Cobb stood before a bunch of reporters on the county courthouse steps of his North Carolina jurisdiction, his shoulders wide and his white-blond hair cut short. "I've finally solved the mystery of the murders at the Lost Springs Home for Boys," Cobb said. "Three boys, now men, killed my brother and another boy. We have no idea what names they might be using, but as kids they were called Ryker, Heath, and Denver...and here are their pictures."

Denver stiffened.

Noni hovered at his elbow. "Denver?"

Pictures of Denver and his brothers flashed across the screen from when they were youths.

Okay. That wasn't so bad.

The cameras returned to Cobb. He smiled, his blue eyes colder than the Arctic. "I've traced these men to the Pacific Northwest. They've been operating a detective agency called Lost Bastards, and they've systematically increased their criminal activities throughout the years. I warn you. They are armed, they are trained, and they are exceptionally dangerous. Here are their current pictures."

Three more pictures moved across the screen. These were current, taken by hidden cameras when they'd rescued Zara, Ryker's fiancée, from Cobb and Madison.

Denver lifted his phone to his ear. "Looks like Sheriff Cobb finally decided to go public," he said to Ryker.

Noni gasped at his side and took a step away from him.

"We thought he might," Ryker said grimly. "His fantasy of catching us and torturing us to death seems to have come to an end. He just wants us caught."

For years Cobb had remained silent as he hunted them, no doubt looking forward to killing them without any trace. But now that he'd gone public, there would be eyes on them.

Denver shook his head. "I bet Dr. Madison has other plans, and she has the trained soldiers. Even if Cobb or one of his cop buddies gets us, she'll figure out a way to take us in. At least I think that's her plan."

She'd never let them go to prison when she could force them to work for her. She no doubt still had many an experiment to conduct as well.

"Agreed," Ryker said. "This puts more pressure on us. You get that, right? These pictures are going to every law enforcement agency in the country. There's nowhere we'll be able to go and not get recognized." He sighed and then he went deadly silent. "Fuck," he snapped.

Denver leaned back from the monitor as a picture of Ryker's fiancée was held up by Cobb next. "Zara Remington, a person of interest," he read. Shit. That would send Ryker over the edge.

"I'll kill him. We should've already killed him, damn it," Ryker growled.

Anya's picture was next. She had been the ultimate prize for the Copper Killer, a serial killer they'd just taken down, so her face had been on TV screens already. Yet she hadn't been labeled a person of interest before. Denver shook his head, anger churning down his esophagus. "This is so bad."

"Definitely. My phone is blowing up from Montana," Ryker muttered, his voice shaking with what sounded like fury.

"It might not be a bad idea to head that way," Denver said, already typing. The brothers in Montana owned several acres with phenomenal security. "We're going to need new IDs. And we have to find Cobb, Ry."

"Agreed. After this mission to find the baby—" Ryker started.

Denver started making up new names for them. "No. You guys find Madison and Cobb. I'll keep on this case, and the second I need help I'll call. We have to work round the clock now on Cobb. You know it's true." His time just shortened to find the baby, because he had to get her safe before he went after Cobb.

The sound Ryker made came from a deep well of what had to be frustration. "All right. But don't for a second do this by yourself. Promise."

"I promise. This can be fixed." Denver turned to see Noni standing close to the kitchen, her pupils wide and her face the color of paper. She was frightened.

He kept her gaze. Not once had he lied to her. Well, recently. He'd admitted he was a killer, but maybe seeing it on television and watching a cop talk about him had changed her mind about him. About trusting him. The idea slammed a fist into his gut. His shoulders straightened.

Too bad. She'd asked for his help, and it was too late to turn back now. Whether she liked it or not.

CHAPTER
8

Noni turned into the kitchen and quickly started cleaning up while Denver did whatever people wanted for murder did on computers to make the whole thing go away. All right. She'd known he had a history, and she'd suspected he was wanted by the law. But murder? Even as a kid, he'd murdered somebody. It wasn't like he'd denied it on the phone with Ryker.

No. He'd been more concerned with messing with the Internet. Probably with his dark web or whatever it was.

The back of her neck hurt, sending a headache right up through her skull. Tension. What should she do? She had to find Talia before Richie hurt or sold or did whatever he was planning with her. The idea of the baby in enemy hands hurt her deep down. She had to save Talia, and she needed Denver's help.

But Denver had enemies—dangerous ones—apparently on both sides of the law. What if she got caught in the crossfire of his world and didn't get the chance to save the baby?

But could she save Talia without him?

She finished in the kitchen, her mind spinning. If she got her pack, she could take the truck. It was in the garage. But what then? She truly had no clue. Maybe it was time to go to the FBI, but if she did that, then maybe they'd let Richie keep the baby. Since he was the father, then he had a parental right she'd have to get taken away, which was difficult and took time. If she was going to be Talia's mother, she had to find the safest path. She set the dishrag on the counter and turned to see Denver leaning against the door frame, watching her.

When he looked at her like that, with those mysterious blue eyes, a hard knot of pleasure slowly unfolded inside her abdomen. She hated that she reacted like that to him—just from a look. "What?" she asked, her face heating.

"Make a decision yet?" he drawled, his voice low and gritty.

That tone. Her nipples peaked, and her breasts felt heavy and full. All of a sudden, her skin seemed too tight. "A decision?" she whispered, her voice hoarse.

He snorted. "Lose the innocent act. You going to make a run for it or not?"

Sometimes she forgot how smart he was and how easily he read people. Probably because he'd spent his life watching them instead of interacting. "I'm still working through the plus and minus columns in my head," she retorted.

"Ah." He flashed his teeth in a primal warning. "Let me help. I'm not gonna let you leave."

Well, now. That certainly took the debate off the table. She bristled. "You're willing to add kidnapping to what appears to be already an impressive list of crimes?"

If she'd meant to shake him or piss him off, she failed.

"Yes," he said calmly. "In a heartbeat."

Shock froze her in place. "You can't do that."

He laughed, the sound lacking in true humor. "Think you can stop me?"

No. Her self-defense class in college probably didn't put her anywhere near his fighting skills, not to mention the fact that he had a hundred pounds of pure muscle on her. "You can't do this."

"I'm not doing anything." He didn't move. "But you asked for my help and got me involved. So I'm involved."

"You have enough going on," she spat. "Or did you not see the news conference?"

He exhaled slowly. "Oh, I saw it. But I also saw what wasn't there."

She frowned. "What?"

"You and me. The picture of us together that you plastered on the Internet. Cobb hasn't found it yet. So we're safe here." Denver's chin lowered. "For now."

"Did you kill Sheriff Cobb's brother?" she asked, hating how her voice wavered.

A muscle visibly twitched beneath Denver's jaw. "Maybe. I might as well have."

"Meaning?" she croaked out.

He sighed, and his voice cracked. "Ryker and Heath swung bats at his head, and he went down hard. But I'm the one who started the fire to burn the place down, and I'm the reason my brothers went down into that basement. If I could've been the one to swing those bats, I would have. In a second."

Not one ounce of regret filled his words. Not one. Noni took a step back. "You were just kids."

"Yeah, we were. Imagine what would've pushed us to that." His eyes darkened, and his shoulders slumped. "Ned Cobb, the owner of the home, beat us. Badly." Denver's hands fisted, and his voice lowered with remembered hurts.

Noni's breath caught. "Denver."

"That wasn't all. It wasn't just the physical pain." Denver scrubbed a hand through his hair, his eyes lost for a moment. "It was the fear. Any day his aim could be off, and we'd take it to the temple. One of our friends could die at any moment."

She ached for him. For the scared child he must've been. "I'm sorry."

He swallowed. "One night Ned was beating the crap out of me and another kid named Ralph, and he killed Ralph." Denver's eyes glazed as he became lost in the past. "Ned was going to blame me, and my brothers ran down into the basement to protect me."

Guilt. That was guilt. "It wasn't your fault."

He blinked. "Ned turned on them, and they swung bats. They killed him *because* of me."

She moved to him, grabbing his hands. "Not your fault."

He shook his head, coming back into the present. "It was my idea to burn the place down. With the bodies." He sounded almost dazed now.

The need to comfort him, the urge to protect him, made her sway. "It's okay, Denver," she said calmly, tightening her hold. It was his idea to burn the place down? With the bodies? How terrified he must've been.

He suddenly turned his head. His entire body stiffened, and he pulled away.

She stilled. "What?"

"Where's your gun?" he whispered.

Adrenaline flooded her. "Which one?"

"The one I gave to you."

She couldn't breathe. "What's happening?"

"Gun?" he asked, more urgently.

His tone prompted her to move, so she turned and opened the utensil drawer to pull out the shiny weapon. "Here," she whispered back.

"Crouch down and point it at the back door," he said.

She did so immediately, her heart battering her rib cage. "What's happening?"

"I'll be right back." Hunching over, he moved into the living room.

She pointed the gun at the innocuous yellow door, wondering what he'd seen. Or, rather, heard. His senses were so strong as to be supernatural. The blood rushed through her veins, pounding between her ears. Taking several deep breaths, she tried to calm the noise inside. What was out there? All she heard was wind and crackling ice.

Less than a minute later, he returned with two packs and tossed hers to her along with her boots and her wool coat. His gun was bigger than hers, with a huge clip thingy. "Put those on. Now."

She set the gun on the scratched linoleum to slide her arms into her coat and then the straps of her backpack before yanking her boots on. Her hands shaking, she picked up the weapon again. "What's happening?"

He shook his head. "I saw three gang members outside, and I don't know how many more are out there. Keep your head down and move toward the garage. We'll drive the truck right over the motherfuckers. I'll go first, and you keep on my six."

Six? What in the world was a six? "Okay." She gulped, feeling way too exposed.

A loud pattering sound ripped through her plan, and wood went flying. She yelped and ducked low as bullets flew in every direction, smashing into the microwave and all across the kitchen. She cried out. The front window shattered in the other room. Computer monitors blew up with loud bursts. Bullets hit the refrigerator, and the door fell off. Milk exploded. Holes covered the top of the door leading to the backyard.

She screamed and covered her head.

Denver grabbed the back of her neck and all but dragged her toward the door to the garage. He opened it and shoved her hard. She tumbled down the two steps and fell against the truck, her shoulder protesting. Before she could right herself, he lifted her by her pack.

He leaned close, his face a hard mask. "We'll be okay. Trust me."

She gulped.

He tugged open the truck door. "The gang found us, damn it."

Bullets ricocheted from outside the garage, pinging against the metal. The front of the truck exploded with a loud hiss. "Fuck," Denver said, slamming the door. "New plan." He pulled her around the truck toward an outside door, ducking as he went. "I'll go first. When I motion for you, follow as fast as you can. Shoot anybody shooting at us."

She looked down at the gun in her stiff hand. How could this be happening?

Denver gingerly opened a rickety door and slid into the darkness. He fired once. Twice. A scream of pain echoed. Then he turned and grabbed her arm to pull her outside. "Run, baby."

She launched into motion, following him through the thick snow and making an instant right turn toward a six-foot worn wooden fence. Without stopping his stride, he turned and lifted her with one arm, tossing her right over. Her arms windmilled, and she fell hard, landing on her back in the snow. Rolling, she was on her feet as he dropped next to her.

Another snow-filled backyard.

The gunfire continued behind them.

A gang member with tattoos all over his face came out from behind a tree, his gun lifting.

Denver pivoted and fired his gun. The bullet hit the man in the middle of the forehead. His eyes opened wide, blood spurted, and then, almost in slow motion, he fell.

Noni stopped feeling. Not the cold snow covering her, not the fear. Nothing. She stared numbly at the dead body.

Denver clasped her arm and pulled her farther through the snow and toward the body. She tried to fight him out of pure instinct, but he was relentless. They reached the back fence.

Sudden silence took over the night.

He paused. "They're in the house."

She turned, the night surreal, and looked the way they'd come.

With a smile that scared the hell out of her and took her from her nice place of shock, he pulled a black square box out of his front jeans pocket.

"What's—" she started to ask.

He pushed a red button.

The entire world exploded. Noni gasped. She was thrown back against the fence, her foot brushing the dead guy. Fire lit the night, and the roof flew off the house she'd just been in. A yell of raw pain screeched toward them.

Denver stuck his gun inside his jacket. He took her gun and tucked it into his jeans before grabbing her by the waist. "Up and over," he said urgently.

Her hands scrambled on the top of the next icy fence, and she tried to balance herself, but she tumbled over and landed on her back in the snow again. Cold permeated her freezing legs, and her hands hurt as she shoved to her feet. Her entire body ached. It took a minute to balance herself in the snow that reached above her knees. Denver landed gracefully at her side, sinking into the snow.

Her shock made the night surreal.

Sirens trilled in the distance. Fire crackled into the sky, even as a light snow began to fall. She looked around a back alley. Rough fences divided small lots and homes across from her. Two had cheerful Christmas lights twinkling. She shook her head.

He leaned down to her ear. "Keep to the fence line and right behind me. I'll clear a path." Without waiting for a nod, he moved in front of her and started running, dragging his feet.

Shouts came from behind them. There were still men with guns. Panic took her and she sped up, trying to keep up with him. He moved silently, gracefully through the snow, his gun in his hands again. Even though it was one of those that could shoot a lot of bullets like the guys chasing them had, he'd only shot once or twice each time.

How many men had he just killed?

She gulped. He'd done it to protect her. She had yet to fire. Her hands closed into freezing cold fists, and she ducked her head against the chilling wind and followed him. They reached the end of the fence line and a quiet street. Denver hustled over to an old muscle car parked near a cottage with snowmen littering the front lawn and forced open the door.

"Get in," he said, sliding into the driver's seat and leaning across to unlock her door.

She opened it and dropped into the seat. Pain flared along her back. Wincing, she leaned forward and shuffled out of her pack, setting it on the floor before shutting her door.

Denver drew a pocketknife from his back pocket, ripped a bunch of wires out from beneath the steering wheel, cut the plastic insulation off some of them, twisted two together, and rubbed two others together. The engine flared to life. He shut his door and pulled out into the street. "Belt."

She scrambled to put on her seat belt, noticing he didn't do the same. "Yours?" she gasped.

"May need to jump out and shoot." He checked the rearview mirror.

She turned and looked to see emergency vehicles, three cop cars, and a fire truck, whiz by on the crossing road, their blue and red lights cutting through the strengthening snowstorm. Their ominous glow contrasted oddly with the happy Christmas lights. "You had bombs in the house."

He took a sharp left turn, and the car slid on the ice. Correcting, he got them back to the middle of the road. "Explosives. I'll miss that truck."

The truck? He was worried about the truck? Tears of pure terror clogged her throat. "Are you sure that was Richie's gang?"

"Yes. Or allies of them." He took another sharp turn, not decreasing his speed any. "How did they find us?" he muttered, his hands relaxed on the steering wheel. "Somebody must've followed me from the hospital, but I didn't see a thing." He hit the steering wheel this time. "Why didn't I see them?"

"I'm sorry." She gulped, the tears filling her eyes. "This is because of me. Because I put up our picture."

He didn't turn her way. "No, baby. This was retaliation because I shot three of them in Greenville and then tortured the same guys in the hospital. But how did they find us?"

But he wouldn't be involved if she hadn't plastered his picture all over the net. She shook her head as he turned another way, her stomach churning. Her body felt like it was on fire with pain. Warmth started to creep into her freezing feet, and icy pinpricks ran along her ankles. She bit back a whimper at the agony of it.

He drove into the main area of town, which was lit with bright Christmas lights on every storefront. Their cheerful colors nauseated her. Less than a mile away, bodies had piled up. She forced down bile.

"Grab the phone out of the front of my pack, would you?" he asked, slowing down.

She reached for his pack in the backseat and pulled out a nondescript black phone to hand to him.

He shook his head. "Find the group 'Pizza Restaurants,' and send a text that says 'Large pepperoni, home address.'"

Her fingers fought her, shaking and tense, but she followed his instructions. "What does that mean?"

He stopped at a stoplight and visibly scanned the entire area around them. "It tells my meddling brothers to stay exactly where they are. That I'm safe but can't talk yet."

Pepperoni meant safety? She slid the phone back into the pack, her voice trembling. "What pizza means 'Get here now'?"

"Pineapple," he said, his shoulders relaxing as the light turned green.

Of course. What else would it be? She let her head fall back against the seat and shut her eyes. Dizziness slammed into her, so she reopened her eyes and took several deep breaths.

"You okay?" he asked gently.

"No."

He nodded. "You will be. Trust me."

The man had just successfully fought off a bunch of gangbangers. Ones who had Talia. Trust him? Yeah. She could do that. He was her only hope of saving the baby, and he was tough enough to do it. "What now?" she asked quietly.

CHAPTER
9

Denver pulled the car into a grocery store parking area, remaining off to the side and out of view of the security cameras. "I hate to do it, but we need to walk from here." He had to ditch the stolen car. "We'll be there soon."

Noni didn't argue and instead grabbed her pack. She'd been silent most of the drive, no doubt dealing with shock. Her adrenaline would be ebbing, and he had to get her into a warm shower to combat the shock and the wet clothing they were both wearing. Later he'd worry about her feelings after seeing him kill without blinking. He grimaced. He'd shot three men. How many had he blown up in the explosion?

Getting out and coming around the car, he opened her door and helped her out. "You okay?"

Her eyes were glassy. She shivered in the cold. "What's our plan?"

"Main plan? I've been monitoring the dark web for any auction. If nothing comes up by tomorrow night, I'll hunt down more gang members and take the fight to Richie. I promise we'll have the baby back soon." Denver would hit the hospital the next day. No doubt several gang members would be available there after the explosion.

Noni stumbled and then righted herself, looking around the snowy area. "Where are we going right now?"

He kept his face calm. They were about to take the biggest risk of the entire night. "Three blocks south." He'd had to leave the automatic weapon in the car because it didn't fit in his pack, and he couldn't very well walk through neighborhoods with it. But his Sig was at his waist, so he didn't feel completely naked. He took her hand. "We need to look like we're out for a holiday stroll in the snow to look at Christmas lights. This neighborhood is nicer than the one we just left."

"Okay." She fell into line beside him, her boots sliding on the icy sidewalk.

He took her through a small subdivision called Apple Orchards, to a cute brick bungalow with cheerful fluorescent lights strung perfectly across every eve. Three glowing reindeer stood over to the right, their lights flickering merrily. He truly hadn't expected this. "Come on, baby."

She stumbled next to him but kept pace. When they reached the door, he set her to the side just in case and then he knocked.

Nothing.

Another knock. The door slowly slid open, and a Glock was immediately pointed at his face. "Sorry to wake you," Denver said evenly.

The door opened farther, and Detective James Malloy stood there in ratty green sweats, his surprisingly cut chest bare. His brown eyes were pissed. "What the fuck are you doing here?" Then he caught sight of Noni shivering next to Denver. The cop's eyes flickered, a multitude of expressions crossed his face, and then he sighed. "Come in." He moved to the side.

Denver drew Noni in front of him and nudged her into the warm home. A Christmas tree took up the far corner of a living room decorated in soft black leather, and a dying fire glowed in the brick fireplace. Christmassy knickknacks adorned every surface. The room was much cozier and friendly than Denver would've thought.

Noni looked around as if not sure what to do.

"Jamie?" a female voice asked tentatively.

Denver jolted and turned. A stunning black woman stood in the hall, her long hair mussed and her brown eyes wide. She wore a bright pink camisole with very short shorts, her long legs smooth and her toenails painted a soft red.

Malloy sighed. "Honey, put on the coffee, would you? Apparently we have visitors. I'll introduce you if I decide not to arrest them."

The woman looked them over and then gave a short nod. "I'll make it strong." She crossed the room and pushed open a newly painted cream-colored door, disappearing into what must've been the kitchen. While Malloy was probably in his midforties, the woman had to be thirty, tops. Interesting.

Denver cleared his throat and toed off his boots. "Noni, this is Detective Malloy."

She jolted and swung wide eyes at him.

"Yeah. He's a cop." Denver helped her out of her boots and then her coat, scattering snow on the entryway tile.

Malloy moved and set his gun on the mantel. "Tell me you're not the one who blew up a house tonight. I heard it on the scanner."

Denver winced.

"Damn it, Denver," Malloy snapped. "I thought you guys were leaving town. You know, for good this time?"

Denver put their packs near the door. "We were. We still are, I think." Trusting the cop was one of the most dangerous things he'd ever done, but Malloy had come through more than once, and Denver had no choice. He hung Noni's coat on a hook. "Can we stoke the fire?" He turned to pull her toward more warmth, and his gaze caught on the bright red covering her right arm. "Noni," he breathed.

"What?" Her head lifted, her pupils seriously dilated.

"Baby, you've been shot." His entire world screeched to a halt, and he turned her to pull up her sleeve. The bullet had passed completely through her forearm, but it was still bleeding.

Her breath hitched, and she slowly turned her head to see the wound. "Shot? I've been shot?" She wavered, her voice shaking. "It doesn't hurt yet."

That was because she was in shock. "You'll be okay." He'd need to stitch her up, and fuck, that was going to hurt.

Malloy was instantly at her side, peering at the wound. "Ouch."

She wavered in place, and her eyelids fluttered closed. Denver caught her before she came close to hitting the floor.

Malloy swore beneath his breath. "Tina?" he called out. "We're gonna need bandages and your steady hand." Clapping Denver on the back, he turned. "My lady is a veterinarian. You have the time it takes her to sew this girl up to convince me not to arrest you. Or shoot you," he added as an afterthought.

Denver's entire chest compressed. He'd let Noni get shot? When? It had to have been in the kitchen. So far he was doing a piss poor job of protecting her, and now he'd landed her with a cop. If Malloy went party line with them, Denver would be in deep trouble. If Richie was the father, Noni might not get to keep Talia.

If he kidnapped the baby then, they'd be on the run forever.

He carried Noni through the happy living room into a newly renovated kitchen complete with a wide wooden table. Setting her down on the table, he brushed hair away from her too-pale face. He nodded at Tina. "I'm Denver, and this is Noni. She's everything important in the world to me."

Tina had already taken out a large first-aid kit and, spotting the blood, quickly grasped scissors to cut Noni's shirt. "I'm Tina." She looked toward Malloy. "Looks like you're making the coffee, babe."

Malloy kept his gaze on Denver. "We might not need it. Start talking. Now."

* * *

Noni came to as she was being lifted from a hard wooden surface. She jolted.

"You're okay," Denver said, his breath brushing her temple. "I need to get you into a warm shower, baby."

Warmth and shower sounded fantastic. She sighed and closed her eyes, resting her head against his hard chest. Heat surrounded her. Her shoulder ached and her head hurt, but the feeling had returned to her extremities, so she'd avoided frostbite. "I feel better."

"Tina gave you a local and sewed you up," he rumbled, walking somewhere.

Tina must've been the pretty woman in the cute pajama set. "She's a doctor?"

"Close enough."

Lights flickered and they leaned in somewhere, but Noni didn't open her eyes. Water turned on, and she was put onto her feet. She swayed and let Denver tug her wet clothes free. Chilled air brushed her, and then she was under the steam. Moments later, Denver joined her.

Her eyelids flipped open, and her body went on full alert.

She faced the spray, and he gently nudged her beneath it. Good lord. Denver was naked behind her. Even though the steam was warm, he was hotter. A presence with power. Okay. She had to clear her head. Ducking it, she let the soothing water wash over her hair and slide down her back. Her groan filled the small space.

He gently tugged her back toward him, and then his magical fingers rubbed coconut-scented shampoo through her hair. He helped her to rinse off.

Fully awake now, she glanced down at the wet bandage on her arm.

"We'll change it before going to bed," Denver said, his breath against her hair.

She was fully awake now and turned around to see him. Did his body look the same as it had a year ago? Did he have any more scars than before? The edge of the tattoo on his shoulder caught her eye. A dangerous looking bird rose out of the fire, its wings spread. Two intricate *B*s combined in the center. She'd traced it with her fingers so many times. "Your tattoo." She touched the only portion visible from the front.

"Yeah. My brothers have the same tat."

So it wasn't a reminder of an odd case he'd once solved. That's what he'd told her. Now it made so much more sense. She wanted to keep touching him, but she was such a chicken. And she definitely didn't look below his chest. "We're staying here?" she asked, her voice echoing off the tiles.

"Just for the night. I don't want to cause problems for Malloy." Denver placed a soft kiss on the top of her forehead.

All she had to do was take a step forward and she'd be flush against him. Her body tingled, this time not from the cold. Man, she needed to think. "Sounds good." Edging to the side, she pushed open the curtain and moved into the chilly room without looking at him.

He sighed. "The guest bedroom is the second door on the left. I'll be there in a minute."

She grabbed a towel, quickly wrapping it around herself. Then she tiptoed into the long hallway and all but ran for the right room. Moving inside, she found another cute nightie set, this one purple, lying on the bed. After drying off, she put it on and jumped into what looked like a queen-sized bed covered with a handmade wedding-band quilt.

The room was cute and definitely had a woman's touch. Pretty vases covered the wide dresser near the door, and matching lamps adorned the heavy wooden end tables.

Somebody knocked softly on the door and Noni jumped. "Come in."

Tina came in, bandages in her hands. "We can't let that stay wet." The woman's movements were gentle as she sat and removed the first bandage. "You feeling better?"

Noni nodded automatically. "Thank you for, well, everything."

Tina grinned, showing a dimple in her left cheek. "Not a problem. Part of dating a cop."

"Even so, I owe you."

Tina sprayed antibacterial ointment over the wound. "Who's after you?"

Noni couldn't blame her for being curious. "I'm pretty sure I can't tell you. We don't want to get Malloy in trouble."

"That sounds ominous." Tina sat back. "So you're a cop or detective?"

Noni snorted. "No. I make lotions." She looked closer at her new friend. The woman was stunning. Tina's skin was flawless and smooth. "Speaking of which, if you don't mind my asking, what do you use on your face?" Maybe she should compare some other products in her work.

Tina's dark eyebrow lifted. "Just hand soap."

Horror filled Noni, the real kind, and she gasped. "You do not. Just soap?"

"Yep." Tina sat back, her eyes twinkling.

"Oh, girl. I'm sending you a care package the first chance I get. I make lotions." Just soap? It was a travesty. "What's your favorite scent?"

Tina chuckled. "Dog fur usually." She cleared her throat. "I'm a vet. I guess I like vanilla? And gardenias are my favorite flower."

Perfect. Noni could totally make a facial cream as well as a body lotion with those scents. As a thank-you. "Expect a box of goodies... sometime." When, she had no clue.

"I look forward to it." Tina stood and handed over a hairbrush. "Jamie is out of conditioner, so good luck with this. You need sleep to deal with the shock of the night. This place is safe. I promise."

Noni grimaced and took the brush. "Thank you again."

"See you tomorrow." The long-legged beauty left the room.

"Hand soap," Noni muttered, yanking the brush through her long hair. Ouch. Yeah, she could've used some conditioner.

The door opened, and Denver strode inside wearing only boxer briefs, their packs in his hand. "We both have clothing for tomorrow but nothing for tonight." He took in her purple cami, and his eyes flared. "I hope you get to keep that."

She shifted, her body heating. Again. The man looked like he wanted to eat her alive. "What's our plan?" She had to stay on point.

He shut the door, dropped the packs, and got into bed with her. "Sleep and then we need to find another safe place tomorrow. We haven't found Richie and the baby, so staying close to the gang who tried to take us out is our best bet for now. I'll question members in the hospital tomorrow."

"Is it Richie's gang?" She hadn't realized the gang was that big.

"Affiliates and drug partners," Denver said, reaching over and turning off his light. The room slid into darkness. "Go to sleep, Noni. We'll figure everything out tomorrow."

Intimacy wound around them, and she snuggled down, her mind spinning. The shock of the night slapped her, and her eyes filled. Man, she couldn't cry right now. God, she was scared and hurt and confused and just lost. She turned onto her side and let the tears fall, fighting so hard to stay quiet.

He gently turned her, pulling her right into his furnace-hot body. "Let it out."

She let herself cry, her body shaking, her tears wetting his chest. "I was so scared," she hiccupped.

"I know. It was scary." His big hand rubbed down her back and up, providing comfort. "You're safe now."

But did he deal with this kind of thing all the time? The idea terrified her. At some point a bullet would hit him. Was this why he'd left her? Because he knew there was a bullet with his name on it out there somewhere? "You need to find a different line of work, Denver," she muttered, sniffing and lifting her head.

His blue gaze lasered through the darkness. "I can't argue with that one, darlin'. I'm hoping to change, but I have two missions to complete first."

One was the baby. The other one dealt with Dr. Madison, whoever she was. "Then what?"

He paused, his mouth close to her forehead. "I don't know. The plan only goes that far."

It was like a fist to the chest. He didn't think he'd survive the second mission. She hiccupped again. "We never really had a chance, did we?"

He studied her, his dark gaze a sharp caress. Regret twisted his lip.

There wasn't an answer to give, and she knew it. But she needed him to say something. Anything. "Denver?"

He lowered his head and brushed her mouth with his. Desire ripped through her, shocking in its intensity after the night she'd had. She breathed out but didn't move back.

A sound rumbled up from his chest that seemed male and tortured. Leaning in even more, he took her mouth.

Hard.

CHAPTER
10

Noni hadn't backed away. He'd wanted to ease her fears, to calm her down, so he'd just touched his lips to hers. And she hadn't backed away. She hadn't moved, holding her breath, just like she had a year ago. The glimmer in her eyes was the same now as it had been then, intrigued and wary. It took him right back in time to the one moment he'd been truly happy.

If he hadn't been exhausted, if he hadn't been furious at the attack, he would've listened to the inner voice that told him to roll over and go to sleep.

But need and awareness bombarded him, and he reacted to the soft touch of her skin. To her scent, even now tempting him beneath the coconut smell of the borrowed shampoo. God, he'd missed her. He'd used a bottle of booze to mask his pain, and it had only dulled it. Living without her, believing he'd never see her again, had been like a physical ache that would never leave.

Yet here she was. Right here and right now.

So he swooped in and kissed her like he'd wanted to for the past day. Hard and fast and demanding. He took, and then he took more. She stiffened and then the tautness deserted her as she softened against him, submitting to his mouth.

It had been that way before. The quiet sound of submission as she let him take, as she started kissing him back, demand on her tongue. Pure sweetness in her taste. The world burned hotter, and desperation tried to claw through him.

But he controlled himself, thinking only of her. He gentled his kiss, giving pleasure. He remembered what she liked, what made her moan. This had to be about her.

He licked along her lips and kissed down her neck, rolling her onto her back. He could take her out of her head and give her some peace, release the tension all but choking them. But this was for her pleasure. She was in shock, she was scared, and he couldn't take advantage of that. He could give her relief, though, which would give him some.

Being with her again was better than he'd dreamed. He didn't deserve another chance; he knew that. But touching her felt right. For the first time since he'd left her, he felt whole again.

His hands pushed up the camisole, and he palmed her breasts.

She arched against him, crying out.

He gently squeezed. Touching her again filled something inside him he hadn't realized had been stone-cold empty. "Noni, you remember me, and you remember this." He lightly tweaked her pretty nipples.

She pushed harder into him and threw her head back on the pillow, pure bliss in her sigh. Yeah, she liked a little bite with her pleasure. He loved that about her. And it worked well, because he couldn't let her tear out her stitches.

"You don't get to move, baby. Move, and I stop." He settled on top of her, forcing her thighs apart. Then he rolled her nipples, and she caught her breath. Good. He had her attention. "Tell me you understand."

"I understand," she breathed, her body relaxing against the bed. "The stitches are fine, Denver."

How well she knew him. He pushed the material up to her neck, baring her. "This isn't about the stitches." Then he took one nipple into his mouth. She tasted so damn good. Sweet and salty with a hint of coconut. Better than his fantasies for the past few months. He sucked hard, and she writhed against him.

He smiled and released her taut nipple. "I said not to move."

The growl of frustration from her widened his smile. He moved to the other breast, licking and nipping, enjoying the trembling of her thighs on either side of his hips. He couldn't help but press his aching cock against her core. Electricity burned him, pleasure cut him, nearly making his eyes roll back in his head.

Her fingers curled over his shoulders, and she dragged her nails down his chest.

The bite was soft but the impact deep. Need rioted through him. He grasped her hands and laid them carefully on the bed. "Keep still. No touching." He had no clue what would tear the stitches, and he wasn't sure he could stay in control if she touched him. He'd be inside her before he could blink, and that couldn't happen. Not after the night they'd had and not until she knew what she wanted.

"Denver, please," she whispered.

He licked beneath her breasts, sliding his other hand down to her shorts and pulling them down. Then he ticked his fingers across her panties, nipping her rib cage at the same time. She jumped against him and he chuckled. Then he maneuvered farther down, kissing her abdomen as it undulated beneath his mouth. Somebody had been working out. She'd been perfect before, but he could feel new muscles. Had she turned to exercise to rid her body of need...like he had? Had he filled her mind like she'd filled his?

He snapped the sides of the panties in two.

She jerked. "Denver! I have only two spare pairs."

Oops. He'd have to hit a store for her. "Sorry." To distract her, he slid his fingers across her, feeling wetness and heat. Oh God, she was fucking perfect. She trembled again, holding her breath. He closed his eyes and sank two fingers deep into her warmth. Her body clenched around his fingers, and she was beyond tight.

The helpless sound she made caught him around the heart and held fast. Her hands clenched on the sheets, but she didn't try to touch him. "You're being very good, Noni," he murmured, sliding farther down and placing a kiss on the top of her mound.

Her entire body shuddered beneath him.

God, he'd missed her. He stretched his fingers inside her, and she gasped. The musky scent of her desire drugged him, and he let himself just feel. Just for the moment.

He slid his fingers free, and she gave a moan of protest. Then he spread her open for him. "Look at me," he said, his voice gritty.

She tilted her head and looked down, those black eyes pools of need.

Keeping her gaze, he dipped his head and licked her. She gasped and trembled. He did it again, and he could swear her eyes glassed over. The taste of her was better than any other on earth. Why had he wasted hours drinking bourbon when this treat was within his reach? How had he left her? The questions bombarded him, so he quelled them the only way he knew how.

He tasted her again.

She groaned and blinked rapidly, fighting something inside her head. "Denver."

He paused, letting his breath heat her clit. "Nothing happens you don't want." If she told him to stop, it'd kill him, but he'd do it. He pressed his tongue right on her clit and swirled it. "Let me make you feel good."

The taste of her was destroying him, and he didn't care.

Her head fell back on the pillow. "I missed you so much."

The words slammed into him, filling his chest. Filling all of him. He licked her again. "I missed you, too."

"Please don't stop," she whispered, her entire body rigid.

He never wanted to stop. He focused on the prize, lashing her clit until she mewed like a little kitten. Waiting until she exhaled, he pressed two fingers back inside her, nearly chuckling when she gasped in air again. Then he bit her thigh. Not hard enough to bruise, but she'd wear his mark the next day. Too much satisfaction filled him at that thought.

Then he lost himself again with her. Nipping and licking, twisting and touching. Her legs clamped to his shoulders, she stiffened, moaning his name.

That sound. He'd never in his life forget the sound of his name on her lips. He sucked her clit into his mouth, and she detonated. Waves crashed through her, and her hands clamped onto his shoulders. He licked her until she came down with a soft whimper. Then he levered up, kissing his way to her neck.

Her eyelids opened, her gaze lazy. "I missed that when you left."

"So did I," he said, kissing her gently before turning her onto her good shoulder and away from him. Her sweetness and honesty flayed him through. "Sleep. Now."

His body rioted, but he'd find relief later by himself. For now, he'd offer comfort and warmth.

"What about you?" she mumbled.

This was more than he deserved. Holding her, keeping her safe— that was all he needed. "Sleep," he whispered.

* * *

Noni blinked, her gaze hazy but her body calm. The man knew how to give a phenomenal orgasm. Denver bracketed her from behind, gently holding her, his erection a firm line against her butt. "Denver—"

"No. You've had a hell of a night. Sleep and we'll talk tomorrow." His voice was firm and rough...need in every syllable. Sometimes he was such an asshole.

"You did this before," she mumbled. "Kept yourself apart and distant. Have you ever let anybody in?"

"Just you," he said quietly.

But that wasn't true. Not really. Everything inside her wanted to understand him. Wanted to really know him, even if it hurt unbearably when he left. "You promised me your story. The true one," she said, her gaze on the dark of the room.

"Now?" he asked.

Snow fell outside the window, and the wind howled through the night. Intimacy cocooned them, and she snuggled closer into his heat. "Yes. Then I'll go to sleep."

He sighed, his hand flattened over her abdomen. "I was a test-tube baby created in a lab by a psychopath named Dr. Madison, as were Heath and Ryker. She experimented and tried to make humans with extra abilities."

Noni snorted. "Denver. Come on." She wanted his real story. Not a make-believe one. "Yeah, right. You're bionic."

"No. Through a bunch of gene splicing I've never figured out, I have stronger senses, reflexes, and strength than the average person. Much stronger. As do Ryker and Heath."

She'd read a journal article about genetic manipulation while in a dentist's waiting room a while back. "Really?" she whispered.

"It's true." His voice didn't waver. "I wish to hell it wasn't, but it is. She and some ex-military guy created supersoldiers in a lab from donated genetic material. You've noticed my reflexes and senses. They're amplified. Genetically."

That was true. How crazy? Genetic manipulation? It wasn't that farfetched to consider these days. But what about the experiments? "How many kids did they create?"

"I don't know. Most they kept and trained to fight and kill, but she let the three of us go and then put us back together when we were adolescents at a home."

How was this possible? Noni shook her head. "Why?"

"To study us. The bitch used us all as experiments. Jory, from the phone the other day, was one of the soldiers she kept and trained. He and his other brothers all escaped years ago, but she's hunting us all." Denver's body stiffened.

Noni reached out and placed her hand over his, waiting until he relaxed behind her.

He continued. "I was supposedly taken by one of the soldiers, and she found me in Denver when I was eight."

So that was how he'd gotten the odd name. "And?" she prompted.

"I was with a guy who acted like my uncle for a while, but even then I knew we weren't really related. He apparently wanted to hurt Madison by taking me. The guy is probably dead now, and I don't care."

How was any of this possible? Noni patted his hand. "How did his taking you hurt Madison?"

Denver shuddered. "I'm not sure. She always said I was special, and I've always been afraid she did something really weird with my genes. Like she incorporated animal genes or something with mine when she was splicing and dicing. If anybody could, it'd be her." He sounded almost bewildered.

Noni snuggled closer into him, trying to offer comfort. He just sounded so...lost. But he needed to get it out. To share his pain. "What then?"

"I ended up with Ryker and Heath at the home, and we bonded just like she thought we would," Denver said.

"I'm so sorry she manipulated you."

He pulled her closer, wrapping all around her. "The home sucked. Ned wasn't the only monster in our childhood. The good ole sheriff liked to show up and use his nightstick as well. He and Dr. Madison were together and I guess still are—now they're searching for us together. I already told you about us killing Cobb's brother, and that's why he's after us."

"So it's all about revenge." What a horrible legacy.

"Dr. Madison wants more than revenge. She wants us to train for her and, ah, donate genetic material for more supersoldiers."

That was incredibly screwed up. No wonder Denver was so closed off all the time. Her heart and the hurt from his leaving her started to unfold. To release. It was a miracle he could show kindness at all. "Is your childhood why you don't like to talk much?"

He shrugged. "The fake uncle punched me every time I opened my mouth, so I stopped opening it."

Pain for him ticked through her, and she made a sound of protest.

He kissed her bare shoulder. "It's okay. Then I learned how much you can see and hear when you're not the one talking, so I kind of kept quiet. After a while, it became normal to remain quiet, so I didn't bother to talk. Then my brothers picked up the slack and made it even easier."

She wiggled to get more comfortable and brushed against his erection. He groaned. "Sorry."

"No problem." The hand on her abdomen heated all the way through to her back. "I'd like for you to, ah, meet my brothers sometime."

The offer shot through her with a thrill that stole her breath. Meet his family? God, she wanted that. But she had to remain calm and not freak out. She could feel his lips against her hair. "You love them."

"They're my brothers," Denver said simply.

Sometimes the sweetness he kept deep down spilled out, and it slayed her. Her heart turned right over and rolled in everything that was Denver. How was she going to let him go again? He was finally opening up to her, but there was a sense of finality to his tone. "You really don't think you're going to beat Madison and Cobb, do you." She'd said it as a statement because it was one.

"Oh, I'll beat them." He nipped her shoulder and sent tingles down her body. "I just don't know if I'll walk away intact. But it's time to take them down."

Ouch. Didn't that sound dismal? "Is there any way I can help?" she asked. Besides praying her heart out for him.

"No."

He didn't even think about it, and much as she tried, she couldn't drum up much anger. They'd just gone through a gang fight, and she hadn't fired her weapon once. All she'd done was point it at a door and then fall over fences. "I wish things were different," she whispered.

"Me too."

"What if you win against them and live?" she asked, knowing it was a question she was stupid to ask. What did she want? Did she want a shot with him? A real one? She was just getting to really know him. What if he said this was still temporary? And hopefully she'd have a daughter to think about. Anybody she allowed into Talia's life had to stay there.

The door opened, and light from the hallway spilled in. Damn it.

Detective Malloy stuck his head in. "Denver? We need to talk."

"I figured," Denver said wryly, planting a harder kiss to Noni's shoulder. "Go to sleep now." Something rustled and then a zipper echoed. He loped out of the room just wearing ripped jeans, his back one long line of muscle. The blood brother tattoo, with its intricate and deadly looking lines, glowed darkly on his skin.

Then he was gone.

CHAPTER 11

Malloy's kitchen smelled like new paint and Sheetrock. The cabinets were yellow, the granite sparkly, and the floor a polished wood. Denver drew out a chair at the table where Tina had sewn up Noni. The slight smell of lemon and ammonia wafted up. Apparently Tina took cleaning up seriously.

"You still drinkin'?" Malloy asked, setting down two crystal tumblers.

"Yeah. Just not as much and not to forget." Denver scrubbed his hands through his messy hair, shoving it away from his face.

Malloy reached into a cupboard above the fridge and drew out twenty-year-old single malt. He poured generously and then sat, his brown eyes hangdog. He'd drawn on a dark T-shirt that showed his impressive biceps along with the same sweats as before.

"You been working out?" Denver asked.

"Yeah. Tina is a health nut," Malloy said, taking a deep drink and then watching him over the rim.

She had looked pretty healthy. Denver grinned and took a sip.

"Shut up," Malloy muttered, flushing. "She's not that much younger than me. Twelve years."

"Love is blind, buddy," Denver said, letting the alcohol warm his chilled gut. "My family, all of them, want you happy."

Malloy sipped slowly. "Your family has been a pain in my ass since the first time I met any of you."

Denver nodded. "We do have that effect, I agree. How long have you been together with Tina?"

"We're not bonding here, numbnuts." Malloy sat back, his gaze thoughtful.

Interesting. Were there wedding bells in the cop's future? Denver took another drink. He liked Malloy, and he hated bringing danger to the cop's door. Especially with Tina there. "What's the intel?"

"According to my people, three known gangbangers are dead from bullet wounds, three more from the explosion. Four taken to the hospital—all in serious condition but not critical," Malloy said, his expression turning pissed again.

Those guys must've been outside when he pressed the button. "I wonder what happened," Denver mused.

"If I search your bag, will I find the gun that killed those first three?" Malloy asked.

"No," Denver returned honestly. He'd have one of Jory's men take care of it.

"Good." Malloy poured them both another glass. "Why is there a gang after you? These guys run drugs and guns. That's not your gig."

Denver took another sip of the good stuff. "They're protecting somebody who has something I want. As much as I'd love your help, I can't tell you anything more than that." He couldn't tell Malloy the full truth or the cop would have to call it in. Denver had to find the baby himself.

"So you're planning on doing something illegal," Malloy muttered, shaking his head. He'd cut his hair short, so it didn't move. But somehow even his hair seemed to bristle at Denver.

"I hope not," Denver said. He wasn't sure if taking the baby from Richie was illegal. "I'm doing the right thing. I promise."

Malloy scratched his elbow. "Did you see the press conference Sheriff Cobb had in North Carolina?"

Denver closed his eyes and then reopened them. Oh shit. This was going to go south and fast. "Yeah."

"Did you kill the kid and Cobb's brother years ago?"

Might as well give Malloy all of it. He seemed like a fair guy, and so far he'd worked with them. "Cobb's brother killed the little kid, tried to pin it on me, rushed my brothers, and they hit him with bats in self-defense." Denver let all the words out in a rush. "I started the fire that burned down that hellhole."

"Fuck." Malloy tipped back his head and drank his entire glass. "What am I supposed to do with that?"

Denver swirled his glass around. "I don't know. It's the truth." Why was the cop even giving him a chance? "Didn't Sheriff Cobb contact you a few weeks ago?"

"Yeah. He visited here for a lunch meeting with me."

Denver stilled. He looked up, shock filling him. "You met with Cobb."

"A week ago Tuesday," Malloy confirmed, his gaze hardening even more. "I didn't like him. Jerk thinks he's too smooth and everyone else is too dumb. Asked me a bunch of questions about you guys and the Copper Killer case."

They'd solved that case and put down a serial killer. Denver swallowed. "What did you tell him?"

Malloy's smile was fierce. "Nothin'. He thought I was a dumb hick cop, and I acted like one. My instincts are good."

Maybe, maybe not. The cop was a good guy who'd decided to trust Denver, and that might be a mistake. "I have a target on my back, and I don't want somebody to hit you instead of me," Denver said.

"Agreed," Malloy said. "But if the shooter is illegal, I take him down."

That was not how it was going to happen. Cobb wouldn't go quietly, and Madison would always somehow find funding to continue her experiments. There was only one way to stop them, and it sure wasn't the legal way. "Of course," Denver said smoothly. "If I had one iota of proof against Cobb for anything, I'd turn it over."

"Why do I feel like I never get the whole story from you guys?" Malloy snapped.

Because Malloy was smart, without question. Denver just shrugged. "Your hick cop act works for only so long. You're not stupid."

"No." Malloy leaned back and opened what looked like a junk drawer to remove a bright purple file folder. He nudged it toward Denver.

Denver stared at the innocuous folder for a moment and then flipped it open to see a picture and background check on Noni. Man, Malloy had run that fast. Just how good were his connections, anyway? He must've taken her driver's license from the pack before Denver had gotten it out of the entryway. "She's clean, Malloy."

"Sure is." Malloy reached out one beefy hand and tapped his finger on the picture. "Why is that woman with you running from shooting gang members? She has no ties to drugs, guns, or gangs. You wouldn't take a girlfriend into a fight with you. Not your style."

"Girlfriend?" Denver kept his gaze placid. "Says who?"

"Says the sounds I heard from your bedroom thirty minutes ago," Malloy retorted.

Denver crossed his arms. "You listened to us? Pervert."

"Look who's talking." Malloy shook his head. "I can see with my dumb hick eyes that you care for her, so knock off the act. There's only one reason you're fighting off gang members, and she's sleeping in my guest room. Tell me the story so I can help her."

Denver finished his drink. "The second I think I can share, I will. For now, trust me."

Malloy's nostrils flared and he drank the rest of his Scotch. Standing, he glared down. "Fine, but I'll keep digging. For now, would you please call your family—all of them—so they stop bothering me? They found out about the explosion, and I don't want to know how. If you guys are hacking into satellites again, I will arrest you."

Denver winced. "Sorry. I sent a text, but they were supposed to hold tight."

"None of you knows how to hold tight." Malloy stomped out of the kitchen and disappeared.

Denver dragged his phone from his pocket and dialed up Ryker.

"What the fuck, man?" Ryker's face was instantly on screen with Heath next to him. Denver should've grabbed his laptop out of his pack for this call. "The safe house blew up."

Denver nodded. "I had the safeguards put in place when we were working the Copper Killer case and hadn't had a chance to disengage them. They came in handy tonight."

"Are you all right?" Heath asked, the green in his eyes burning.

"Fine. Noni got shot in the arm, but she's okay." Denver glanced at the half-full bottle of Scotch. He didn't need another glass. It tempted him, but he was stronger than that. He had to be—for Noni.

Ryker leaned in. "We're heading your way."

"There's nothing for you to do here yet," Denver countered evenly. "I'm not even sure if Richie and the baby are here in Snowville. What I can't figure out is how the gang found the safe house."

"They must've followed you from the hospital," Ryker said, not sounding convinced. "But it's odd you didn't notice something."

Heath snorted. "His mind isn't on the op, now, is it? We never should've let you go alone."

Denver ground his back teeth together to keep from snapping. He would've felt the same way if Heath was in danger and he was safely at home, but there wasn't an alternative right now. "Listen. Sheriff Cobb came here to meet with Malloy a week ago Tuesday. One of you start hacking and see if you can find where he flew from, *if* he flew. If there's no record, we'll start hacking into traffic cams to see where he drove from."

Ryker stiffened, his eyes darkening. "You think we can find where Cobb and Madison have set up shop?"

"I hope so." Denver tapped his fingers on the table. They'd been searching for Cobb and Madison, who'd set up a new lab, for so long. They had to find those bastards. "This is the best lead we've had in ages. Maybe ever." They were so close. It was time. The Scotch caught the dim light from the stove clock, looking delicious. He licked his lips and kept his hand away from the bottle.

Heath cleared his throat. "What are you staring at?"

"Nothin'." Denver hunched in his chair, his focus back on his brothers. "Just thinking the problem through. I told Malloy what really happened."

Ryker sighed. "You probably didn't have a choice. It's better he hears the truth from us before investigating further, which we know he'll do. You're not safe staying there, regardless."

"Agreed." Denver scrubbed his face. "I lost the truck." Damn it. He'd loved that truck. "It was in the garage when the house blew."

Heath winced. "Sorry."

"Me too," Denver murmured. "I'll need clean transport. The Montana gang sent money and provisions, so I just need to buy something off the street." There had to be a local magazine with cars for sale around the house somewhere. Malloy seemed like a car guy.

Ryker opened his mouth, no doubt to argue, and Denver cut him off. "There's no plan, guys. I can't include you until I know where Richie and the Kingdom Boys are. For all I know, the assholes could be heading in your direction. Keep up your searches, I'll keep up mine, and we'll see what happens. I'm safe and fine." And armed. "Trust me."

His brothers both looked at him, their gazes worried.

"Fine," Heath muttered.

"Agreed," Ryker said, his voice no happier than Heath's. "We need a plan. Saving the baby takes precedence over any other op, even our main one. Find that baby and get in touch with us."

"Roger that. Call me the second you find either Cobb or Madison," Denver said, disconnecting the call. He had to find Talia—time was running out. He leaned back and sighed, thanking God once again for his brothers. A part of him believed that they would've found one another even without Madison's interference, because they were family, and that was that. Speaking of family. He dialed another number.

"Are you all right?" Jory Dean instantly filled the screen. "The safe house blew up and Malloy wouldn't tell me anything. He enjoys being a dick."

"Can't blame him. We never tell him anything," Denver said slowly. "I'm fine. I blew it up, we ran, and we're safe right here. Stay where you are, keep your brothers there, and I'll call if I need help."

Jory snarled. "Don't brush me off. You're out there alone, and that doesn't work for me."

"I'm not alone—"

"Yes, you are. Whether we're brothers or not, we're family. We never leave one of us alone. Never alone." Jory's gray eyes turned stormy.

Denver blinked. Had he just hurt Jory's feelings? The guy was a bulldog and deadly soldier—one of the deadliest alive. His training had started at birth. Who knew he was so sensitive? "I'm sorry if I was curt," Denver said hoarsely.

Jory rolled his eyes. "Don't be a jackass." He paused. "I, ah, I have the results of our genetic testing."

Denver stilled. His breath caught. "What does it say?"

Jory glanced down. "I haven't opened it yet. Thought we should do it together."

Denver swallowed. "This is as close as we're going to be for a while. Open it."

Jory nodded and the sound of an envelope being ripped open came across the line. He glanced down to read, his eyes starting to darken.

Denver caught his expression. "We're not brothers." A fist dropped into his gut. Until that second he hadn't realized how much he wanted that genetic link.

Jory looked up, his eyebrows down. "I don't give a fuck what a test says. We're family. At least one of your brothers is a half brother to my one of my brothers—"

"Jesus." Denver snorted. "Okay. We're family. Stop with the confusing brother talk." His chest ached, and he fought the urge to rub it. The Scotch bottle beckoned him again, and he gripped the table to keep from reaching for it. Man, he'd wanted to be Jory's brother, too. "It's okay, Jory."

"Promise we're family," Jory said, looking much younger all of a sudden. Like a wild wolf who'd been cornered and was trying to decide whether to nudge forward or attack with teeth bared.

Denver blinked as he let go of the dream of a genetic link with another person. He was fine making his own family in life, so why not give Jory the words? Jory was a good guy, and Denver liked him. "We're family." Yeah. It was true.

Jory cleared his throat, looking congenial again. "Okay. Enough with the mush. Did your truck survive the explosion?"

Denver's jaw tightened.

"Ah, sorry man. That sucks." Jory leaned to the side. "I'll have my guy bring you a car tomorrow. What do you want?"

Denver leaned back. "Business is that good?" The Dean boys owned several businesses throughout the country that provided military-like services in the private sector.

"Yep. It's great. You should come on board after this case is over," Jory said.

Denver ignored the Scotch that was so damn near his hand. "I'll keep it in mind. Have your guy bring something fast and good in the snow, and I promise I'll pay you back."

"No worries. Call in when you get to the next safe house." Jory sobered. "Family means everything. You guys know that, right?"

Denver let the words ring true. "Yeah. It's all we know."

Jory grinned. "How is Noni?"

"Night, Jory." Denver clicked off, a genuine chuckle rising up. The first part of his life had been shitty and then he'd found Ryker and Heath. Life had gotten shittier, then they'd escaped, and life had gotten a whole lot better. Now he had an entire family in Montana also.

Man, he hoped he lived through his next two missions.

Then there was Noni.

As if on cue, she moved into the room, her dark eyes grumpy and her hair all over. She slid his laptop onto the table. "The thing keeps beeping." Without waiting for a reply, she turned and stumbled sleepily out of the kitchen.

Denver watched her the whole time, not sure what to say. His body sprang to full life, and his cock perked right up. Oh, he wanted to be back in bed with her.

His laptop beeped.

Frowning, he flipped open the lid and went through his extensive security to reach the searches he was still conducting. A few minutes later, he was on the right site on the good ole dark web.

A line caught his eye. An auction. He knew it. Damn it. His patience had paid off, but he didn't like what he read.

"There you are," he murmured. He kept reading, his blood freezing in his veins. The gang was auctioning off the baby, just like he thought they would. A picture of Talia, her baby eyes so innocent and vulnerable, filled the screen.

God.

CHAPTER
12

Get dressed, sweetheart." Denver gently tugged Noni up, turning her to examine the bandage on her arm. "This will keep. We have to go," he whispered.

She instantly awoke and looked around. It was still dark outside. "What time is it?"

"Five in the morning. We have to go before Malloy wakes up." Denver tossed clothing onto the bed for her.

She shrugged into a thick sweater and pulled on her jeans before quickly braiding her hair down her back. "Why are we sneaking off?"

Denver handed over her pack. "Malloy is a cop, and we have to make this easy on him."

"I wondered how long we could stay." The detective would probably have to fight his conscience to just let them go and not drag them down to the police station. "But I still want to say thank you to James and Tina." Noni stepped into her boots.

"You can send them a fruit basket later." Denver motioned her toward the doorway. "Follow me."

Smart aleck. Noni stopped by the bathroom quickly to take care of business and brush her teeth. Denver was waiting for her right outside. "Let's go."

She shook her head but did as he said, following him down the hallway and through the living room. The Christmas lights still twinkled happily in the corner. Would she ever have this with Denver? Was it possible? She was off balance, and somehow sad. Leaving the comfortable home made her feel chilled. He opened the door, and more cold instantly slammed into her. Barely keeping herself from grumbling, she grabbed her coat and shoved her arms in before heading out into the darkness.

Denver took her hand and led the way down the walk to the street, where a man leaned against a deep green SUV. He pushed off as they approached. A hat sat low on his head, and in the darkness she couldn't really see his face. He handed Denver the keys and a piece of paper, turned without a word, and trudged down the sidewalk.

Noni watched him go. This was all so weird. "Who was that?" she whispered, even more off balance than before.

"Get in." Denver opened the passenger side door, and she climbed in, then he walked around and got in too. He ignited the engine, and they drove away from the detective's house.

Noni secured her seat belt. "Where are we going?"

"There's a motel on the outskirts of town." Denver maneuvered through the subdivision and reached the quiet main road before flipping on the light above the mirror. He unfolded the paper the man had given him. "Or maybe not."

A male voice suddenly came over the speaker. "You get the present?"

Noni yelped and shoved back in her seat. Her heart sped up. She put her hand to her chest. "What in the world?"

Denver sighed. "Noni, meet Ryker, my brother. Apparently he hacked into the vehicle's phone system."

"Nice to meet you," Ryker said, his voice deep.

Noni blinked. "It's like *Knight Rider*," she murmured.

Ryker laughed. "Good one. Did you get the paper?"

"Affirmative," Denver said. "Figured it was from Jory, though."

"We coordinated through the night. The messenger was one of his guys, though. We found a different safe house in Coeur d'Alene. We bought it, and it's now registered to a shell corporation that can't be traced to any of us," Ryker said.

Noni's mouth gaped. "You managed a land exchange in the middle of the night from somewhere else. Just what kind of connections do you guys have?"

"The owner was motivated to sell," Ryker said dryly. "He's had three deals fall through, and he has already relocated to the Florida sunshine. It wasn't that difficult."

Sure it wasn't.

Denver took a left turn around a series of commercial businesses that were still closed. "I'm not going to ask how you found the money. Did you get the e-mail I sent?"

"Yes. What do you need?"

"I don't know. When I do, I'll call." Denver scanned the roads and the few vehicles already out and about on the dismal morning. "Thanks, Ry." He hung up.

Noni turned toward him. "What's going on? What was in the e-mail?" She was finally waking up completely, and he looked seriously tense. A vein pulsed down his neck, and his hands were anything but relaxed on the steering wheel. He held it so tightly his knuckles were turning white. "You need to talk to me," she said, her heart thundering.

He took another turn, glancing at the GPS in the dash. "I found the auction site for the gang on the dark web. They're auctioning off the baby, and the bids are up to three hundred thousand dollars."

Noni's stomach cramped as if she'd been punched, and she leaned over. "Oh God. Who is bidding?"

"No clue, and the gang doesn't care." Denver took another turn down a quiet, icy road.

Noni swallowed several times. "Are you sure it's Talia?"

"I'm sure," he said grimly. "Her picture is up, and it's the same baby. She looks okay."

"Wait a minute. That's illegal. Nobody can auction off a baby, especially a known drug gang. This is proof that Richie is still a bad guy. Should we call the FBI?" Noni clasped her hands together. What the hell should they do?

Denver nodded. "That's one route. We could call the cops."

Noni tried to wet her too-dry lips. "But?"

"How are they going to get to Richie? You can't find bidders on the dark web, and whoever wins will be contacted directly." Denver took another turn out of the main Snowville downtown area.

"So we bid," she said softly. "Don't you need special virtual money?"

"Not for this," Denver said. "They'll want real cash."

She didn't know how to do this. "I don't have any."

"I have some but not nearly enough." Brightly decorated storefronts bracketed them right before he opened the throttle and burst onto the interstate. "We'll have to bluff and just take them out at the drop point."

"What if they don't bring the baby until they see the cash?" she breathed.

His mouth tightened. "Good point. Okay. We'll have to figure something else out. Maybe I can get that kind of cash. If not, it'll be the bluff of the century."

"When is the auction finished?" she asked, her head aching. How was this possible? Where was the baby?

"Tomorrow evening at five, PST," Denver said, his voice hoarse. "As soon as we get to the safe house, I'll set up a bidding profile. Well, after I create an identity or two." He scrubbed a rough hand through his thick hair.

A black sports car whipped by them on the right, fishtailing several times.

"Idiot," Denver muttered, slowing down. He glanced in the rearview mirror and tensed.

"What?" Noni gasped, twisting to see behind them. A couple of trucks followed them, their lights cutting through the early morning.

Denver's shoulders settled down, and an odd calmness permeated the vehicle. For some reason that pricked every nerve in Noni's body to life. Her palms grew sweaty. "What's happening?" Something definitely was going on.

"Baby? I need you to make sure your seat belt is fastened securely," Denver said calmly.

She fumbled and double checked the strap across her chest. She gulped. "Okay."

"Now I need you to plant both feet on the floor and set your spine against the seat. Face forward, don't twist, and try to somehow relax your body. No tenseness," he said, his grip visibly loosening on the steering wheel.

How was he so focused? The calmer he became, the more she wanted to jump out of the car screaming like a wild woman. She tried to relax her body and instead tightened every muscle.

"Relax," he murmured, flicking his blinker and moving over into the slow lane.

She scrunched down a little to see in the side mirror. The trucks behind them remained in the fast and middle lanes, abreast of each other and not speeding. They looked like well-equipped working trucks complete with thick grilles. "Please tell me what's going on."

"I'm not sure." He punched in a series of buttons on the GPS in the dash. "Get ready to hold on to something, but try to keep your body aligned forward, okay?"

She could barely breathe. Was he losing his mind? The trucks hadn't changed speed or trajectory at all. They weren't even in the slow lane. "I think you might be paranoid."

He shook his arms out. "Just because you're paranoid doesn't mean they're not coming for you." While his voice remained light, a thread of tension wove just beneath the surface of each word. He reached for a gun in his waistband and pulled it out. They drove past an exit.

At the sight of the weapon, her mind fuzzed. "Wait a minute. Just—"

Denver yanked the steering wheel and they crashed down a snowy embankment, swerving at the last second to catch the side of the exit.

Noni screamed, slamming her hands onto the dash. Her neck snapped to the side, and she scrambled to remain in position, facing forward. If they crashed, she would be safer not twisting.

The SUV bumped and jumped down the hill, throwing its back end up. Pain ricocheted up her spine as they slid and hopped toward the off-ramp.

Denver barreled down the exit and ignored the stoplight at the bottom. He made a hard right through the red light, and the SUV skidded on the ice, spinning out in a full circle. A car honked and shot out of the way. Denver slammed the SUV into reverse and whipped it around, his foot pressing the pedal.

Noni panted and turned to see the two trucks sliding down the hill and catching the exit. "They're coming."

"I know," Denver said. "We need to lose them, and then we'll get to the safe house."

She reached for the gun in his hand. "I can shoot them out the window." Could she? She'd never shot at anybody before. Her stomach lurched.

"I'm driving too fast."

She swallowed rapidly. "I'm sorry I got you into this. It has to be the Kingdom Boys and Richie."

He frowned into the rearview mirror. "I don't think so. These guys are too good."

Pings echoed off the metal body of the SUV.

"Get down." Denver grasped the nape of her neck and pushed her face down.

She struggled to breathe as the seat belt tightened across her torso. "They're shooting?" Adrenaline ripped through her veins, bringing everything into way too sharp of a focus. Her breathing. The tick of the heater. Denver's total sense of calm. "Oh God."

Something crashed into the back of the SUV, throwing it into a wide tailspin. The seat belt across her lap constricted her, shooting pain through her abdomen. "No airbags?"

"Any SUV left by my family would've been modified in case of, well, this," Denver muttered, pulling on the steering wheel and trying to correct. The driver's side door smashed into a blue postal mailbox, and he instantly hit the gas pedal, spiraling them back onto the street. "They rammed us." He drove up onto the sidewalk and whipped around a building into a dark alley. They flew by garbage cans and metal doors.

"If not the gang, then Cobb and Madison?" she asked, her hands shaking.

"It would make sense. I have a bad feeling Cobb has been watching Malloy just in case we contacted the cop again." Denver took another turn onto a street and nearly smashed into one of the trucks. "This has nothing to do with you." He clipped the truck's back bumper and swerved.

A man jumped from the back of the truck, landing on the roof of the SUV. His body thumped hard above them, and the metal protested.

Noni's mouth gaped, and she turned toward Denver. "Who are these guys?"

The man on the roof leaned over the passenger side and punched her window. Glass flew inward. She ducked and screamed as a piece sliced into her neck. Pain slashed down to her collarbone.

Denver swore and aimed his gun up at the roof, firing rapidly. The percussion exploded in the SUV, and Noni clapped her hands over her ears. Her entire head rang.

The man on the roof rolled to her side and kept on falling, leaving a smear of blood on the jagged remainder of her window. Snow and ice blew in with the blood. She tried to stifle a scream and covered her mouth with her hand. Tears filled her eyes. "You shot him," she said numbly.

"Yeah." Denver angled his head toward the back window. Blood dripped from a cut above his cheek.

The sight of his blood shot the entire scene into focus. Those men were trying to kill them. Noni shook her head.

Denver coughed. "Good. One truck is picking him up, so they've slowed down."

Was the guy dead? She hadn't been able to tell. Cold air blasted inside and forced her away from the numbness shock provided. She turned to look out the back. Both trucks were now speeding toward them.

Denver swung the SUV in an arc. "Duck," he yelled.

She yelped and pressed her head to her knees. Gunshots echoed above her head, and she shut her eyes, trying not to scream again.

Bullets plowed into the SUV, and the back window shattered. Something hissed.

The vehicle rocked back into motion.

Sucking in air, she slowly lifted her head and looked around. Pain filled her neck. Denver had shot out the front windshields of both trucks. Blood covered the front hood of one truck. A man leaped from the other truck, already firing with what looked like a fully automatic weapon. She'd seen one on television.

Denver pushed her down again and took a sharp turn around a brick building.

Noni struggled to breathe and her body started to shake. "A guy jumped on the roof," she said, almost in a daze. "The people after you are crazy. Are these genetically altered soldiers?"

"Maybe." Denver sped through town way too fast for the conditions. "Genetically altered or not, these guys are trained, and they have to be from Cobb and Madison. They're on me, not you." He swung the SUV in another circle and spun into the empty parking lot of a sewing shop. The car had barely stopped when he shoved open his door and stepped outside. "Stay here."

She shook her head, trying to grasp reality. Her fingers fumbled with the belt, and she finally removed it. So now not only was the gang after them but Denver's past had finally caught up? It was all too much at once. Way too much.

Denver strode forward in complete control, his gun pointed at the quiet road.

One of the trucks turned the corner wide and lifted onto two tires, coming down with a hard thump. Denver aimed his gun and fired. Low-pitched pings filled the air, a front tire blew, and the truck flew almost in slow motion through the air, flipping onto its roof and sliding several yards down the icy road.

Noni gasped and pushed herself over to the driver's side to see better. Almost as an afterthought, she yanked her gun out of her pack and pointed it toward the hissing truck.

The second truck careened around the corner, this one closer.

Denver dropped to one knee, aimed, and fired rapidly. His bullets sprayed across the grille toward the gaping hole where the windshield had been. The driver's body recoiled as if he was shot, and he turned the wheel, bashing the truck into a telephone pole on the other side of the street. Denver calmly shot out both front tires while the driver's body hung out the front. The passenger fired back, and ice spit up all around Denver. He returned fire, and the other guy went down.

Without missing a beat, Denver turned and strode toward her.

Noni gasped and scrambled back into her seat, her ears ringing. Denver closed his door and set the SUV into motion. "Hold on, Noni." Without another word, he drove into the darkened night, the snow and freezing air pouring through the broken windows and bullet holes.

CHAPTER
13

Goddamn motherfucking soldiers." Sheriff Elton Cobb kicked a chair out of his way as he stomped into his love's office.

She looked up from behind her glass-topped desk, her blue eyes clear, her black hair pulled back into an intricate braid. "Really, Elton."

He slammed the door and moved the brocade chair back into place, taking several deep breaths to keep from losing his mind. "Really? How can you be so calm? Your damn soldiers missed Denver. Again. We had the motherfucker. We had two trucks, four men, and we lost him." To have finally been so close, to have had a visual on the target. Cobb's hands clenched into beefy fists.

"I find emotion unnecessary." Isobel Madison was the epitome of class and sophistication in her blue silk blouse and gray pencil skirt. Her ever-present white lab coat hung on an antique coat hanger over in the corner. Stunning oil paintings of the Old West covered the walls, and delicate trinkets lined glass shelves behind her. Her numerous framed diplomas and awards took up the wall to the west. "The good news is that we've found Denver as well as the woman who put that picture on the Internet."

Cobb dropped heavily into the chair. "Why didn't we also post that woman's picture when I had the press conference?"

Isobel sighed, her red lips pursing. "Because we didn't want Denver to know we'd found her. However, I told you keeping an eye on Detective Malloy would be useful." Her fine eyebrows angled down. "I *also* told you the press conference was a bad idea, but you wouldn't listen."

Bad idea? Bullshit. Finally the entire law enforcement community was looking for Denver, Heath, and Ryker. Oh, he'd get to them first, or he'd end up with them, but either way, he was going to strip the skin from their bodies. After he destroyed everything and anything they loved. "Tell me about the girl."

Isobel nudged a manila file across the desk. "Her name is Noni Yuka. Inuit for 'bright star.'"

Cobb flipped the file open. The woman had dark eyes, even darker hair, and pretty pink lips. "She's stunning."

"Yes." Isobel leaned back in her chair. "Yet she has no backbone. Trying to track Denver down in such an obvious manner since he deserted her a year ago."

Elton stiffened. "You've traced his past year?"

"Yes. He had a job in Anchorage, where this woman runs some lotion and candle business. Apparently there was a brief affair, he did his job as a lowly private detective, and then he left." Isobel sniffed. "She posted all over the Internet to find him."

"Yet he found his way back to her." Cobb rubbed his cleanly shaven jaw. "There must be a reason. Either he cares for her or there's something else going on."

"Obviously he cares for her," Isobel said, her pert nose in the air. "That's why he left in the first place. But you're correct. I need to do more digging into what's going on now. He wouldn't be with her unless there was a compelling reason." Her voice had risen.

Cobb glanced her way. She'd always had a soft spot for Denver, the little asshole. He turned back to the photos.

The next picture he found was of Denver. The boy had grown into a large man with angry blue eyes. At least Cobb saw anger. "I wondered if he would grow into those feet." Oh, Cobb would make that bastard pay for killing his brother. In ways that made even him sick to his stomach. "He outfought your soldiers, Isobel." Something nearly impossible to do.

She clicked her tongue. "I'm aware."

Was that pride in her voice? Cobb's gaze narrowed as he now watched her.

Her eyes darkened as she took in the picture. "He looks strong. And smart. I made him that way, you know. I made every one of my soldiers that way."

All of the science crap made Cobb queasy. "You enjoyed yourself." The woman liked to play God.

"Yes," she said, pulling the picture toward her to study. "Many of my records were destroyed, as you know. But I remember making Denver. He's special."

Her possessive tone straightened Cobb's spine. "You can have all the pride you want, but never forget. Denver, that little fucker, is all mine." They had come to an agreement.

She sighed. "After I take his genetic material, you can have him." Then she smiled, the look feral. "If you can take him."

Cobb sat back. Fire lanced through him, and he bit it back. He refused to feel jealousy for a man who was as good as dead. The woman was always challenging him, and he usually liked it. Not right now, however. "I'm going to kill him, Isobel."

She pushed the photo back toward the pile. "Noni is going to lead us to Denver, and then you'll have your chance."

Noni. Even the name had nice peaks and valleys. It had been too long since Cobb had tortured a woman for the night. "Do you want to watch this time?" he murmured.

"Not really." Isobel swept her hand out.

That kind of thing had never interested her. Pity. Cobb rummaged through the papers in the file. "Noni has an aunt...who's married to another woman."

Isobel tapped red nails on her desk. "I'm trying to find them now. They seem to be on the move, but the second I get them, we can use them as leverage."

Cobb looked up and focused. "Lesbians," he mused, finding a picture of the women. He pointed to a fifty-something woman with dark eyes. "This one looks like the girl."

"That's her aunt."

He nodded. "They got married. What do you think about that?" He and Isobel so rarely discussed anything but their future plans. Other people's lives didn't factor into their thoughts usually, and sometimes that was okay. Every once in a while he wished for more. Could he make Isobel look at him the way she looked at her creations? With pride and possession? "Sweetheart?"

"Fine by me," Isobel said, her voice cultured. "What a pity to miss out on the male species, however. You're all so easy to...love." Her head tilted.

What had she really meant to say? He narrowed his gaze at her, not fooled by her placid expression. His blood started to pump faster, even as his chest ached a little. "I believe the word you were looking for is 'manipulate.'"

She rolled her eyes. "I meant the word I used. I always do."

He stretched his biceps after working them hard that morning. "You never talk about your family." Except her daughter, and that talk was usually clinical.

"Nothing to say. My mother was weak and died in childbirth. My father was a soldier. A great one." She smiled, and her chin lowered, giving her a sultry look.

"I already knew that." Why couldn't she give him more? Just a little bit.

"I grew up in boarding schools. He died when I was twenty." Her gaze remained clear, but a small tremor had gone through her words.

Cobb's gaze sharpened. "It hurt you. His death."

"He was my father."

So she could be hurt. Was that why she'd chosen her work? He opened his mouth to ask more questions but stopped when she waved a hand.

"The past is irrelevant." Her perfectly painted lips twitched as she stood and sauntered around the desk toward him. Her scent of roses came with her. "You know I don't manipulate men. I love everything about the males of this species. Their strength." She dropped to her knees between his legs. "Their determination." Her palms smoothed up his legs to unbutton his pants. "Their courage."

Desire slammed into him. Hard. Even though he understood her mind, even though they often had opposing goals, she had him here, and he knew it. So he grabbed her hair and yanked the braid free, letting the glorious mass cascade down her back. In her midfifties, she was truly stunning.

She released him from his pants and stroked him, her skin softer than silk. "We need to proceed slowly, Elton. No more crazy news conferences."

He barely kept his eyes from rolling back in his head. "We'll talk later."

"Now." She leaned over and let her heated breath brush the tip of his dick. "My soldiers have regrouped. They're going after the cop."

Cop? What cop? Cobb tried to focus and instead spread his legs more. "Wait. I met with the cop a short time ago. Malloy. He didn't know shit."

She sucked the tip of him into her mouth, her grip strong at his base. "No matter. We're taking him alive for information. Well, probably." Then she swallowed him whole, forcing him to the back of her throat.

He should protest, but his head fell back and his eyes closed. Then, as she no doubt wanted him to, he completely forgot everything but her heated mouth.

* * *

Denver kept an eye on the quiet woman in the passenger seat, taking back roads in a long circuitous route to make sure they weren't being followed. Freezing wind blew in through the shattered windows and bullet holes. He couldn't believe Madison and Cobb had nearly caught up to him with Noni in the car.

Damn it.

He'd known he would be a danger to her. And he'd been right.

She huddled in her seat, her gaze sightless out the window. No doubt in shock. He turned up the heat to battle the open air and took another icy corner. "We'll get you into a hot shower soon, sweetheart."

She barely nodded.

He reached for a burner phone and called Detective Malloy.

"What?" Malloy snapped.

Denver winced. "Ah, we left your house and got into a bit of a skirmish. Enemies from my past, from the Gray brothers' past, have obviously been watching you." He waited for Malloy to explode, but the cop remained quiet. "You should get out of town. Take Tina on a vacation."

Malloy finally breathed out. "Who are these people?"

"Can't tell you." Denver said. "They have to be watching you. That's the only way they could've found me."

"Then they can come and get me," Malloy said darkly.

Denver sighed. Since he'd left Malloy, the cop was probably safe. But he and the Gray brothers needed to cut all ties with the detective for his own safety. "Just think about a vacation." He hung up.

Man, he hoped Malloy listened. One problem at a time, though.

He focused on the dark and snowy morning, his memories tumbling back from the quiet. Yeah, he'd known Dr. Madison would someday find him. She'd told him as much.

He was eight years old, sitting on an examination table while the doctor took his blood pressure. They were using a local doctor's office for physical tests today, and Ryker and Heath were somewhere in other rooms. He wished they could all be tested together, but that never happened.

"So perfectly steady," she said, unwrapping the cuff. "You also performed very well on your calculus test earlier today. Equations and also spatial relations is going to be a snap for you." Gently, almost kindly, she ran a hand down his hair. "You're everything I could've hoped for, Denver."

He swallowed, entranced by her gentle touch but wary of the sharp gleam in her too-blue eyes. "Thank you."

Approval lifted her dark eyebrows. "You've been so strong and silent the last two times we've met. I like when you talk to me."

He looked around the small room, absently counting the cotton balls he could see through the glass jar on the narrow counter. "Okay." Kicking out his legs, he thought again about her real name. He hadn't seen her in two months, and he wondered what she knew about his life. He extended his arm, showing a myriad of bruises cascading to his wrist. "These hurt."

She looked at the bruises, her eyebrows lifting, her hand still on his head. "Mere contusions. You're strong enough to banish the pain."

He blinked. Did she care or not? "Ned hit me." Then he watched her. Carefully.

Her bright red lips pursed. "Hit him back." No emotion, no concern was in her voice.

"He's too big," Denver whispered.

She let go of his head and moved away, making him feel cold. "You'll be bigger someday." Then she leaned against the counter and crossed her arms over a light pink blouse. The silky kind. "You have to fight your own battles, Denver. It's the only way you'll get strong enough."

"For what?" His ears rang. She wasn't going to protect him or Ryker or Heath. She didn't care.

"For your life and what you must do in it. You're unique." She reached for a notebook. The damn lady was always taking notes.

He scowled. "Where do you live?" Why was she studying him? If she didn't care, why was she even here?

She scribbled something. "That's not your concern."

He couldn't see beneath her surface. Why not? "Do you care about me? About us?" Was there a way to make her care? If Ned hit Ryker in the head again, he might kill him. "Do you?"

She looked up, her eyes burning. "I care more than you know. We're tied together forever. All of us."

He shook his head. "I'll run away. I will."

She smiled then, her teeth white and straight. "Oh, Denver. You'll never get away from me. That much I promise you."

Denver jerked back to the present as the vehicle slid. He quickly corrected, looking to make sure Noni was all right.

She blinked, huddled closer to the heat as snow blew inside the vehicle. "You okay?"

He slowly shook his head. "Not even close, sweetheart."

CHAPTER
14

The place outside Coeur d'Alene was a small cabin fronting a lake, away from any main street. Denver drove carefully around the lake road and down a long forested drive to reach the log A-frame. Snow billowed down, and across the lake, shimmering Christmas lights glowed from three widely spaced mansions as dawn began to lighten the sky. Between them, smaller cabins, dark and empty for the winter, dotted the hill.

He stepped out of the vehicle, noting defensive positions in rock formations and thick trees. Wind and snow battered him, and his boots crunched the ice. "The cloud cover is strong. If they were tracking us via satellite, they had a rough time. We're safe here."

Noni didn't move from the vehicle.

He leaned down to see her staring numbly out the front window. His heart stuttered. What had he just put her through? He had to find the right words, but they escaped him. So he resorted to action. "We're okay now. Let's get you warm."

Her face was so pale it looked waxen. But she opened her door after grabbing her pack. She left the small silver Lady Smith & Wesson he'd given her on the seat.

He stepped closer to the vehicle and gently secured the weapon, tucking it into the front of his waist. Shutting her door, he took her hand and led her across the frozen ground to the cabin, which was unlocked.

"It's dark," Noni murmured, her shoulders shaking.

He stepped inside and flipped on a light. The quaint entryway held a long bench and hooks for coats. He shrugged out of his leather jacket and took Noni's wool one to hang up. "Boots off." He kicked his off and then gently set her on the bench before dropping to his haunches and taking hers off. She allowed him to do so without saying anything. "Baby? I think you might be in shock." He gently rubbed the thick socks covering her small feet.

She just stared at him.

The blank look sliced into his heart. His past was threatening her now. Fury at himself nearly choked off his breath, but he didn't have the luxury of feeling anger. He calmed himself. There were so many promises he wanted to make her, but he wouldn't lie to her ever again. He just couldn't. So he'd stick with the truth. "I'm not gonna let anything happen to you. I promise." Not once in his life had he meant a promise more.

She swallowed and then nodded.

Good. He stood and took her hands, pulling her to stand. Then he led her into a cozy great room complete with a plush sofa and chair set in front of a stone fireplace. Wide windows looked out at the darkened lake and houses on the far side. He pressed her onto the couch and then turned to quickly make a fire from the logs and paper set to the side. It soon crackled merrily and filled the room with warmth. "I need to check out the generator and make sure we're set," he said, turning to face her. "It's on and working, so there's probably warm water. How about a hot shower?" That might help ease her out of the shock. The woman had seen him kill again. His entire chest hurt at the thought. But for now, he had to get her warm.

She rose shakily to her feet and looked around.

An L-shaped kitchen, complete with granite countertops, sat in the west corner, and to its left were three doorways showing a bathroom and two bedrooms. "I'll be right back," Denver murmured, striding for the outside door again, grabbing his jacket on the way. The wind slashed into him when he stepped outside and crossed around the side to check the generator. A small shed safely ensconced it along with a couple extra containers of gasoline. Good. He was just closing the shed door as his phone buzzed, and he lifted it to his ear. "Denver."

"Hey. It's Ryker." His brother's voice was hushed. "Everyone is still asleep here, but I wanted to check in."

"Madison and Cobb found me," Denver said simply. "I just outran their soldiers on icy roads."

Silence ticked for a moment. "Are you sure it was Madison and Cobb's soldiers and not Richie and the Kingdom Boys? That gang found you somehow at our safe house. Maybe they followed you?" Ryker's tone was a low growl.

Denver pinched the bridge of his nose and leaned against the freezing log cabin. "Not a chance. The soldiers I just fought with were well trained and armed beyond any local gang. One man actually jumped on the roof of our SUV while I was driving."

"Fuck."

Yeah. That pretty much summed it up.

"Are you secure?" All emotion deserted Ryker's voice as he went into battle mode.

"Yes. We're at the safe house."

"Good. We'll create an extraction plan. May need to borrow a Blackhawk from the brothers up north." Movement sounded over the line.

Denver shook his head and then remembered Ryker couldn't see him. "Negative. I have to stick with one op at a time, Ry. Madison and Cobb will have to wait."

"They're too close to you now."

Opposing forces pulled at Denver, trying to rip him apart. He had to settle himself. *Focus, damn it.* "The window for saving that baby is too short. If she's around here, and my gut says she is, then I have to stay in place." The baby had to come first. "She's an innocent, Ryker. There's nobody else to protect her."

Ryker breathed out. "I agree. She has to come first for all of us. If not, what the hell have we been fighting for?"

Denver closed his eyes. Thank God Ryker got it. "So we remain in place. Keep with the plan. You guys find the headquarters for Madison and Cobb, and I'll focus solely on reclaiming the baby while trying to stay off Madison's radar. Then we'll go from there." The weight of keeping everyone safe landed like boulders on his shoulders.

"You'll need backup with the exchange," Ryker said evenly.

"I won't." Denver tapped his head back on the log wall, his body hurting. His head aching. "Trust me."

"I do," Ryker said. "What about Malloy? They only way Madison and Cobb could've found you would be if they had been watching him. Which we kind of expected."

"I know. I told him to take a vacation, and he told me to basically fuck off." Denver sighed.

"Then we have to cut ties with him. To keep him safe," Ryker said.

"Yep. Agreed. Let the group in Montana know," Denver said.

"I will. You sound...off. Besides the obvious, what's up?"

Denver started pacing. Tension uncoiled inside him, wanting out. Now. "Shit, Ry. I wasn't going to tell you this, but Jory and I took a test. We're not blood." He couldn't hold that in.

Silence.

"Ryker?"

"You have brothers, Denver," Ryker said, his tone hoarse. "Me and Heath. We're yours."

Yeah. Denver stopped and shut his eyes. "I know." It was true. They were blood. He opened his eyes again to look at the scar along his palm. "I do know it, Ryker." For so long he'd had only his brothers. Everything eating him up inside came pouring out. "There's more. Noni saw me kill, Ry. Cold. Again."

Ryker exhaled across the line. "Oh."

"Yeah. I mean, I had to or we would've died. But I killed fast and without any struggle." Though would it have made a difference? Probably not. The end result would've been the same. "She's been in shock since."

"Get her into a hot shower."

Denver swallowed, his hand tightening on the phone. "I did."

"Ah man, Denver," Ryker breathed. "You did what you had to do to save you both, and she'll either get that...or she won't. It doesn't change who you are."

That was the problem. "I'm a killer." Had been for years. He hung his head since nobody could see him. Exhaustion weakened his knees. The backs of his eyes stung. The world was too heavy on him. "What happened. Before. That was my fault."

Silence had more weight. Then..."Are you kidding me?" Ryker barked.

Denver winced. This was definitely not the time for this discussion. "No."

"Too fucking bad. Explain."

He never should've opened his damn mouth. This is why he chose not talking over talking any day. But he also knew his brother, and there was no getting out of this one. And it was time to atone. To at least say the words that cut through him with a sharpness that stole his breath. "Ned Cobb. If you guys hadn't been trying to save me, then you wouldn't have been there. He wouldn't have died, and we wouldn't have gone on the run for so long. I'm sorry." For years he'd wanted to say those two last words but had never gotten up the balls. His eyes itched. "I'm so fucking sorry, Ryker."

"Jesus, Denver." Ryker was way too quiet for a minute. "None of that was your fault. Everything bad that happened to us was on Ned and the sheriff's heads. And Isobel Madison's. All we did was try to survive, man."

"I know, but if it had been just me, then you guys could've had normal lives." Denver's throat started to hurt. Enough words. He couldn't control them. "Without me—"

"Without you, we'd be alone in life," Ryker said quietly. "You made us a family. The three of us. Suddenly we had a brother, a younger one to protect, and we did it. It was a shitty time and a shitty place, but we survived together. The three of us. That means something, and I thank God—who I thought had forgotten about us—for helping us find one another. For you."

Tears, actual tears, clogged Denver's throat. He'd reimagined that day a million times, trying to figure out how he could've spared Ry and Heath. Why was life so fucking hard? "I'd be dead without you guys."

"We'd all be dead." Ryker sighed. "But we're not. So lift your head back up and go check on your girl. If she's somebody you care about, she's strong enough to handle what you did. It's that simple."

Life was never that simple. But Denver couldn't handle any more emotion. He was close to short-circuiting as it was. "All right. I'll call in tonight after I start bidding on the auction." The idea of bidding for a baby nauseated him. "And Ryker? Thanks."

"Love you, brother." Ryker clicked off.

Yeah. That was truth. Denver straightened up and wiped the snow off before clomping into the cabin. Noni was stretched out on the sofa in front of the fire, her wet hair splayed across the pillow, her eyes closed, and her breathing even. Good. She'd showered. He reached for a knitted blanket to place over her.

Her soft skin was pale against that black hair. He couldn't help running a finger over her high cheekbone. When they'd been together in Alaska, a little kid had seen her coming out of a store. The kid's eyes had widened, and he'd whispered to his mom that Pocahontas was there.

Noni had snorted.

But Denver had seen what the kid had seen. With her long dark hair and stunning eyes, there was something absolutely magical about her. Not just in the way she looked but in her smile. In the way she spoke and in the kindness that seemed to surround her.

He forced himself to turn away from her and grabbed his laptop to work over in the chair closer to the fire. He sat, and his entire body ached.

Sucking in air, he punched in the necessary keys and found the site. His fingers going stiff, he typed in a dollar amount to bid on a baby. Talia.

His stomach lurched, and he swallowed down bile.

Somebody instantly countered his bid.

He needed to throw up.

A tremble slid down his arm, and he clenched his fingers into a fist, opening and closing it. Then he breathed in and out, forcing himself to go cold and concentrate.

He bid again.

CHAPTER
15

Noni finished cleaning the kitchen after a quiet and very late dinner of sandwiches with a surprisingly good Shiraz. Denver's brothers had somehow stocked the kitchen with staples right after purchasing the cabin. They had connections that were impressive. She'd slept for a while in the morning and then had watched Denver work the dark web as if he had done so a million times before.

As he bid on the baby throughout the day, the price kept going up. Somebody kept outbidding him.

Who wanted Talia that badly and why?

Noni tried to remain calm, but a scream kept trying to rise in her.

They'd been polite to each other all day, but he'd been focused, and she'd hustled around cleaning in a freaked-out frenzy. Where was that numbness from the night before? She couldn't find it.

The wind whistled through the trees outside as the temperature dropped to nearly zero. She moved from the kitchen to stand near the fireplace. Denver sat on the sofa facing her with his laptop on his legs and his feet planted on the coffee table in front of the roaring fire. His broad shoulders took up an inordinate amount of space. In his dark shirt and faded jeans with bare feet, he brought back memories that had been etched in her heart.

"I didn't realize it got so cold here," she murmured, trying to ignore how quickly her body attuned to his.

He glanced up, and his blue eyes focused. "I don't think it usually does. But the cloud cover moved away, so it'll be chilly for the night."

Good Lord, they were talking about the weather. Tension rumbled around them, competing with the crackling of the fire. She jerked her head toward the laptop. "How's it going?"

Stress emphasized the lines at the sides of his mouth. "Good. Right now I'm the high bidder, but there are two other determined bidders."

A lump settled in her throat, and she swallowed several times. Her heart rate picked up. "Well, why don't we just bid really high? I mean, higher than they'd ever counter?" This whole thing made her want to puke. To think people were trying to buy Talia.

He studied her in that way he had, as if he were trying to see inside her. To see how much she could take. "We can't be obvious. If we bid too high, that'll raise suspicions, and I don't know what will happen. The Kingdom Boys could just contact one of the other bidders directly and cut us out."

What if they didn't get to Talia? What if one of the other bidders actually won and got their illegal hands on that baby?

"Stop thinking like that," Denver said quietly, his gaze softening. "You have to believe we'll get her."

He'd always been good at reading her facial expressions, not that she was holding anything back. "I don't think I can make it until tomorrow evening," she said, tears pricking the backs of her eyes. The poor baby. Was she warm? Fed? Feeling safe?

"You'll make it." He turned the laptop so she could see new pictures of Talia in a bright green outfit. "She's okay."

Noni nodded, her heart filling. Okay. That was good. She had to believe Talia was safe or she'd lose her mind.

Denver set the laptop on the side table and patted the seat next to him on the sofa. "Come talk to me."

That low voice. So inviting. She moved toward him and sat, staring at the fire.

He slid an arm over her shoulders, casually and just to offer comfort. She tried to keep herself from leaning into him, but his warmth was too enticing. Barely biting back a soft sigh, she allowed him to take some of her weight.

"There you go," he murmured, his gaze still on the fire.

The scent of the forest, wild and free, surrounded her. The forest was probably because he'd scouted outside. But that dark, elusive, all-male scent of pure wildness? Yeah. That was Denver Jones. Not once had she wanted to harness or tame him. But, man, she'd wanted to keep that scent around her. To keep him around her and with her. What he didn't know was that she'd heard his conversation. The one in which he'd apologized to his brother for earlier mistakes.

Had he lived with that guilt his entire life? Deserved or not, that was a heavy burden.

"Why do you think you're going to fail at taking down Dr. Madison?" she asked, closing her eyes and letting her head rest on his chest.

His breathing remained sure and steady beneath her cheek. "I won't fail. It's just...I don't know that I'll survive. Even if I live, I'm, ah, not sure."

Noni's eyelids opened. The fire popped a deep orange with dark blue hues. "Because of Madison." Could he kill a woman in cold blood? Even that woman? "Can't you turn her in to the authorities?"

His barked laugh lacked humor. "No. She has enough connections she'd be free and creating more soldiers in a lab in no time. There's only one way to stop her."

Shouldn't those words scare her somehow? Noni tried to hold on to reality, but all she could feel was Denver. All she could sense was his emotion, his pain. Every cell in her body wanted to be mad at him and wanted to hold a grudge for his hurting her. But he'd come to her rescue, and now he was going to challenge a gang to save a baby he'd never met. One he had no connection to and probably would never know. What if he died? What if he survived and then died trying to go after that crazy doctor?

Would Noni have any regrets?

Yeah. If she never saw him again, which seemed a definite possibility, she'd regret not taking every moment she had with him and riding it through. Oh, he'd destroy her, and she knew it. But did she care? Really? There were worse ways to go, and maybe she'd somehow save him. A part of him. "My thoughts are going way too deep," she whispered.

He chuckled, his body moving hers. "Life, eternity, ever after?" His voice wove around them, soothing over her skin.

"No. Here and now. Regrets and promises. Moments and reality." Now she wasn't speaking in complete sentences, either.

But he caught her meaning. She could tell because he stiffened, just slightly. If she hadn't been pressed against him, she never would've noticed the change.

"Not a good idea, baby," he rumbled.

"I'm well aware," she said slowly. "Who said every idea has to be a good one?" She was so tired. Tired of missing him, tired of being scared, tired of being lost. Life changed in a second, and she knew that firsthand. Right now she was in a cozy cabin with the badass of her dreams. "I'd give anything for one more minute with my parents. With Sharon. With the cat I lost when I was ten." She'd give anything to escape reality for just a few moments.

Right or wrong, she needed him. More so, he needed her. She could *feel* it.

"I've hurt you enough," he countered softly.

She moved, turning and straddling him, her thighs outside his hard ones. Atop him, facing him, was exactly where she wanted to be. "Maybe this time I'll hurt you."

His chin lifted, and his eyes darkened to a dangerous blue. Intensity, so sharp it hurt to see, swirled there. "You've already slayed me through, darlin'."

Why were those words sweet? Because they came from the truth and somewhere deep inside him he didn't try to conceal from her. Life sucked, and this hurt, but the truth held strength. Maybe it even held a promise, thinly veiled, of something good. Something possible. "I didn't hurt you."

"Leaving you hurt me. Losing myself in a bottle didn't help, either." He held himself perfectly still as if fighting himself.

A bottle? "You rarely drink."

He breathed out. "I tried it, but even that didn't erase you. Nothing could."

Power flushed through her. No more fighting this—for either of them. She ran her palm down the side of his neck. "I love your neck."

One of his eyebrows rose, and his upper lip twitched. "My neck?"

"Yeah," she breathed, feeling the corded strength along his jugular. "It's so tough. So male."

He held himself still, his muscles barely undulating beneath his skin. As if he still tried to hold himself back, as if he tried to tether his control.

Oh, that wouldn't do. She slid her hands up and into his thick hair, tightening her fingers in the strands.

"Noni—" he started.

"Shut up, Denver." She leaned in and kissed him. His inward drawn breath spurred her on, and she tilted her head, increasing the pressure. Finally Denver. The taste of him, so familiar, exploded on her tongue. Wine and…Denver. She moaned and scooted closer, her core settling against the obvious bulge in his jeans.

The man lived with regrets from his past, and she lived with lessons from hers. This was a moment she'd never get back, and she was taking it.

He kissed her back, following her lead, his hands clenching the sofa on either side of them. Finally, she couldn't breathe, so she broke free. They were both breathing heavily.

"Are you trying to seduce me?" His voice was glass in a tumbler, his gaze curiously hot.

"No," she whispered, pressing her thighs against his and moaning at the delicious contact. The pulse between her legs demanded relief, forcing her to grab on to control with both hands to keep from rubbing where it hurt. "I'm trying to fuck you."

The crude language obviously caught him hard. His head jerked, and his eyes flashed. "Noni."

She'd never been coy and had no idea how to act like a damsel in distress. "I know what I want, and you want me just as bad." This time she did rub her sex against his erection.

Red flushed dark across his rugged cheekbones. "This is a mistake."

"Who cares?" Her nipples sharpened to points against her plain cotton bra. "I don't care who you've been with this last year, and I don't care who you're with next year. Right now, tonight, you're with me."

His bizarre reflexes kicked in, and he instantly tangled a hand in her hair, forcing her head back. "I haven't been with anybody. There isn't anybody but you. Never will be."

Her heart lurched. *No, no, no*. None of that. No emotion. "I haven't been with anybody since you, either. So we're due," she whispered, trying to return to just this moment. Her head was captured by his hold, and she couldn't move it an inch. The forced immobility shot liquid need through her entire body, forcing a primal hunger through every nerve. "Denver?"

Warning and lust crossed his face. With a low growl, he jerked her to him and took her mouth.

The carnal kiss erased every thought in her head, turning her into one long line of pulsing need. Too easily, he lifted her by the waist, setting her on her feet between his legs, even as he deepened the kiss. She wavered and grabbed his arms for support. He ripped her yoga pants down her legs and settled her back on his lap before she could take another breath.

Then he finally released her mouth. "I ain't playin', Noni."

Neither was she. Grasping the hem of her T-shirt, she whipped it over her head. He instantly grasped her wrists behind her back, holding her in place, careful of the bandage near her elbow.

She gaped. "Denver?"

His smile was all determination. "Like I said." Using his free hand, he pushed her panties to one side, exposing her. Cool air brushed her tender parts, and she moaned. Then he slid his knuckles over her slick folds, pressing gently and then easing a finger inside her. White-hot lightning burst pleasure through her, and she bit her lip to keep from begging.

How had she forgotten this part? Forgotten how easily he took control and made her feel so much? Too much? "Den—"

"Look how tight and wet you are, sweetheart. All for me," he murmured, stroking inside her.

She moved her hips, jerking as he added another finger inside her. Stretching her. Her shoulders rolled in an effort to release her arms, but he held fast. The slight struggle only increased her need. Her hunger.

"I've missed you, Non. Missed this." His fingers moved, sliding out and then back in. Deep and slow with perfect control.

Warning bells—finally—trilled inside her head, but it was way too late. She'd missed this. The feeling of vulnerability and helplessness as he took her places she'd never imagined.

"Ah, you're remembering." His knuckles tapped across her clit. She cried out, and he smiled. "This is where you don't have to be in control. Don't have decisions to make. Nothing is on your shoulders." He leaned in, kissed across her jaw, and bit beneath her ear.

She jumped and gasped.

"In fact, you don't get to be in control." Leaning back, he studied her bra, his hand at her core cupping her. "Pretty." Then his gaze caught hers and trapped it. "I'm gonna let go of your wrists. You keep them there, where I have them. Got it?"

Defiance, somehow, flared up inside her.

His eyelids half lowered, giving him the look of a predator. "You move, you get spanked. You really want that tonight?"

Wings beat through her abdomen. He'd spanked her once, and she'd orgasmed so hard that night she'd been in a daze for hours. But she didn't want a daze. She wanted here and now and memories. "Not tonight," she breathed, her voice shaking with need.

"Then, baby, do what I say." He released her wrists, and she kept them in place. "Good girl." His gaze dropped to her bra. The air around them, between them, ignited.

Her thigh muscles began to tremble, and when he released her sex, she whimpered in protest. Both his hands went to her bra, and he tore in it half. Nothing in her protested as the material was flung across the room. Cold air wisped across her bare nipples, sliding down to her clit, even with the heat pouring off him.

He leaned back, taking her in. "God, yes. Perfect." Lust and hunger glittered bright in his blue eyes along with a primal possessiveness that should've given her pause. Instead, she drank it in. The man was staring at her as if he wanted to take her hard and keep her forever. Her fingers twitched behind her back, and she clenched them together to keep them in place. The control cost her, but the pleasure curving his lips made it worthwhile.

"Lift," he murmured.

She used her thighs to lift up, allowing him to jerk down his jeans and briefs, before falling back down, her bare skin against his rock-hard erection. "I want to touch you," she breathed.

"No." The word was ragged but the tone firm. "You still on the pill?" he asked.

She nodded, her nails digging into her palms.

"Good." He grasped her hip, slightly lifting her. His other hand, with those dangerous fingers, spread her open.

God, it was too unbelievable. She closed her eyes, trusting he'd keep her safe. Then he slowly pushed her down on him, his hard shaft instantly seeking entry. Her flesh stretched, surrounding him as her body trembled. Pleasure rushed through her, edged with pain, mingling into a sensation so intense she could only feel. Her hands released, and one of his was instantly banded around her wrists, keeping them pressed against the small of her back.

Her eyelids flashed open.

Determination and lust stamped hard on his angled face. "Don't. Move."

She swallowed, her body vibrating, her breasts so heavy they ached.

Finally, her butt rested on his thighs. She tried to lift up, tried to move, tried to dispel some of the need ... and he held her in place. She could do nothing but take what he was giving. Wait until he gave more. Even his gaze trapped her in place. The reality of his strength and her vulnerability uncoiled sparks inside her, starting an internal trembling.

"No." He tapped her clit.

She arched against him, raw fire ripping through her.

"Not yet." The fierce expression on his face commanded obedience. Somehow, shockingly, her impending orgasm paused. His fingers around her wrists were iron hard. His massive chest heaved as he caught his breath.

Good. He was as affected as she was. "Take off your shirt," she said, trying to keep from begging for it. She wasn't sure she was successful.

He yanked his shirt off and dropped it. Somewhere.

Smooth and hard, his chest made her salivate.

He cupped her breast, rubbing his thumb across her needy nipple. Then he shoved up inside her farther, his hips controlling hers. She arched her back against her own wrists, losing herself in the vicious pleasure. He did it again, the glide of him inside her brushing nerves she'd forgotten about. Nerves that only Denver had ever owned. As if they belonged to him. She pulled against his hold, instinctively trying to release herself and find some control. Escape this hold he had on her.

One she'd forgotten was so damn intense.

"I've got you, baby," he said in a rough voice. "You're safe."

She was nowhere near safe, but at his low voice, she eased into his hold.

"There you go. Let me show you." He moved, his hand sliding down to her hip, his strength easily allowing him to lift her to meet his thrusts. Her thoughts scattered, and her nerves focused on the devastating sensations spiraling out. He pinched her nipple, the rough pain pulling her deeper into his spell. His thrusts grew harder and faster, deeper inside her.

Her fears and concerns faded away, replaced by the hard cock inside her, the strength of the body surrounding her, the determined fingers on her breasts. There was a gentleness to him, a sweetness she'd barely glimpsed before. The rise to ecstasy was sharp and edged with pain, and yet she kept trying to climb. Finally, she caught on the edge, teetering before falling into nothingness.

"Go over," he murmured, pinching her other nipple.

Lightning flashed hot and sharp up her spine and exploded in white-hot light in her head, flooding her body with a primal sensation so raw she actually screamed. He released her hands and grabbed her hips with both hands, hammering faster and deeper. Finally, he dropped his head into the crook of her neck, his powerful body shuddering with his own climax.

She slid both hands around his shoulders, kissing his salty neck. Her heart beat rapidly against his, and they both breathed quickly. She blinked but didn't lift up, her entire body boneless. She'd wanted a release. What she'd gotten was so much more.

But what now?

CHAPTER
16

The early sun rose over the mountain across the lake as Denver sat in front of the fire, legs out, typing furiously on his laptop. He'd just upped the bid on the baby and had needed something else to occupy his mind. So he'd gone out and repaired the SUV as much as possible by covering the broken windows with plastic.

Now he was back inside searching through traffic camera footage in Snowville for the date Elton Cobb had visited Detective Malloy. Cobb had to be on camera somewhere. Denver's search for plane tickets hadn't found anything.

So Cobb had driven.

What did that mean? Was Madison's new headquarters close to Snowville? If so, was Noni safe in Coeur d'Alene? Denver closed his eyes and used his enhanced hearing to check the area around the cabin. Snow falling, deer moving, wind rustling pine needles. No people. So far, nobody knew where they were. Could he keep her safe?

He heard her at the doorway before she moved into the room. Partially turning his head, he watched her carefully. After taking her on the sofa, he'd moved them into the bedroom, and they hadn't gotten much sleep. It was as if he couldn't get enough of her. Every sigh, every moan, every cry had dug into his heart and planted hard. This morning she'd put on yoga pants and a thin green T-shirt, sans the bra. Her movements were slow and a little stilted, and he winced. "Too much?" Of course it had been too much. He'd barely let her catch her breath before taking her again. And then again.

"No." She stepped barefoot across the thick rug and headed for the coffee in the kitchen. "But I no longer have a bra."

He couldn't see that as being a problem. "We can get you a new one."

"Humph." She poured herself a cup and turned, her dark hair a wild mass down her back. Her lips were swollen from his, and a slight whisker burn had pinkened her cheeks.

Probably her inner thighs, too. At the thought, his groin hardened. Possession flushed through him with a hard edge. How could he ever let her go again?

What about the baby? Noni had committed to being a mom. He had no clue what to do with a baby. With his life, anybody close to him was in danger. Until he took out Cobb and Madison. He shook his head, trying to dispel the onslaught of thoughts he couldn't control. What was wrong with him? "There's sugar in the cupboard above the coffee maker."

She took a sip of it black, her gaze over the cup. "Why are you up so early?"

He lifted a shoulder. "A lot going on. I'm trying to track safe houses for the Kingdom Boys in town, trying to keep an eye on the FBI, and trying to monitor emergency frequencies just to make sure nobody has found me."

Her eyes sharpened. "That's a lot."

"Yep." He started to set the laptop to the side when a traffic cam near Malloy's caught his eye. Three suited-up men in a truck, driving slowly. There was something wrong about them. Something he couldn't quite put his finger on. Heat coated his esophagus, and he lunged for his phone.

"What—" she started to ask.

He held up a hand as Malloy's voice-mail message came on the line. After the beep, he finally spoke. "Malloy? Get the hell out of your house. It looks like unfriendlies are headed your way, and they've had time to regroup and send reinforcements. Get Tina and get out." Denver jumped to his feet and ran to pull on his boots. "I have to go."

Noni hustled for her boots and started dragging them on.

"No." He grasped her arm to halt her movements. "You're not coming."

She jerked free. "The heck I'm not. I started all this, and you may need backup. I can point a gun and shoot if necessary." Panic paled her face. "What if we put Malloy and Tina in danger?"

Oh, they'd definitely put the cop and his lady in danger. "You have to stay here."

Noni reached for her coat. "Not a chance. Geez. Don't you ever watch television?"

Denver gripped his leather jacket. "What are you talking about?"

She pulled on her coat, her eyes wide. "It's always the chick left behind who ends up taken and used for leverage. You know. What if they managed to trace us here?" Leaning down, she starting lacing up the boots.

He zipped his jacket. "Too much cloud cover. No satellite vision."

"You think." She straightened and poked him in the chest. "You can't be a hundred percent sure. Or what if they hacked your phone call with your brother? Or your computer?"

He jerked back, oddly affronted. "*Nobody* hacks my computer."

"Says you." She tucked her hands in her pockets. "Maybe the guy who gave us the car is working for them and secretly followed us."

Every scenario she played out got crazier, yet there was always a slim chance. "You're nuts."

"Maybe." She turned for the door. "But you and I are sticking together. Period."

Having her close to him helped him to concentrate, and he couldn't guarantee her safety if he left. Damn it. He opened a cupboard by the door and drew out several weapons, handing her a gun. "No safety on it. If you point, you shoot. So don't point unless you want to shoot."

She swallowed and turned the weapon over in her hands. "I think I like having a safety."

"Too bad. When we get there, you do what I tell you to do." He handed her his burner phone and opened the door, adrenaline surging through his veins. "We know that Cobb and Madison have found us, and by now, they know who you are. When we get in the car, call your aunt and tell her to get out of Portland. Have them use cash only and start driving toward South Dakota." He had to get those ladies safe. At the moment, nobody in his life was remotely safe. "Got it?"

She paled even more but followed him out into the freezing air. It was only about five in the morning and darkness still ruled.

Next time he went on an op, he wanted it to be somewhere warm. "Follow me. We'll have to hurry." God, he hoped he could get to Malloy in time. Running through the snow, he jumped into the SUV and waited until Noni had secured her seat belt before hitting the gas and speeding up the icy lane. "Sorry about the plastic on the window, but at least we're warmer now." There wasn't anything he could do about the bullet holes in the ceiling.

He listened as she called her aunt with the terse directions and then hung up after exchanging I love yous.

What would it be like to automatically have that sentiment from her at the end of every call? He rubbed his chest and focused his attention back on the disaster at hand. "We might not get there in time." If the cop or Tina got killed because they'd helped him, he'd never forgive himself. "Hand me the phone, would you?"

She slipped it into his hand.

Oh, Malloy was gonna kill him if this was a mistake. Denver dialed 911 and spoke in a high voice. "Hello? Yeah. Um. There's something going on at 2124 Meadowlark. You know? Where that cop lives with the pretty lady with long legs? Men with guns. They have on face masks. Hurry." Denver clicked off and handed the phone to Noni. "Break that apart and throw pieces out the window toward the lake every several yards."

She gulped in air but took the phone and pulled it apart before setting it on the floor and smashing it with her boots. Then she followed his instructions. "Malloy is going to be pissed if we're wrong."

"Yeah, but at least he'll be alive. If Madison's guys are there, then the local cops will go in hard and fast."

Noni retaped the bottom of her window. "You don't think Madison and Cobb would go after a cop, do you?"

Denver gritted his teeth. "They'd absolutely go after a police officer. The good news, kind of, is that Dr. Madison wouldn't want Malloy dead. Yet."

"What do you mean?" Noni asked, her voice shaking.

Denver wanted to reach for her hand, but he had to keep both of his on the steering wheel. The twists and turns of the icy lake road demanded his full attention. They slid around a corner, and he stopped breathing but couldn't slow down. "They'll want to question him about us. About me." Tina could be collateral damage, however. Also, Malloy would definitely fight back, so he might be killed. Denver increased his speed, his mind spinning. "There should be a few more burner phones in the glove box. Grab one, would you?" He took a turn too fast, and the car fishtailed. Swearing, he brought it under control.

They traveled the rest of the way toward Malloy's house in silence with Denver driving way too fast for the conditions.

"Do you need the phone?" Noni finally asked.

"Not yet." The second he turned the vehicle into the subdivision, his gut sank. Flames licked into the dawn, and sirens wailed from every direction. "Fuck." He slowed down and drove through the streets, coming upon Malloy's house engulfed in fire. Cops, firefighters, and neighbors milled around.

An ambulance roared by, heading for the main street.

A car followed it with Tina hunched over the steering wheel.

Thank God. She was okay. Denver squinted to see better. A man in black sat in the passenger side, facing her. Ah shit. Denver swallowed, forcing control through his veins. He'd put a defenseless veterinarian into danger.

He drove down the street a ways and turned around in the plowed driveway of a small ranch house. His heartbeat thundered in his ears. "Sweetheart? Tina's in trouble." He kept his voice low and drove sedately past the melee before punching the gas. Within minutes, he was behind Tina's car, which was racing behind the ambulance.

Noni leaned forward. "Why do you think she's in trouble? She's following the ambulance. Oh no. Do you think Malloy is in the ambulance?"

"Yes." Denver bit back panic. The guy next to Tina was tall and wasn't dressed like a cop. Denver reached for the phone and quickly dialed Jory. They had to get Tina free. Now.

"What's going on?" Jory asked without preamble.

"I think they came after Malloy, but I'm not sure." Denver sped up, trying to get closer to Tina's car, spinning over the ice.

Something clicked over the line. "What can we do?" Jory asked, his voice low.

Denver took a deep breath. "We have to get him out of here. I need transport for Malloy, if he's able. If not, I still need transport for his girlfriend, Tina. I also need all the on-hand cash you have. I wasn't going to ask, but since you're sending a copter, add the cash. I'll pay you back." The world was squeezing him, and he was letting everyone down. Danger was everywhere. The list of people he needed to save kept growing while his time did not.

"Copy that," Jory said, all business. "Give me a minute."

Denver put the phone on speaker and slapped it onto the seat before yanking his gun from his waist. "I'm going to run her off the road, baby. Try to stay loose and get ready. Don't point the gun."

"Okay," she said.

"Denver?" Jory came over the speakerphone clearly. "We have a helicopter heading your way. I'm sending coordinates to this phone. It'll be there in thirty minutes for whoever wants to get on, and I'm having them bring all the cash we have from that location. Then I'm coming your way."

"Not yet," Denver said. He couldn't look out for one more person.

Jory's growl was full of frustration. "We'll see. If you need help with the baby drop, I'm there. Just say the word. Let me know the second you have intel on Malloy. He's one of ours, whether he likes it or not."

"Agreed." Denver shook out his arms. He had to calm himself. Now.

The phone went quiet and Denver clicked off the call.

"You guys can just get helicopters?" Noni asked, her knuckles white from her grip on the gun.

Denver shook his head. "I can't. But my relatives in Montana have a kind of protection and private military business. That's how we have the supplies and guns. And helicopters."

"Crazy." She straightened up, tension pouring from her. "What if that's a cop with Tina?"

He grimaced. "Then we're fucked." Waiting until the road around them was clear, he moved to pass on the right side, took a deep breath, and swerved into the rear of Tina's car. Metal crunched loudly, and he slid on the ice. The small compact jerked and then spun, turning around several times before crashing into brick pillars of another subdivision. Within seconds, Tina was out of the car and running for him, blood flowing down her face.

Denver leaped from the car, his gun out.

She reached him and grabbed his arms, incoherently coughing. He shoved her behind him just as the guy in the car shook his head as if dazed. Then he snapped up and leaped from the car.

"Get in," Denver ordered, lifting his gun.

The man lifted his hands, a gun visible in his waistband. Bruises already formed along his temple, but his eyes were clear. And un-afraid. Definitely one of Madison's soldiers.

Tina yanked open the back door. "We have to get to Jamie. The ambulance driver isn't a real one. I mean, he's one of those guys. Who are those guys?" Her voice had risen to a panicked shrillness.

With barely a twitch, the guy went for his gun.

Denver fired, hitting him center mass. He flew back into the pil-lars, dropping onto his face.

Tina screamed and jumped into the car.

Denver slid back inside and gunned the engine. "He's probably wearing a vest." In that case, he'd be out for a little while. If not, well, he'd be headed for hell. Denver pulled back onto the road. "How bad are you hurt?"

Tina lifted her shirt and wiped the cut above her eyebrow. "Not bad. We were in bed, and then everything went crazy. The police burst in every door."

Denver sped up, trying to find the damn ambulance. "The police got there first?"

Tina gulped, still wiping her face. "Yeah. So we got out of bed, and suddenly somebody started shooting through the window with guns and a flamethrower."

Denver's hands tightened on the wheel. "A fucking flame-thrower?"

"Yeah. Jamie got shot, all the cops shot back, but they didn't get the guy. So we got out of there while everything started on fire." Her voice broke on the last. "An ambulance came, and they loaded Jamie. Then I was going for my car when that guy grabbed my arm and pushed me inside." She swiped a hand across her tears. "Jamie's friends from the force are expecting us at the hospital. I said I'd meet them there." Tears mingled with the blood on her cheek. "I should've just gone with one of them, but I wanted my car. So stupid."

"No. Not stupid," Denver countered, his breath heated. "If you'd gone with them, we wouldn't know that somebody else has Malloy. How did you know he was in danger?"

She gulped. "The guy with a gun to my side told me. He said we were taking a little trip."

Denver nodded grimly. All right. He had to get to that ambulance. "How badly was Malloy hurt?"

"I don't know," Tina whispered, her voice trembling. "I just don't know."

CHAPTER
17

D_{r.} Isobel Madison crossed her legs and typed quickly, trying to bring up a satellite feed. Nothing. She clenched her fingers into fists and then tried again. The U.S. government was getting so much better at protecting its resources. She took a deep breath and reached for a cell phone. "Status," she said coolly.

"Have the cop, and we have the girlfriend in a car following the ambulance," came the short response. "Cop's been shot."

"How bad?" Isobel snapped. It wouldn't do to lose Detective Malloy before she had time to interrogate him.

Her soldier cleared his throat. "One in the arm, one in the leg. We stabilized him at the scene before leaving. He figured out we weren't legit, so I had to give him a sedative."

"That's all right," Isobel said. "Time until rendezvous point?"

"Thirty minutes."

The rendezvous point was an abandoned lot on the other side of the mountain where her one and only helicopter could land. There was a time when she'd had a fleet of them under her command. She sighed. "All right. Don't let him die."

"Copy that." The line went dead.

She bit her lip and turned back to the computer.

"Sounds like we have the cop," Elton Cobb said from the doorway. "I won't allow him to be killed, Isobel."

She turned back around. "There are always casualties in a campaign, my love."

Elton shook his head, his blue eyes so dark, sizzling. His blond hair was trimmed short, and in his light T-shirt with camo pants, he looked like a soldier. "Malloy is a cop, and that means something."

Oh, for goodness' sake. Why must she soothe male egos all the time? It was tiresome, but she slid on a smooth smile. "I understand you were a sheriff, dear, but Malloy is working with Denver. With Heath and Ryker. The men who killed your brother." She kept her voice calm when all she wanted was to give him a good slap. But he was useful, and even more so, Elton Cobb was dangerous. She needed to remember the existence of the man he kept carefully banked. The one who'd kill without mercy.

"I know," Elton snapped.

She breathed in slowly. "Are you going to protect Detective Malloy at the expense of getting justice for your sweet brother?" Ned Cobb had been a weak, pathetic loser who'd beaten kids to make himself feel like a man. "He deserved better than to die the way he did." She almost choked on the words.

Elton's chest heaved. "You're right."

"I've been laying our trap across the Internet the last couple of hours." The idea of finally catching all of her boys nearly made her giddy. She was born for a purpose, a grand one, and that was to create them. Beyond science and beyond even faith, she'd taken the male form and improved it. From brainpower to muscle to heart—she'd done that. Pride and something deeper filled her. Something beyond mere mortal.

If her boys thought they could leave her, could just go live *normal* lives, they were wholly mistaken.

She wasn't delusional; she knew she wasn't a god. Yet God, if one truly existed, had given her gifts to change the world. And she was going to do it, one male specimen at a time. "Elton?"

His focus cleared. "Sorry. I was thinking about what I'm going to do to Denver. His silent, innocent act never worked on me."

She nodded. "He was very clever." Of course, she'd made him that way. "I have a plan that will glean both of us justice, my love." Not for one second would she allow Elton to harm Denver. But there was no need to tell him that.

His eyebrows rose. "Is that a fact?"

She barely kept from clapping her hands together. "Yes. I'm formulating it now and will get you up to speed once I figure it all out." She glanced toward the picture of her daughter on the desk. "Audrey will be giving birth soon." Audrey had married one of the Gray brothers and turned her back on everything important. "I must get my hands on that baby." To think that one of her soldiers had procreated. The child would be something…new.

"All in good time," Elton said. "First we get Denver, Ryker, and Heath. Then those three will get us the Gray brothers."

That was somewhat her plan with a couple of mutations thrown in.

Elton cleared his throat. "So have you, um, decided?"

She lifted her chin, rather appreciating his temerity. "Yes. I already had my eggs harvested last month when you were touching base with your department in North Carolina."

His eyes flared. "I was retiring, Isobel. In order to give our projects here all of my time, as you requested."

He was retiring from being a simple sheriff, which was good. The man had more potential than he realized, or she wouldn't care for him. He wouldn't interest her to this degree. "You're still in the prime of your life, darling," she said, letting her voice go breathy. "We have a bigger calling, and you'll do more good with our new enterprise." Of creating and training the next generation of soldiers. "I already have three requests for our soldiers from different governmental entities." She needed her boys back first.

Elton swallowed. "You harvested your eggs?"

"Yes." Thank goodness she hadn't gone through menopause yet. She'd take her samples and make new babies. Oh, she'd give Elton one just to keep him tied to her. But her other material would be combined with her earlier creations. Those soldiers who were so much more that she'd ever hoped. "Would you like a boy or a girl?"

"Why would I want a girl?" he asked, his frown deepening.

Why indeed? "Then I'll make sure we have a boy," she soothed. "As soon as we get my soldiers into place, we'll find surrogates like before. I'll find just the right one to carry our child."

Elton patted his very flat belly. "I'm not too old to have a child."

"You're barely over fifty, my love. These days, that's young. Very young." Maybe she could splice the insecurity out of whatever child they created. It was so tiresome. That was one reason to have a girl. Women were so much stronger than men. Naturally. Of course, she'd changed that with her boys. What could she do with a female she created in the lab? Audrey had been an unfortunate accident, so Isobel had just let her be. She tapped her finger against her lip.

Her egg with one of her soldiers. Interesting. It'd be difficult to choose which one. She could use specimens from several, but the idea of having several teenage girls running around someday made her blanch. One. She'd just choose one for a girl.

Her laptop let out a sharp alarm, and she swiveled to read the code flashing across the screen.

"What is it?" Elton asked, snapping to attention.

Her chest filled with the thrill of the chase. "It's Denver. I think I can find what he's been up to." She set her nails on the keyboard and started to type.

Oh. Her boy was good, but she'd taught him everything he knew. She had him.

Yes.

* * *

Noni held the gun tightly, fine trembles coursing through her arms. This was crazy. They were chasing a speeding ambulance down back roads and definitely away from the city with a bleeding veterinarian in their backseat. She turned to check on Tina. "How's your head?"

"Fine," Tina said, her hand pressed above her eye. Her thick black hair had been tied at her nape and out of her face. "Bleeding has almost stopped. Now tell me who has Jamie. What is going on?"

Denver leaned over the steering wheel, his focus absolute. He didn't utter a word.

Noni bit her lip. "Somebody who is after Denver thinks maybe you and Malloy have information about finding Denver and his brothers." She didn't care if it was a secret. Tina had been shot at and kidnapped. She definitely deserved some truth. "We'll get Malloy back. I promise." No, she couldn't make that promise, but again she went on instinct. "Right, Denver?"

"Right," he said grimly. He looked toward her. "Can you trade places with me?"

She gaped. What was he talking about? This wasn't a television show. "Sure." This was crazy. She gingerly set her gun on the dash. His seat was all the way back, so she nudged over and almost sat on his lap, putting her hands inside his on the steering wheel. He smoothly slid out from under her, and her butt hit the warm seat. She tried to scoot forward to touch the gas pedal.

"Use the button," Denver said patiently, keeping his foot pressed to the gas.

The snowy world sped by outside.

She looked and found the button on the door, pressing it forward until she could reach the pedal. Then she set her foot next to his, and he let up.

She kept the pace going.

"Whew," Tina muttered from the backseat. "You two are insane."

Noni clutched her sweaty hands to the steering wheel. "What's the plan?"

He took out his own gun and shoved the temporary plastic away from the passenger side window. "I'm going to shoot the tires. As soon as they stop, you stop. The two of you stay in the car." His hand looked steady as he pointed the gun out the window. "Try not to hit the ambulance if we go into a slide."

Panic clicked through her until she couldn't speak. So she nodded instead.

Denver glanced over his shoulder. "Tina? Seat belt." Then he took in Noni. "You too."

They both fastened their belts.

Denver turned back to the window again, aimed, and fired. Even though the gun was outside the window, the sound was deafening. He shot again. The right rear tire of the ambulance blew into pieces. The vehicle swerved crazily, smashing up the snowbank into the hill.

Noni pressed on the brakes and the car skidded. She kept control and rolled to a stop on the passenger side of the ambulance.

Denver was out of the SUV and firing toward the front of the ambulance before she could take a breath.

Tina screamed and scrambled out of her belt. "Don't shoot Jamie."

"He won't." Noni released her belt and grabbed her gun, pushing from the car. She pointed it toward the back of the ambulance and slowly walked toward the rear doors.

Denver was instantly at her side, shoving her behind him. He reached the back and yanked open the door, staying behind the metal.

"What the holy fuck?" came from the back.

Denver peered around the door. "Malloy?"

"Yeah. Get me the hell out of here."

Tina rushed forward and leaped into the back of the ambulance.

Noni peeked around Denver to see Malloy sitting up and hugging Tina. His legs were strapped to the gurney, but it looked like he'd gotten his arms free. "I'm, ah, drugged. Who did you just kill?"

Noni gaped and looked beyond Malloy to a man in all black slumped over the steering wheel. His head was turned and his dead eyes seemed to look back at her.

"We have to go," Denver said, jumping into the vehicle and releasing Malloy's legs. "Can you stand?"

"Yes," Malloy snapped, his brown eyes somehow both cloudy and furious. He stood, and Denver shoved a shoulder beneath his arms.

Tina scrambled around and grabbed several medical supplies from bins. Noni braced her feet and helped Denver get Malloy out of the ambulance, then into the backseat of the SUV. Before she knew it, they were speeding in the other direction, Tina double-checking Malloy's bandages.

"I need to get to the station," Malloy barked, his face pale.

"You're getting out of town," Denver returned, taking a sharp turn on the ice. "All of you. There's a helicopter that will provide transport, and you're taking it."

Noni shook her head. "I'm not leaving."

"Not a chance," Malloy said wearily, setting his head back on the seat.

"I'm staying," Tina added, taking a good look beneath a compress on Malloy's arm. "This one was a through and through. Not sure about the leg yet."

Denver cut Noni a furious look, and she sat back in her seat, not breaking eye contact. He finally had to turn away to watch the snow-filled road. Nearly thirty minutes later, they pulled into what looked like a cut-down wheat field to see a helicopter waiting, silent and ready. Three men flanked it, all armed with really big automatic guns like the ones on television.

"Are you kidding me?" Malloy muttered. "Who are you people?"

Denver stopped the car, took his gun, and jumped out. "Everyone out. You're going to safety."

"Not until we get the baby," Noni returned, grasping her own gun.

"Damn it." Malloy groaned as Tina helped him out of the SUV.

One of the armed men reached into the helicopter for a silver briefcase and jogged over. He was dressed in black and had various weapons visible along his body. His chest was wide, made wider by a bulletproof vest. "You Denver?"

"Yes," Denver said.

"This is all we could come up with in the short timeframe. We can get more by tomorrow—just let us know what you want." The guy's dark buzz cut caught snow, and his eyes were hidden by aviator glasses. But he moved like he could fight. Smooth and graceful. "Is there anything else you need?"

"Your vest," Denver said. "I could really use that."

"Sure." The guy released the Velcro and shrugged out of it, handing it over. "Anything else?"

Whoa, this was just weird. Noni took a step back.

Denver visually scouted the area before answering. "Yeah. These three need to be taken to safety. When they're in the air, contact Jory and find out where to take them. I also have two fifty-something women en route to South Dakota who will need to be picked up at some point."

Malloy watched the exchange, his eyes hard. "I'm not going anywhere. I should arrest all of you."

Noni winced.

Denver sighed. "Malloy? You've been shot, and your lady is in the crosshairs. Stop being a hero and get on the fuckin' helicopter." He turned toward Noni. "I'll get Talia and bring her to you. This has become way too dangerous, and you need cover."

"No," Noni said softly, knowing if she left she'd never see him again. Oh, she trusted he'd find Talia and send her to Noni, but he'd be gone. "I'm staying. My baby will need me." A good mother would never desert her child. She was going to be a good mother.

Malloy leaned against the SUV, his face pale with what had to be pain. "I'm a cop, dumb-ass. Somebody just shot and kidnapped me. That means I stay here and fight." He turned toward Tina and tugged on a piece of her long hair. "I don't know these guys, sweetheart. I think we can trust them, but you're not leaving, either. You'll get full protection from my people."

Denver looked at all of them, fury in his gaze.

Noni swallowed and walked around the SUV to get in the passenger side. Chills swept her, but she held her head high. "Let's go," she ordered.

CHAPTER
18

Denver's anger grew as he drove back to the safe house on the lake. Sweat broke out on his forehead as he tried to rein in his fury. How was he going to keep everyone safe if they didn't do what he damn well told them to do? Madison and Cobb had seriously upped their game in trying to take the cop, which showed they were either desperate or getting too close. Madison didn't seem like the desperate type.

When they arrived at the icy parking area outside the cabin, he parked and tuned in his senses. Nothing.

He and Tina helped Malloy inside, and he watched as she checked his wounds again. The arm wound was easily bandaged, but the leg still had a bullet in it.

"We have to get you to the hospital," Tina said, her dark eyes worried.

"Take it out," Malloy countered. "It's not deep or near an artery. Just take it out, T."

Denver gritted his teeth. "Knock it off. Let's call your people and get you to safety."

Malloy's eyebrows lifted. "Oh, I'm not leaving. I've had it with this shit. I want to know the entire story. Now." His forehead was sweating, and pain etched into the sides of his mouth, but his gaze was clear. "Or I'm arresting you."

Denver fought a grin. The cop couldn't arrest a gerbil at the moment, but his determination was admirable. "Well, we might be able to come up with a plan." He moved to the table where Malloy already sat. He'd like to see the baby-trafficking gang taken down completely, and Malloy could accomplish that. "All right. But everything you hear, you keep to yourself. Forever."

As Noni put together a breakfast of eggs and bacon, and as Tina sorted the medical supplies she'd nabbed from the ambulance, Denver gave the entire truth of his life to Malloy. All of it. He held nothing back. The words flowed from him and something released.

It felt good to finally be honest with Malloy. He was a decent guy. If he still liked Denver, or at least still tolerated him, after knowing everything, then maybe the truth wasn't so bad. Maybe Denver wasn't so fucked up.

The cop listened, no expression on his face, until his chin just dropped. "That's the craziest thing I've ever heard. Supersoldiers? Government spies? Genetic manipulation?"

Denver dug into his eggs, his shoulders feeling lighter, and then told Malloy the full story about Noni, the gang, and Talia. He tried to banish the irritation he still felt about Noni refusing to go to safety, but it lay there, just under the surface. Along with guilt.

It ate at him, and he let it in so he could deal with it. His ears burned, but he forced himself to continue. He'd seen a cop nearly be killed, and the idea of Noni getting harmed pricked awareness along his every nerve like he'd been stung by fire ants. So he kept his voice level and answered every question Malloy had.

Malloy eyed his eggs but didn't eat. "I take it that my knowing this puts me in the crosshairs of the Gray brothers? They're coming for me?"

Denver shook his head. "No. They think you're family."

Malloy paled even more, for the first time showing emotion at the entire story. Was that panic? "Shit."

Denver coughed out a laugh. "Yeah. So. Welcome to the family." He looked at Tina. "Can you get the bullet out?"

She winced, stress darkening her eyes. "I can, but it's going to hurt. I have only a local in the materials I took from the ambulance, and that won't diminish the pain enough. There's also the chance of infection. We should go to a hospital."

"Not a chance," Malloy said. "I need to start coordinating our plan for tonight. When we get the baby."

Denver leaned forward, his mind rapidly calculating the facts. "The bidding closes at five, and I'll make sure I'm the high bidder. The exchange probably won't be until tomorrow. They'll want to get everything in place first."

"You're right," Malloy said thoughtfully. "But you can't do it alone now. A gang this large, one spanning states? You need the authorities to get them all and do it fast. You can't take the next fifty years to go after them one by one. You need me."

Denver paused. The detective was probably right. He couldn't spend his life going after each member. But the cops could. All right. Time to coordinate. "I'm doing the exchange, though. That's non-negotiable."

"I won't get that past my superiors." Malloy winced as he moved his leg.

"You'll have to," Denver said simply. "Say the sellers know my face and they'll only exchange the baby for me."

Malloy studied him. "Do they?"

"They might," Denver said. "Since I've been having issues with them for days, they won't be surprised to see my face. My bidding to get the baby will make sense to them. They won't care as long as I have the cash." He reached for the briefcase that the Montana boys had sent and flipped it open.

Malloy whistled. "Wow. How much is that?"

Denver quickly inventoried it. "Three hundred thousand." If he put paper in the bottom, he could make it look like more. "The bidding is at four hundred thousand right now." By the time the gang counted the money, he'd have the baby.

Malloy shook his head. "You know how dangerous this is, right? They might take one look at the money and then just shoot you."

Denver nodded. "We'd better come up with a good plan, then." His gut hurt, and his temples pounded. What if the gang had contacts in the police department? What if the gang saw cops? At some point they'd cut their losses and lose the baby. Would they really kill a baby? Some people were evil enough to do just that, and he knew it.

Noni cleared her throat. "They wouldn't hurt a baby, would they?"

Denver couldn't lie to her. The clock was counting down, and this had to go perfectly.

Malloy coughed. "I don't like the wildcard element here." He wiped his brow. "Shit. I should clarify which wildcard I mean." Tension sizzled off him.

"Madison and Cobb," Denver said, on the same page. "I know. The Kingdom Boys' motivation is clear and their trajectory foreseeable. But Madison's soldiers? They know who you are, who Tina is, and they know we're in town. We have to lie low until it's time for the exchange." Even so, he had no clue how much Madison had figured out about his plans. There was a chance she knew about the baby. Tracing Noni's movements and ultimately her motivations wouldn't have been too difficult.

"If Cobb and Madison figured out why you're here and what

you're doing, they could outbid you in the gang auction," Malloy said quietly.

Denver could feel the walls pressing in. His two ops might've just combined into one big one, but he had no way of knowing anything right now. "One threat at a time. It's a live bid, so I'll keep upping it." He glanced at the clock, which seemed to be speeding up. They had several hours until the bidding closed. "How much time do you need to get a plan in place?"

Malloy breathed out, his wide chest shuddering. "From the moment we have a location? I'd like a couple of hours."

"You're probably not going to get it," Denver said, the itch between his shoulder blades intensifying. Telling the cop everything might've been the biggest mistake he'd ever made. What had he done?

Malloy sighed. "I'm aware." He looked over at Tina. "You ready to take this bullet out or what?"

* * *

Noni finished cleaning the blood from the table as Malloy rested on the sofa with Tina next to him. The bullet removal had been surprisingly quick, but the cleanup was taking time. "Are you sure he hasn't lost too much blood?" she called out.

Tina glanced over the back of the sofa at her. "He'll survive." She rubbed her hand down his jaw. "He'd better."

Noni tossed the paper towels in the trash and tried to keep from freaking out. A clock on the mantel ticked ominously. How had she not noticed it yesterday? Today it seemed to tick away her chances of finding Talia. Her knees shook, so she locked her legs.

Denver was in the chair next to the sofa, his concentration absolute on his laptop. "Three minutes to go," he muttered.

"You ahead?" Malloy asked.

"Bid is at five hundred K," Denver said, his fingers poised over the keys. "Two serious bidders left."

Tina extended her long legs onto the coffee table. "I don't understand why the police can't track this."

"Anybody on the dark web can track it, but only online. There's no way to follow the participants into the real world. No way to find them," Denver said grimly.

Noni moved up behind him to see another picture of Talia, this one with today's newspaper next to her. At only three months, she was bright eyed and smiling with a purple bow in her hair. The image almost dropped Noni to her knees. "She's okay," she breathed.

"Yes." Denver didn't turn around.

He'd been cranky all day since everyone had refused to board the helicopter. In fact, he'd barely looked at her. She fought a rising irritation and tried to focus on the baby. Soon she'd be back in safety. Noni had to believe that. *She had to.*

Denver stiffened. "Damn it. Three new bidders." He started typing faster.

The entire room seemed to hold its breath.

Flashes of color showed across the screen.

"Fuck," Denver said, typing even faster. Then the entire screen went black.

Noni stopped breathing. "What happened?" She leaned over his shoulder to see just a blank screen. "Denver?" Her voice trembled. Had they lost? Was Talia gone? Oh God. She gripped his shoulders.

Malloy grabbed his phone. "I'll call for help."

Denver held up a hand. "Wait. Not yet."

Noni swallowed rapidly as bile rose in her throat. What was happening? She blinked.

A three-dimensional box suddenly spun into existence on the screen. Denver clicked on it. Words exploded:

You have three minutes to send a picture of your final bid.

Then a clock appeared on the screen, already counting down.

"Shit." Denver set the laptop down and ran for the briefcase. "Malloy. Phone." He somehow snagged the phone out of the air without even looking when Malloy threw it. Then he yanked open the briefcase and snapped several pictures before taking the micro SD card out of the phone. He hustled back to the laptop and inserted it, bringing up the pictures.

As Noni watched, he manipulated two of them to change the briefcases, the angle of the money, and even the denominations so they all looked different. So it appeared as if they had three times the money they really did. Wow.

The clock counted down, now at *twenty-two seconds. Twenty-one. Twenty.*

She pressed a hand to her mouth to keep from screaming. If they didn't win, she might never see Talia again.

Eighteen seconds. Seventeen. Sixteen.

Then Denver typed some weird code, the pictures blinked, and then fizzled.

Noni's eyes filled with hot tears. Talia. The people bidding might want to hurt her. Use her. God.

Seven seconds. Six. Five. Denver typed some more.

Finally, with two seconds to go, he pressed the ENTER button.

Noni grabbed the back of his chair to keep herself standing upright. Her entire body hurt. "Denver?"

He shook his head. "I don't know."

Malloy leaned forward. "If they asked everyone for pictures, they might be playing a con. Getting money from everybody and then running."

"I know," Denver said, his voice grim. "We'll have to play it out."

Nothing. The screen went black again. Silence. It was as if the entire Internet paused.

Then a blue goblin came on the screen. "What the hell?" Malloy said, leaning toward Denver.

The goblin opened its mouth, and words poured out:

Congratulations. You are the high bidder. Be at this address
at exactly 4:00 a.m. tomorrow. Only one person may come.
Wear a red shirt.

An address scrolled across the screen next. "Where is that?" Noni breathed.

Malloy leaned in farther. "That's the old abandoned Louis gas station at the edge of town. Good place for an exchange."

Denver shook his head. "That'll probably only be the first stop. Whoever is running this thing is pretty smart. They'll already have surveillance in place."

Malloy breathed out. "Agreed. We'll have to suit up and be prepared to move in as soon as it's safe. We'll need a tracker on you."

Denver turned toward him, his body tense. "We have to prepare here. The gang or Madison or both will be watching the police station and the FBI for any movement. You know it. This thing is put together too well."

Malloy wiped a hand across his eyes. "I get that." He reached for his phone. "Then we'll mobilize under the radar. How's the cloud cover?"

Denver shook his head. "Still too thick. Satellite won't be useful."

"Ah, but traffic cameras will." Malloy sat up, wincing and then rolling his shoulder. "We'd better get to work."

CHAPTER
19

Denver finished scouting the area outside the cabin for threats, finding nothing. Darkness had fallen along with even more snow. Christmas lights twinkled again across the lake, their merriment in direct opposition to his mood. As he reached the front door, he took several deep breaths. In a few too many hours, he'd know the fate of that innocent baby. There was a chance—a good one—that the gang wouldn't hand her over. There was also a chance that Madison and Cobb had found him, which put Noni and Talia in danger.

Either way, he had to get his priorities straight. Squiring Noni and the baby to safety was the only thing that mattered. It was that simple.

For the first time he was willing to put something else in front of his need to take out his past. Somebody else. Noni and the baby had to come first. No matter what. He hadn't been given a chance at a good childhood and his adulthood was questionable, considering he knew how to torture and kill. And had. He was who and what he was because of his past. He wouldn't let anybody force Talia into an existence she had to wonder about. She would be saved. Period.

He pushed open the cabin door and stomped the snow off his boots.

Noni was waiting for him, seated in front of the fire, her eyes pools of concern. Of course she was scared. His chest thumped. He left his jacket on a hook and moved into the warm living room.

"Your brothers called on Malloy's phone," she said quietly.

Denver looked over to the table where Malloy and Tina were going over the maps he'd downloaded of the area around the deserted gas station. "Did you tell them the plan?"

Malloy nodded absently, his gaze not moving. "They didn't like it."

Figured. Denver rolled his aching neck. The tension there had dug in and spread until his shoulders felt like rocks. "Here's the deal. Noni and Tina, you're staying here tomorrow." He'd leave them with enough firepower to protect a small village.

"No," Noni said, her chin lifting. Fire lit her dark eyes, and pure stubbornness firmed her jaw.

His entire body heated to a slow burn. He'd sacrifice anything but her. Saving her was within his control, and he had to do it. "Yes."

She stood then, crossing her arms and moving around the sofa toward him. "Not a chance. This is my fight, and I'm getting that baby."

His temper uncoiled like a live wire. Too much uncertainty and danger slammed into him, releasing the tight hold he'd had on his control. No more. "You don't want to push me any more today," he said, giving fair warning.

Malloy cleared his throat. "On that note, Tina and I are going to get a couple of hours shut-eye." The cop sounded exhausted, but he shoved to his feet and lurched toward the hallway. "Which bedroom?"

"On the left," Denver said evenly, his gaze not leaving Noni's. The woman should've gotten on the helicopter like he'd told her to do. If she was safely in Montana, he could fully concentrate on the job, or jobs, he had to do. There was almost a zero chance somebody wouldn't die in the morning. But Noni had to be safe. "Noni."

She faced him squarely as Tina quietly shut the door to the bedroom behind her and Malloy. "You can't seriously be arguing about this," she said, sweeping her hands out. "I've been in car chases. Shot at. Nearly kidnapped. For goodness' sake. This baby is *mine*. I'm not leaving her and hiding somewhere."

Hers. Yeah. Of course he got it. She already viewed the baby as her daughter. She'd stated that intent. Of course she'd fight to the last breath to protect Talia. But how could he protect Noni at the same time? "They said to come alone," he said lowly, shaking out his hands to prevent him from curling them into fists. The pressure on him, from every direction, upped in power.

She breathed in, her chin down. "I know what they said, and we'll follow the plan. But I'll be right alongside Malloy so I can hold my baby the second we have her. That's nonnegotiable."

Her defiance was having the untenable effect of waking the beast inside him. The one that still railed against the unfairness of the world. The one he kept so carefully in check. Even the air around them tasted of danger. Of the myriad of precise blades and guns even now being prepared. He could feel them. Could sense their intent. Heat unbanked inside him as fear and fury combined. How could she not see the danger? "You don't understand what's happening."

She flung her arms out wide. "How could I?" Her voice rose. "Everything that is happening is crazy. I'm stalking a gang to take back a baby who became my daughter in a split second. You're a super-secret genetic experiment being chased by the people who created you. I have my aunt and her wife driving who knows where to meet who knows whom."

In fury, she was glorious.

She slapped her hands against her hips. "We just watched a veterinarian dig a bullet out of a cop on a kitchen table. Then we bid on my baby against monsters on the dark web—whatever that really is. There's no way to understand this world." She rubbed her forearm. "I've been shot, Denver." Her voice wavered on the last.

Ah hell. He reached her in two strides and wrapped his arms around her. "I know, baby." Shoving his emotions aside, he held her close and placed a kiss on the top of her head. "You've been through enough." Now she had to see his point of view.

She lifted her head, and tears glimmered on her long dark lashes, her tone broken. "We've all been through enough. But we have further to go."

Those words dug deep. He'd lived his entire life thinking them. "You can stay safe," he whispered. The woman had no idea how much he needed her to stay safe. No clue. Perhaps he hadn't, either. But now he did. Everything good in him he'd already given to her. "Trust me."

"I do." She placed her hands on his chest. "But I'm coming tomorrow, and there's no way to stop me."

He blinked. Her defiance just pissed him off. Right or wrong, his temper took over. "You'll do what I tell you to do."

She tried to step back and he didn't allow it. "Listen, Denver—"

"No. You listen." Emotions ripped through him so quickly he couldn't grasp just one. "This is an op involving gangs and cops and probably soldiers who want me taken." He hated talking. This is why he didn't do it. "You'd be just collateral damage to them." When she was everything to him. He'd known it from the first time he'd kissed her. Sinking into a bottle hadn't helped even ease his pain at leaving her. How could she not understand that one simple fact?

She opened her mouth to argue, no doubt. So he went on instinct and stopped her, his lips covering hers. She stiffened, her hands still against his chest. Then she made a helpless sound in the back of her throat, and those fingers curled into his shirt with a little bite of pain. Her body softened, leaning into him. He took the kiss deeper until she opened her mouth, letting him in. Her mouth was hot and tasted of the wine from dinner and of something else, something sweet, something that was just Noni.

His girl.

He was tired of pretending otherwise. Tired of pushing her away and trying to be a good guy. Tired of being alone.

God, she tasted like heaven. Oh, he'd probably never get there, but this was close enough. This was perfect. He explored her, his hand flattening across her lower back, bending her into him. She slid her hands up over his shoulders, pressing her breasts to his chest. His cock jumped and nestled into the sweet warmth between her thighs.

Too damn perfect. The lust always present when she was around, the hard-edged desire she brought out in him, ignited into a demanding ache. Sharp and intense.

They had to stop this. His control had snapped, and he'd felt that release deep inside. She wasn't safe with him, and that knowledge cut deeper than any scalpel ever could. Nobody was safe near him at the moment. So he leaned back, releasing her mouth, panting.

Her eyelids opened to reveal those stunning black orbs. They slowly cleared. Need shimmered there along with a dark defiance. "That all you got?" Her voice was husky and taunting.

The animal inside him, the one that tracked and hunted, leaped alive with a hunger so sharp it craved. His chains released. "No. I've got more." Awareness finally crossed her face, but it was too late.

Way too late.

* * *

Noni realized just a second too late that she'd gone too far. Oh, she'd felt it in his kiss. The barely restrained hunger, the snapping of his control. She'd wanted all of him, or she thought she had.

One of his hands still spanned her lower back, holding her easily in place. Her lungs compressed as if breathing was too much effort with the tension clogging the air. Slowly, deliberately, he ran a knuckle down the side of her face. Just one soft touch...but the look in his eyes. Feral and determined. A wild bolt of elemental fire burned right down her spine.

Everything inside her knew she'd pushed him too far. Yet...every nerve inside her sparked from the lightning she'd just unleashed. Intrigue, the most dangerous kind, kept her hands on his shoulders. She wanted this.

A voice of reason tried to interfere with her desire as the wildness between them grew in force.

"One chance," he ground out, his voice not sounding remotely like him. "Go to bed."

She knew what he meant. "No."

He blinked, and his hand somehow heated across her flesh. "I'm not in full control here."

A warning. Definitely a warning.

"Good." She lifted her chin, mesmerized by the primitive glint in his eyes.

He released her. "Take off your shirt."

She glanced toward the bedrooms. "Shouldn't we—"

"No. Take off your shirt." His tone lowered and roughened. "Don't make me tell you again."

Red-hot desire cut through her, nearly shocking in its intensity. Why? Why would his order, his command, even his determination weaken her knees and throw flutters down her abdomen to her clit? A part of her, one she didn't trust, wanted to defy him. Just to see what he'd do. This dark side of herself—of him—thrilled her to the edge. The other part had at least a sliver of self-preservation. Yet still. She wouldn't be so easily tamed. Slowly, deliberately, she reached for the bottom of her shirt and drew it over her head. Then she lifted both eyebrows in the most smart-ass expression she could summon, considering her nipples were obviously diamond hard beneath his sharp gaze.

"See? You don't need that bra I ruined," he rumbled, his smirk full of male satisfaction.

Challenge rose in her, heated and strong. "You're right," she whispered, grasping her nipples and groaning at the sparks of instant pleasure.

His hands immediately grasped hers and pulled them free. "Oh no, baby. I do the touching."

Triumph filled her. "If you say so," she breathed, trying for nonchalant. She didn't make it.

He shook his head slowly, studying her, satisfaction curving his lips. As if he couldn't quite believe her daring...or his opportunity. "Take off those yoga pants before I rip them off you."

She was running out of clothes, so she didn't hesitate. They hit the ground, and she kicked them aside, leaving her in a silky pink thong. She reached for it, and he stopped her.

"No. I like that." Without preamble, he dropped to his knees and set her ass on the back of the sofa.

Vulnerability swept her as she looked directly at the darkened doorways. Malloy or Tina could come out at any moment. "Denver? We should go to the bedroom," she whispered.

In answer, he nipped her sex through the silk. His hands caressed down her legs, his strength and gentleness both obvious.

She jumped, her thighs trembling. It was too decadent. "I don't think—"

He snapped the thong in two, and then his mouth was on her. She leaned back against the sofa, her eyelids fluttering shut. It was more than she could take. He licked and nipped, his fingers joining his mouth and talented tongue. Her legs trembled, and fire flashed through her, but he wouldn't let her topple over. She kept trying to open her eyes to watch for movement in the doorway, but they kept closing.

His thumb pressed against her clit, and his fingers stroked inside her. She shook, her knees feeling like Jell-O. Sparks of pleasure zipped through her, and she tried to push against him and gain more friction.

He chuckled, the sound vibrating through her core.

She gasped and opened her eyes, the feelings too incredible to stop. "Shhh." God. What if they woke Malloy?

Denver looked up, his eyes a sizzling blue of intensity. He leaned back. "Worried?"

She shifted her weight, panic and desire smashing into her abdomen. "They could come out." Her voice was way too breathy.

He smiled then, the sight dangerous. Warning bells clanged fully alive in her head, and she held out her hands. He stood suddenly, and she leaned farther back. "You wanted to play, baby." Barely ducking his shoulder, he lifted her against his chest, cradling her.

She bit back a yelp and then relaxed in his arms. Good. They were going to the bedroom.

He moved around the sofa toward the fireplace, and she stiffened. "What are you doing?" she breathed.

For answer, her quiet protector set her on her knees on the sofa seat, facing those doorways, her belly against the back cushions. Her elbows settled on the sofa back. If Malloy came out of his room, he'd see her fully bare breasts. "Denver?" she whispered.

His hand was instantly between her legs from behind.

She gasped, her hips instinctively tilting to give him access. He chuckled again, the sound low and rough as he pressed his knees to the sofa behind her.

"No," she said, shaking her head, trying to focus. The sensuality, the danger, wrapped around her with desperate heat.

"Yes," he corrected, his knees nudging her thighs farther apart. "You're about to learn self-control and obedience, sweetheart."

She trembled from the dark promise. Why wasn't she pissed? Her body was one long nerve of need, and all she could do was vibrate in place. He was so sexy, and she wanted everything he had. All that he was. This was part of him, and she craved more.

His big hands palmed her thighs and he lifted her up. "We're gonna need leverage."

She caught hold of the back of the sofa, her hands curling over the fabric, her gaze on the darkened doorway hiding the other couple. This was insane. Then the tip of his cock touched her clit, and she cried out from the raw pleasure.

His teeth sank into the back of her shoulder. "Quiet," he whispered, his voice melted sex.

She blinked, her body shaking with need. Tremors ran down her arms, and she lost her balance, falling onto her left forearm, protecting her bandaged right one. Only his strong hold on her kept her from tumbling over the back of the couch to the floor on the other side.

"Better." Using his thighs on the sofa for balance, he shoved up into her while also pulling her down.

Pain and sharply edged pleasure exploded inside her, and she bit her lip to keep from crying out again. Her vision hazed. Using both hands, he tilted her butt toward him, forcing her up and slightly over the sofa. Then he slammed back home, his mouth nuzzling her neck.

She arched her back as sensations ripped through her. Keeping quiet was killing her. This was torture. He was torturing her on purpose, and he was enjoying it. "You are such a dick," she gasped.

He stopped nuzzling. "Oh, you're going to apologize for that," he warned.

She shivered.

He released her hip and reached around to toy with a nipple. Ecstasy rippled through her, landing squarely in her clit. She squirmed against him, trying to move, but he held her in place. Then he moved to the other nipple and pinched.

She gasped and pressed against him. "Denver."

"Apologize for calling me a dick." Amusement darkened his tone. His fingers tapped from her punished nipple down her abdomen. She sucked in air. He kept going, his touch hot. Oh God. He was heading even farther down.

"I'm sorry for calling you names" she breathed right before he reached her clit.

He sighed and then gently rubbed her. "Fair enough. Now you be quiet, or they'll hear you and come out."

Her eyes opened wide and she pressed her lips together.

Denver lifted her up again, apparently done with playing. His thrusts were hard and fast, filling her completely. Each strong stroke pushed her over the back of the sofa before he yanked her toward him again, making her breasts jiggle with each movement. Just when she couldn't take any more, he hammered even deeper.

So much desperate pleasure filled her it was all she could do not to cry out. Forcing herself to be quiet just enhanced every feeling, every sensation. Finally, his lips brushed her ear. "Now, baby."

As if her body had just been waiting for his command, she detonated. The room flashed white and then hazed while wave upon wave of raw electricity ripped through her. He thrust faster, his hands bruising her hips, his mouth against her neck. Finally, she came down and went limp with a soft whimper, no longer caring if anybody heard.

He shuddered and then kissed her neck. "There we go," he murmured softly.

She murmured something in a sensual fog. Cold air brushed her face. The ticking of the clock permeated her cocoon.

Slowly, she lifted her head. Her body, even still wrapped in his, chilled.

It was time.

CHAPTER
20

Denver shifted his shirt beneath the bulletproof vest and made sure he had free range of motion while wearing the stupid thing. It had been some time since he'd put one on. He stood near the sofa and tried to banish thoughts of what had happened there last night. He still felt Noni around him.

If they survived this, if he lived through the coming showdown with Cobb and Madison, could he hope for a life with her? Was it possible? Hope was a dangerous drug, and he'd tried to keep it away for so long. What if?

He had to focus. "What time is it?" he asked Malloy, who sat at the kitchen table.

The cop glanced at his watch. "One in the morning. I have a force ready to move on our command, and my men have scoped the area. It seems quiet, which probably isn't a good sign."

There was little chance Cobb and Madison hadn't taken notice of Malloy amassing a force. Hopefully they wouldn't have time to gather their forces before Denver had blown town. But when had luck ever been on his side? Denver tightened the vest. "Copy that. The road conditions are going to slow us down a little."

The bedroom door opened, and Noni stepped out.

His chest took a hit from an invisible anvil. Every primitive feeling he'd ever had rose to the surface fast and hard. His. Everything about her was his—and he wanted to keep her. Bad.

She'd dressed in jeans and a sweater, having pulled her dark hair back in a braid. "We ready?" she asked, studiously ignoring the sofa.

Denver couldn't take his gaze off her. Neither one of them would probably look at a fabric sofa the same again. "Yes." He wanted to argue with her again, but he'd promised to let her stay with Malloy on the op. If Denver got the baby, he could immediately turn her over to Noni. And Malloy would keep her safe.

Tina opened their door and came out, a bandage in her hands. "We need to change your arm bandage, Jamie."

A sound caught Denver's attention. He stiffened and turned his head toward the door.

"What?" Malloy asked, shoving to stand on one leg.

Denver closed his eyes and reached out with his super-hearing. "One large vehicle, going slow, heading our way down the driveway from the lake road." He hustled toward the light switch and turned it off. "They're trying to be quiet." *Shit, shit, shit.*

Malloy reached for a gun from the back of his borrowed jeans. "Tina? Go back into the bedroom."

Denver jerked his head for Noni to do the same. "Take the gun that I gave to you out of the drawer by the fridge," he whispered.

She paled but did as he'd said.

Denver angled toward the front door and looked out at the cold landscape. His breath heated, and he calmed down into battle mode. No emotion—just calculation. "We'll have to take them out. It's too cold for us to run anywhere." Plus, Malloy couldn't run.

A large SUV rolled to a stop.

Denver tensed. "One vehicle only." Shadows could be seen, but he couldn't count them. He quietly opened the door and pressed his gun out into the darkness. "I'll take one out right away."

The driver's side door opened, and a man jumped to the ground.

Denver paused. Ryker? Emotion bombarded him as his instincts recognized family.

"Don't fuckin' shoot," came clearly through the whistling wind. Ryker shut the door and gave a smart-ass wave.

Denver's entire body relaxed, and he pulled the front door fully open. "It's my brothers," he said to Malloy, shocked as hell at the gratitude and relief slamming into him. He tucked his gun into the back of his waistband and strode into the storm, straight at Ryker, to envelope him in a strong hug. God, he'd missed them. He clapped his brother on the back. "I told you not to come."

If Madison and Cobb had found them, this was going to be a trap. Ryker couldn't be caught in it. But Denver didn't want to let go. Having Ry at his side made the world better—and safer.

Heath exited from the passenger side and made his way toward them, also giving him a hug. "Since when do we listen to you?"

Denver leaned back, the world righting itself. He hadn't realized how off he'd felt without them. "I'm glad you guys came." It was as close as he could think to express himself. To let them know how much he counted on them and needed them. While he'd wanted them safe, he needed them at his back. They'd help get the baby. And if this was their last stand, if Cobb and Madison showed up, they'd be together to fight. Where they belonged. "Thanks."

"Where else would we be?" Heath asked, his eyes dark. "It took longer than we'd hoped, but we had to secure the South Dakota property better before leaving."

Denver paused. "You shouldn't have left Zara and Anya." Guilt swept through him.

"They're safe. I guarantee it," Heath countered, nodding toward the cabin. "I take it we're on op?"

"Yeah," Denver said.

Ryker tugged on the vest. "Nice."

Denver nodded. "Borrowed it." He turned, his step lighter than it had been in days. His brothers finally got to meet Noni. Suddenly, oddly, his palms started sweating. His palms never sweat. What if she didn't like them? How could she not like them? They were amazing men.

"You're thinking awfully hard," Ryker murmured, walking alongside him toward the door. "Are you worried about the gang and the baby exchange?"

Denver pushed open the door. "Yes."

Malloy was waiting, standing by the fridge on one leg, his gun pointed at Denver. "Damn it," he muttered, although his gaze showed relief. "You guys promised you'd stay out of Snowville."

Ryker stepped past Denver and strode for the cop, quickly shaking hands. Without seeming to, he somehow got Malloy to sit back down and get off that leg. "It's good to see you again."

Malloy frowned.

Heath shut the door behind them. "How's the leg?"

"Fine," Malloy snapped. "It appears your enemies are now my enemies."

Denver winced. "I told you we were sorry about that."

Ryker wiped snow off his jet black hair. "You have a standing invite from the brothers in Montana to relocate there. Something about a sheriff's position opening up."

Malloy's chin lowered. "You think I want to be a country fucking sheriff?"

Denver grinned. "Why not?"

The bedroom door opened, and Noni poked her head out. "Denver?" she asked, her face pale.

He straightened and moved for her, gently taking her hand and leading her out. His shoulders stiffened. "Noni? These are my brothers, Ryker and Heath." He brought her over to them, feeling like he'd brought a girl home for dinner for the first time.

Her eyes widened and then she shook hands with both. "It's nice to meet you."

Ryker smiled, all charm. "You too."

Heath grinned as well, his gaze searching. "What you're doing to find the baby, to save her, that's brave."

She shuffled her feet. "I don't feel brave. Just determined."

"Even better," Ryker said.

Heath grasped a manila file from beneath his jacket and handed it over to Denver. "I did some research, and if at all possible, get Richie to sign this. We've already had it, ah, notarized. It'll hold up in court, I promise."

Noni blinked. "You know about Richie?"

Heath stretched his wrist. "Yes. He's listed as the birth father on the certificate, so he'll need parental rights terminated in order for your rights, per the will, to be followed. This is the easiest path but not the only one."

"Heath is a lawyer," Denver explained. Although Heath didn't like practicing law, it sure had come in handy once in a while.

"Oh," she said, glancing at the papers. "We have to get Talia first."

Denver's chest settled. For the first time he thought he might actually have a chance of surviving this. "All right. Let me explain the plan to you guys." Hopefully they wouldn't think he was crazy.

* * *

The plan was crazy.

Noni slowly sipped her coffee as Denver and his brothers went over it detail by detail. Malloy, Heath, Tina, and Denver sat at the table, looking at maps, while Ryker stood behind Heath.

As they talked, she took a moment to study them. She'd felt the scars when they'd shaken hands. Their blood brothers scars.

It was a simple act, really, but it obviously had held so much meaning to them. They were truly a family. She liked seeing Denver as part of a family—as not being alone. Even if they couldn't find a future together, he had people. That mattered.

Just like she had Franny and Verna. She rubbed her chest. Man, she wished they could see how hard Denver was working to bring Talia home to them. How much he was willing to sacrifice to save the baby. When she'd wondered if he'd be able to love a baby, to love her, she'd been wrong.

Denver was more than capable of love. His brothers proved that.

Ryker had black hair that curled over his collar and sparkling bluish green eyes that seemed to take in everything at once. His features were more angled than Denver's but not as much as Heath's. He was just as tall as Denver—maybe about six foot four. Heath seemed just as tall too, with brown hair and greenish brown eyes.

Ryker pointed out defensive positions, Heath opined the best offense, and Denver seemed to put it all together into a workable plan. They often spoke in shorthand, but they apparently understood one another. Malloy interjected several times with plans for the police presence while Tina kept an eye on his injuries; the arm had suddenly started bleeding again.

It was odd to see Denver work so effortlessly with his brothers, but it made a nice kind of sense. He seemed like such a lone wolf that observing him with people he loved, with people he trusted, gave her hope that someday he'd find peace. Was there a chance he'd find that with her and Talia?

If not, she'd leave him with a kiss and go become a single mom. But…what if?

At the thought, she straightened her shoulders.

Denver turned toward Malloy. "I think we've got this."

Malloy snorted. "I'm a cop. You should know me by now."

Ryker cut Heath a look.

Tension rolled through the room.

Malloy seemed to relax. "I also know you guys."

Noni shivered, caught by the undercurrents. "What's going on?"

Malloy focused on her. "Your boys here are trying to figure out a way to keep me out of this. To keep the authorities out of this." If anything, the cop sounded cheerful as he announced the news.

Denver crossed his arms. "Say what you're going to say."

"I already set the plan in motion." If Malloy had been a more dramatic guy, he probably would've twisted an imaginary mustache. "SWAT is ready to roll."

"Damn it," Heath snapped. "Sheriff Cobb has our faces all over the news. Our pictures are probably stuck on bulletin boards all across the country."

Malloy nodded. "Yep. The only way I can make this work and not make you guys true fugitives is to do this within the law and say you're working with me. Cobb has your pictures up and has put out BOLOs, but he's in a different jurisdiction, and I can plead ignorance. For a while, anyway. Long enough."

Denver shook his head. "Let's get the baby and worry about our fugitive status next. You two will have to take up sniper positions as soon as we have a location. Then get out as soon as possible. If I get taken in, we'll deal."

Noni gulped. "You're assuming we'll get Talia." God, she had to believe them. She had to. The idea of not getting her baby, of Talia in a monster's hands, was too terrifying to imagine.

Denver sent her what he probably thought was a reassuring smile. "The ear communicators my brothers brought with them will keep us in contact with one another. This is good."

They'd also brought a box of bulletproof vests, more guns, and several wicked-looking knives. Denver's eyes had gleamed at the knives.

She shivered. The more she listened to the plan, the more her stomach began to hurt. "You think the gang is going to try to double-cross you," she murmured, finally catching some of the subtext.

Denver shook his head. "The smart thing for them to do is honor the deal."

Heath looked up from papers on the table, his gaze serious. "There's an odd code to the dark web—one they shouldn't want to violate. If word gets around that their auctions, any of them, are rigged, then nobody will bid on their items. And they make a lot of money from selling drugs on the dark web."

Were the brothers trying to reassure her? If so, they were in perfect sync with one another. "Right," she mused. "That's only if you can make it back to the auction site to report them or talk about them or whatever. If you die, then nobody will know you were double-crossed." She wasn't born yesterday, for goodness' sake.

Ryker grinned from his position of leaning against the fridge. "Smart. Denver said you were smart."

Heat climbed into her face. Denver had talked about her to his brothers? She kept her gaze level and tried to stop blushing. "He was gone so quickly from Alaska that I hadn't thought he'd noticed." Yeah, she was being a smart-ass. He had deserted her, after all.

Ryker bit back a snort, and Heath grinned, keeping his gaze down on the papers.

Denver looked at her. "I noticed." His tone was level, but his gaze burned.

Was there a warning in those stark blue eyes? Noni lifted her chin. "Oh." Lame comeback.

Heath cleared his throat. "He noticed a lot about you."

Denver cut him a warning look.

Noni straightened, curiosity rippling through her. "Really?"

"Yes. Black hair, black eyes, voice like a song," Heath murmured.

"Stubborn, with a great love of alexandrite," Ryker chimed in.

Her blush heated more.

"Shut up, you guys," Denver said, hunching his shoulders. "We need to concentrate right now." He tapped his finger on the map. "I still don't like this area toward the hills. It's not covered well enough."

"The terrain is rough," Malloy agreed.

What a nice job he'd done of changing the subject. Noni crossed her arms. So he'd told his brothers about her. About her love for the pretty greenish purple stone. What did that mean? Did that mean anything? Why did she care? The man had said he was leaving, and he never lied. Why would she open her heart up to him again? But...he had talked about her. When he'd said he cared, that he hadn't been able to forget her, he'd meant that, too. Her heart stuttered.

Her heart was wide open for him.

Denver looked up. "All right. It's time to go."

That quickly, she forgot all about her heart. This was life or death.

God, she hoped Richie and the Kingdom Boys brought Talia, and that nobody got shot. Her legs trembled, but she moved toward the door. Would they all survive?

CHAPTER
21

Denver waited in the empty parking lot in the crappy subcompact he'd stolen from a junkyard on the way, since his SUV was toast. He was taking directions from the gang, and he wouldn't be needing speed.

He'd also broken into a luggage store on the way and stolen a case large enough to hold the auction money. Hopefully the gang would think he'd combined the three briefcases into one case. He'd also left money at the store for the case as well as the broken window. Now here he was.

A rusty sign had fallen to cover the door to the ramshackle building. Ice and very fresh snow blanketed the deserted parking lot with hills and trees spreading out on the other side. There wasn't another building in sight, thus no streetlights. At the predawn hour, night still ruled, and the snow still fell lightly. It was a good spot for a meet, but so far he couldn't sense anybody but the ones he'd brought with him. Even the cops were on standby more than a mile away.

Malloy's arm had continued bleeding, but he'd insisted on having a cop buddy pick him up so he could remain on the periphery—a mile in the other direction. Noni was safely in his backseat along with Tina. Nothing would happen to them.

So he kept vigilant, his super-hearing tuned in. A phone started to ring.

He slid his window down and listened. Over by the sign. "There's a phone," he said quietly, using the ear communicator. "I'm exiting the vehicle." He stepped into the freezing dark, eyeing the area around him before stalking over to the door. A burner cell phone had been taped to the back of the sign. He lifted it to his other ear. "Yeah."

A male voice came over the line. "Get the money and walk out to the main road. Leave this phone on the ground." The line went dead.

He dropped the phone, grabbed the one case, and strode through thick snow to reach the icy road. Nothing. Five minutes passed. Then another ten. He kept still, banishing any thoughts of being cold. If nothing else, having been genetically spliced to be strong, he could handle time in freezing weather. Even so, his ears started to burn a little.

Twin headlights finally cut through the dark fog down the road.

He widened his stance.

A small truck came into view, pulling alongside him. Keeping his face calm, he opened the passenger side door to face the barrel of a sawed off .22LR rifle. A kid of about twenty, gang tats down his face, stared at him from the driver's seat. His aim remained steady. "Take off the clothes."

Denver looked around. Tension rode him, but he hid it. "It's ten degrees."

The kid shrugged. "Or I shoot."

Oh, he could take the gun from the little fucker in about two seconds. Denver tugged off his leather jacket, tossing it behind him. Somebody had better grab it—he'd had it for years. His pants and boots followed. Then the shirt and bulletproof vest.

The kid lifted a pierced eyebrow. He had short brown hair, dead brown eyes, and another piercing in his lip. "Nice vest."

Without a word, Denver tossed it over his shoulder. No way was the kid getting the vest. Finally, he stood there in his boxer briefs and socks. "You can't want to see more, kid."

"Show me the money."

Denver lifted the case and partially opened it, hoping the kid didn't want to rifle through. The bottom was paper. But he kept his hands steady when they wanted to tremble. Time to disengage and just work. Emotion would harm him. So he banished it.

The kid texted something on his phone. "Get in."

Denver slid into the truck, setting the case on the floor. They drove off immediately. Maybe the gang wasn't planning on violating the auction rules. "Where's the baby?"

The kid scratched what looked like a new tattoo across his neck. "No clue. I have orders."

That wasn't helpful. "Where are we going?"

"Why you want a baby, anyway?" The kid cut him a sideways look. "You a pervert?"

"Nope." Denver watched snow-laden trees fly by outside the truck. "I'm just the middle man. My clients want to adopt a baby. Nothing creepy about them."

"Right," the kid drawled. "If you say so." He managed to drive with one hand while controlling the rifle with the other.

"You can put down the gun. I'm not going anywhere," Denver said easily. Or he could just take it from him. But then he wouldn't be cooperating, so maybe he'd let the kid keep the gun for a while.

"No." The gang member drove toward town, and store lights started to show sporadically. Finally, they pulled into the far reaches of a parking lot of a twenty-four-hour market.

"We're shopping at the mini-mart?" Denver asked quietly, letting his team know his location.

"We took out the security cameras, so don't worry." The kid stopped the truck next to a black van. "Get out."

Denver opened his door just as the side door of the van slid open. Two more gang members pointed guns at him, one with a Glock, the other with a Sig. The kid with the Glock had *Richie* tattooed across his neck. He'd tattooed his own name? "I take it you're Richie?" Denver asked, shutting the door of the truck behind him. Great. A moron with a gun. They were the most dangerous types.

Richie nodded. "You with the cops?"

"No. I'm for hire—by the parents wanting this kid." That would explain the vest in case there was any question. If Richie even knew about the vest. "I'm in my underwear, man."

Richie pushed from the van, standing to about six feet tall. He had blue eyes and dark hair with several tattoos down one side of his jaw.

Denver tried to keep from punching him in the face for putting his own kid up for sale. For torturing Noni into not being able to sleep because she was so worried about the baby. Her baby. "We doing this or what?"

Richie smiled, showing what looked like a ruby glued to his right incisor. "So you're a professional."

"Of sorts." The cold was beginning to creep into his bones, and his damn socks were sliding on the ice. Where the hell was the baby? "I'm about done playing. Where's the kid?" He didn't need to try to make his voice hoarse. The cold was doing it for him.

"In time." Richie moved in. "Take out the earbud."

Denver lifted an eyebrow. As a professional, he would have an earbud. The kid wasn't that stupid. So he easily took out the earbud and handed it over.

Richie threw it high and wide before turning back to the van. "Get in."

Denver followed, set the case down, and sat on it. "My clients are going to get impatient and fly right off. We need the exchange."

The driver, a thirty-something gang member wearing all the colors, ignited the engine, and they started to drive. Denver kept a bored expression on his face. Hopefully his brothers had traced them to the store from his description when he'd first arrived. It had to be almost five in the morning, and meager traffic had started to fill the road with folks on their way to early shifts.

Good. Where was the baby? Was she warm enough? "I had wondered if you guys would adhere to the rules of the auction," he said.

The kid with the Sig didn't twitch.

Richie breathed in. "The Kingdom Boys don't welsh on agreements."

Good to know. "Then we'll make sure to leave you five stars on the site," Denver said congenially. He could get both guns and pistol-whip the snot out of these jerks before they could suck in a breath. If only he knew where the baby was being held. God, she had to be okay.

Richie looked him over. "You don't even look cold. You some type of soldier?"

"I just get the job done." Denver rolled his neck. "Are we almost there?"

Richie shrugged. "Soon enough." He tucked his gun into loose-fitting jeans while the guy with the Sig kept his pointed at Denver. "Why do your clients want a baby? Really?"

"Adoption takes too long," Denver lied. "Whose baby is it, anyway?"

Richie snorted. "I'm on the birth certificate, but who the hell knows. The mom was a skank, man."

"What if the baby is yours?" Denver had no reason to try to find humanity in this scum, but he couldn't help it.

Richie lifted a narrow shoulder. "You think I should keep a kid?" He grinned at his buddy.

"Good point," Denver said. "I can assure you, the people who want to adopt the baby only want one to love. Nothing skeevy."

Richie snorted. "For the kind of money they're paying, I don't give a shit."

Oh, he was going to kill this asshole. Denver's hand fisted. He coughed out, trying to control himself. "Good." Denver glanced toward the driver. After another ten minutes of driving, they pulled up outside a dilapidated motel on the other side of town. The kind of place that rented by the hour, if it rented at all. "Tell me you don't have a baby here." The urge to run inside and save the baby coursed through him.

"Don't be picky." Richie yanked open the door and jumped out. "Be careful on the ice. With socks, it's going to be slippery." He laughed and started moving toward the doorway to room number five.

The kid with the Sig motioned for Denver to get out.

Denver stepped out, careful of his balance. He grabbed the case and followed Richie, fully aware of the gun at his back. A quick glance around showed the place to be deserted. The wind picked up, chilling his bare skin. He could hear cars and movement all around, but many people were heading to work. Was backup near?

He couldn't make a move until he saw that the baby was safe. "You guys have to know. If you double-cross me, my people will hunt you across the globe and rip out your eyeballs."

Richie kept going and knocked three times on the door. It slowly swung inward. "Go."

Denver took one last listen around and then stepped into a room that smelled like mold. Filthy shag carpet covered the floor, and peeling wallpaper covered the dingy walls. Two men sat at a rickety table, guns in front of them and gang tats all over their faces. One appeared around fifty and the other thirty. A woman sat on the one bed, a baby in her arms. The woman from the pictures he'd shown Noni. He looked closer. The baby was dressed in pink with a bow in her mass of hair. She slept peacefully, and she looked clean. A healthy tinge covered her little cheeks.

Relief nearly dropped him to his knees. Only training kept him in place.

Richie shut the door, remaining outside with the others. Probably to scan for threats.

Denver concentrated on the danger inside the room. He'd deal with Richie later and after Talia was safe.

The older man nodded at the case. "Open it." His voice was raspy as if he'd been smoking three packs a day his entire life.

Denver turned to place the case on the bed. He opened it slowly. Rows of cash showed clearly, with the paper beneath hidden.

He moved to the side and closer to the baby as if to give a clear view of the money.

A closer examination showed the woman's pupils to be dilated and her jaw slack. Whatever she was on obviously didn't affect her ability to hold the baby. Even so, Denver's arms itched to take the infant and get her to safety.

The younger guy stood up and crossed to the case.

Denver angled closer. He could grab the gun, or he could grab the baby. If he got the gun, would the woman harm the baby? His only choice was to go for the gun and hope the woman was too stoned to think.

His muscles bunched.

A flurry of movement sounded outside. Were more gang members right outside? How would he get the baby out? He couldn't just shoot his way out with a baby in his arms.

The gang member reached the case and started filtering through the money. Denver stiffened and prepared to strike. The second the gang member found the paper, he pivoted around, his mouth opening to yell.

Denver was on him in a second, grabbing his gun even as the older guy lifted his. Using his momentum, Denver yanked the younger guy in front of him, pointed, and fired. Several bullets hit the guy he was holding, jerking his body against Denver's. Denver hit the shooter in the center of his head, and blood splattered all across the wall.

Without missing a step, Denver dropped the dead gang member and pivoted, his gun pointed at the woman.

She blinked, her eyes wide.

He hustled toward her and grabbed Talia as gently as he could, whose face had scrunched up. A piercing wail came from the little one. Denver nudged the woman toward the bathroom. "Go in there and duck down."

She stumbled toward the bathroom, shutting the door.

Taking a deep breath, Denver eyed the two dead men. Okay. What now? He glanced down at the screaming baby and tried to bounce her a little. His other arm hurt, but he didn't have time to worry about it. Could he put the baby in the case? It wouldn't stop a bullet. Nothing in the room would stop a bullet.

His body would stop bullets from hitting her, though.

So he ducked down on the other side of the bed, his gun toward the door. Surely Richie and his buddies had heard the gunfire. Where were they?

The darkness outside suddenly lit up with red and blue swirling lights. Rapid firing filled the air. A gap in the curtains showed men in SWAT gear battling gang members wearing bright gang colors. It was mayhem.

Then...silence.

He slowly stood and moved toward the window, nudging the remainder of the torn curtain aside. Malloy was barking orders while leaning against a cop car. Richie and his buddies were handcuffed, facedown over another car.

Denver caught sight of his brothers on the periphery, and then they were gone. Escaped into the darkness. His shoulders settled, and he patted the screaming baby. Then he gentled his hold. She was so damn breakable. "It's okay." At least Ry and Heath were safe.

Holding the baby gingerly, Denver yanked open the door and strode outside. He caught Malloy's eye. "We need her checked out." He held her like she'd shatter, but he wouldn't let her fall.

An ambulance roared into the lot, and he hustled toward it, waiting impatiently until it parked. The second the EMTs stepped out, he handed over the baby to an earnest-looking blonde in her early twenties.

Malloy tossed him his clothes. "We grabbed these on the way."

Denver pulled his jacket into place just as Noni and Tina emerged from another police car. Noni ran toward him across the ice, and he held out his arms. She lunged into him, panic on her face. "Talia?"

He gently turned her toward the ambulance. "She looks good to me. Go check."

Heath instantly came around the other side of the ambulance, dressed in full SWAT gear.

Denver paused. "Get the hell out of here." They couldn't get caught now.

Heath shoved a file full of papers toward them. "Do what you need to do, and then run. You can't stay." He then tapped his ear as if getting an order and turned to stride toward a SWAT vehicle. He veered at the last moment and soon disappeared in the darkness.

Denver glanced toward the motel room, where the police were swarming. He'd never get to the money. It was gone.

This was a fucking shit-storm. But at least he had the baby—and she was all that truly mattered right now. He strode toward the car and yanked Richie up by his arms. "Uncuff him."

Malloy nodded toward a uniformed police officer, who quickly uncuffed Richie.

Denver grabbed the kid by the throat. "Sign this. Now."

Malloy handed him a pen.

The kid coughed out blood and then grabbed the pen, shakily signing his name

"What is it?"

"You just gave up any right to the baby." Denver shoved the kid back at the cop and turned for the ambulance. The paper wasn't exactly legal, but it was something to help with Noni's case. It was doubtful Richie would show up and contest it.

Malloy grabbed him by the arm. "Give me the papers."

Denver handed them over, his entire body rioting.

"Get out, now. I'll get your girl to the hospital," Malloy said urgently as more police began to arrive. "The FBI will be here any second. You'll have to trust me. Now."

Denver's lungs compressed. Malloy was right. If Denver stayed, he'd be arrested and of no use to Noni. But what could he do? He couldn't leave her.

Malloy moved past him to the ambulance. "This is your one shot," he muttered.

Damn it. The cop was right. Denver looked around, feeling eyes on him. Had Madison's soldiers found him? It was a stretch to think they hadn't at this point, and they could be just lying in wait. He had to get free of this feeling of being watched, and leaving Noni might be safer for her. At least Malloy would have her covered. It physically hurt for Denver to turn away from Noni and stride into the darkness to find his brothers.

He'd see her at least once more before he faced his past. But the déjà vu he felt in walking away from her again made him want to puke.

She'd hate him for this.

CHAPTER
22

Thank God Denver had gotten away. There was a little déjà vu in his leaving, but she had to let that go. She had to believe that he'd be back this time. That he wouldn't just desert her. He'd have to check on Talia at the very least.

She sat in the hospital examination room with a young female doctor, who was gently checking Talia. Armed police officers stood sentry at the doorway. It was nearly nine in the morning, and Noni's stomach growled. How could she even remotely be hungry right now? Her life was a complete disaster.

At least the baby gurgled and kicked her feet on the table. She looked around, already so alert.

A rush of maternal love washed through Noni, and she stood closer, touching Talia's hand. Nobody would ever hurt this baby. She said the vow inside her head, her entire heart full. Would Denver want to be a part of their lives? Suddenly she wanted that with a clarity she'd never had before. Oh, she'd always wanted him, but now she felt a trust in him she hadn't had before. He'd risked his life for Talia. That meant something. Was there a chance he could be a part of their family? Of their future?

Dr. Laraby smiled and finished replacing the baby's purple dress.

"Talia is in good health, and I can't see any sign of abuse. Whoever has had her this last week actually took fairly good care of her." She lifted the baby and handed her over to Noni.

Noni's knees almost gave out, her relief was so strong. Her mind had wandered to some pretty dark places on what evil people could do to an innocent baby. Thank God they hadn't abused her. She cuddled the snuffling baby close and held her tight, where she belonged. "Why does she keep crying?"

"Her general health is good." The doctor pushed black curls over her shoulder. She had to be around thirty and was strikingly beautiful with dark coloring and Asian features. "However, she does have an ear infection, and I'll write you a prescription for antibiotics. Also give her infant Tylenol for the pain."

Noni stiffened. She had no clue what she was doing. She had to find books on motherhood. "Ear infection?"

The doctor grinned. "It's quite common. Don't worry. Just follow the directions on the medication, and if you have any questions, give me a call."

Detective Malloy hitched on crutches through the door. "Hey, Doc."

Laraby's dark eyebrows rose. "Malloy. Somebody finally kicked your feet out from under you?"

Malloy rolled his eyes. "A couple of bullets can't stop me. What's the news?"

"The baby is fine. Slight ear infection." Laraby scratched on a notepad and handed the prescription over to Noni. "She'll need antibiotics and rest. No flying for a couple of weeks, but I'm sure that's not an issue."

Noni shook her head. All right. That may be an issue. "It's okay, baby." She soothed Talia.

"Nope," Malloy said. "Noni and the baby have a date in court first thing tomorrow morning." His brown eyes were serious and lacked any semblance of a smile. "It's the only way I could keep Child Protective Services off you at the moment."

Noni's lips trembled, but she forced a smile. The awesome responsibility that just descended on her nearly dropped her. But she could do this. The baby needed love and protection. "I understand." Would they take the baby away? What should she tell them? She suddenly felt so alone the room went cold. She needed Denver. Then Talia sniffled, and Noni looked down at her smooth face. No. She didn't need anybody. This baby was her responsibility, and she'd protect her. "It's okay," Noni whispered. It was all going to be okay. No matter what she had to do.

Malloy gestured toward the hallway. "Let's get going. We have a safe house ready for you as we finish rounding up the gang members, and the FBI wants to interview you. Like, right now."

Noni swallowed. The walls seemed to close in, and the atmosphere grew heavy. "We'll need, ah, supplies." She looked down at the trusting baby in her arms. Talia looked back, her dark eyes already serious. "Um, diapers, food, and stuff." Stuff? She'd just said *stuff*. She had no idea how to care for a baby all by herself without Sharon's guidance. The thought of Sharon was like a punch to the stomach. She'd died way too young. Man, she missed Sharon. This was crazy. She was crazy.

Malloy patted her arm. "Not a problem. Tina is at the store right now. She has a bunch of nieces and nephews, so she knows all the shit we'll need. You've got to concentrate on the immediate issues."

Oh yeah. The fact that Denver was gone. That a whole stack of money had just been confiscated by the FBI—money she couldn't trace to her business or anywhere else. There was also the dark web and the obvious fact that she'd been on it to make a deal to buy a baby. "How much trouble am I in?" she whispered.

Malloy shook his head. "You don't want an answer to that question."

Noni smoothed a hand down Talia's back. "I need to call my aunt." If Noni ended up in jail or detention or wherever, she had to make sure Talia was safe. They couldn't put her into the system. What if Noni never got her back? Even when Sharon made the colossal mistake of dating Richie, Noni had been there for her. They'd been close—Sharon was her foster sister. She'd promised Sharon she'd protect Talia, and even if Noni went away, Franny and Verna would take care of the baby. "Please."

Malloy moved with purpose. "You can call her on the way to the FBI office. I told the FBI they could interview you at the safe house, but they disagreed and got all threaty. So we're off to the FBI office."

Noni stumbled as she followed him from the room. At the last second, she turned. "Thank you, Doctor."

The doctor watched with obviously curious eyes. "Any time. I meant what I said. Call me if you have any questions or concerns about the baby." Then she smiled at Malloy. "Don't get shot again, Detective."

"No promises," Malloy said dryly, moving with ease on the crutches.

Noni shook off her fear and self-doubt. "What did the doctor say about your wounds?"

"I'm fine, but I have some explaining to do with my superiors," Malloy said grimly.

"How much trouble are you in?" she whispered.

He shrugged. "Not sure. I let Denver and his brothers slip away, and it was obvious that I'd been shot before the take down. But we did just bring in an entire drug-dealing street gang, so we'll see. First things first. Let's make the FBI happy by showing up for your interview. Think of a good story, if you can."

Her story? She had a story? "All right." Her entire life she'd been a terrible liar. Wasn't it actually a felony to lie to the FBI? She recalled reading something about Martha Stewart and federal charges from lying to a federal agency. "This is so not good."

"Preaching to the choir here," Malloy agreed.

He led her through the hospital, and the police followed. Then he loaded her and the baby into the back of a nondescript brown car with a few dents in the side. "We don't have a car seat yet, but Tina is picking one up. Just, um, hold tight."

Noni winced. She was already a terrible mother. "Okay." She gently rocked Talia back and forth until the baby finally fell asleep. She called her aunt and Verna, and discovered they were only an hour away. Apparently they hadn't rushed right off to South Dakota like instructed, no doubt wanting to help get Talia back. Malloy gave her the address for the safe house, and she rattled it off. Good. They'd be with her soon.

After a quick trip to a pharmacy, they finally drove through town and ended up at a stately brick building. She allowed Malloy to assist her from the vehicle and quickly followed him into the building, through a couple of secured doors, and ultimately into a rather nice interrogation room.

She sat just as Tina poked her head in.

"Oh, what a cute baby." Tina came inside and leaned down. "My buddy at the FBI let me in since I promised to help with the baby while you're interviewed. I have a little crib thingy for her. Why don't I take her into the other room, give her the medicine, and let her sleep a little? She could probably use some food, too."

Noni looked at her new friend. She trusted Tina, but even so, it felt wrong to give up the baby. "All right." She handed her over, and Tina cooed and rubbed Talia's little face. "I really appreciate your help," Noni said.

"Of course," Tina said, her adoring gaze not leaving the baby as she left the room. "I don't know, Jamie," she murmured. "We might be ready for one of these."

Malloy paled.

Noni bit back a smile. Smiling felt inappropriate at the moment.

Footsteps approached outside the door, and then a large man with deep brown eyes and slightly darker hair came into the room. He wore a blue power suit with a green striped tie, and he moved like he could seriously...move. "Miss Yuka?" The guy slapped a manila file on the table. "I'm Special Agent Fred Reese." He pulled out a chair and took a seat. "Malloy? You can go."

Malloy snorted and dropped into a chair off to the side. "Not a chance. This is my case, and I brought you in only because of the federal charges against the Kingdom Boys gang. My witness isn't staying with you."

Reese barely smiled. "We'll see about that."

Noni shivered. The agent didn't seem like a guy she wanted to mess with. How could she explain everything without giving Denver and his brothers away? She'd have to lie, and she wasn't sure which direction to take. If crying and turning into a sobbing mess would help, she'd do it. But one look at the agent's implacable face, and she realized that wouldn't work. "So."

A scuffle sounded outside, and a huge barrel of a man lumbered in. "Questioning stops right now," he ordered, his Southern-accented voice booming.

Noni jumped in her seat, her breath catching.

"I haven't started," Agent Reese muttered.

"Good," the man roared. He had a couple of files in his hand, and he opened one to toss a piece of paper in front of Reese. "I'm Carl Symington the Fourth, attorney out of Alaska." Then he threw down another piece of paper. "I have reciprocity here in Washington." His plain brown suit had certainly been purchased at the big-and-tall store. His entire torso was just…large. No beer belly, just a lot of girth. A dark brown beard covered the lower half of his face, but his jowls still jiggled. Tinted glasses veiled what looked like deep brown eyes, and his hair was a mix of brown and gray, slicked to the side. He shambled around the table, laboriously drew out a chair, and settled his impressive bulk into it. "I represent Miss Yuka."

Noni's mouth gaped. Who in the world was this guy? The smell of pipe tobacco and mint gum wafted toward her. "Hello."

He gave her a short nod, his large head moving with effort. "Hi. Don't speak."

She blinked. "Gladly." There was something familiar about him, but she couldn't quite place him.

Reese glared at the lawyer. "All right. Let's start here. Where did your client get the three hundred thousand dollars we found in the motel?"

Noni stiffened.

Symington just calmly reached for another piece of paper to nudge across the table. "My client hired a firm called Krill Associates."

Reese leaned back. "I've heard of Krill."

Noni barely kept the surprise off her face. She opened her mouth to speak, and her lawyer shook his head. Oh yeah. Silence.

"I have no doubt," Symington murmured, handing over another paper. "Here's the agreement with signatures, and here's a trace of the cash to the corporation's account. They'd like that back as soon as possible, by the way."

Malloy leaned forward. "I haven't heard of Krill."

Reese sighed. "Krill is an international security firm that specializes in kidnap prevention and hostage release services. Usually overseas but apparently sometimes in the States." He dropped his chin and focused on Noni. "How in the world did you find them to hire?"

Symington shifted in his seat. "She posted information online, and the firm found her. They don't like street gangs kidnapping babies. I'm sure the FBI doesn't, either."

Reese studied the attorney for a moment and then took something out of his own folder. "You're telling me this guy works for Krill." He shoved a picture of Denver across the table. The picture looked like it had been taken by a security camera when he'd been in the truck driving with a gang member early that morning.

A pit formed in Noni's stomach.

Symington shrugged. "I don't know the players. Never seen that guy. If he is a Krill operative, he's long gone. You know that."

Reese's lip curled. "This guy is being sought by the law in North Carolina. Supposedly killed an owner of a boys home years ago."

"Don't know anything about that," Symington said. "Sorry." He handed over a stapled set of papers. "Here's the correspondence on the dark web about the gang, their site, and the baby exchange. You can use this to find their drug trade."

This time, Reese didn't even look down. "Right."

Noni's hands started to shake, so she set them quietly in her lap. This was crazy. Who was this lawyer guy? She scooted away from him just a little. The pipe smell was getting a little overwhelming. She cut a look at Malloy to see fire burning in the cop's eyes. He was furious. Oh, this was so not good.

Symington kept acting like nothing was amiss. "All righty, then." His accent somehow deepened.

"How did a Southern attorney end up in Alaska?" Reese asked, his gaze sharp.

Symington smiled. "My mama married a fisherman. It's the oldest story in the book."

Reese frowned so hard, lines cut into his forehead. He obviously didn't like what was happening, but there didn't seem to be much he could do about it. "I want the Krill employee, or your client is in a world of trouble."

Symington shook his massive head. "Sorry, but I have no clue where he is. He's probably already on another case, perhaps in Colombia. Krill is the international kidnapping champion, you know."

Reese slowly lowered his chin, obviously not liking the sarcasm. "Your client is going to need to cooperate if she wants to keep that baby."

Noni gasped. Wait a minute. "Hey—"

"No," Symington said smoothly. "No talking. I have the hearing tomorrow covered. This is just a threat, and quite frankly, it's beneath you, Agent Reese."

Color clashed across Reese's hard face. "If your client is impeding a federal investigation, she has much bigger worries than finding the right diaper."

Symington scratched his beard. "She's obviously cooperating with you." He shoved the second folder toward Reese. "Here is the will from the deceased mother as well as the signed form relinquishing parental rights from the father listed on the birth certificate. Oh. That's there as well. Just for your records." He turned and groaned as he stood. "Let's go, Miss Yuka. We have to prepare for tomorrow morning's hearing."

Noni flattened her hands on the table and stood. The FBI was letting her go? "Okay," she whispered.

Reese also stood. "Malloy? You're in deep shit. Tell me what's going on here."

Malloy blinked, suddenly wide-eyed. "Agent Reese, I used proper channels to create an op last night that saved a baby and shut down a dangerous drug-running gang. I think I'll survive this one."

"We'll see," the agent said grimly. "For now, I'll go through these documents and no doubt have more questions for you, Miss Yuka. At least then I'll know what exactly to ask you, and I expect you to answer for yourself. I take it you're staying in town for now?"

Malloy nodded, using his crutches to stand. "Yes."

Noni swallowed. Okay. She had to get out of there. The room swirled around her, and she shoved down the dizziness. To focus, she looked down and took several deep breaths. Her gaze caught on Symington's boots.

Boots beneath a suit?

Wait a minute. She turned and held out her hand. "Thank you for your help."

Her attorney looked at her hand and then took it, shaking gently.

The very clear ridges of a blood brother scar rubbed against her palm. Heat fired through her. She looked closer. Holy crap.

Was that Denver?

CHAPTER
23

Denver finished scouting the small apartment the cops apparently used as a safe house. It was on the third floor, so anybody wanting to infiltrate would have to climb. Or scale down.

Malloy directed his attention to a couple of uniformed cops. "Take position outside."

Noni sat in an overstuffed green chair in the small living area with a sleeping baby in her arms, her gaze wide on Denver.

He turned toward Malloy as the other cops shut the door when they left. "If you don't mind, I'd like a moment with my client."

Malloy looked at him, glanced toward Noni, looked back, and burst out in laughter. "If nothing else, you assholes never fail to bring the fun." He wiped his eyes and dropped onto a clean-looking sofa, setting his crutches to the side. "I know that Heath has the law degree, but...my guess it's Denver."

Well, hell. Denver exhaled loudly. "How did you know?"

"This ain't my first rodeo with you guys," Malloy said, losing his smile. "You just committed fraud with the FBI. How good are your documents?"

"The best," Denver said. Should he grab Noni and run now? "Krill actually exists, and we have connections to it." In fact, it was one of the businesses owned by the Gray brothers from Montana.

But Malloy didn't need that much information. "Since we're speaking freely, you and Tina need to take a vacation as you mend from the bullet wounds."

Malloy's jaw firmed. "Tina is in danger?"

Denver unbuttoned the large suit coat. "I don't know. But you're both on Madison and Cobb's radar, so you need to go under. Just until we take them down."

Malloy grabbed his nearest crutch. "You know I'm a cop, right? If these assholes are breaking the law, then I'll take them down. You have to understand that."

Denver sighed. "They're not exactly breaking the law yet, at least not that we can prove. Also, Madison has connections. Good ones."

"I don't care. We're doing this the right way," Malloy countered.

Denver struggled to remove the body suit. "You're in enough trouble."

"I'll be fine. At the end of the day, we brought down a gang," Malloy said evenly.

Denver groaned as he dropped the suit. "God, this is heavy."

"Serves you right," Malloy grumbled.

"Okay. We'll work with you. First let's take care of Noni and the baby." Denver gingerly pulled off the fake beard. He'd need it again tomorrow. "Then we'll formulate a plan." He had absolutely no problem lying to the cop. That was something he should probably be concerned about. Later. "We'll work together, Malloy."

Malloy's expression didn't change. So much for trust. "Who's the makeup artist, anyway? My guess is Heath."

"Ryker," Denver said, easing the wig off his head. "The guy has a knack for it."

Malloy's phone buzzed, and he glanced at the face. "Apparently Aunt Franny and Aunt Verna are downstairs." He sighed. "I'll have them sent up."

Denver barely kept from grimacing. "If you'll excuse me, I'll get out of the rest of this getup. Then we need to talk about the hearing tomorrow." He nodded at Malloy. "We'll need full protection not only en route but there." His gut told him Dr. Madison was about done with biding her time. She'd make a move on him soon and wouldn't care who got caught in the crosshairs. The fact that she'd been waiting at all made him want to throw up. That couldn't be good.

Malloy nodded. "Oh, you'll get it."

Denver grabbed his bag, brushed a hand across Noni's hair, and then loped into one of the two bedrooms, shutting the door. He quickly divested himself of the rest of the outfit, showered in record time, and drew on ripped jeans and an old T-shirt before booting up his laptop. After going through security measures, his screen lit up, and Ryker's face came into view.

"We clear?" Denver asked.

Concern glowed hot and bright in Ryker's eyes. "We have a problem."

Of course they had a problem. They always had a problem. Movement could be seen behind Ryker, and as Denver focused, he could see Heath rapidly packing in the background. "What's up?" Denver asked, looking for his gun in the pack.

Ryker typed in some keys. "Couple of things. First, we traced Sheriff Cobb's movements the other week when he drove to see Malloy. He came through Idaho."

Denver's breath heated, and the urge to hunt flowed through his veins. "Do we have a starting point?"

"Not yet, but I have searches running." Ryker glanced behind him. "Second, sensors and alarms are going off on the South Dakota property."

Denver stilled. The world silenced. "Where Anya and Zara are?"

Oh God. His brothers came to help him, leaving their hearts behind. "How bad?"

Ryker held up a hand. "Not sure. I've checked everything, and I can't find proof of human tampering or anybody in the vicinity. Anya and Zara are fine…and armed to the gills. Plus, there's a hell of a storm going through. But…"

Denver paused. But nothing was ever quite what it seemed. "You have to get home, Ry. Now."

Ryker nodded, his gaze torn. "I know. Heath is going now, and I'm going to cover you at the hearing and then we'll jump on a helicopter."

Denver shook his head. "No. You need to go now. Heath might be heading right into a trap. He'll need backup before I will. I have Malloy, and he's solid. His people are solid."

Ryker opened his mouth to argue. "I'm not leaving you, brother."

"I'm safe. Malloy is good backup." Denver cut him off. "The baby has an ear infection and can't fly, so we'll drive and meet you in Montana. You have to get out of South Dakota right now in case Madison has found you." The woman still had excellent resources, and they were fooling themselves if they thought they were safe while she was alive. "What about calling in reinforcements from Montana?"

Ryker sighed. "I don't know. If we've been compromised, which seems likely, then I can't lead Madison to Montana and the Gray brothers. I just can't." He bit his lip. "If this is a trap, Heath and I can handle it. If not, then we'll call them in."

This sucked. Denver scrubbed both hands down his face.

Ryker leaned in. "Listen. After the op last night, there's no way Madison and Cobb don't know where you are. They know. They're waiting to make a move."

Yeah, but they could also be making a move in South Dakota at the safe house. "I know," Denver said. "But we have to go to this hearing to clear Noni with the baby." They could manipulate and circumvent the law left and right, but at some point they needed real documents. A true history. And a situation in which the FBI wasn't hunting down their asses.

Cobb had made it difficult with the law enforcement community, but his BOLO was only from North Carolina. So far, no other agencies had really taken up the hunt. It had to stay that way. If the FBI got involved, Denver and his brothers were screwed. "Go home, Ry. I promise I've got things covered here." He started calculating a good plan in his head. It'd piss off more people than he wanted to, but he really had no choice.

Female voices sounded from the other room, and he moved farther away from the door.

Ryker's sigh was full of frustration. "I can't leave you."

"Zara needs you more than I do. I'm trained. She's not," Denver said simply. "Trust me."

Ryker's eyes darkened. "I do." He lifted his head as the sounds in the other room got stronger. "What's all that?"

"Aunts Franny and Verna are here," Denver whispered, trying not to blanch.

Ryker snorted. "Don't they hate you?"

"Yeah. Thanks for the reminder," Denver said dryly, his heart rate speeding up. He set the laptop on a rickety dresser with no knick-knacks on it. Not even a television. "Call when you get home, Ry."

Ryker's bluish green eyes sizzled. "Keep yourself safe, brother. We're too close to the end of this thing to get hurt now."

The closer they got, the more danger came for them. Denver took a moment. "Thank you," he said simply. For making them a family. For being his brother. For everything.

"You too," Ryker said, his voice dropping. "We'll make it through this."

Maybe. Maybe not. "I know. For now, I need a favor. Will you call and arrange something for me with the Montana contingent?"

Ryker sighed. "Tell me you're not going to do what I think you're going to do."

"I am. Will you help?" Denver held his breath.

Ryker waited a beat. "Of course. Always."

* * *

The shower started in the other room as Noni stood and rushed to her aunts.

Franny had long black hair liberally sprinkled with gray, and her dark eyes were a match for Noni's. She held out her arms and hugged both Noni and the baby close. "I'm so proud of you. Everything you did to find this babe." She leaned back and cupped Noni's face. "You're such a smart girl, Non."

"My turn." Verna grasped Noni and pulled her in for a hug. While Franny smelled like huckleberries, Verna always smelled like vanilla cookies. Somehow. She had a short gray bob that went perfectly with her sassy blue eyes. She cut a look to the side. "Who's the cop?"

Malloy cleared his throat. "I'm a friend."

Verna looked more directly at him. "Humph."

Noni smiled as her world finally righted itself. The baby slept soundly in her arms after her first dose of medication.

Verna took Talia with a soft smile, cooing as she went over to sit down. "Isn't she just perfect?"

Noni nodded, feeling not so alone. "She is, but she has an ear infection."

Verna took off the pretty white socks and counted each toe. "She's okay. Healthy." Looking up, tears glistened in Verna's eyes. "Thank God."

Emotion swamped Noni's chest. "I know," she whispered.

"We'll make sure she's never scared again," Verna said, setting the socks back into place.

Aunt Franny slid an arm around Noni, giving support and comfort, just like she had Noni's entire life. "So. Where's dickhead?"

Malloy barked out a laugh. "Are you ladies hungry? I can order out for some food."

"Yes," Verna said, her gaze still on the baby in her arms. "But Franny is watching her cholesterol."

Franny rolled her eyes. "She is driving me crazy with that," she stage-whispered to Noni while pulling her over to sit on the sofa. "A pizza would be great, er…"

"Detective Malloy," Noni supplied, settling against her aunt's side. "He's a good guy."

"Why is he on crutches?" Verna asked, rocking the baby back and forth.

Malloy used said crutches to stand. "I got shot." Without waiting for an answer, he headed for the door. "I'll go check the troops and order pizza. Loaded?"

"Yes," Franny answered before Verna could.

"Okay." Malloy moved outside on the crutches and then shut the door.

Franny shifted against Noni. "My turn, Vern."

Verna stood and very gently set the baby in Franny's arms. "Isn't she pretty?"

"Yes," Franny whispered. "And she checked out? Everything good?"

Noni had already reassured her several times. "Yes. The doctors were very thorough. Except for the ear infection, she's perfectly fine." Thank God. "Richie and his Kingdom Boys pals have been arrested." Well, the ones who weren't shot dead. "So it's over." But it wasn't. Not until Denver got free of Madison and Cobb. "We might need to take a little vacation for a while, though."

Franny lifted her head and narrowed her gaze. "Why?"

"Because I've put your daughter in danger," Denver said evenly from the bedroom doorway. "Maybe you two as well."

Noni jumped as all gazes swung toward him. He'd showered all the makeup off, and his dark hair curled wetly around his ears. In a dark T-shirt and faded jeans, he was the epitome of danger. His blue eyes studied them all, softening when his gaze landed on the sleeping baby. "I'll get you to safety while I take care of the threat."

At least he didn't try to ease them into the truth. Noni cleared her throat. She tried to smooth over his rough edges and calm her aunts. "There's a dangerous faction from Denver's past that now knows about us."

"So?" Franny asked just as the baby started to fuss. She raised Talia to her shoulder and patted her lower back, her movements natural and gentle. "What about us?"

"They might use you to get to me," Denver said, leaning against the doorjamb, his tone gentle. "I want to reassure you I won't let that happen."

Verna scoffed. "Listen, dickhead. We don't need your help."

Noni grimaced. Apparently her aunts weren't ready to forgive Denver.

Denver's lips twitched. "Actually, you do. I'm sorry I hurt Noni when I left. I've regretted it every second since."

Noni straightened. He regretted leaving? Or he regretted hurting her? Those were two very different things. "What are you saying?" Her voice rose.

"Oh, for pete's sake," Verna groused, her full lips pursing. "You've slept with him again."

Noni's mouth dropped open.

Franny turned her way. "You didn't. I mean, after everything, you did not." She turned a stink eye on Denver. "You're cute and all. The muscles are nice. But I just don't see it."

Heat flamed into Noni's face. "Auntie," she murmured.

Denver blushed.

The man was blushing? Actually blushing? Noni could only stare.

He eyed the door with what looked like longing. Then, drawing himself up, he moved into the room to take a seat on the only remaining chair. "Ladies, I understand you're angry, and you have every right, but we have to think about Talia and the hearing tomorrow."

Verna glanced at Franny.

Franny lowered her chin. "All right. Talk." Her voice had softened, as had her eyes.

Denver detailed the court proceeding, how they all three might need to testify, and explained what documents he'd hand to the judge.

About halfway through his explanation, Franny stood without warning and moved to hand him the baby. "Your turn."

The panic crossing Denver's face filled Noni with a glee she probably shouldn't have felt. Yet she couldn't help it.

Denver gingerly reached out and cuddled the baby, looking down at her with unease. She looked right back up as if fascinated. "I don't want to break her."

"Then don't," Franny said simply, returning to her seat on the sofa.

Denver held himself stiffly, the baby watching him. She reached up a chubby hand and slapped his chin. His eyes widened, but he didn't even twitch. She smacked him again. He laughed, the sound free and quiet, but he didn't move as if still afraid to jostle her. "She's got a good right cross."

Okay. It was absolutely adorable. Noni's ovaries actually swelled inside her. She cleared her throat and settled back against the cushion. He was trying so hard to be gentle with his huge body and hands. How could anybody not see the sweetness that lived in Denver?

"I guess he's not that bad," Franny said grudgingly.

Talia giggled, apparently in agreement.

Quieting his voice, Denver continued playing out what would happen the next day, his body naturally relaxing and starting to rock the baby. When Talia started to fuss, he instinctively stood and rocked her more, not pausing in his explanations. His big hand, so gentle, covered her entire back in absolute protection.

Yep. Noni watched him with the baby, her heart turning to goo. Game over. She wanted that with him. Long-term.

Franny watched her with sharp eyes. "Just so you know, you're sleeping on the couch tonight, Denver."

Noni's face heated.

Denver coughed. "I understand." He glanced toward the bedroom doors. "It'll give me a better protection point. Guard dog sleeps by the door."

Franny nodded smugly.

Noni cut her a sharp look, and her aunt rolled her eyes. Damn it.

CHAPTER
24

Denver lumbered out of the courtroom with Noni behind him and Malloy behind her. Franny and Verna followed along with Tina, who'd held the baby during the hearing. The hearing had been closed because of Talia's age, so he hadn't had to worry about unwelcome threats.

"I can't believe it went that smoothly," Noni said, holding the sleeping baby. "I mean, it just happened."

Actually, they'd had all the necessary documents as well as the testimony of a cop. Malloy had come through and big time. Now that it was done, the cop was safe. The paperwork was authentic.

"We're almost legal," Noni whispered to Talia again.

Denver straightened. She was right. "You have temporary custody and will need to do the actual adoption in Alaska." Heath had explained jurisdiction ad nauseam, but that was the gist of it. "So you'll need all the same documents up there. But you'll be successful." Man, sometimes things worked well in the court system when the welfare of a kid was at stake. It almost gave him faith in the system again. Almost.

The hair on the back of his neck prickled, and he looked around the hallway of the courthouse. Was he being watched? Lawyers, clients, some people just hanging out. Maybe jurors on a break. He tried to study them and find anybody out of place. They all blended.

That wasn't good.

His instincts were, though. Somebody was watching him—watching them. He had a plan to execute, and it was going to piss everyone off. But he had to get moving to get it done.

He slowed to be closer to Noni. Damn it. He had to get out of this fat suit. "Are we covered outside?" he asked Malloy quietly.

The cop apparently caught the undercurrent, because he sped up on his crutches. "We are." He gestured at two uniformed officers waiting at the front door. "We don't have all the gang members rounded up, so a protection detail was easy to obtain."

Denver kept his body between Noni and the exit. "Are you still in trouble?"

"Some but not as much. Taking down an entire gang kind of increased my worth around here." Pain cut lines across the cop's forehead.

"You need a rest, Malloy," Denver said, opening the door and scouting the outside. In fact, the cop was taking a break whether he liked it or not. Malloy's crappy car waited, guarded by two patrol cars. "Did you even take a pill?"

"No. I'll rest when this is done," Malloy said.

"I could use a rest, too," Denver said, leading the way to the vehicle. He hoped he didn't lose Malloy's friendship over this. Sucking in air, he took the baby from Noni, gave her a little kiss on her little head, and settled her in the far back car seat that Tina had picked up. Talia giggled, and his heart melted.

Who was going to kiss her knee when she fell riding a bike? Or scare off teenaged boys when she was old enough to date? Noni would do it and well, but alone? And who'd protect Noni?

He swallowed, wanting them. But he couldn't put them in danger. Couldn't get them hurt.

Noni sat next to the baby while Franny, Verna, and Tina sat in the middle. Malloy limped into the passenger side, folding his crutches, and Denver stretched into the driver's seat.

"To the safe house," Malloy said. "I've told the protective detail to wait and then follow, making sure nobody else follows us."

Denver looked around, unable to shake the feeling of being watched. His body tensed. Everybody in the car needed protection, and he had to be ready. "Somebody is out there." But hell. It could just be the FBI. They were certainly keeping an eye on him, if the two agents he'd made inside the building were indicative. He drove slowly out of the lot and started heading in the right direction. Malloy's gun was in a shoulder holster that apparently didn't bother his wounded arm. Or if it did, he didn't seem to care.

Denver calculated the distance. Oh, this was going to be ugly.

Malloy searched outside, keeping an eye on the surroundings. "I don't see anybody following us."

"Neither do I," Denver said, moving through the center of town and appreciating the Christmas lights sparkling from every storefront. The women were too quiet. He'd scared them. He had to get their minds off the danger. "Any plans for Christmas?" he asked Malloy.

Tina piped up. "We're supposed to head to Tahoe for a ski vacation, but I'm thinking that is out of the question now."

"I can ski," Malloy said stubbornly.

Denver sighed. "I like you, Malloy."

The cop partially turned, his eyebrows rising. "I'm taken."

Smart-ass. "I know." Denver drove past the mall and took a deep breath. This wasn't going to go well, but it was too late to turn back. In one smooth motion, he unholstered Malloy's gun, pointed it at him, and yanked the wheel to turn the vehicle into a parking garage.

"What the fuck?" Malloy bellowed.

Denver pressed the pedal, speeding around and around, finally ending up in a quiet corner on the fifth level. "I'm sorry." He shut off the engine, keeping the gun on the cop, meaning the words. So damn sorry.

Malloy glared. "You're gonna have to shoot me, and I don't think you will."

"What in the world are you doing?" Franny smacked him on the back of the head.

Denver winced. "Ow."

"Put that gun down right now," she snapped, pinching his ear.

Pain roared through his entire head. "Noni? Tell your aunt to let go." Did that sound like a whine? It kind of did.

Noni patted Talia's knee in the back of the SUV, her eyes wide. "What are you *doing*?"

Man, when she sounded like that, she was really mad. He couldn't explain right now, though.

Malloy reached out to grab the gun, and Denver smashed his knuckles.

"Ouch," Malloy roared, pulling back his hand.

"Denver!" Tina leaned over and pushed his shoulder. "You stop it."

This was unreal.

Suddenly, all four doors opened.

Malloy's body went rock tense. Men in ski masks and combat gear, fully loaded for war, gestured them out.

Denver slid out and then moved to assist Franny, Verna, and Tina. Their faces had gone pale, and Tina's arm trembled. "It's okay," he whispered.

It took two men to get Malloy out of the car, and it sounded like he broke one of their noses in the process. He nailed the other guy in the balls, and that guy bent over with a cry of pain.

"Malloy, stop being an asshole," Denver said, herding the women toward a nondescript van.

"Denver?" Noni called from the vehicle, starting to scramble over the seat.

He ducked as Tina aimed a pretty decent cross at his face and kept pushing her. "Stay there, sweetheart," he called out. "Keep the baby safe."

Noni instantly blocked the baby from the melee. He didn't want to scare her, but he needed her out of the way for just a couple of moments.

Verna hit him in the gut with her purse, and in that second, he'd had enough. "Everybody get in the fucking van. Whether you like it or not, you're going somewhere safe," Denver bellowed.

Three men forced Malloy, his hands bound behind his back, into the van. The words he strung together were truly inspired. Denver sighed as soon as everybody had been shoved inside. "Listen. I know this sucks, but you all need to get to safety. Noni and I will follow with Talia." If the baby could take an airplane, she and Noni would be in the van, too.

Tina looked warily at the masked men.

"They're okay," Denver said, nodding to the tallest one.

"I'm going to kill you," Malloy shouted from his seat, struggling furiously.

"I know." Denver leaned in. "Paperwork has been submitted from both you and Tina at your jobs that you've gone on vacation. It's up to you if you want to back that up with phone calls or not. If you don't, then you're putting a lot of people in danger." He turned toward Franny and Verna. "I'll keep them safe, and we'll see you soon. I promise."

All of the men except one jumped into the van. The remaining guy shut the door.

Denver's head dropped. "Thank you."

Jory Dean lifted his face mask. "Ryker called and arranged all of this. On your orders?"

"Yes," Denver said. "Please try to keep from killing Malloy."

Jory grinned. "No promises. The blue sedan over in the corner is for you. Take it."

Man, Ry had thought of everything. "We'll be along as soon as possible," Denver said.

"I have a copter waiting. We'll be in Montana within an hour," Jory said, his voice low and dark. "I could stay with you."

"No." Denver grinned at this new family he'd met just recently. "Get them safe, and we'll plan our next move."

"Fine, brother." Jory grabbed him for a hard hug.

Denver returned it, ignoring his fat suit. They weren't brothers, not really, but who the fuck cared? Why the hell not?

"Noni is pretty," Jory whispered.

Jesus. "I know." Denver released him. "Stay safe…brother."

* * *

An hour after the most bizarre kidnapping in history, Noni yanked the brush through her wet hair in a hotel on the edge of the Idaho-Montana border, more than an hour away from Coeur d'Alene. They had a small bedroom and larger living area. "I still think you made a big mistake in forcing Malloy to go with Jory." She wanted to understand, but her temper had just kept getting stronger and stronger ever since it had happened. She bit her lip to keep from swearing.

Denver nodded from where he sat on the bed, rocking the baby after having fed her a bottle. He'd already showered, and his wet hair still curled over his collar. "I had to get him out of town. Anybody who knows us could be used as bait right now."

She tried for reason, but her hold on the brush tightened. If she hit him across his stubborn head, would he understand? "You don't have the right to make that decision for everyone else."

He blinked. "I had no choice."

"No, you definitely had a choice." Sure, she would've preferred Franny and Verna go somewhere safe, but she never would've forced them to do so.

"This is my mess, Noni." He had no right to look so sexily adorable while rocking a sleeping baby.

Yep. She was going to have to hit him. Hard. After he put down her daughter. "But it's their lives. My life. You can't just tuck me away somewhere safe until you're ready to deal with me."

He stood and walked to a corner of the living area to place the sleeping baby in the portable crib. "I'm getting the feeling that you're pissed."

Oh, he did not just get sarcastic with her.

She ignored him and moved over to cover Talia with a blanket, running a finger down the baby's smooth cheek. How was it possible to love anything this much? Turning, she tried to hold on to that strong feeling. It was just as strong with him.

Denver crossed his arms, pure stubbornness firming his angled jaw.

Nope. Strong feeling gone. "You are such a dick," she whispered, keeping her voice low.

"Name calling?" His biceps flexed. "I did what I thought was right."

"You had a cop kidnapped," Noni hissed.

Talia snuffled.

Denver pressed his lips together and drew Noni toward the bedroom. She stumbled and looked over her shoulder at the baby. "She's fine," Denver whispered. "We can hear if she makes a peep."

Noni glanced toward the triple-locked door. Denver had taken back roads the entire way there, and he was sure they hadn't been followed. "Fine." It was time they had it out anyway.

He left the door open a couple of inches. "I take it you're feeling emotional."

Fire nearly blew off her head. "Are you kidding me?"

He sighed and scrubbed a hand across his eyes. "Listen. I get that you're pissed. You're also overwhelmed. We've been shot at, hauled into the FBI, and then faced a judge. Then I had your aunts kidnapped by guys in masks. You have every right to feel everything. But do we have to fight?"

She hated, *hated* that he had a point. She was overwhelmed. Not only by everything they'd gone through but also by the baby in the other room. She was a mother now. Oh, she had to get the paperwork stamped in Alaska, but it was a done deal. She felt like a mother. And she had no idea how to be one. What if she screwed up? What if Talia already had problems because of the kidnapping? Then there was Denver and her feelings for him. She couldn't even organize those into a semblance of anything that made sense. Her shoulders slumped. "I don't want to fight."

"Good." He straightened. "I'm sorry for everything I've done wrong."

But he'd do it all again, wouldn't he? She sighed. "My aunts are going to kill you."

He slowly nodded. "I know, but you'll be with them tomorrow, so you can help them plan." His slight smile was a bit too charming for fairness.

It hit her then. This might be their last night together. "You're leaving me in Montana." She had to do what was right for Talia, and being in a safe place for now was right. She got that. "To go after your enemies."

He just studied her.

She slowly shook her head. A part of her wanted to beg him not to go. To stay in Montana with her and Talia. To stay in their lives. To not put himself in danger and possibly die. Her body ached for him.

As if he could read her mind, his blue eyes darkened. "They'll never stop coming for me. For Ryker and Heath." He rocked back on his heels. "Jory and his family. None of us are safe until Madison and Cobb are stopped."

"Malloy and the FBI could help," she argued, wanting him to live. Even if it wasn't with her, she needed him to be alive out there somewhere.

"No." Denver shook his head. "I'm sorry, but they can't. Madison is too well connected, and there's no proof against either of them."

A battle like this, she didn't understand. One fought in the darkness, on the periphery of the rest of the world. Like the dark web but in real life. Most people wouldn't get it. Just how many people on earth lived in this other world? One where law and order were not what she'd been taught. She suspected more lived and worked there than she'd like.

Denver was one of them. Maybe through no fault of his own, but he navigated there freely.

"I'll miss you," she whispered, her chest aching. Miss the way he seemed to dominate everything and everyone around him without twitching a muscle. Even though he truly had ticked her off, there was a sense of safety she felt in his orbit.

His gaze darkened.

She shivered. Maybe not safety. That wasn't the right word.

"I'll miss you, too," he said quietly.

She knew then exactly why she'd wanted to fight with him. Why she'd wanted to push him over the edge—so he'd do the same thing to her. It was too difficult to be up front about what she wanted. What she needed.

If this was their last night together, she wanted it to last. He meant something to her, whether he wanted to or not. She thought she might mean something to him. It hurt to think this might be their last time. He was going to leave her in Montana the next day with her family. Maybe she'd never see him again. That thought left a hollow ache throughout her chest.

Whatever it was, they had only hours. So she moved toward him.

He uncrossed his arms.

Several steps later, and his scent washed over her. She slid her hands up his shirt and curled her fingers over his shoulders. "I guess this is good-bye, then." Levering up onto her toes, she nibbled across his mouth.

With a low growl, he wrapped his arms around her waist and took over the kiss.

CHAPTER
25

Denver was stealing time, and he knew it. They should rest. But the idea that this could be their last time, that he'd never see her again, spurred him on. He deepened the kiss as her scent wrapped around him.

There was a rawness to the kiss, to the moment, that slashed through him. How could he let her go again? The last time had nearly killed him. This time it might. Everything in him hurt at the thought. If this was good-bye, he needed to slow the hell down.

But he couldn't. He thrust his tongue into her mouth and swallowed her small moan. He kissed her, demanding more. Right or wrong, he wanted all of her. Even if it was for only one night. Nothing held back. Just them.

Her kiss was just as demanding, and he gave her everything. Every emotion he couldn't express. Every word he didn't know how to say. Every dream he'd ever secretly kept.

For the moment, it was all hers. He was all hers.

His hands swept down her body. All of her. He wanted to touch every inch and pull her even closer. The idea of life without her pierced too deeply, so he concentrated on right here and right now.

She was perfect.

From her brain to her huge heart to her sexy body. She was everything.

He lifted her shirt over her head. Her nipples tightened before his eyes. "God, you're beautiful," he murmured, planting his hand across her chest. Slowly, he slid his palm between her bare breasts, allowing his fingertips to graze those nipples.

She shuddered, and her dark eyes seemed fathomless. "Denver."

The way she said his name. He loved it. There was no better sound in the entire world.

There were promises he wanted to make. Vows. But he could guarantee only one. "You have to know. You're safe. No matter what, I'll make sure you and Talia are safe." It was all he had to give, and he'd do it. Even if something happened to him, his brothers would cover her. Always.

He lifted his hands and caressed both breasts. They filled his palms as if made just for him. Staying as gentle as he could, he removed the rest of her clothing and then backed her toward the bed. Her legs hit, and then she fell backward with a slight chuckle.

The sound. Husky. Sexy. Sensual.

His.

Then he took a second—one he would carry with him for the rest of his life—to just look at her. Her thick hair was spread out behind her in a black mass. Her eyes were even darker, mysterious and full of desire. Her cheeks were flushed, and her lips were full and red.

Alive or dead, he'd somehow keep this image of her. "I've never met anybody so perfect," he said.

Her blush deepened. "Denver." She reached out her hands in welcome. Pure welcome.

He shed his clothing, dropping it to the floor. Even so, he took another second to tune in to the outside world. To check for threats. Nothing. Good. He slid onto the bed and covered her, careful not to crush her. She was so delicate. He wanted to savor her, show her how much she meant. "I'd do anything to keep you with me."

Her lips pursed, and she ran her hands through his hair. But she didn't argue. He could tell she wanted to, wanted to tell him to stay, but she remained silent.

He kissed her again, taking her deep, memorizing her taste. "Noni."

She breathed and shifted her weight, spreading her legs so he could settle more firmly against her. Wet. She was definitely wet. He stroked her, his fingertips touching everywhere, learning every spot. She arched against him, trembling.

Tears gathered in her eyes, and he kissed them away. His body ached, his heart clutched. He couldn't stand causing her tears. She was sweet and soft and kind…and he wanted to give her everything he could. But he held himself back, pleasing her. Touching her until she moved against him, asking for more. When she moaned, it was his name on her lips.

Slowly, he entered her, kissing her deeply, his hands captured in her hair. He had to pause several times to let her adjust, and his body rioted. His cock ached with a demand so strong it pulsed in time with his rapid heartbeat. He was a guy who could control his heartbeat if he tried, but at the moment, he was subject to it. There was no slowing it down.

Even if he'd wanted to try.

She lifted her legs and clasped her ankles at his back, her nails scraping down his sides. "Please, Denver." Her soft plea nearly broke him.

He thrust inside her, and her internal walls clamped around him. His eyelids closed, and he pressed his forehead to hers, pulling out and pushing back in. God, she was perfect.

Her internal muscles gripped him, cascading around him.

"Denver?" she whispered.

He opened his eyes to see her darker ones on him. Focused. Seeing everything he was and would ever be. He increased the speed of his thrusts, diving deep, his vision nearly hazing.

Her release hit, with her entire body tightening around him almost to the point of pain.

He withdrew and hammered inside her as far as he could. The world exploded inside his head, outside his body. Pleasure swamped him, pouring through him with the most powerful release of his entire life.

He paused still inside, his forehead dropping to hers again. "God, Noni."

She went limp beneath him, and her arms fell to the side. "I know," she panted.

He rolled to the side and curved around her, his hand flattening across her thigh. "You okay?" he rumbled.

She nodded, and the back of her head caught his chin. "Sorry."

"No worries." He cuddled her close, trying to keep in the moment. "You always smell so good."

"I make lotions and potions," she murmured, her voice sleepy.

"Why is that?" He ran a hand down her arm, enjoying the softness of her pretty skin. "I know you make a good living, but I've never asked why lotions." He hadn't wanted to get too close when they'd been together before, and now he wanted nothing more. "Tell me."

She sighed. "I like creating." Her fingers played along his hand. "It's fun making up recipes—the right one for each person. And some of them have been passed down through my family. Through my people."

It was the first time he'd heard her talk about her lineage, and there was definite pride there. Love. A connection to people of the past. He wished he had that. Even a semblance of that.

But at least he had his brothers and now. That was more than he'd ever expected to have.

"Denver?" she asked quietly.

"Hmm?" He pressed a kiss to the back of her head, trying to stay in the moment.

"There's a baby in the other room I have to be strong for. Brave," she whispered.

He wanted to help her. To shield them both. He had to stay calm and focused, but his heart started to pump faster. To propel him to act. He could lose them both, and his control started to unravel. "I know."

"So I should start now. Being brave." She wiggled her butt against his groin, awakening it. "Don't answer. But I have to tell you. Just once and tonight. I love you."

Tears slammed into his eyes, and something clogged his throat. He couldn't breathe.

She snuggled closer and tucked her face into the pillow. "I just wanted you to know. Before you left." Then, with a sigh that almost sounded like relief, she fell into a peaceful sleep.

Denver held her, alternating between needing to snuggle her closer and wanting to get up and punch a wall. Life was so fucking unfair. The fact that she loved him, that she trusted him with not only her safety but her daughter's too, put her in danger. The real kind.

He dropped his face into the nook of her neck, breathing deeply. It truly didn't matter if he was ready to kill Cobb and Madison or not—he couldn't harbor any doubts. To ensure Noni and Talia's safety, he'd become the monster they'd created him to be.

The killer they'd genetically engineered.

He was in an empty classroom with the lady doctor. He still didn't know her real name, but he knew her.

"You did so well on the aptitude tests," she said smugly, sitting on the teacher's desk, a bright red high heel dangling from her foot.

He sat in the front row, his hands on the wooden desktop. A couple of pieces of gum were stuck just under the edges, and he was careful not to touch them. Outside, boys yelled in a vigorous game of kickball, and he had to force his gaze to stay away from the wall of open windows.

The smell of freshly cut grass and new summer wafted inside. He waited quietly.

She arched a dark eyebrow. "You're becoming more and more quiet, Denver. Each time I see you, you say less, and we both know you're not mute. You can speak any time you wish."

He'd never talked much, and considering Ned Cobb beat the crap out of him on a regular basis, why talk? Even the sheriff liked to get in on the fun with his nightstick. The sheriff and Ned were brothers. Now, that was a fuckin' gene pool to avoid. "Sorry," he said as she let the silence draw out.

"Are you?" she asked quietly, smoothing down her slim black skirt.

He shrugged. Not really. Silence had always been his friend.

She tugged on her white blouse, which was so pressed it had its own lines. "I, ah, I brought you something."

He tensed. In his world, presents were always bad.

She reached into a big black bag and drew out a handheld video game. "One of the other kids I study created this in his spare time. It's a rather complex spatial relations game." She held it out.

A game?

He swallowed and stood, moving around the desk and approaching her like he would a snake about to strike. When she handed over the game, he stood there, unsure where to go. What to do.

"What do you say, Denver?" she asked quietly, her blue eyes sparkling.

He glanced at the game and then up at her. "Why?"

She blinked. "Excuse me?"

"Why did you bring me a present?" His breath heated, and his stomach hurt. It didn't make sense. People didn't give him things. Ever.

A very small pink blush colored her high cheekbones. "I thought you'd like it." She smoothed her hair back from her angled face. "Do you?"

"Yes." He glanced down. Ryker and Heath would love to play with a game. He almost smiled. They'd have fun. Catching himself, he made himself meet her gaze. "Thank you very much for the present."

Pleasure lit her face. "You're very welcome."

He shuffled his feet. At ten years old, he really wasn't sure how to talk to adults. To anybody but Ryker and Heath, actually. "Why me?" he whispered. She hadn't brought gifts to Ry or Heath, and she studied them, too.

"You're special. I've told you that from the beginning." She watched him as if taking mental notes on every movement he made. "You understand that, right?"

No. There wasn't a damn thing special about him. He didn't want to lie to her, so he didn't answer.

She sighed and looked around the dismal classroom, one of several at the boys home. "I know you don't get it right now, but I have to believe someday you'll put the puzzle pieces together. It's obvious if you ask me."

He shook his head. "I saw your suitcases by the door." When she stayed there, so did the sheriff, which just meant more pain for Denver. "You're leaving."

She reached out and cupped his cheek.

His stomach revolted.

"I am leaving, but I'll be back. You and I are going to work to-gether forever, Denver. I promise." She smiled.

Denver's phone jerked him out of the dream and into the present. "What?" he whispered as he answered.

"Den? It's Ryker. We found the evidence that we've been compromised in South Dakota," Ry said, the sound of rapid movement coming over the line.

Denver sat up. "Can you get to Montana to meet us?"

"Yes. We have a clear escape that they can't trace or follow, so we're heading to Montana. We'll meet you there by tomorrow night," Ryker said tersely. "Where's your location? Jory will monitor all of us via satellite. He'll watch your area as well."

Denver gave his location. "Be careful, brother."

"Ditto. See you soon," Ryker said, hanging up.

Denver breathed in Noni's orchid scent. As soon as he got her to safety, he was going hunting. There really was no other option.

* * *

Noni jerked out of a deep sleep. Her body was pleasantly sore, and her heart ached. They'd had sex plenty of times, but last night had been different. The whole sex-versus-making-love debate now made sense. It had been more than sex.

She lifted her head and listened. Denver breathed softly at her back, his arm wrapped around her waist. Silence came from the other room. Even so, she slid from the bed.

He shifted slightly in the bed.

"Just checking on Talia," Noni whispered, tugging his T-shirt over her head. For good measure, she found clean panties and drew them on. "Go back to sleep."

His breathing deepened. It was probably exhausting planning a mass kidnapping attempt. She bit back a chuckle and tiptoed into the other room, closing the door behind her.

She switched on a small lamp and moved quietly toward the baby.

Talia gurgled, kicking out her legs.

"Oh, you're awake, are you?" Noni asked, reaching down to lift Talia to her chest. "Wonderful. A night owl." The baby snuffled into her neck, and Noni ran a gentle hand down her back, moving to the nearest chair.

There she sat and rocked the baby, turning her so they could look at each other.

"So. Guess I should tell you some things." The feeling of love nearly took the words away from her, but Noni persisted. "I don't know what I'm doing."

Talia kicked her legs again and giggled. Was that a giggle? Maybe. It was more of a gurgle. But definitely a smile. Yep that was a smile.

Noni breathed out, the feelings overwhelming her. "But I want you to know that I'll do my best. No matter what, it's you and me." She tilted her head. "And Franny and Verna."

The baby squirmed and seemed to look toward the closed bedroom door.

"Not him," Noni whispered. The baby had no clue what she was talking about, but she felt the need to say the words out loud. Just to hear them. "He's leaving." She cleared her throat, rocking gently, the words feeling like glass in her mouth. Painful and sharp. "Not all men leave, and we're not going around calling them all 'dickhead.'" She winced. That probably wasn't language she should use with her daughter. "See? I don't know what I'm doing." God forbid, Talia's first word would be *dickhead*.

Talia found her hand and stuck it in her mouth.

"I love you, baby," Noni whispered. Geez. Twice in one night. She was getting sappy. "Those are words I'll say every day." That seemed like a good plan as a mom. It was the only plan she had. Survival and love. She could do those things. "How about one day, after you earn your doctorate, you find a nice quiet banker to love? Or maybe a dentist." It'd be helpful having a dentist in the family. "Just not a renegade, rambling vigilante. Trust me. They break your heart."

Talia snuffled again.

"Not sure I'm a good example in the area of love," Noni said. "It'll be more of a 'Do as I say' situation." See? She was getting this down already. Kicking her feet out onto the table, she leaned her head back and closed her eyes. This was a pleasant way to sleep. She was just so tired.

A sound, some sort of rustle, had her eyes opening. She lifted her head.

The door to the outside burst open.

She jolted and jumped up.

Smoke filled the room.

She turned to shield the baby. Adrenaline, hotter and faster than she'd ever felt before, rushed through her veins.

Three men in all black and wearing gas masks ran inside, guns in their hands.

Denver burst through the bedroom door, buck-assed naked, fury on his face.

The nearest guy fired twice, and Denver leaped to the side and just as fast took the guy down in a hard tackle. He slid an arm around the guy's neck and something popped. The guy's neck?

The man flopped unconscious and hadn't even hit the ground completely before Denver was up and fighting the second soldier hand to hand.

Noni screamed, moving to get behind him to protect the baby.

The third guy grabbed her injured arm, yanking her toward the door. Pain shot up her bicep. Tears streamed down her face, and her throat clogged. The smoke was terrible.

Talia started wailing, her arms and legs flailing.

Noni stumbled, and the guy righted her. She turned to see Denver break the other guy's arm and then hit him hard in the gut. The guy doubled over, crying out in pain.

Noni struggled, holding the baby tight.

The soldier holding her lifted a hand and shot Denver three times. Were those darts?

He started to go down.

"Secure him," the soldier holding her yelled.

The other soldier dropped to his knee, his broken arm against his ribs. "Can't," he coughed out, blood dribbling from his mouth.

Sirens trilled in the distance. Thank God. Somebody had heard the fight and had called the cops.

Denver flopped onto the floor and tried to move closer to the guy.

The wounded soldier shoved to his feet and stumbled toward them, more blood pouring from his mouth. "Get out of here before the police arrive."

"She'll kill us," the guy holding her said.

"No choice," the second guy yelled. "Run now."

Noni struggled hard, trying to loosen his hold while still protecting Talia.

Denver growled and tried to crawl toward them. She glanced frantically at him but couldn't see blood on his body.

Fury lanced through her. She kicked the guy next to her in the knee, and he pivoted, clapping her over the ear. Pain sparked behind her eyes, flashing bright. He reached for the baby, and she fought him, all the way to the door.

With a low snarl, he ducked and lifted both her and Talia up, turning to stride into the billowing snow. She screamed louder, and he ignored her, planting her in the back of a dark SUV. She struggled to both hold Talia and push on the useless door handle, pressing her face against the cold darkened window to look for help.

The last thing she saw was Denver stumbling out the doorway, darts still in his chest. Terror screamed through her. Then he dropped to his knees and fell face-first onto the ice.

"Denver," she whispered, terror taking her. Something sharp pierced her neck and then darkness descended all around her as she slipped into unconsciousness.

CHAPTER
26

Denver woke to the sound of a person wailing. And corn nuts. Loudly crunching corn nuts. Something was also beeping.

He opened his eyes to see he was in a hospital bed. Muted lights shone down, an IV pumped liquid into his arm, and his other arm was handcuffed to the bed. His entire body felt like it had gone through a cement mixer and was still coated with heavy rocks. He could barely move. His brain seemed to be firing too slow to catch a thought.

Where was he?

"Mornin'" came from his left. "You've been out cold awhile."

He partially turned to see a country deputy complete with cowboy hat, munching on corn nuts, seated in a plastic yellow chair.

Denver blinked. "Who is screaming?"

That quickly, it cut off.

"Dead great-grandma down the hall," the deputy said, continuing to chew, his brown eyes seeming bored. "Makes folks sad."

Denver shook his head. He was supposed to be somewhere else. Everything was fuzzy, and his tongue was thick. This wasn't right. "Where's Noni?"

"Dunno." The guy had to be about thirty. He stretched his long legs out and crossed his cowboy boots at the ankle as if he had all the time in the world. "She the baby? We saw baby stuff in the hotel room."

The baby! Denver tried to sit up but his body wouldn't work. Panic rushed through him. He banged his cuffed hand on the rail. Hard. The morning fight filled his mind. Three men, dart guns, gas masks. They had worked like a superior fighting unit. Oh God.

"Doc said you had enough tranq in you to knock out a grizzly." *Munch. Munch. Munch.*

Jesus Christ. Denver barely held on to his temper. He was stuck in a fucking Stephen King novel all of a sudden. "I have to get out of here."

"Nope." The guy scratched his chin. "Sheriff Thistle is on vacation in Hawaii. Won the Elk's raffle this year, you know."

Denver blinked and tried to clear his head. There was so much to do. Where were his brothers? Could he get to a phone? The idea that Noni and Talia had been taken churned his stomach. No time for emotion. He had to think. "Listen, Deputy, ah, listen, pal."

"Barney. You can call me Barney."

"Funny." Denver shook his head and tried to move his arms. His body felt like it weighed a thousand pounds.

"Why is that funny?" The cop tilted his head to the side.

Denver paused and studied him. Was he for real? "You don't know?"

Barney shook his head. "Should I?"

Jesus. "I guess not. Listen. You can't keep me here." He had to work this guy, and now, to get free.

Thick eyebrows rose. "I kinda think we can. You were in a hotel room that was busted open, filled with tear gas, and somebody shot you full of a tranq. There's obviously a missing baby, and based on the pretty panties we found on the floor, her mama is missing, too."

Noni. Denver yanked against the cuff. They had Noni and Talia. Fucking Madison and Cobb. Those soldiers were too well trained to work for anybody else. "Maybe I got in a fight with my woman, and she plugged me full of darts. That makes her the criminal and not me. I'm the victim." He was babbling now, but he had to get free. He had to find them. Were they okay? They had to be terrified. Fury swept him, hazing his vision. "Just uncuff me."

"Nope. I'm thinkin' that's not the way to go." The cop shook the bag of nuts and then reached inside again.

The hospital was quiet now that the wailing had stopped. A quick glance toward the window confirmed it was still dark, so maybe around five in the morning? The hospital would be short staffed, and apparently this was the only guy guarding him. If Denver was going to make a move, it had to be soon. "Where am I, anyway?"

"Hospital." Barney leaned over, his brow furrowing. "You get hit on the head? The doc said he couldn't find anything but the darts in your chest. Speaking of which, you're lucky a trucker saw you outside in the snow. You should be dead from frostbite and exposure."

He wasn't sure he could die from that. Well, probably, but it would most likely take longer for him than for most people. "So the trucker called you?"

"No. The trucker called 911." The cop shook his head. "They called an ambulance and us. When I saw your face, I remembered the picture that was sent across the wires from North Carolina." His chest puffed out. "I've never caught anybody like you. You're an international fugitive."

Denver blinked. "North Carolina is in this nation." He almost felt bad planning to hurt this guy.

"Yeah. I know."

Enough chitchat. "All right, Barney. What's your plan?" The feeling was rapidly returning to Denver's legs like sharp needles poking out from his veins. He shifted them restlessly, trying to move the process along.

The cop just looked at him.

Damn it. Another five minutes, and Denver would have to make his move. If he could kick the covers off, he could swing and catch the deputy in the face. Then it'd just be a matter of taking him down to the ground and getting the keys. "This is a mistake." It'd be so much easier to just reason with the guy.

"I don't think so," the cop said. "We have your picture on the bulletin board in the office. You're wanted in North Carolina."

"I'm not wanted. The sheriff is just trying to work a case. There's no warrant," Denver said. There probably wasn't a warrant, right? Maybe Cobb hadn't issued one and had just sent person-of-interest photos around. The video hadn't specified, which was just like Cobb. It gave him plenty of wiggle room. Bastard. Heat coated Denver's throat, and his hand fisted against the cuff. He was losing it.

Barney the deputy sighed. "All I know is that I did my job. A good one. Haven't even called the sheriff in Hawaii. The guy needed a break."

Denver forced calmness through his muscles when all he wanted to do was yell. Terror poured through him, making the world finally come into sharp focus. Noni and Talia needed him. They were vulnerable and at the mercy of psychopaths. The reality of that made it hard, nearly impossible, to keep from losing his mind. But he had to stay calm. Somehow. "Come on, man. Let me out of these cuffs."

"Not a chance. I already called this in."

Denver needed Malloy and now. But fuck. He'd had Malloy kidnapped to Montana. That had seriously backfired. There was only one chance. He didn't know the guy, and he probably couldn't trust him. "I need to call Special Agent Fred Reese from the FBI."

"I hardly think that is necessary," came a low voice from the doorway.

Denver's bones chilled. He looked up and the biggest monster from his childhood stood there, blond hair cut short, blue eyes gleaming. The world narrowed to right here and right now. "Well, now, Sheriff Cobb. What a surprise," Denver said quietly.

* * *

Now that the moment had finally arrived, Elton Cobb wanted to savor it. Truth be told, he'd figured he would be full of adrenaline and already punching. But this was better. Like when he'd torn wings off butterflies as a kid. Slow and satisfactory.

The hick cop shoved to his feet, taking his time with it. When he reached his full height, Cobb had to look up. Several inches.

"Sheriff Cobb." The cop held out a hand. "Deputy Barney Acres."

Barney? Cobb stared to make sure he wasn't being made fun of. "Like Barney Fife?"

"Who?" the cop asked, frowning.

Cobb studied him. Nope. The kid's eyes were clear and earnest. "Forget it." He took the offered hand and shook. "You've done a hell of a job here, Acres. This is one dangerous fugitive."

Denver snorted from the bed.

Cobb's shoulders straightened. "Would you mind if I interviewed him before we get the paperwork going?"

Acres shook his head. "No problem. I'll head down and get some coffee." He glanced toward Denver. "You stay put." Chortling at his own joke, he left the room in a slow lope.

Cobb made a production about shutting the door and then turning the chair around to straddle it. He'd probably have to kill that young cop, but he couldn't wait to get started on Denver first. He'd figure out a way to frame Denver for the cop's death, and then he'd be in the clear. But first things first. He was going to enjoy these moments. He'd earned them. "How's the head?" He couldn't help his smile.

Denver just looked at him, no expression on his face.

Cobb had forgotten the little shit could do that. Even as a youngster, the asshole could look right through him, even while being beaten with a police baton. The kid had definitely grown into his huge feet, and any sense of looking lost or innocent was absolutely gone. A killer looked back at Cobb, and he had to concentrate to keep from moving the chair back a foot.

Denver didn't break eye contact, though the promise of death lingered in those eyes as if it just lived there daily.

Cobb swallowed. "You knew we'd end up here."

The degenerate didn't even twitch.

"I have your woman." Those words would do it.

Nothing. No movement, no color in the face, no eyes widening. The fucker didn't even blink.

"I don't think you're human," Cobb snapped. How frustrating. He'd earned this moment, damn it, and the prick would give it to him. There had to be a way to reach inside Denver's solid rock of a head and incite fear. Cobb was a man to be feared. Why wasn't Denver showing the terror he must be feeling? Cobb gritted his teeth.

The machine—the one tracking Denver's vitals—beeped slow and steady. Maybe he really *wasn't* human. Who the hell knew what Isobel Madison had done while splicing and dicing genes and crap.

Cobb rested his elbows on the back of the chair. "Have you wondered about your genetics? If Isobel put in animal genes or something crazy like that when making you in petri dishes?" The idea was kind of gross. Maybe he shouldn't let her create their own kid that way. But that was the only alternative. "I mean, you look like a pussy. Maybe you have kitty cat genes."

Actually the man looked like one of Isobel's killing machines. Denver had filled out in the years. Blankets covered his legs, but his bare chest was visible. Broad and wide. A lot of muscles. Definite strength and a history of killing.

Cobb wouldn't be scared. Not in a million years. His hands started to sweat, even while chills slid down his spine. Maybe he was coming down with something.

He forced a smile—his mean one. "Still don't talk much, huh?" Truth be told, that had always creeped him out. "That's okay." Reaching down, he pulled his favorite Smith & Wesson Survival Black camo knife from his boot. He lifted it to the light, and his dick hardened. "Isn't this a beauty?"

No change from the bed or the monitors.

Cobb looked up, tilting his head to the side. Studying the man on the bed. "This knife is sharp enough to actually peel skin from a body." His voice roughened, and he coughed to clear it. "I used it on a woman once. She was just a whore off the streets, and nobody missed her." Then he leaned in. "Don't tell Isobel. I don't think she knows." Maybe. It was possible she knew. The woman was frighteningly brilliant. His woman. "If I kill you, she's gonna be so angry with me." He looked forward to their fight. Angry makeup sex was one of their specialties.

"You're not gonna kill me, Cobb."

Cobb jumped and then tried to cover the movement by shifting his weight on the chair. "I knew I'd get you to speak again." The kid's voice had seriously deepened through the years, sounding low and rough. "I'm definitely going to kill you. And your brothers."

If anything, Denver suddenly looked bored. "She has you on a leash, and she wants us alive." He rolled his eyes, which were just as blue as they'd been decades ago. "We both know that bitch is in charge."

Cobb's head snapped up. Oh, he knew what Denver was trying to do. Even so. His blood started to pump faster. "She's occupied with your lady and the baby right now." He pushed back from the chair and stood, feeling better looking down from a higher height. "Even I got chills when I heard her plans for—what's her name, Noni?" He lowered his voice. "No plans for the baby. She's ordinary and expendable. Probably in a Dumpster right now somewhere."

Those words should've gotten a response. Yet again, Denver revealed nothing. What kind of fucking self-control did a man have in order to remain calm with those threats hurled at him?

Cobb's gut felt tight. The need, the basic urge, to plunge the knife into Denver's chest made his hand tremble. "Apparently you don't care."

No response. With just one wrist handcuffed, he was still dangerous. Oh, Cobb had trained his entire life and could take him, but it wouldn't do to be complacent. This was too important. He was smarter and stronger than Denver and his brothers. It was a fact, and it was okay he reminded himself of it. Isobel wouldn't love him if he wasn't the strongest. That was for sure.

Denver watched him. Quiet and waiting.

"Where are Ryker and Heath?" Cobb asked. He twirled the knife, getting ready to use it. Hopefully he'd get to take his time before Denver gave him the information he wanted. Then he was going to shove that knife through the killer's throat. All the way to the hilt. "Tell me where they are, and this will be quick."

"My brothers?" For the first time, Denver smiled. The look was feral.

Cobb swallowed rapidly. The younger man was cuffed securely.

One swipe of the knife, and it'd be over. No matter how strong Denver might be. "They're not your brothers."

Denver's vitals remained so steady it was a mockery. "Sure they are. Brothers are the best, right?" His eyebrows drew down. "You should know. You had one."

Fury grabbed Cobb around the throat. "You killed him."

"I surely did," Denver said easily, his smile widening. "Nearly took his head off with one swing of the bat."

Cobb's blood actually felt like icicles pumping through his veins. The jerk was lying. He hadn't been big enough to kill with a bat at that time. "We both know it was one of your brothers."

"No. Then I started him on fire with lighter fluid and gasoline and a match from the Dixie Motel in town," Denver said quietly. "You ever seen a body burn? Man, it stinks."

Cobb lost it. With a roar, he lunged toward the bed, his knife already slashing down.

CHAPTER
27

Noni's head lolled on her shoulders and she coughed. The sound woke her more. She lifted her heavy head. Were there weights on her head? She opened her eyes to darkness.

Blinking several times, she tried to grasp reality. Slowly her vision began to focus. A yellow fluorescent light in the ceiling illuminated what appeared to be a small office. She faced a paneled wall decorated with several black-and-white photographs of early airplanes.

Cold. Her entire body was freezing.

She tried to move…and couldn't. A quick glance down confirmed that zip ties secured her wrists to a leather chair. She struggled, quickly realizing that her bare ankles were tied as well. She leaned to the side to see a similar zip tie attaching her right ankle to a wooden spoke above the chair's roller. Her legs were slightly spread, and considering she wore only Denver's T-shirt and thin panties, a devastating vulnerability washed over her.

"Ah. You're awake finally." High heels clipped, and the chair was turned around. "Hello."

Noni blinked up at a woman, waiting until her vision cleared. "Dr. Madison," she murmured, recognizing the woman from the manila file she'd found in Denver's pack. "Where the hell is my daughter?" Fury and fear nearly choked Noni, but she struggled against the bindings anyway.

Madison took a couple of steps back. "My records show the adoption hasn't gone through yet. You have to finish the paperwork in Alaska."

"Wrong." Maybe the paperwork wasn't finished, but Talia was her daughter, and fierce maternal protectiveness nearly choked her. "Bring my daughter to me. Now."

"No." Madison studied her, head to toe. "You're not much to look at. What is Denver thinking?" She tapped a red nail to her very red lips.

The judgment in the woman's tone was like a wake-up slap. What a bitch. Noni looked frantically around. The office held a heavy oak desk complete with stapler, tape, and pencils. Was that a letter opener? She could use it to stab. A leather sofa was across from her. Maps and the pictures of airplanes covered the walls. An open doorway led to a wide concrete hangar housing a quiet white jet. She was in a private hangar? How long had she been unconscious? "What did you give me?"

"Just a simple sedative," Madison said, taking a seat on the sofa and crossing slim legs. She wore a heavy blue sweater over a thin pencil skirt and high-heeled boots. "It should be clearing your system now, although you've been out for quite a while."

Noni pricked up her ears. "Where. Is. Talia?"

"She's sleeping in the plane," Madison said easily, her gaze sharp. "Do what I tell you to do, and I won't toss her out into the cold."

Fear gripped Noni's heart like a fist made of pure evil. "I want to see her."

Madison arched perfectly shaped dark eyebrows. "What you want is irrelevant."

Noni shook her head, trying to concentrate. Everything still felt a little numb. "Why did you take us?" She tried to curl her toes and push away, but she couldn't get purchase on the smooth floor. "I mean, why drug Denver and take us?" It didn't make any sense.

Madison sighed. "That's a long story, and I doubt your IQ is high enough to grasp the intricate concepts. The drug was just to subdue Denver. My soldiers had orders to take him as well, but the boy lived up to his potential. Killed one and seriously injured another." She smiled, pride in her eyes. "I finished that one off for him. Rather, I ordered it done."

God, the woman was nuts. "Listen, lady. Unbind me and get me to my daughter, or I swear to God, I'm going to rip out your condescending tongue and shove it up your ass." Noni yanked against the restraints, and pain cut into her wrists. Even so, she couldn't stop fighting, struggling as hard as she could. Finally, she subsided with a hard glare toward the bitch on the sofa.

Madison shook her head. "Denver's surrogate was a free-spirited artist. Brilliant, with an impressive IQ, but a dreamer nonetheless. Apparently that created a type for him." She sighed. "I guess I should take that into account with the next generation of my creations."

Noni paused. "Denver's mom was an artist?"

"No. Just his surrogate was. We took genetic material only from the best, but babies have to cook, you know. We used women who needed money." She flicked lint off her skirt. "His maternal donor was gifted intellectually."

Noni's stomach lurched. "Is she still alive?"

"I hardly think that's any of your concern." The woman looked her over as if she would be the next one to throw into a volcano. "That boy is special even among the special. You're trash and don't belong with him. Ever."

The bitch was insane. "Wh-what about his father?" Noni asked, curious without wanting to be so. Plus, the longer she kept Madison talking, the more likely Talia would wake up and start wailing. Noni needed proof that her daughter was near. "Who was the sperm donor?"

"A soldier out of MI6, actually," Madison said, seemingly fine about chatting. "He left the British and worked for us. For the commander, who was my partner." She crossed and recrossed her legs. "Truth be told, I had a rather energetic weekend with him in Bora Bora that I still remember fondly." She pushed a stray strand of dark hair away from her smooth skin. "Before you ask, we didn't kill him. He died on a mission for us. Somewhere in Fallujah."

Noni swallowed, her chest hurting. "What about the so-called uncle? The one Denver stayed with as a kid in Colorado?"

Madison frowned and then her forehead cleared. She rubbed the still-visible lines as if remembering not to create lines in her face. "I'd forgotten about him. He was a former soldier, one who'd washed out of our program and took off with Denver." She frowned and uncrossed her legs, tapping one foot on the ground. "I made sure he was killed—violently—after we found Denver again."

"You're evil," Noni said, her voice trembling. Talia still hadn't woken. Was she really in the plane? What about her medicine? "My baby can't fly. You have to know that."

Madison shrugged. "I saw the medical records. She's been on medicine for more than a day, and frankly, if her eardrums burst, I don't care. Her only use to me is temporary."

Bile rose in Noni's throat along with fury. "I'm so going to kill you. With pain."

Movement sounded, and a soldier with several guns strapped to his body appeared in the doorway. "The airport is secure, and the pilots are ready any time. There's a storm brewing, and our window is only during the next hour."

Noni fought against the bindings. "Help me, please. Let me out."

The soldier ignored her.

Madison eyed him. "Has Sheriff Cobb reported in?" Her lips thinned into a white line, made garish by her bright red lipstick.

"Negative," the soldier said.

"Get my bag from the plane, please," Madison said, her eyes turning harder than any stone Noni had ever seen. The soldier instantly moved away from the doorway.

Noni dug deep to find calmness. She had to think clearly to save Talia. "You seem unhappy with Sheriff Cobb. Trouble in psycho-lovers-ville?"

Madison eyelids lowered slightly at the sarcasm. "If you must know, we had a very good plan that Elton apparently has dismissed. He was supposed to fetch Denver from the hospital and bring him here."

Noni stiffened, her body aching. Her toes were so cold she could barely feel them. "So where is he?"

Madison sighed, a small catlike smile playing on her full lips. "If I had to guess, and I really don't, he's trying to kill your boyfriend right now." She stomped her high-heeled boot. "He'd better *not* succeed."

* * *

Denver rolled quickly to the side, and the knife plunged into the pillow next to his head. The IV was yanked out of his vein, and he ignored the pain. Without losing momentum, he swung back and struck Cobb in the ear, hitting him with a closed fist as hard as he could. The impact echoed loudly through the hospital room.

Cobb hissed and leaned back, grabbing his ear. His eyes were swirling pools of raw hatred.

Denver kicked off the blankets. Thank God they'd at least put a hospital gown on him. He swung out for Cobb's head.

Cobb swiped down, smashing the knife hilt against Denver's knee. Pain shot through Denver's legs, attacking his nerves. Denver swung for Cobb's wrist, hitting solidly, and the knife fell to the bed.

"I'm going to kill you," Cobb said, keeping his voice low.

Good. No yelling. The cop didn't want witnesses. Denver would have to silence him before he decided to call for help. Denver tried to sit up, but his body still fought him. Whatever had been in the darts wasn't completely out of his system yet. "Why did your soldiers leave me alive?" he asked, grabbing for the knife with his free hand.

Cobb clubbed him square in the mouth and grappled for the knife. Agony spread through Denver's skull, and he struck out, dropping the knife.

"Isobel's plan involves using you on the outside," Cobb gasped, lunging and winning the knife as Denver kicked him. The kick momentum threw Cobb back against the wall, and he hit hard. Sucking in air, red flushing his pale face, he regained his balance. "My plan involves something entirely different. Mainly, you gutted and bleeding out."

"Your missus isn't going to like that." Denver pretended to sag back on the bed while wrapping his hand around the bar. He tugged. No give. "She's not exactly the forgiving sort."

Cobb straightened his denim shirt. In the blue shirt and jeans, he no longer looked like a county sheriff. Denver studied him. The guy had been working out. He even moved smoother than he had before.

"Don't tell me. She has her soldiers training you." Denver forced a wheeze into his voice. Fuck it. He might not win this fight. He struggled to get his focus back, but the ringing in his ears wouldn't stop.

"I'm training them." Cobb puffed out his chest and inched closer to the bed. "You don't sound too good."

Yeah, he still felt like shit. "How about you release this cuff and we have a fair fight?"

"I don't really care about fair." Cobb angled to the side and up toward Denver's head.

"I remember," Denver said softly. "You like hitting kids. Just like your loser of a brother did."

Cobb's nostrils flared. "My brother gave you a home. Food and a bed. And you killed him."

Denver scoffed, rage heating through him so quickly his lungs burned. "Your brother was a weak limp-dicked asshole who picked on people smaller than him just to feel better about his loser life."

Cobb snarled. "It's not going to work again."

Wasn't it? Denver was losing his own temper, and he had a good grasp. The sheriff never could control himself. "No sheriff uniform? Did she make you quit your job?" False sympathy coated his words.

"You're stalling." Cobb shifted his weight and slipped the knife into his other hand. His good hand. "Still feeling the drugs?"

Yes. Definitely. "Nope. I'm good." Yet he made himself sound breathless. "I could do this all day."

"Sorry. I can't." Cobb took another step, his gaze alert. "I need to get to your lady. Isobel should be finished with her soon...and then it's my turn." He smiled, flashing a jagged incisor Denver had never forgotten. "Isobel is going to be mad at me for killing you, and we're going to have a big fight. Then I'm going to take my aggressions out on your little bitch."

Denver smiled then, when all he wanted was to wrap his hands around Cobb's throat and squeeze. "Noni will kick your ass."

"We'll see," Cobb said almost breathlessly. "I had your brother's girl—Ryker's woman—in a cinder-block shed. She smelled like roses."

Denver bunched his muscles. "I'm aware. I also know that she got free and away from you before you could touch her. That had to hurt you."

"It did." Something gleamed in Cobb's eyes. "I had to find another woman, one off the streets in the city, and I made her scream just to get over losing Zara like that." He rubbed his dick. "But it was almost worth it. I'm ready again, and this time Noni is going to feel my blade." He closed his eyes as if savoring a treat. "I can't wait to make her scream."

The more Cobb spoke, the calmer Denver became. Dealing with the psycho as a kid had been good training for this fight. "Your brother—what did you call him? Neddy?"

Cobb stiffened and opened his eyes. "Shut up."

"That's right. Neddy." Denver's lips peeled back, and he showed his teeth. "He cried when the fire started. Did you know that?"

Cobb swallowed and his body vibrated in place. "Stop it."

"Yeah. The bat to the head didn't really kill him." A total lie. When Ry and Heath swung those bats, Ned's head had exploded like a watermelon. "After I hit him with the bat, he fell, but his eyes were still open." Denver tensed, readying himself, lying again about who'd killed Ned. "When I started the fire, I guess he didn't cry. It was more like a pig squealing."

"Fuck you." Cobb struck then, going for the throat.

Denver slid to the side and kicked out a leg.

As if he'd been expecting the move, Cobb dodged, slashing his knife down Denver's torso.

Pain exploded through Denver, and he swiped his free arm down, grabbing Cobb's wrist. Holy crap. He was losing strength and fast. His armpit to his ribs burned, and then his vision hazed.

He struggled, yanking Cobb down on top of him. A twist of Cobb's wrist, and the knife went flying across the room.

Cobb levered up and punched him in his bleeding ribs.

Denver hissed, stars detonating behind his eyes. His vision fuzzed even more. He had to gain control and now. Levering his legs around

Cobb's torso, he compressed the man's arms to his sides. Then, giving in to temptation, he wrapped his hands around Cobb's neck and squeezed.

Cobb floundered, trying to get in a punch. He made desperate grunting noises.

Denver tightened his hold. Damn it. The man wouldn't submit. Cobb managed to dig a finger into his fresh wound. Pain exploded throughout him, and only raw fury spurred him on.

Cobb stopped fighting, his chest heaving.

Denver loosened his hold just enough to let the guy breathe. "Where is Noni?" he gasped.

"Doesn't matter," Cobb growled, his face trapped against Denver's chest. Somehow Cobb shifted and dug his fingers in more.

The pain was so intense Denver nearly blacked out. He squeezed harder, fighting Cobb, until finally the sheriff went limp.

"One more time. Where is Noni?" Denver ground out.

Cobb shuddered. "Long gone—already in Coeur d'Alene. The soldiers took them to meet Isobel, and I was supposed to be there, but I came here." He snorted, the sound slurred. "She wouldn't have waited for me and is now long gone. You're too late."

"That's okay with you?"

Cobb coughed. "It's what we have. A constant battle, and when I win, it's really good."

What a nutjob. Denver choked him again until Cobb fell into unconsciousness. Blood—Denver's blood—covered them both.

God. Denver shoved him to the side and searched his pockets. No key. Figured the asshole wouldn't have a key.

Denver grabbed the bar and swung his other arm to the floor, patting for the knife. There it was. He lifted it and made quick work of the handcuff lock. It sprang free, and he shoved from the bed. His knees wobbled, but he managed to hold himself upright.

He turned, flipped Cobb around, and used the handcuff on him. "Wake up." He slapped the cop hard.

Cobb didn't wake up. His chest moved, so he was still breathing, but the psychopath was out cold.

Denver yanked off his hospital gown and pressed it to the gash along his side. Then he searched Cobb, finding a phone.

The door opened, and Denver pivoted to see the deputy walk in. The guy's eyes widened.

Denver leaped for him, taking him down in a surprise move. He grabbed the cop's big ears and smashed his head into the tile floor. Those blue eyes hazed and then his eyelids fluttered shut. "Sorry," Denver muttered, his body heaving. He dragged the cop over to the bed and used his handcuffs to secure him as well.

Time was way too short. Everything in him—*everything*—wanted to kill Cobb right then and there. He punched the wall, and plaster flew. Pain detonated in his hand.

Kill. He had to end the fucking monster.

But he might not be able to find Noni. And if he killed Cobb, he'd either have to kill the seemingly innocent deputy or have a cop know he'd committed cold-blooded murder. He couldn't do that. He couldn't run forever.

He quickly divested the deputy of his uniform. "Sorry about this too." It hurt like hell, but he forced himself into it. The boots were a perfect fit.

Then he lurched toward the door and took one last look at the former cop on the bed. "We're not done," Denver ground out. He'd deal with Cobb later and under the radar. "I promise."

CHAPTER
28

Noni tried to keep calm as she faced the crazy doctor. "No way will Denver go down easy. In fact, if I had to bet, I'd say your man is the one bleeding out right now."

"They're both my men," Madison said, her voice cultured and smooth.

Bile rose in Noni's throat, and she swallowed it down, the burn sharpening her focus.

The soldier returned and moved into the room to place what looked like a doctor's bag in front of Madison. "I want to recheck the perimeter," he said, quickly exiting.

"Where are we?" Noni whispered.

Madison looked around the small office. "Because of the snowstorm, we had to drive to the Coeur d'Alene Airport. You were out for the entire drive through the pass."

Noni opened her mouth to scream for help.

"It's a small county airport," Madison said, forestalling her. "There's nobody else around for miles. In fact, I'm having a crew plow the runway before we can even take off, and none will be the wiser."

"I'm not going anywhere with you. Get my daughter. Now." Noni tried to listen for anybody out there. The world was silent.

Madison opened her bag. "You know, unlike Elton, I'm not one for torture."

Noni gulped down air and looked frantically around. "That's nice to hear." Shouldn't Talia be awake by now?

"But I do need some answers from you." Madison took out a syringe and a vial of something pale.

Noni pressed back in her chair. "What is that?"

Madison looked up and smile. "It's a nice concoction, dear. It will encourage you to tell the truth, if it doesn't kill you."

Fear made Noni's ears ring. "Why would it ki-kill me?"

"It's my own recipe." Madison's voice turned almost singsong. "Let's say it hasn't been vetted by the FDA."

Oh God. "You can't just shoot me up with experimental drugs." Noni tried to shove her chair away. If she died, nobody would protect Talia. Oh God. This couldn't happen. "That's illegal. And crazy."

"We're way past illegal," Madison said coolly, pressing the needle into the vial and pulling the plunger to fill the syringe.

"Didn't you take some sort of an oath as a doctor?" Noni whispered. "Do no harm?"

Madison pulled out the needle and pushed the plunger; a little bit of liquid came out the top. "I believe in the bigger picture. All great scientists do. In fact, all great revolutionary figures believe in the bigger picture and not the mundane details."

Mundane? Like her life? Noni struggled again, ignoring the ties digging into her wrists. "Don't do this."

Madison stood and walked toward her, instantly inserting the needle into her vein.

Pain flared, and warmth instantly spread from the injection site. Noni swallowed rapidly, and her tongue felt thicker. "This won't work." Was she slurring?

"You know about truth serums?"

"Not really."

Madison removed the needle. "They really don't compel people to tell the truth."

"Huh?" Noni asked, her ribs feeling funny.

"Yes. They make a subject very susceptible, and they lead to the truth. But it's not what you see on television." Madison returned to her seat on the sofa and crossed her legs again.

Noni's ears grew hot. Really hot. Then her limbs went weak. But her toes finally warmed up. She giggled.

"How are you feeling, Noni?" Madison asked, her voice sounding very far away and in a tunnel.

"Good." Noni tried to kick out her feet, but they didn't move. Maybe they moved. Who was to say what moved and what didn't move? What was a move? She hummed a song from childhood.

The pretty lady on the couch leaned forward. "That's a nice song."

"Uh-huh." Her whole body felt tingly. What a lovely moment. Confusion clouded her, but she didn't much care. "Who are you?"

"I'm your aunt." The lady morphed and looked like a unicorn with sparkles.

Noni blinked. Seconds later, her aunt sat there. "Aunt Franny." So much joy whipped through her she tried to clap her hands. Did they clap? She couldn't tell. Not that it mattered. "You're so pretty."

"Thank you." Her aunt changed into Auntie Verna with green stripes through her hair.

Noni tried to nod. Did her head move? She wasn't sure. "Pretty stripes."

Aunt Verna turned back into the dark-haired lady with red lips. She stood and glided across the room, then lifted Noni's eyelids. "How are you feeling?"

"Ph-ph-phenomenal," Noni sang. A voice, way deep down, tried to tell her something. Was it another song? Maybe the world was singing and she just needed to listen. Listening was good.

"Noni? I need your help. Denver needs your help." The woman crouched down, and their faces were close together. Her face morphed in and out, wavering as if it was in a cool mirror. "You want to help Denver, right?"

Noni's head lolled. "Denver," she drawled. "So handsome." The image of his torso, bare and strong, slid across her mind. "Perfect."

"Yes. He's perfect." The lady tapped Noni's cheek. "Concentrate. Where is Denver?"

Noni bit her lip as images ran through her mind. Was Denver making snow angels? "In the snow?"

"Right." The lady patted her knee. "Very good. Where are Ryker and Heath?"

Ryker and Heath? "Denver's brothers." They were handsome, too. Where had that unicorn gone? The world needed more sparkles. "Let's get a kitty."

The woman slapped her across the face, and Noni's head flew to the side. "Ow," she said slowly. Did that hurt? It might not have hurt. What was a hurt, anyway? "No hitting." That sounded right. Aunt Franny had said that once. No hitting. Was kicking okay? Probably.

"Noni." The lady shook her arms. "Listen to me. Where is Jory?"

"Montana," Noni said automatically. "You're there, too." The lady looked like Aunt Franny again.

The lady nodded, her face in a smile. "That's good. I am there. Where is there? Where in Montana?"

"Dunno." Noni looked around. Where was she? This was weird. Was this weird? Why were colors flying through the air? So many of them. "Why don't they all sparkle?" she murmured, watching closely.

The lady sighed. "Are Ryker and Heath in Montana?"

"Dunno." Where were Ryker and Heath? Wasn't Montana close? Wait a minute. They were somewhere else. She should tell the lady. They were in a south place. Right? Weren't they in a south place?

"Have you been to Montana?" the lady asked.

"Yessss," Noni said gleefully.

The lady caught her breath, her fingernails tightening on Noni's legs. "That's good. Where in Montana?"

"To the park," Noni said, her head starting to loll. It was too heavy. She couldn't keep it on her neck any longer. "When I was sixteen." The family vacation had been so much fun. Parks were fun.

The lady slapped her face again, but she just couldn't care. Her eyelids closed. Yeah. That was better.

"Damn it." The voice came from far, far, far away. Maybe where Prince Charming lived.

Noni snorted. Prince Charming. Dude had blond hair. She liked dark hair. Like Denver's hair.

A male voice pierced her clouded mind. "We need to go now. Are we taking her with us?"

"No," said the lady. She asked more questions, and Noni may have answered. There was talking, but her brain seemed removed somehow. The lady even slapped her a few more times.

Noni didn't open her eyes.

"Sheriff Cobb said to bring the girl after you were finished with her," the man said.

What girl? There was a girl? Noni tried to open her eyes, but they wouldn't lift. Girl. Talia. Where was Talia? She had to get to her.

The lady sniffed loudly. "Elton chose to go against my wishes when he failed to bring in Denver. If he shall not cooperate, neither shall I."

Neither. What a fancy word. The lady used fancy words. Noni

breathed out, her chin hitting her chest. Tired. She was so tired. Where were the unicorns?

"What are you going to do with her, then?" the guy asked, his deep voice vibrating around in every direction.

"Oh, I have plans," the lady replied. "We'll return her to Denver in a way he'll never forget." She laughed then, her voice tinkly. "She's going to get me everything I want. Soon."

Noni frowned as darkness surrounded her. The laugh had been tinkly, but something had been off about it. "Bad laugh," she slurred. Very bad.

* * *

Denver stole a phone off the nurse's desk before exiting the hospital and quickly hot-wiring an old car sitting on the edge of the parking lot covered with snow. Hopefully it was owned by a patient who wouldn't know it was missing for a while. Gritting his teeth against the pain in his side, he drove out of the lot and turned west. Cobb had said Noni and Talia were in Coeur d'Alene. But Denver wasn't focused enough to drive through a mountain pass while it was storming.

He took the nurse's phone and dialed his brother.

"Hello?" Ryker answered the unknown number by raising his voice several octaves.

"Ry. It's Denver."

Ryker's breath rushed through the line. "Thank God. Where are you? What's going on? Your phone is off, and—"

"They have Noni and Talia." Black dots danced across his vision, and Denver shook his head to clear it. "I need help."

"We know. Jory was monitoring your area and saw it go down. We changed course and headed that way immediately. Where are you?" Ryker asked urgently.

Denver's chest heaved. His brothers were there. Of course they were there. That's what brothers did. Relief and gratitude warmed through him. For a second. Holy shit. His vision went completely black. He swerved the car over and shook his head again. The world cleared. "I think I'm going to pass out."

"Get somewhere safe," Ryker ordered. "Denver. Now."

Denver swallowed down bile, his head ringing. He took a turn into a residential area, drove around, and came out the other side. Driving several blocks, he pulled into a parking area at a fast-food restaurant. "I'm at the McDonald's in Bordertown, Idaho," he mumbled, trying to shift his weight so his ribs stopped hurting. "Might wanna bring a first-aid kit."

He cut the engine and leaned his head back on the seat. Silence surrounded him. Snow dropped onto the windshield in big fluffy flakes, soon covering it. That was good. His brothers would come. He trusted them.

Swallowing, he tried not to think about Noni and Talia. Yet his thoughts kept going to them. They had to be safe. Noni would fight to the death for that baby, and so would he. He'd give his life for either one of them. Where were they? He should've stayed and tortured Cobb, but there hadn't been time. God, his heart hurt. Was Noni still alive?

He had to find her. Digging deep, he opened his eyes. He leaned over and grabbed Cobb's phone, quickly disengaging the GPS. Maybe they could find Madison with it. Find wherever she'd taken Noni and Talia. He had believed Cobb when he said Isobel would've escaped without him. She was a snake.

His side hurt like a bitch, and the smell of his blood filled the car.

The door was suddenly wrenched open, and Ryker stood there with Heath by his side.

So much relief filled Denver he couldn't speak.

Ryker winced and bent to help him from the car. "Dude. You're bleeding all over."

Denver gritted his teeth to keep from groaning. "Need stitches." He allowed Heath to set a shoulder under his other arm. They moved through the snow to a dark green Suburban, where they put Denver in the middle seat. Heath sat next to him.

He tried to turn and smile at Anya and Zara in the far back. Their eyes were wide. "Hi. Missed you guys," he mumbled.

Zara handed over a blanket. "How bad is it?" she asked.

"Just a flesh wound," he lied, his vision going again.

Anya patted his shoulder, her gaze concerned but her voice level. "You'll be okay."

Ryker grabbed the phones from the other car and ran to get into the driver's seat, then quickly pulled out of the lot. "Where to?"

"Cobb said the soldiers took Noni and the baby to Coeur d'Alene to meet Madison," Denver said, his entire body in pain.

Ryker coughed. "Then it's a trap. Somewhere."

"Yeah, but we have no choice," Denver said, his ears ringing. And it was a shitty trap since he didn't even know where to go.

"Okay," Ryker said grimly. "Can you make it about an hour to the Coeur d'Alene safe house at the lake? We should regroup there."

Denver closed his eyes. He'd failed them. "Yeah."

"Madison isn't just sitting around here in northern Idaho," Ryker countered. "She's probably already gone from there, but at least we're headed in the right direction."

Denver couldn't think any longer.

Heath ignored them both and started unbuttoning Denver's deputy shirt. Denver didn't have the strength to fight him and it was irritating his wound, so he let his brother discard the shirt.

"Whoa," Heath said, giving a slow whistle. "Knife wound, looks like." He balled up the shirt and pressed it against the long wound. "I'll sew you right up."

Denver fought a groan and tried to ignore the sharp pain. "They have Noni and Talia. Soldiers took them," he whispered, his voice hoarse.

Ryker studied him in the rearview mirror. "We know."

"We'll get them back," Heath said, his hand firm on the wound. "Is that how you got stabbed?"

Denver wanted to hang his head, but he kept staring straight ahead. "No. Cobb stabbed me in the hospital."

Heath jerked. "Cobb? You fought with Sheriff Cobb?"

Zara gasped quietly.

"Yeah," Denver said. "I think he was there in defiance of Madison's wishes. He was there to question and then kill me."

"Is he dead?" Ryker asked tersely.

Denver flushed, his face heating and then cooling. "God, I'm sorry, but no. We were in the hospital, and there was another cop, and I couldn't kill them both." He'd let his brothers down again. Cobb had been there, and Denver had had the opening to end him.

Heath squeezed his good arm. "You did the right thing."

Ryker drove through the mountain pass to get back to the Coeur d'Alene safe house. "Agreed. You kill a cop, or you kill Cobb with a cop knowing, then we're on the run for life. When we take the fight to Madison and Cobb, we'll end them without a trace."

Denver set his head back on the seat. "I know, but I had him. In my hands. I could've ended him." Finally. He could still see the bastard's sneering face.

"You did the right thing," Ryker repeated, speeding up through the snowy forest. He held up the two phones Denver had had with him. "Can I toss these?"

Denver opened his eyes. "Toss the blue one. I stole it."

Ryker slid down his window and threw the phone into the snowy trees. "What about the other one?"

"It's Cobb's. I disabled the GPS already. Maybe I can hook it up to the laptop and somehow find where they've been."

Heath pulled the fabric away from the wound. "Ry? I'm gonna need to stitch this up now. An hour is too long to wait."

"Want me to pull over?" Ryker asked.

"No." Heath reached beneath his seat and drew out a bright red first-aid kit. "Keep going. We need to get as far away from that hotel and hospital as possible." He grasped a bottle. "This is gonna hurt, brother."

Denver leaned his head back again, shut his eyes, and lifted his arm. "Do it."

The sound of a bottle being squeezed echoed two seconds before unbelievable fire consumed Denver's rib cage. Antiseptic was a bitch. He kept perfectly still and didn't make a sound, holding his breath for a few moments. The pain ebbed, slightly, and he let his lungs relax.

Then a needle pierced his skin.

"You're doing well," Heath said, drawing the thread through.

Man, it hurt. Denver kept his body loose and allowed the pain to flow through him. It wasn't his first injury, and it wouldn't be his last.

Cobb's phone suddenly rang.

Denver's eyelids snapped open. Heath's shoulders straightened, but he kept sewing.

Ryker pressed a button on the phone. "Yeah."

A female voice said, "Is this one of my boys?"

Nausea poured through Denver's gut. Dr. Madison sounded exactly the same as she had when they were kids. God, he hated her.

Ryker glanced at him in the rearview mirror, and Denver nodded.

"What do you want, Madison?" Ryker asked.

She giggled. Not a chuckle or an educated laugh. The bitch giggled like a little girl.

Denver fought to keep from puking and looked at Heath. He'd gone a little green around the edges, but he continued to pull the thread through Denver's flesh, his hand steady as he sewed up the knife wound.

Ryker's shoulders visibly tightened. "Talk now, or I throw the phone out the window."

"You smart boys have already disabled the GPS," she said smoothly. "Elton just called in, and apparently his phone is gone. I figured my Denver was smart enough to take it."

Denver forgot all about the pain in his side. "Where are Noni and Talia?"

Madison giggled again. "If I just told you, what fun would that be?"

"I swear to God I'm going to kill you," Denver said, heat flowing through him.

She sighed. "You were such a nice mannered young man. Oh, all right. Your last location was the hospital with Elton, so I'm guessing you're still on the Idaho-Montana border."

He kept silent. They all did.

"You're about an hour away from the Coeur d'Alene Airport. They're there."

So there was the trap. She'd laid it perfectly. "Are they okay?" Denver asked, unable to help himself. His voice cracked, and his body shuddered. They had to be all right.

The line went dead.

CHAPTER
29

The drive to the small regional airport was made in record time with Ryker speeding way too fast. Denver and Heath suited up with tactical gear Ryker and Heath had brought, and as soon as Ryker pulled into the main parking lot, he did the same. The entire place was silent, and the small main building dark. Huge snowflakes continued to fall, whipped around by a wind making shrill whistles. Lights from Coeur d'Alene illuminated the sky to the south, but the immediate area was dark.

Heath gave Zara and Anya guns. "Stay in the car, and if anybody approaches, just shoot them. We'll come running."

Anya nodded, her gaze serious. "Not a problem."

Denver scanned the area for threats as he gingerly eased from the vehicle and followed Ry to the nearest hangar.

Ryker handed him a Sig, and Denver took it, carefully controlling his breathing. He'd had to put his bloody shirt back on, and it stuck to him beneath the vest. His injured side pounded in pain, but that was nothing compared to the raw panic ripping through him. Had Madison killed Noni? The crazy scientist wouldn't have just told him where to find her. Either this was a trap or he was about to get his heart sliced from his chest.

"Let me take point," Ryker said quietly.

"No." Denver leaned against the metal building and closed his eyes. "Do you guys hear anything?"

They all silenced their breathing.

He tuned in, trying to find signatures. Breathing, heartbeats, anything. All he got was the wind. Giving the signal, he moved around the building toward the rear, his gun at the ready.

Again, nothing.

When they reached the rear, he looked around. The nearest runway had been plowed. "She took them," Denver said woodenly, his gut aching. Then he looked to the south. Private hangars, quiet and still, lined the way. His breath caught. The fourth one had its wide hangar doors open. Oh God. Breaking into a run, he was barely cognizant of his brothers on his six.

"Slow down," Heath hissed. "This might be a trap."

God, Denver hoped it was a trap. If it wasn't, then Madison wanted him to find bodies. So he slowed. "Sorry."

They reached the building and fanned out outside the door. The main lights in the hangar were off, but a small light showed in the back. Was there an office?

"Let me go first," Heath said, his face grim.

Denver almost let him. "No." There was no way Noni or Talia had been killed. They were alive. There was no other option. He had to believe that or he'd lose his mind. He swept in, his footsteps silent on the smooth concrete. He scouted the area. Nothing. Giving a hand signal, he moved toward the office in the back.

The second he got close, he could smell her. Wild orchids. "Noni!" he yelled, bursting inside.

Then he stopped cold, unable to process what he was seeing. Cut zip ties were still on a chair, but it was empty. He swung around, his heart pounding. "Noni?" he whispered. "Talia?" He could still smell Noni. How long had she been gone?

Ryker looked around, his gaze hard. "There's no clue here. Why would Madison want us here?"

Heath shook his head, keeping his gaze outside the room. "Doesn't make sense unless she's just messing with us."

Denver looked at the floor, trying to focus. "Okay. Think." Normal office stuff was on the desk in the room. Tape dispenser, file folders, flight maps. No computer, though.

He leaned down, and something silver on the floor caught his eye. He grunted and grabbed a letter opener. Standing, he looked from the sharp metal object to the ripped zip ties. "Wait a minute." What if? He turned and started running for the doors, yelling for Noni, with Ryker and Heath following him. She wouldn't have just taken Talia out into the storm, would she?

Maybe. If she thought she was escaping Madison.

"They weren't at the main building," he said tersely, looking around frantically. Where would she go?

Ryker ducked his head and squinted into the swirling snow.

Denver followed his gaze past the plowed runway to a second one blanketed in snow. Was there a figure? He started to run, his boots slipping on the ice, his arms pumping. He leaped over a snowbank and then another one, finally focusing on a person farther down, barely discernible through the storm. "Noni," he yelled. Was it her?

He ducked his head and kept running, his brothers covering his back.

"Noni!" he yelled.

She turned, and her hair fanned out. Then she stopped moving, just stood in the snow.

He made it to her in seconds, grasping her up. She was wearing only a T-shirt, which was already wet. The woman felt like an icicle. "Noni?" he leaned back, his instincts flaring to the point of pain.

She blinked up at him, snow landing on her face. "Denver?" Her voice was low. Confused.

He looked around crazily. "Where's the baby? Where's Talia?"

"Huh?" Noni wavered, looking around. "What?"

He shook her and then stopped himself. "Noni. Sweetheart." He pulled her in, his heartbeat thundering in his ears. "Where's the baby, honey?" If the baby was out in the snow, he was too late. He'd never find her.

Noni swayed and clutched his vest. "Talia." She shook her head. "They, ah, took her. In a plane." Noni turned her head and looked up at the sky. "Gone."

"You're sure?" He was already picking Noni up and running back toward the vehicle, stretching his new stitches. He didn't care. If he didn't get her warm, she'd die of pneumonia. Or frostbite. Her damn feet were bare. What if he was too late? "The baby is in the plane?"

Noni dropped her head against his chest. "Yes. In the plane." She still sounded lost and bewildered.

He fought the storm to get around the building, and Ryker was already there, opening the Suburban door. Heath jumped in on the other side. Zara handed up a nonbloody blanket from the back as Ryker started the engine, and heat began pumping.

Denver held Noni on his lap, tugged off her shirt, and wrapped her in the blanket. "Baby? Talk to me."

Her head fell back, and she looked at him through hooded lids.

"Holy shit." Heath leaned over and lifted her eyelid. "What the hell did they give her?"

She was drugged. Denver took a deep breath and checked her pulse. "Slow, too slow, but steady." Whatever it was, the crap was working its way out of her system. The warmth started to permeate, because her teeth began to chatter. "Let's get out of here, Ryker."

Denver let Heath help him out of his vest so he could hold her closer and let his body warm hers.

The heaters beat heavily as Ryker drove away from the airport.

She rested her head on his shoulder. "I couldn't find her, Denver." Tears clogged her voice. "Talia. I looked everywhere, and she was gone." A sob escaped her. Then her body went limp, and she dropped into a drug-induced sleep.

Denver barely kept from losing his mind. He held her close, trying every technique he'd learned through the years to stay calm. If he'd been just ten minutes later, he would've lost her. Or if she'd fallen into a snowbank, he never would've found her. "I'm going to kill that bitch Madison," he muttered darkly. He was grateful to have Noni back, but his mind wouldn't leave Talia. Where was the baby? He kept rubbing Noni's back, trying to push warmth into her.

Heath paused, fury glittering in his gaze. "Dude," he breathed, tugging down the blanket.

"What?" Denver asked, fear gripping him again.

Heath reached up and turned on the interior light. "Her back."

Denver swallowed and slightly turned Noni over to see black marker written on her. Madison had left him a message? Fuck. He sucked in air and read the entire thing.

DENVER. YOU WANT THE BABY, AND I WANT YOU. IT'S TIME TO COME HOME. I'LL TRADE THE BABY AND LEAVE HEATH AND RYKER ALONE. IT HAS ALWAYS BEEN YOU, MY BOY. XOXO ME

* * *

Noni woke up with a gasp, her entire body feeling like somebody was pricking her with needles.

"You're all right," Denver said, his voice low and controlled.

She blinked several times and took inventory. Soft sheets. Warm male. No clothes. "Denver."

"Yeah." He held her tight, her back to his front, his body warming hers. "Are you back with me?"

That quickly, flashes from the entire night went through her head. "Where are we?"

"The cabin at the lake."

She closed her eyes as dread rolled down her to land in her stomach. "She took Talia."

"I know." He pressed a kiss to the back of her head. "I promise you, I'll get that baby back. No matter what."

Noni bit her lip and slid her feet along his calves. She was still chilled. "I can't remember everything," she whispered, her heart feeling like somebody had stabbed her. Why was everything still so hazy?

"You were drugged," he said, holding her even tighter. "If you're up to it, you can tell me everything. Anything you remember might help."

Her shoulders jolted, and she shoved against him. Panic tried to take hold of her. "We have to go find her. We can't be in bed."

He didn't relent and easily held her in place. "We don't know where to go yet, and you need rest. You have to warm up, baby."

She curled her toes, still feeling the pain. "Why am I so cold?"

"You don't remember?" His breath brushed her hair.

She blinked and tried to remember. Moments and pictures wound through her memory. "There was a unicorn."

He caressed heat into her hip. "Maybe start before that."

Good point. "I can't just lie here, Denver." There had to be something she could do.

"I have multiple searches going on right now on the Internet. I'm tracing Cobb's movements a week ago as well as those from yesterday. We have buddies in the FAA looking for the plane. There is nothing you can do right now but heal. I promise." He kept caressing her as if he couldn't stop touching her. "What you can do is tell me everything. Just tell me what happened, and maybe something will spark. Trust me."

She wasn't sure she could remember. For Talia, she'd try. "After the hotel, they gave me something. I fell asleep and woke up in the hangar with Dr. Madison, and she injected me with something else."

He stiffened and then slowly relaxed behind her. "I know. Did she tell you anything?" A fine tremor rode his hard voice.

"I didn't see Talia. Not once. Madison said she was in the plane, but I never saw her." Noni's throat clogged, and her heart curled in. "I don't know where she is."

"Madison said she has the baby, and she's telling the truth," Denver said firmly. "The baby is leverage. She's safe."

Tears gathered in Noni's eyes. "That poor baby has been leverage since she was born." God, it hurt. The fear was so real she could taste it. "What does Madison want? Why not take me?"

"Madison is crazy and wants all of us. She didn't take you because she has the baby." Denver moved Noni's hair out of the way and kissed the nape of her neck as if trying to give comfort. There was nothing sexual in his touch or kiss. It was all promise and comfort. "Seeing you in pain is supposed to motivate me," he said quietly.

Noni swallowed. "Is it?"

"Hell yes, it is," he said quietly. "Keep talking. Was there anybody else with her?"

Noni blinked and tried to remember. "There was a soldier and I guess pilots. Um, I can't remember much after she shot me full of stuff. Some weird drug. Everything turned sparkly."

"Did she ask questions?"

"I think so." Noni reached up and rubbed her aching eyes. "I think she did." It was all such a bewildering blur. "I think she asked about Ryker and Heath?" None of it was coming back. "Maybe something about Franny being in Montana?" God, had she told Madison where everybody was? "We have to warn them." She tried to move again, but her body just wouldn't cooperate.

Denver continued rubbing feeling into her arms, his movements gentle. "My brothers are here at the cabin, so even if you told her about South Dakota, it doesn't matter. Nobody is there."

Noni's breath caught. "What about Zara, and, um..."

"Anya," he murmured. "They're here as well. Everybody is safe."

She tried to focus again. It was like a blanket across her brain. Nothing. "What about Montana?"

"They've been given a heads up," Denver said, his lips near her ear. "Everyone is safe there. Not only do they have land mines and missiles, they also have escape routes that are undetectable."

Wow. That was a little crazy. She took a deep breath, surprised that even her throat felt cold. "I can't remember what I told Madison."

"All right. At what point did she untie you from the chair?" he asked, his tone soft and soothing.

Noni shook her head. "No. That's not right." It's like the entire night was one dark pit in her head. "She left me, and I rolled over to the letter opener." She coughed, her brain fuzzing. "I think I ran out trying to follow the plane." God, she felt stupid. "I was so out of it." Her chest felt like it was trapped in a vise. "Denver." His name came out on a sob.

He turned her, pressing her face into his neck and rubbing his broad hand down her back. "Let it out, baby."

She couldn't help it. While she wanted to be tough, she needed this moment. The tears started and wouldn't stop. She cried for Talia, for fear, for everyone being hunted by Madison and Cobb. She cried because she and Denver might not win.

She was cold and scared, and her daughter was lost.

In the end, she just cried.

CHAPTER
30

Denver let himself out of the bedroom quietly, noting the snow billowing around outside in the cloudy daylight. His brothers used twin laptops, typing and reading the screens while sitting on the sofa, legs extended, in front of the crackling fire.

Ryker looked up first, his bluish green eyes weary. "How is she?"

"Terrible but asleep," Denver said, moving to the fresh pot of coffee on the counter. His body still felt like it had gone through a cement mixer, and his heart hurt. There was no other way to describe it. "I'm pretty sure she told Madison about South Dakota, so we need to scrub that place."

"Already did," Heath said, tilting his head toward his screen. "Fried the entire security system and then changed all ownership documents. There's going to be a house fire in about an hour. Had to hire local muscle, but they don't know who we are, and they'll get out of there soon."

Ryker rubbed his hands down his face. "I liked that house. Too bad we have to burn it."

Denver poured himself a large mug of the thick brew. "There will be an investigation."

Heath shook his head. "These guys know what they're doing. It'll look like an accident. Faulty wires in the garage next to paint cans. And paint remover."

Denver took a big drink and grimaced at the strong taste. Ryker enjoyed his coffee in a jet-fuel type of way. "I can tell Ry made the coffee."

Heath grimaced. "No shit."

Denver took another big gulp, over the rim of his cup watching his brothers watch him. "What?"

"You okay?" Heath asked, his greenish brown gaze narrowing. "You can't be."

"Of course not," he said, gravity seeming to pull him down with more force than usual. "But she's asleep and doesn't seem to have frostbite, so I'll take the win for a second." He leaned back against the counter. "I now have no problem killing Madison, however." Sometimes even a woman needed to be killed. That one did.

Ryker leaned forward to study his screen and then settled back. "Why do you think her soldiers left you at the hotel?"

Denver shrugged. "There were only three soldiers, and I killed one and incapacitated a second, while the cops were fast to arrive. They couldn't get me as well as Noni and the baby in time with the police arriving. So she sent Cobb to take me from the hospital, and he had his own plan."

"He didn't even bring backup?" Heath asked.

"No. He wants me dead too badly," Denver said, his mind turning things over. "I think they're working against each other at the moment."

"Do they know it?" Ryker asked thoughtfully.

Denver nodded. "Madison knows it, of course. Cobb? Not sure. He probably doesn't realize she'll sacrifice him in a second to get what she wants. It's who she is."

Heath typed what looked like a set of commands. "She needs him right now, I think. She's lost the commander and several of her top soldiers lately."

That psychopath didn't need anybody. "How are the searches going?"

"Good," Ryker said. "We're hacking all traffic cams, bank cams, and security cams from the area of the hospital you were in and tying them to the shots we have of Cobb when he visited Detective Malloy in Snowville. We'll find him on one of these feeds. I just know it. That'll help us trace Madison's current base of operations sometime today."

Heath gestured toward the silent phone on the table. Cobb's phone. "The message on Noni's back has me confused. Why does she want just you?"

"I don't know," Denver said, having thought of nothing else for hours. "She's playing yet another game. I don't know what it is. Maybe she's bluffing and just trying to catch us off guard." Though she'd always treated him as special. Why? He didn't see it. He looked around. "Zara and Anya are sleeping?"

"Yeah." Ryker tilted his head toward the other bedroom. "I figured they should get rest while they can. This is about to become crazy."

Cobb's stolen phone rang.

Denver jumped. He took several deep breaths as his brothers stood and moved toward the table. "Well, shit." His body went on full alert, but he forced himself to move slowly and pick up the phone, then push the speaker button. "What?"

"Who is this?" Madison's voice came clearly over the line.

"Denver," he said without preamble.

"Did you get my gift?" she asked on a giggle.

Rage rushed through him so swiftly he could barely think. "Your gift? You mean my girlfriend half frozen in a snowbank? She hasn't woken, you crazy bitch." He had to see how much the evil doctor really knew.

"What in the world are you talking about?" Madison asked.

Denver lowered his head and tried to listen through the line. Was there any sound of a baby anywhere in the background? He couldn't tell. "Noni was half naked in the snow out on the tarmac. Did you do that?"

Silence came for a moment. "Interesting. No. I left her on the chair for you. The silly twit must've gotten loose and gone walking. In bare feet." Madison tsked through the line. "You really could do so much better, Denver."

Denver's hand tightened on the phone with enough force the screen started to crack. Heath grabbed it and placed it on the counter, his own jaw tight with what looked like raw fury. Denver cleared his throat and tried to sound unaffected. "Well, I found her in the snow, and she's still in bed trying to get warm enough. That was quite the message you wrote on her back."

Madison giggled. "I know. It was like being back in college and doing a prank."

Denver reached for the phone, fury consuming him.

Ryker walked right into him, using his body as a block. Denver fought for two seconds and then regained his fucking brain. He gave a short nod, and Ryker moved to the side. "Why the hell do you want me so badly? Why me?"

"Why you? Come on. You know you're special." Madison sounded almost gleeful.

Denver barely kept the rage out of his voice. "Special my ass. This is just another of your mind games."

"Language," she admonished. "Be polite."

Polite? His fingers curled into a fist he would've loved to plant through the nearest wall. "What *the fuck* do you want?" he hissed, his chest filling.

She sighed heavily. "Sometimes you're so blind."

Did she sound miffed? "Then enlighten me. Please."

"Stop playing games," Madison snapped. "You forget. I have the baby."

"Do you?" Denver tried to sound bored. "Not sure I believe you on that one."

Movement sounded, and then high heels clicked on concrete. The gurgle of a baby came through the line, and then the phone dinged. Denver pushed a button, and a picture of Talia appeared, her dark eyes looking up from some sort of crib.

His knees almost buckled.

The screen went black, more heels, and then silence. "Are we finished playing games?" Madison asked, her voice cool and so damn cultured.

"I'll exchange myself in a heartbeat," Denver said, shocked when his voice remained steady and calm.

Ryker shook his head.

Madison exhaled. "Why? Because you know you belong here with me? Or just for that stupid baby?" For the first time, maybe ever, her voice had risen with what sounded like emotion.

What was her problem? Denver fought down nausea. "For the baby."

"You'll pay for that," she said.

What kind of game was this? Denver pounded his closed fist against his forehead as quietly as he could. He didn't trust a thing she said. "What makes you think I won't just turn you in to the authorities for kidnapping a baby?"

"We're past that, and you can't find me. Take me off speaker. I can tell the difference."

He glanced at his brothers, and Heath gave a short nod.

Denver swallowed. He clicked the speaker button off and slowly lifted the phone to his ear. "Whatever you tell me isn't a secret."

She laughed, this time the sound low. "Haven't you wondered? Through the years?"

He blinked. His stomach clenched. "Wondered about what?" His voice broke.

"You know. You've always known," she crooned.

His lids half lowered, and he braced himself. He wiped a hand across his eyes, and it trembled. This was happening. His worst nightmare. "Say the words."

She sighed. "Fine. I'm your mother."

* * *

"You let the woman go?" Elton Cobb burst into Isobel's office, his pale face flushed a deep red.

Ah. She'd heard he'd secured transport back to Boise. She sat back in her chair and lifted her legs to the desk, crossing her ankles to reveal high-heeled red shoes. "I did. Yes."

He slammed the door and leaned back against it, impressive muscles flexing in his arms. "I told you I wanted time with her." Rage sizzled in his overly blue eyes, giving him the look of a shark circling a swimmer.

Isobel pushed her keyboard to the side and faced him directly, her heartbeat so calm she didn't need to even take a deep breath. "And I told you I wanted Denver retrieved from the hospital. It was the perfect plan." Having the local cops assist Elton in securing Denver would have put to rest the national manhunt, and then all of her boys could have just disappeared into her program. Yet Elton had disappointed her. The son of a bitch had tried to murder her son. Against her direct orders, no less. "Instead, you tried to kill him."

"The bastard killed my brother," Elton said, his hands in fists.

"Yes, I know." She barely kept from rolling her eyes. "I truly don't understand why you want a quick kill. He hurt you, thus you destroy him. You can't do that if he's dead." Why did she have to explain things in such simple terms? The commander had understood nuances. Lord, she missed him. Although he'd never known of Denver's lineage, he wouldn't have wanted the kid dead.

A vein pulsed across Elton's forehead. "Hence, the woman. I want to take my time with her and teach Denver a lesson."

Elton was completely missing the fact that if he'd killed Denver, then Denver could no longer care what happened to Noni, so torturing her wouldn't hurt Denver. "Elton, if you want to pursue your own agenda, I can't stop you." Isobel tapped her red nails on the desk. "However, I shall just pursue my own as well." She had been willing to keep Noni for Elton to play with if he'd brought in Denver. Since he hadn't, she would employ her own strategies. "This has been your choice."

"I stabbed him." Elton's eyes glittered, and his nostrils flared. "He bled like a stuck pig."

"He's fine now," Isobel said. For God's sake. She had engineered her boy to survive. A simple knife wouldn't take him out, and it was time to stop coddling the sheriff. If he wanted in, he needed to grow a pair. "I just spoke with him, and he sounded perfectly fine."

Elton shoved away from the door. "You just spoke with him."

"Yes." She tilted her head to the side, studying the bulging in that vein. Maybe she should do an MRI of him. "He stole your phone, dear."

Cobb's mouth tightened until his jaw really had to hurt. "And you've been talking to him. Did you even try to track the phone?"

She rolled her eyes, unable to stop herself. "They disconnected the GPS, and as you know, it's a satellite phone. So I can't trace it." Good thing he had muscles, because he didn't come close to having brains. Oh, there was a darkness in him that called to her, one that heightened orgasms. But really. It was time to employ strategy, not emotion. "I did, however, leave a message across Noni's back."

That earned his full attention. The vein stopped bulging. "You cut her?" His voice roughened and went breathless. A quick look confirmed his penis had hardened against his jeans.

A thrill ran through Isobel. There was that edge of his that kept a woman like her intrigued. "No. But I did use dark marker all across her bare skin."

He half lowered his lids. "You did?"

"Yes." Her smile felt a little catlike, so she softened it. "Told him he'd have to sacrifice himself."

Cobb frowned, studying her. Expressions crossed his square face—lust, satisfaction, and curiosity. "So he comes home. Back to us." His gaze narrowed, and he moved closer to the desk. "He's always been your favorite. Why?"

"He's brilliant." She waved the issue away. Knowledge was power, and she couldn't allow Elton to have any over her. He could never know she'd donated her own eggs to create Denver. "There are more experiments to do on him."

"With pain?" Elton said slowly.

"Sure. Why not?" This cat and mouse with Elton shot energy through her.

He planted his hands on the desk. "Wait a minute. You don't want me to kill Denver to avenge my brother, but you're willing to give him pain?" His head snapped up.

"Sure." She sighed and uncrossed her ankles. Her son would be able to withstand any pain or torment. Her designer heels clicked on the desk. Her nipples hardened.

Elton leaned toward her as if pulled. His brows drew down into a fierce line. "You know Heath and Ryker won't allow Denver to sacrifice himself."

"Denver is smarter than those two, and he'll figure out a way. Or we'll capture all three of them." She moved one leg far to one side, effectively spreading her legs on the desk.

Elton's gaze flared.

Yes. No undergarments. Her breathing sped up. She scooted her buttocks forward on the chair, giving him an even better view. "Understand?"

Elton didn't look back up. "Um, yeah."

"Besides, just think of the punishments I could create for Denver defying me. How badly I can make him regret running from us." Wetness instantly coated her thighs. Her boy would be back in line and training as an obedient soldier in no time. She'd break him first.

Elton's nostrils flared, and he moved around the desk, grabbing her leg and swinging her chair around. He grasped her other leg and spread her even wider, stepping between her knees and holding her ankles with his strong hands. "Your only leverage is that baby down the hall."

"I know," Isobel said, reaching for him. God, she hoped he was still angry with her. "Just imagine what I could do to break Denver for good."

Then Elton was on her.

CHAPTER
31

Noni stumbled out of the bedroom, her head still cloudy. Her toes burned even in the thick socks Denver had left on her. She lifted her nose. Coffee. There was coffee near. She was almost to the carafe when she noticed two women sitting at the table, both eating cereal. Her stride hitched. "Hi."

"Hi." The first woman had black hair and sapphire blue eyes. "I'm Zara, and this is Anya."

Anya was a stunning redhead with tired green eyes. "Morning, Noni." She pulled out a chair. "Sit."

Noni blinked and took the seat, gratefully taking the mug of coffee Zara handed over. She couldn't quite grasp a thought, so she got right to the one that made the most sense. "Where is Denver?"

Zara took a sip of her coffee. "Denver went for a run, Ryker is scouting the area outside, and Heath just jumped into the shower." She set her mug down. "For the moment, it's just us girls."

Anya patted Noni on the arm. "I'm so sorry about last night and the baby being taken. We'll get her back." Concern darkened her eyes.

Noni bit her lip to keep it from trembling. It was stunning how empty her arms felt considering she'd only had custody for a couple of days. But she'd loved that little baby from the second she was born. "I know. We have to get her back."

Zara cleared her throat and lifted her mug in the air. "On another note, welcome to the club of having been kidnapped by the psychotic Dr. Madison."

Anya snorted and lifted her mug, waiting until Noni did the same before clinking. "First of all, you weren't kidnapped by the bitch. Neither was I." She leaned in. "I was kidnapped by the Copper Killer."

Noni blinked. "The serial killer?"

"Yep. Turns out he was a soldier who worked for Dr. Madison. Unfortunately, I did end up spending a little time with that witch." Anya's pointed chin firmed.

Noni swallowed and looked toward Zara. "And you?"

The brunette lifted a shoulder. "I may have jumped into a helicopter en route to her lair."

"As it was hanging outside a second-story window," Anya said, her pink lips curving in a smile.

Zara grinned. "I had places to be."

Noni listened to the interchange, her mind spinning. Who were these women? "Are you guys spies or something?"

Zara laughed out loud. "I'm a paralegal, and Anya is a psychology professor. So close enough." She munched on her cereal for a moment. "The one good thing about Madison is that she won't give up an opportunity. She'll keep the baby safe and healthy, Noni."

Noni nodded. "I have to believe that." But she knew Madison cared little for the baby or for human life. Her obsession was with the men she'd created and them only. It didn't take a shrink to figure that one out. "Are we any closer to finding Madison?"

"Not yet." Anya pointed toward a couple of laptops on the sofa table. "They're running through data as we speak." She motioned to the cereal box. "Are you hungry?"

"No." Noni softened the refusal with a smile. "I need a phone, though. To call my aunts."

Zara shook her head. "Montana has gone dark. No calls in or out."

Noni's stomach swelled and cramped. "Because of me. Because I probably talked to Madison."

Anya poured more coffee for her. "No. Not your fault. But your aunts passed on love before it went dark. That Franny is spunky."

"Yeah, she is." Noni leaned back. "So we're dark, too? I mean, I can't check on the business?"

"We're dark as well. No Internet business," Zara confirmed. "Speaking of which, when we were still using the net freely, I checked out your site. Very cool. How did you get into making lotions and perfumes?"

Noni blew on her refreshed coffee cup as steam billowed out. "Aunt Franny had always made her own lotions, so she taught me using family recipes." She shrugged. "I guess the business later flowed from that. I miss it. Miss creating." Would she get a chance to pass on that history to Talia? She had to.

The bathroom door opened, and Heath strode out wearing dark jeans and a faded T-shirt. His gaze immediately caught hers, and he faltered. "How are you feeling?"

"Better." She sat up, conscious she hadn't even brushed her hair. Why was he looking so intently at her? "Thanks for finding me."

"Of course. Um, Denver is probably going to need to talk to you when he gets back." Heath loped across the room, all muscled grace, and his hands settled on Anya's shoulders. He leaned down and pressed a kiss to the top of her head. "Morning, beautiful."

The redhead smiled and tilted her head back for a kiss.

Noni looked away. As a couple, they were striking looking and obviously in love. What would it be like to have that security? To plan an actual future with somebody? She breathed out. Enough.

"Is the shower free?" she asked, her knees still a little wobbly as she stood and moved her chair back under the table. "Hot water might finally warm me all the way up."

Heath straightened. "Uh, yeah. But why don't you wait for Denver?"

Noni coughed. Heat filled her face. "I think I can shower by my-self." No way was she having a shower with him with everyone in the same cabin. Almost belatedly, tension caught her. Zara was look-ing at her cup, and Anya had a sympathy in her eyes that threw Noni's balance.

"What's going on?" Noni asked.

Heath's scruffy jaw firmed. "Nothin'. I just thought that maybe you'd like to wait till Denver got back. He'll need a shower as well."

Zara pushed away from the table. "Don't lie to her."

Noni's legs trembled, and she grasped the back of her chair. "What's going on? Something is. Tell me." Her voice rose on the last.

"Denver has to tell you part of it." Zara winced. "But we can tell you some. Try not to freak out." She stood and gently tucked a finger into the neck of Noni's borrowed shirt.

Noni stilled. "What the hell?"

Zara pulled. "Madison wrote a message on your back."

Noni partially turned to see dark ink down her back. Her breath heated and expanded in her lungs. Fury and fear grabbed her. "She did what?" Noni's voice shook, and she pulled away to run into the bathroom and take off the shirt. Turning around, she tried to read the message in the mirror, but it was backward.

Zara followed her and leaned against the door frame. "Denver is furious, which is why he went running. Well, one of the reasons."

"Why does that bitch want him so badly?" Noni shook her head, reality crashing around her. Vulnerability and the sense of being violated hit her sharply. She turned and jumped into the shower, turning the water on and scalding herself. "Help me get this off," she yelled.

"I've got it." Denver was suddenly in the doorway, his sweats and sweatshirt soaked with snow and perspiration. His hair was wet, and his tractioned snow boots covered in ice.

Zara quickly disappeared.

Noni let the panic sweep her and started scrubbing the areas she could reach, not caring if she scratched her skin off.

Within seconds, Denver was inside the shower with her, his hands on her wrists. "Stop."

"I can't." She struggled against him, her body feeling like ants were crawling across it. Her voice rose high with the panic. "The bitch marked me. She *marked* me. I have to get it off."

Denver pulled her against his hard body. "I've got you, Non. Deep breath. We'll get it off. Gone. I promise."

Noni closed her eyes and tried to slow her racing heart. A sob rolled from her chest. "Get it off, Denver. Please."

* * *

If Denver had been more furious in his entire life, he couldn't remember it. But he kept his hold gentle and turned Noni around, grabbing the soap and a washcloth. "I'll make sure it's all gone," he whispered, his voice soft while his hands trembled with the need to punch something. Hard. Instead, he rubbed circles across her skin with the soap and then the washrag, rinsing it out several times. The offensive ink swirled down the drain.

"Tell me it isn't permanent marker," Noni said, her voice low. Hurt.

"It isn't," he said, wiping right above the twin globes of her butt. She'd been marked because of him, and he felt that to his core. That responsibility and primordial sense of possession. She was his, and they'd hurt her because of it. But now wasn't a time for fury. Oh, that would come later. "The ink is coming right off."

Her shoulders slumped, and her head lowered. "What else did she do to me?"

His breath hitched like he'd been punched. Thank God her back was turned to him. It took several seconds for him to be able to control his voice. "Nothing, baby. I'm surprised she had time to write the message before taking off." Of course, Madison had plugged her full of drugs as well. "The message is just her messing with us." And showing Noni how fragile she was—in addition to proving to Denver what kind of havoc Madison could create. "I'm so sorry about this," he whispered.

"Not your fault," Noni said, her head lifting. "Don't for a second think this is your fault." She rubbed her feet on the tiles and warm water. "We should hurry. There's only one shower in this house."

"No hurrying." He finished with her back, making sure not one spot of ink remained. "It might be my fault." His voice broke.

She settled. "Impossible."

Right. How the hell could he explain this to her? He tuned in to the outside world to make sure it was safe. Heath and Ryker would return to the searches while Zara organized the data and Anya tried to get inside Madison's head with the notes she'd already collected. At the moment, his only job was to make sure Noni knew she was safe and had faith that they'd get the baby back. He reached for the shampoo to work through her mass of hair.

She let her head fall back into his hands. "That feels good."

Everything about her felt good around him. He wished he had the words to explain that to her, but maybe his touch could convey that. The silken threads wound around his hands, and he rinsed them off, moving next to the conditioner.

His body reacted to her, even with the stress surrounding them. It was totally inappropriate, and he tried to force need for her away. Truth be told, he could be half dead in a coma and her scent would arouse him. There was something about her—something made just for him. On a level he didn't understand, one too primal to describe, he recognized her. And he wanted her, just one more time, before he told her all of it. That he was made from evil.

"You warming up?" he asked.

"Yes," she breathed, her voice soft in the steam.

"Good." He kept his administrations gentle. This was about comfort. Period.

She turned then, her cheeks rosy. "You went for a run?"

"Yes." He washed soap off her shoulders.

Her teeth played with her full bottom lip. "Had to get away from people for a while?"

He stared into her eyes. Clear and focused. Good. "Yes."

"I'm sure you're tired of speaking and need a break." She took the soap from him and frowned at the small amount of ink still on it. Leaning over, she washed the darkness away, leaving only the white. Then she ran the bar across his upper chest.

Pleasure spread from her touch as well as how easily she read him. How well she knew him. Sometimes solitude was not only necessary but crucial for him. But he'd give that up—he'd give anything up—for her. "What happened, it is my fault." He'd force words out for her.

"No." She washed his chest and shoulders before sliding the soap down his good side. "That bandage will need to be changed."

He sucked in a breath, trying to control his body's response to her. "It is my fault." Madison had been able to read him since day one, and she knew what Noni meant to him. Fuck. She knew him. They shared genetics. She knew what marking Noni, what scaring her, would do to him. It was a psychological attack of a kind he couldn't describe, even if he wanted to try.

Noni stepped flush into him, her skin against his. With deliberate slowness, she slid the soap back onto the ledge before planting her hands on his upper chest. "Neither of us is to blame for what's happening. We're the solution, Denver." Levering up, she feathered a kiss across his lips.

Desire liquefied through him, washing over nerves. Heating them. "What are you doing?" he asked, his abdomen clenching.

She blinked away water and shook her hair away from her face. "Stealing a moment. I'm so scared. You're so angry. There's nothing we can do right this second."

He knew that. Those facts, those very same facts, are why he'd gotten into the shower with her to offer comfort. He slid a wet piece of hair away from her cheekbone, marveling at the softness of her skin. She deserved gentle and sweet, which were two things he'd never be. Especially right now. Right now he was furious and murderous. "We should go back to work," he whispered.

"To do what?" she asked, her hands sliding lower. "Watch the computer output?"

Well, yeah. She reached his dick with her soft hands, and lightning ripped down his spine. "Noni." It was a warning. His control was an illusion. "This isn't a good idea."

"I know," she said softly, the steam rising around her stunning body in an image he'd never forget. "But I don't care." Stroking him base to tip, she used both of her hands. "Take me out of here, Denver. Just for a few minutes."

At that plea, at those soft words, his control snapped.

CHAPTER
32

She'd meant to make him lose control. His mouth took hers, hard and rough. Even so, she could feel him try to remain gentle.

When he'd washed her clean, when he'd taken that ink from her body, he'd done it as a way of claiming. He tried to hide it, but she could feel his possessiveness. His absolute fury that somebody had hurt her in order to hurt him. His anger was going to get him killed, and she needed him to be clearheaded so he could survive. So they'd all survive.

More than that. After the terrifying night she'd had, after getting lost in the snow and not knowing her own name, she needed to escape.

If there was nothing they could do right now by the computers, then she'd take this moment. She'd help him and ease his pain. In doing so, she'd calm her fears, so she could plan. So they could be settled and strong.

His tongue swept inside her mouth, and he kissed her like she was the only thing holding him to the world. That quickly, she stopped thinking just to feel.

His hands gripped her, wandering everywhere, his tongue becoming demanding. Not letting her hide or hold back. She moved even closer into him, her belly cushioning the long line of his erection. He growled into her mouth, and the entire sound, the vibration, rolled down through her body to make her core clench with need. With want. With an ache only he could satisfy.

"I knew you'd come for me last night," she whispered when he finally released her mouth.

He murmured something, kissing a trail to her ear and licking down her throat. A nip to her jaw and then he moved along her sensitive neck, nipping and kissing. "Mine," he whispered, kissing her chin and then taking her mouth again.

The one word shot a pang through her heart. *Mine*. He'd never said anything like that before. Not once. Oh, it had been in his eyes. Even his touch. But never on his mouth.

His hands gripped her hair, and he partially bent her back, his kiss turning forceful. She allowed him to bend her, knowing he wouldn't let her fall.

"Need you," he muttered against her mouth.

She moaned and rubbed herself against his shaft. These emotions, this passion, it was almost too much. If they lasted a century together, it would still be like this. He'd make her want this badly. He'd get her out of her head and away from fear with just one touch. From chilled to white hot in seconds.

His fingers found her sex, and she almost fell. But he kept her upright, an arm banding around her waist, just like she'd trusted he would. He plucked at her clit and pushed two fingers inside her, forcing her to accept him.

Ecstasy rippled through her, and she let her head fall back. It felt too good. "Denver."

"You're wet for me," he rasped against her neck, his fingers moving in and out. "Already. Just for me."

She gasped and tried to push out words. "Now. God. Now."

He flipped her around, and her hands slapped the stone bench set against the wall. Firm hands gripped her hips, and he kicked her legs farther apart. The simple act rippled need through her, pulsing between her legs. She dropped her head and arched her back.

His hands flexed on her hips, and his cock nudged her open. She sucked in air. Holding her firmly, he pushed inside her, not giving her one second to adjust. Pleasure, lava hot, mixed with pain and made her moan. He kept moving, pushing, holding her until he was finally fully embedded in her to the balls.

She sucked in air, her torso panting as she took all of him. There was so much of him. "You're so big," she rasped.

He chuckled, his torso resting along her back so they touched down to their thighs. "Don't let me hurt you."

She closed her eyes at the rough plea. Didn't he get it? "You can't hurt me, Denver. Give me all of you." She wiggled her butt against his groin.

He sucked in air, his chest moving against her shoulder blades. "Slow."

"No." She widened her stance and arched her back, tilting her pelvis.

His hands tightened on her hips, leaving bruises. Then he withdrew with a gentle, torturous stroke.

She moaned and shut her eyes. He slid one hand up her side and toyed with her breast, tugging on her nipple. Showing control. He had it, and he wanted her to know it.

Biting back a sob of need, she tensed. "More."

He held her tightly, his movements slow, the drag of his cock into and out of her a slow torment. For so long. He kept her on the edge, playing with her breasts, his legs behind hers.

Her need built, hot and fast, moving like a monsoon inside her. Water and lava and electricity. There were so many feelings, and she could take them all. Somehow. Finally, she needed more. "I want you," she whispered.

His teeth clasped the shell of her ear. "You have me."

"Then let go," she said, her body shaking with the need to explode. "Just let go—all of you," she whispered into the billowing steam.

He paused as if trying to control himself. As if preparing to give her just enough.

Her eyelids flashed open, and she clenched every internal muscle she had.

He stiffened, and his dick hardened even more inside her.

Planting a hand on the wall in front of her, she pushed back and did it again, internally gripping his cock so tightly it almost hurt. His control snapped with almost an audible sound.

He pulled out and then hammered back in, fucking her hard. Faster and deeper, he pounded into her, thrusting with such power she just shut her eyes to feel. She couldn't think, she couldn't speak, she couldn't even see. *This* is what she'd wanted. What she'd needed. She could feel herself climbing, her nerves firing, and then she fell.

The orgasm hit her hard from multiple directions, and she cried out his name. Just his name. Knowing he'd keep her safe. He kept powering into her as she rode the waves, chuckling as finally she went limp.

The second she did, he grabbed her hip, angled up, and thrust inside her completely, forcing her up onto her toes. He shuddered behind her, and his teeth sank into her shoulder. She threw back her head and cried out, his orgasm throwing her into another one that came out of nowhere. For several long moments, he pulsed inside her, prolonging the sensations.

Finally, every ounce of tenseness left her, and she relaxed back in his hold.

He kissed the nape of her neck and slowly withdrew, turning her in his arms. She settled her cheek against his chest to hear his heartbeat hammering. Her body still quaked, and she gave herself a moment to calm.

He smoothed the wet hair back from her face, his large body blocking her from the spray of water. "Are you all right?"

She tilted her head back, satisfaction pouring through her. "Yes. You?"

"Yes." He leaned down and pressed a soft kiss to her mouth. "The other day. You said something."

She caught her breath. "Yeah."

"I love you, too." He slid both hands into her hair, cupping her head. "I don't know what that means for us or what's gonna happen next, but I wanted to say the words." Then he kissed her again, the gentleness from such a deadly man bringing tears to her eyes.

All too soon, the water started to chill.

She savored the moment, feeling the truth of his love. Whatever happened, she held his heart. Even though they were in danger, and even though she was scared to death, she took a moment. Just to feel something so good.

He blinked.

She caught his eyes. Somber. Scared. Sorry. "What?" she whispered.

"I know why Madison wants me back so badly." His voice cracked.

Noni stilled. All emotion fled, leaving her cold. It had to be bad. Really bad, or Denver wouldn't look like he was about to throw up. The truth hit her harder than any punch ever could. She replayed her conversation with Madison. Every word and every hint. "Wait a minute. Oh, man. She's your mother."

Denver's jaw firmed to rock, but his face remained pale. "Egg donor. She was my egg donor."

Oh God.

* * *

The homemade chili Anya made for dinner had been delicious, but it still sat in Denver's gut as the midnight hour approached. He'd worked most of the day and evening on the computer, trying to trace Cobb's movements. He was getting so damn close.

His brothers kept eyeing him, obviously lacking words. He couldn't blame them. There weren't any. Of course he'd told them the truth the second he'd learned it.

He'd finally had to force Noni to go to bed when she couldn't keep her eyes open. The woman had been drugged and then nearly frozen to death and needed sleep, whether she liked it or not. She'd tried to soothe him about his new reality, about his genetic link to Madison, and he'd let her believe he'd come to grips with it.

But there was no accepting it. Not really.

Heath had similarly talked Anya into getting some sleep since she'd been going through psychological profiles all day of pretty much everybody involved. Madison seemed to fascinate and scare her all at once. She'd gone in with Noni to leave a bedroom for anybody else who needed sleep.

Hell. They all needed some sleep.

At the moment, Zara muttered to herself over at the kitchen table, reading her many reams of color-coded notes and making sure the title search for the South Dakota property would never lead to them. Ryker was checking the outside perimeter while Heath and Denver worked the laptops.

Heath typed for a minute. "We should probably talk about this."

"What the fuck is there to say?" Denver exploded, slamming his fist onto the table with enough force to make it jump. Fury roared through him so quickly his entire head heated. "I come from pure, psychotic evil."

The front door opened, and Ryker walked inside, snow covering his jacket. He looked around, taking in the scene.

Zara hustled his way and leaned up to place a kiss on his cheek. "I'm heading to bed," she whispered, glancing over her shoulder at Denver. "I think you guys might want to have a talk."

Ryker kissed the top of her nose. "Got it." He shut the door as Zara moved into the free bedroom and then he tossed his coat onto the bench. "So."

Denver turned a glare his way. "I'm fine."

Ryker lifted a dark eyebrow and looked at Heath. "He going on about coming from the she-devil?"

Heath nodded, his eyes somber. "Yeah."

Heated blades spun through Denver's torso, and he clenched his fist again. The need to hit something was a physical burn.

Ryker crossed his arms. "You tell him we all probably come from someplace bad?"

Heath drew in air. "I was getting to that part."

"Did you tell him—"

"Knock it off." Denver grabbed the sofa cushions near his legs to keep from launching up and tackling his brother. "I'm right here."

"Yeah. You are," Ryker said, moving forward and dropping into a seat. "We're all here, and we're us. No matter what genetic material they spliced into us. We're *us*."

Denver tried to shrug off the panic engulfing him. "I think I knew," he whispered, his tone going hoarse and his throat hurting from the heat. "There were times, when she treated me differently, that I thought…"

Heath reached over and clasped his shoulder. Hard. "It doesn't matter. She doesn't matter."

But she did. She always had. "Did you know? Suspect?" He looked at his brothers.

"No," Heath said, his voice hoarse.

Ryker didn't answer.

Denver sat back. "Ry?"

Ryker's jaw stiffened. "I wondered." He scrubbed his hands over his eyes. "She treated you a little differently, and you have similar eye color and eye shape." He paled.

Denver couldn't breathe. "Why didn't you say anything?"

"Why?" Ryker's chin lowered. "Why would I?"

Good point. Denver breathed out. "She knew about Ned and the sheriff. She knew they hit us," Denver said, feeling eight years old and all alone again. How could his own mother—the person who was supposed to love him, to care—leave him with monsters? How could he come from such a monster? Yeah, he'd always been dark. But that dark? "We're nothing but an experiment to her. I'm *nothing*."

"You're my brother," Ryker said simply. "We made ourselves, Den. She has nothing to do with who we are and what we want. What we love."

Denver's arms trembled. He wanted her to hurt. To pay for everything—to regret not loving him. To regret not protecting him and his brothers. Everything inside him, all the darkness she'd given him, rose to the surface.

And a part of him, way down deep where hopefully nobody ever could see, wanted her to love him. Somehow. Guilt flushed him at that thought. He shouldn't care about her. He really shouldn't. It felt somehow disloyal to his brothers. So enough of that.

He swallowed. *Think, damn it.* "You're right," he said, focusing on his brothers and forcing himself to climb out of the pit. "We made ourselves. To survive."

Heath released him and sat back. "Exactly."

"So that's what we'll do." Determination rocketed through him. Two could play at her game.

Ryker's chin lifted. "The look on your face. I'm not sure I like it."

Even Denver's smile felt mean. "Let's see if she gives a shit at all. Let's play her."

Heath straightened. "You want to try and manipulate Madison? Really?"

Denver looked up. "I think Madison will sacrifice Cobb for the good of the organization."

Heath nodded. "Definitely." His gaze sharpened. "You have an idea?"

Denver gulped down air. "What if I show vulnerability? I mean, try to hide the fact that I'm freaked out about Noni and the baby? I've gone from being alone to having responsibilities." That was the absolute truth. But he wanted that responsibility. He wanted to protect Noni and Talia—needed to do it. But those were human emotions, and Madison didn't have those. She surely couldn't understand those.

"I don't know," Ryker said, leaning closer as if to offer support. "Madison won't fall for it. She knows you, Denver. Or she wouldn't have written on Noni's bare and very vulnerable back."

Denver frowned. "Yeah, but that could open the door for a weakness Madison could pounce on. She has to think I'm vulnerable from learning the truth."

"You are," Heath said in a low tone.

"Yeah, but we can use that," Denver said, nausea swirling through his gut. "Though she's not just going to meet me somewhere." Messing with Madison like that was a long game. Talia couldn't stay in

Madison's clutches that long. The baby wasn't safe. "There isn't time for that."

Heath rubbed his temples. "You calling Madison might still knock her off balance a little. She gave a number for when you're ready to sacrifice yourself, right?"

"At least now I understand better how I can figure Madison out," Denver said. Did genetics give him that ability? Or was it just a co-incidence?

Ryker's lips firmed. "I don't like this, but throwing her off even just a little would be good for Talia. Even that would keep the baby alive and in Madison's care."

Denver hated that those words actually made sense. "I've never been good at keeping her out of my head," he admitted. She'd treated him differently, as if there was a puzzle he needed to solve. Now he saw the whole picture, and he wanted to put his head through a wall.

"You were just a kid last time you tried," Heath countered.

"Yeah." He wasn't a kid any longer, but he sure as shit felt like one. Denver set the laptop aside and looked at Cobb's satellite phone. He was unsettled, and he wanted nothing more than to climb into bed with Noni and snuggle her close. Considering Anya was in there, he'd probably get punched by Heath if he tried. Yet he had to *do* something.

His brothers waited patiently for him to decide. Covering him. Just being with him. Yeah. They had created themselves, and they'd formed a brotherhood. Madison couldn't destroy that. Shaking out his hands, he reached for the phone and dialed the number.

"Denver," Dr. Madison said smoothly. "How is my special boy?"

He stretched out his legs and let the fire lull him. "Why didn't you ever tell me?" His chest hurt when he started talking. He was trying to out-manipulate a master, and he wasn't that good. Nobody was.

"Your IQ is in the genius range, and you needed to figure it out yourself," she said. "I'm rather disappointed you didn't."

He couldn't find it in himself to care if he disappointed her. That was good, right? He tried to focus on his role. "Why are you up?" he asked wearily. Wherever she was, it was at least midnight. "It's late."

She chuckled. "I have work to do. Why are you up?"

"Can't sleep," he said somewhat honestly. "Finding out I have a mother who didn't give a crap about me makes it hard to close my eyes."

"The crass language is beneath you," Madison said. "I cared, and I still do. That's why I want you to come home."

The words slithered around him. A dream that wasn't true. She didn't care about him and she never would, no matter how much he wished she did. His chest ached. He had to protect his brothers. They were his family. Period. He closed his eyes and leaned his head back against the sofa while his brothers remained silent. "Who was my father?"

"An MI6 soldier who died on a mission," she said easily. "Good man, thoughtful lover."

Denver heaved, and he swallowed down bile. "Did you love him?"

"No."

Okay then. This woman had always frightened him—mainly because he felt a connection to her. Now he knew why. In his darkest hours, he'd tried to figure her out with no luck. If he could do so now, maybe he could finally be free of her. "Are you capable of love?" Vulnerability washed through him like a cold bath.

"Of course. In my way." Ice clinked in a glass across the line. "You, out of all of my creations, are the one I did personally. You come from me." She swallowed something. Probably a very expensive Scotch. "You don't belong out in the world alone."

He wasn't alone. After all this time, how could she not realize that fact? Her words chilled him. She'd never understand, would she? "Let Noni have her baby, and I'll come in." He meant every word. If she'd give up the baby without a shot fired, then he'd gladly sacrifice himself. "It's simple."

"You're speaking much more freely," Madison said thoughtfully.

He blanched.

"Is it because of Noni? Are you in love?" Madison asked in her doctor voice.

He shuddered at the tone. "You think I'm capable of love?" She kind of knew him, right? Was he capable of love? Considering not only his lineage but his life? Yeah. There was a real honesty to the question.

She was silent for a moment. "No. Not really. You're incapable of being with people long term. You'll destroy any woman or child in your life because you won't be accessible to them. Then you'll leave them." She sighed. "I understand you and want to work with you."

He swallowed over a lump in his throat. The doctor had studied him since birth, and she had a pretty good grasp on him. But did she really see everything? There was no way to reach her. No way to reason with her. Worse yet, she was probably right. The idea made his entire torso hurt, and for a crappy second he felt eight years old again. Vulnerable and lost.

He was beyond fucked up. *Love* was just a pretty word for him. Reality was dark. But he couldn't let Madison win. He wouldn't.

As he thought the problem through, Heath's laptop dinged. Heath stiffened and then spun it around, his mouth gaping.

Denver read quickly. Holy shit. There she was—somewhere in the south. Heath had finally found Sheriff Cobb on traffic cams and a couple of ATM cameras located between Snowville and Boise. They knew where Cobb and Madison were located.

He had to clear his throat to sound normal. "I want that baby safe."

"Babies, babies, babies," Madison muttered. "I am happy to give this child, this ordinary child, back to her mother. All I want is you."

Denver frowned. Were there other babies Madison had taken? "What you said—about babies. What was that?"

She chuckled then, and the sound skidded over his skin like a razor blade. "Oh. You haven't put it all together." Her chuckle turned into a giggle that was freakishly odd considering her age. "Funny."

He looked at Ryker, who shook his head. "What? What have I missed?"

Madison sighed. "I'm sure the news of your parentage has caught you a little off guard. But Denver? I have a daughter. Audrey."

Denver's vision went black at the edges. He'd totally forgotten. Nate Dean, the second-oldest Gray brother, had married Audrey, who was Isobel Madison's daughter. And now she was also pregnant. They were safe up in Montana right now. "I forgot," he said, his voice so low even he could barely hear it. He had a sister. A vulnerable, pregnant, delicate sister who was still hiding from their mother.

His chest filled. Oh, he had a duty, and he'd meet it. Nobody would harm Audrey or that baby.

"Yes, well. You're going to be an uncle. Congratulations." Madison clicked something in the background. "After you come home, we'll create a plan for Audrey and the baby to live with us. I really must study that child."

Denver jolted upright.

Ryker shook his head and motioned for him to calm down.

Adrenaline flooded Denver's veins, and his focus narrowed as his emotions finally shut down. "Let me know when you want to do the swap. Me for Talia." His voice didn't even sound like him.

"Good night, Denver," she purred. "I'm looking forward to the future." She clicked off.

He stared at a satellite feed of Boise, Idaho. She was somewhere in that vicinity, and he was gonna find her. "Oh. That's going to be sooner than you think," he murmured softly. He had not only Noni and Talia to protect but his sister too. A pregnant sister he hadn't even known he had.

Yeah. It was time.

CHAPTER
33

An hour before they reached Boise, after a surprisingly excellent burger from a mom-and-pop joint, Noni settled back in the passenger seat of a truck Denver had borrowed. Okay. Stole. It was about ten years old but in good shape, and it very much needed snow tires. Heath and Anya drove a SUV while Ryker and Zara followed in another truck. Three vehicles, all stolen from the north so they hopefully wouldn't be discovered too soon in the south.

Ryker had done some switching of plates that looked way too smooth to have been his first time boosting vehicles. Plus, they'd stored all their gear—guns, knives, bulletproof vests, baby stuff, and food. Once they hit Boise, which was turning out to be a nine-hour drive from Coeur d'Alene because of the heavy snowfall, they were going off the grid.

Noni cleared her throat as the white world sped by outside. "Did I ever tell you that I have Aunt Verna's smile?"

He cut her a look. "You're biologically related to Franny, not Verna."

"Not by blood, no." She rolled her neck, wanting so badly to help him. His mouth was drawn, and from where she sat, his shoulders looked tense. "But I have her smile. She raised me, and somehow I mimic her."

He kept driving, his gaze forward. "Okay."

"You and Heath move the same way. Across a room."

He slightly tilted his head. "We do?"

"Yes." She warmed to the subject. "And you and Ryker, somehow you have the same laugh." It was slightly off-key, actually.

Denver looked her way and smiled.

Her heart stuttered.

"Thank you," he said softly before concentrating on the road again.

She relaxed. "You haven't told me about your discussion with Dr. Madison last night."

He shook his head. "She's too smart to manipulate."

Yeah. Noni had figured. "Did she say anything about Talia?" Just saying her baby's name made her heart squeeze.

"No, but she'll keep the baby safe." He switched lanes as the world became even more of a whiteout on the nearly deserted road. "Trust me."

She did. Completely. "So, um, should we talk about the shower? I mean, what you said?"

He kept his alert gaze on the storm, and his hands seemed relaxed on the steering wheel. "It's the truth. Doesn't change anything."

She gaped at him. "You still think you're not going to make it."

He frowned. "I just can't make promises. I have to make sure Talia is safe before I do anything, and I can't plan until then. Can't fight until then."

She understood putting the baby first. They both had to do that. Plus, their entire romance was first created on a lie and then full of intrigue and danger. What would they be like in an ordinary life? Could Denver even have an ordinary life? She studied his profile. In the overcast afternoon, his features were all angles and hard edges. Could he take his skills and rough history and be a family man? Was it even possible?

Or was it the rebel in him—the man who faced danger and fought with guys holding knives that intrigued her? She sighed and settled back in her seat. Maybe he was right and discussing their relationship, such that it was, right now was silly. But still. She had things to say. He cared for her, and they needed a chance together. She couldn't let go of that hope. "I don't want you to sacrifice yourself. I want us all to live through this."

"That's the goal." He still didn't turn from the road.

Yeah. Terse sentences and no help. The man had been distant and preoccupied for the entire trip. No doubt he was planning his raid, but it seemed like something more. "Why won't you tell me how you feel about having a sister?" she whispered.

He leaned over and flicked the heater to a hotter temperature. "Your seat should be heated. Do you have it on?"

"Yes," she snapped, her chest aching.

"How are you feeling? I mean, after the time in the cold?" he asked, also increasing the speed of the windshield wipers.

So he didn't want to talk. She'd learned that sometimes he needed to process before talking. Perhaps he was mulling over his conversation with Madison and just wanted to figure it out before sharing. Of course, being so understanding last time was how Noni had ended up alone and wondering where he'd gone. "I'm fine. My toes still ache a little, but I have feeling in them, so I'm not worried." Should she let him off the hook or should she push him?

"Open the laptop and bring up a map I downloaded of the Boise area, would you?" he asked.

Her shoulders tensed, but she did as he asked. "There are tons of ranches and acreage around Boise and up against the Payette River," she murmured. "How are we going to find where Dr. Madison has started to build her new compound?"

"Land records," Denver said simply. "Once we get settled at the ranch house Ryker hopefully is leasing right now, I'll hack into the local land-use organizations and trace companies that don't look quite right." He rubbed his chin and stared out at the swirling white mess outside. "Or maybe businesses that look exactly too right."

She tried not to feel isolated. They were together right now, and they were headed to get Talia. Somehow. "I want to go on the raid." Her daughter would need her.

He didn't answer.

That was kind of an answer all by itself.

"Denver?" she asked.

"No."

All right. Now he'd answered. "I don't want to go in guns blazing, but I want to be there the second you find her." Noni's arms felt useless without the baby, but explaining that would just sound crazy to somebody who wasn't a mom. And she considered herself a mom. She really did. Fear made her voice tremble. Was her baby okay? "I have to be there for her, Denver."

He switched lanes again when the potholes on the slow side got too deep. "I understand."

"I can be behind you guys but still have a gun." She had to believe they'd find Dr. Madison, so it was good to make plans for that eventuality. "I need your support in this."

He turned down the heat.

Temper and fear competed in her chest. "You're not talking to me right now."

"I'm thinking and trying to drive in conditions we shouldn't be driving in," he said calmly, not looking at her.

The roads were pretty bad, but he could still talk. Though perhaps giving him some quiet time would convince him to include her in these plans. In his thoughts. Heck. In his life. "Fine," she mumbled.

He drove for about twenty more minutes and then reached over and took her hand.

Warmth and strength instantly enveloped her, running up from her palm straight to her heart. It was a small gesture, but it was something.

Perhaps it was a start.

* * *

Denver finished hooking up the computer in the home office, more than a little impressed with the Internet connection. The four bedroom ranch was off the beaten path and surrounded by beautiful and snow-covered trees. It had been remodeled recently with comfortable furnishings and high-end appliances. "This place is great," he said to Ryker, who was standing in the doorway.

Ryker nodded. "Agreed. Even the alarm system is top-notch." He rocked back on his heels and brushed snow off his hair. "I had to use our actual Lost Bastards accounts to qualify for the lease, so those are all burned once we're done. Just a heads up."

"Got it." Denver connected the two laptops.

"Noni seems a little out of sorts. Is she okay?" Ryker asked, his eyes sober.

Denver looked up. "Yeah. This is just…a lot."

"Isn't it?" his brother asked quietly. "That baby is going to need a father, Den."

Denver's breath caught, and he sat back in the leather chair. The words punched him in the gut. He'd do anything for the innocent little one. Include walking away. "I don't know about babies. She'll need somebody who can express, you know, emotions."

Ryker rolled his eyes. "She needs somebody who protects her, defends her, and loves her. Maybe one who teaches her computer skills." He shook his head. "Everything Madison said to you the other night, let go of it now. She's a master at getting in our heads. You know that."

"Yeah, I know," Denver said. He wasn't like Madison, no matter what she said. But the future wasn't something he could worry about right now. Nothing Ryker said could change the fact that they were going to run right into hell as soon as he had a location. There was a slim chance they'd all make it out alive, and he had to cover his brothers' backs.

"Stop blaming yourself," Ryker exploded, fury darkening his high cheekbones.

Denver jerked. "I'm not."

"Yes, you fucking are." Ryker crossed his muscled arms. "You always have, and I'm done with it. We lived in hell, and we got out. Heath and I killed Ned Cobb."

"You came down to the basement to save me," Denver burst out, his body jerking. "Remember?"

"Yes." Ryker sighed. "The same as you would've had it been one of us. Ned killed that kid. He was going to kill you or one of us."

It was the truth, and Denver knew it. "How can you make promises to Zara with what we're about to do?" Ryker had gotten engaged. Ring and all. "We might not make it."

Ryker studied him. "I know. If I die, I want my ring on her finger when I go and I want her to know I loved her with everything I ever had." He wiped a hand across his jaw. "My hope is that she'll move on and find a good life for herself. Find somebody to love, because that woman is full of love. But if I'm leaving her, she's going to know the truth. That she meant everything to me."

A lump settled in Denver's throat. "Does she know that?"

"Yeah. And before we go in, I'm gonna remind her." Ryker shook his head. "Let the past go, man. We have right now and we have the future."

"That's exactly what Madison hinted at," Denver said slowly, his temples starting to thrum.

Ryker barked out a laugh. "Yeah, we also have one another. We're brothers." He held up his hand, revealing the scar line across his palm.

Heath poked his head into the room. "What's going on?"

"Just telling Denver to let go of the past and live for the now," Ryker said easily.

"Ah." Heath settled in the doorway next to Ryker. "Is he still blaming himself for our being on the run since we were kids?"

Denver frowned. Had his brothers been discussing this?

"I'm not sure," Ryker said. "Denver? Reach any conclusions?"

He studied his brothers, his chest filling. Together they were secure and strong, no matter what the world threw at them. They weren't alone. From day one, Ryker and Heath had included him as family. Then they'd all formed lives together. Even if he left this world soon, he had been loved. He'd had family, and that meant everything. "I don't blame myself any longer." If nothing else, he'd give his brothers that. His voice choked. How had he been so lucky to have found them? "Everything we've gone through has been worth it to become brothers."

Ryker's eyes darkened. "Damn straight."

"Amen to that," Heath added. "Family is all that matters."

Ryker nodded. "And that's why we're going to beat Madison. She doesn't understand that—she never has. It must drive her crazy, not truly understanding what motivates us. What she's missing in life."

Denver breathed out. "Cobb understands."

"No. He just understands revenge," Heath countered. "That's all he wants, which is why we're going to beat him as well. He and Madison don't have the same goals in this, and they're not really working together. As kids, we didn't get that. As adults, we can see how to beat them."

Maybe. But Madison's troops were well trained. It didn't take understanding or awareness to pull a trigger, and that was the unfortunate truth. Denver had to come up with a way for everyone to survive. "I understand what you're saying. How about I finish up with the Internet searches here, and then we have dinner and plan?"

"Sounds good." Heath pivoted and disappeared, no doubt going to look for Anya.

Ryker pushed off the door frame. "As soon as you have a location, we'll need to let the Montana contingent know. The more backup we have with this, the better."

"Agreed." For a full-blown fight against Madison and Cobb, they needed the Montana brothers. Denver returned to uncoiling some wires as both screens flashed land searches in rapid succession. When he looked up again, Ryker was gone.

Denver sat back, his mind spinning the entire conversation over. He didn't have a right to keep himself from Noni in an effort to protect her in case he got his head blown off. Letting go of the past hurt in an odd way, maybe because it had been with him for so long—the guilt and the fear. Now that the time had come, he was ready and oddly calm. No fear. No guilt. Just determination.

Feelings for Noni, full and deep, welled up inside him. He couldn't keep himself from her any longer. No matter what happened, he had to let her know how much she meant to him. She was everything to him, and she deserved to know it.

The left screen caught his eye, and he leaned forward, reading the text. A drumming sounded in his head. Grabbing the keyboard, he typed in a series of commands, reading each result with his breath heating. A fifty-acre parcel, purchased five years previous, stopped his typing. Noting the location, he hacked into satellite maps and scrolled through the last five years, looking for changes. For additions. A building. Then two more. Then large metal shops. And fencing. Then odd changes to the landscape. Finally...what looked like a training field.

Ryker appeared in the doorway again. "Hey. Dinner will be ready in a couple of hours. Homemade stew in a Crock-Pot."

Denver took a deep breath and looked up at his brother. He could barely breathe. "I've found them."

CHAPTER
34

After dinner of a truly delicious stew, Noni finished filling the clip of yet another gun—this one a 9 millimeter. Well, what she thought was a 9 millimeter. After a while the guns all looked the same. She sat on a bed in one of the many bedrooms of the ranch house that had come fully furnished in an overly strong Western theme.

First things first.

She looked around for another project. Tension hung throughout the house. How were they going to beat the sheriff, the psychotic doctor, and their trained soldiers? Denver and his brothers had been preparing for decades, but still.

Zara appeared in the doorway, her mounds of hair secured on top of her head and her pants somehow pressed. "You hungry? I made brownies for dessert."

Noni forced a smile. "Thanks, but no."

"Me either." Zara's shoulders slumped. "This is so stressful. I mean, I've known the moment was coming for a while, and here it is, but you know? It's life or death." She rubbed her chin. "Literally. I've used that expression before, but I've never really meant it. Not like now." Concern fanned out from her eyes.

Noni nodded. The idea that any of those strong brothers might be killed cut through her. They were tough, but bullets were tougher. "I know." She tried to find the right words. Also, Zara and Anya had folded her into the family, and she didn't know how to express her gratitude. "No matter what happens, thank you. For, well, everything."

Zara smiled, but her lips trembled. "Family is family, and tonight is going to go well. It has to." The smile slid away.

"I know," Noni whispered, steeling her shoulders.

"Okay. Stay strong, and that baby will be home by morning." With an encouraging nod, Zara turned and continued down the hallway.

Seconds later, Denver stepped inside and shut the door. "Hi."

Noni straightened. "Hi. Do we have a plan?" She'd watched him and his brothers pore over maps while on the phone with the family in Montana, nailing down entry points and a bunch of stuff that sounded like a raid on television. The Montana guys were already in the air for the two-hour helicopter flight. "Finally?"

Denver walked over to a pile of stuff he'd dumped in the corner when they'd chosen their bedroom at the ranch. "Yeah. Ry, Heath, and I are going in from the south while Jory and his brothers are coming from the north and fanning out. They're dropping from a helicopter a few miles out and running, and we'll park and do the same."

"Won't they see you coming?" Her breath felt chilled in her lungs.

"No." He dropped his jeans and pulled on a pair of black cargo pants with what looked like a lot of pockets. "The snowstorm has increased, which will give us cover. If we leave vehicles miles away and go on foot, we should be okay."

It would be freezing. "What then?"

"We have the plans of the entire compound, and we'll breach from every direction. The baby will be in the main building, and we'll get her to safety first. That's the main priority."

She swallowed. "Then what?"

He didn't answer, and his face went blank.

Okay. Whatever he was planning, he didn't want to share. She wouldn't judge him for wanting to end the threat over his head. "What about me?" she asked. Waiting a few miles away was better than waiting an hour away.

He reached for a pair of combat boots and slipped his feet in, leaning down to lace them up.

She waited for him to answer, but he seemed so focused it was as if he wasn't really in the room. "Denver?"

He moved to the bed and the myriad weapons he'd laid out, choosing a sharp knife with a jagged edge to set gently in a sheath strapped to his right calf. A darker knife with twin blades went into a sheath on his left. "Where is…there it is." He grabbed some odd concoction of Velcro and strapped it around his right thigh before reaching for a big gun with a large barrel to place in its holder.

She looked around and found a similar-looking Velcro gun holder to toss his way. He secured it on his other leg and reached for another version of the same gun to set in place.

Whoa. Two knives and two guns. But he wasn't done. Three cylinders went into holders near the guns.

"What are those?" she asked.

"Tear gas." He flipped open a box he'd put on the floor and drew out several other odd-shaped silver things. "Flash grenades," he said before she could ask, also setting those in pockets. Then he strode back to the corner and grabbed a bulletproof vest, wincing when he pushed his arms into it.

This was unreal. To think Ryker and Heath had all this stuff in their vehicle when they'd driven from South Dakota. The devastation he was already wearing blew her mind. "How is your side?" Obviously the stitches were pulling.

"Fine," he said, securing the vest.

Heath suddenly appeared in the door. "Talked to Jory, and they have snow camo suits that will blend in with the storm better. But they'd have to stop here first."

Denver paused. "No. Stay on plan. It's dark and we'll be fine."

"Agreed." Heath gave Noni a nod and then moved away.

Noni swallowed. "Why not get the suits?"

Denver reached for the 9 millimeter she'd just loaded to place at the back of his waist. Spare clips went in even more pockets. "The plan is detailed to the last second, and we have to come from opposite directions. Madison is waiting, and I don't want any delay." He caught her gaze, his blue eyes glittering with determination. "Trust me. We'll be fine. It's dark anyway."

A lump filled her throat. She didn't seem to have much of a choice. So she stood and grasped a jacket off the bed, moving toward him to hand it over. "No weapons in the jacket?"

"Maybe just a couple." His lips twitched, and he took more stuff out of the box to put in his jacket. "Did you count the weapons on me?"

"There are a lot," she whispered.

He nodded. "See why you're not coming?"

So she wasn't a fighter, and she wasn't trained. If they left the cars miles away in the snow, she'd need to turn on the heat to keep warm. Anything could give the position away. Didn't mean she liked it, though. "Waiting is the hardest part."

"I know." He brushed her hair away from her face and placed a soft kiss on her nose. Then he paused. "Did I leave my pack in here? The one with C-4 in it?"

Her stomach dropped. "Um, no. Haven't seen it."

"Must be in the office." He rolled his shoulders back.

She just looked at him. God, he was big. Tall and muscled, so deadly looking in his combat gear. She'd never been this close to so much danger—not really. But instead of seeing Denver as bringing danger, as she had a week ago, she now saw him as a shield. Even a protector. He'd do everything he could to save the baby. "Please be careful." Fear was ice-cold inside her. Fear for him, for Talia, for all of them. This was *real*.

His eyes darkened past blue into something deeper. "I will. We're leaving you all with weapons." He jerked his head to the two guns remaining on the bed. One was the gun he'd given her just days ago, and the other one looked identical to it. She also had the gun she'd started with, and that was in her pack. "You just point and shoot them. Just in case," he said.

She looked at the two silver guns, and a pit formed in her stomach as she focused back on him. "No problem."

"Noni." His stance was wide, his jaw hard.

"What?" she asked.

He cleared his throat. "I'm not that good with words."

Well, no shit. "I know."

"I've been trying to hold back since this is so dangerous and I don't know what's going to happen." The more he spoke, the faster the words were coming. "But I meant what I said."

"I know." All of it. She was well aware of his fears and his love. Her heart hurt, and her eyes stung. But she had to be strong. For him and for Talia. "I get it, Denver." Right now he needed to concentrate. "We'll talk when you get back."

He grimaced. "Okay. But—" He reached inside the case where he'd gotten the flash grenades and pulled out a velvet box.

She stopped breathing. Completely. No air.

He flipped it open to reveal a ring sparkling with alexandrite surrounded by a whole lot of diamonds. "I want you to have this. I mean, it's yours."

She could only blink. Emotion washed through her, stealing every thought but one. Just one. He'd bought her a ring? *A ring?*

"I, ah, saw it and thought of you a while back, and I couldn't help but buy it." He sounded bemused, and he shuffled his feet in those big boots. His voice was low and sure. Intent. "It's a promise if I make it through this. If I don't, it's something to remember me by." Taking the ring out, he grasped her hand and slid it onto the ring finger of her right hand. "For now."

Tears filled her eyes, and she blinked them away. "It's beautiful, Denver." It truly was. Her favorite stone and diamonds...from Denver. She just stared at the sparkly gem. From Russia, like her paternal grandfather, a man who'd died long ago. It was a stone made of hard times and cold winters and strength and pressure and hope and faith. Denver had bought it for her when he wasn't sure they'd ever see each other again. The tears went deeper than her eyes. They filled her. "You have to make it back to me." Her voice cracked on the end.

"I will." The promise was solid, his tone strong. He took one last long look at her and turned for the doorway, stopping right before leaving.

Her eyes filled again.

"Damn it." He pivoted and was back in front of her, his fingers spearing through her hair. His mouth descended, and he kissed her deeply, so much emotion in his touch that he took everything she had. Releasing her, he pivoted and strode away.

In a flash, he was gone.

* * *

The freezing trek through the trees, blinded by swirling snow, took Denver's mind off the constant ache in his side. The knife wound was healing, but the heavy gear on him kept pulling the stitches. He had no doubt he was already bleeding, and they'd just arrived in the center of the compound. The barbed-wire fencing had been easy enough to dispatch, while the traps set along the way had been a bit more difficult.

One hole holding spiked limbs had nearly taken Heath out, but Ryker had tossed him to the side in the last second.

They had to take care of three sets of two-man patrols, knocking them out and tying them up. No need to kill them. There was no doubt they were just hired muscle and not Madison's small special force of supersoldiers. It had been too easy to take them down.

The difficult part of the op was coming up.

Finally, now they were in position.

There were three standing targets. The first was the main facility, where hopefully Madison was staying with the baby. The lab was in the same building, based on the floor plans he'd studied. The second building contained fuel, supplies, and weapons. Probably. The third was a barracks that housed soldiers.

All had to be destroyed. The remaining outbuildings didn't concern him.

He stared at the main building and settled himself. No thinking. No feeling. Just action. Heath was at his right and Ryker at his left.

Out of the mist, without a wisp of a sound, Jory Dean appeared.

Only training kept Denver from moving back. Jesus. The guy could really come out of nowhere. "Hey."

"Hi." Jory shucked his pack, handing over earbuds. Then he dug deeper and brought out three pairs of night-vision goggles.

"Nice," Ryker breathed, taking a pair.

Jory grinned. "They also can detect heat signatures. Do not ask how we got ahold of the technology."

Denver didn't want to know. He really didn't. He accepted the goggles. "Is everybody in place?"

"Affirmative." Jory clapped him on the shoulder. "Per our discussions, Shane and Nate are on the supplies depot, and Matt and I will take the barracks. The main building will be guarded, and after we take out the other threats, we'll converge behind you to clean up. You've got five minutes before we blow the explosives and they know we're here for sure."

Denver stuck the earbud in his ear. "My priority is the baby."

"Yes." Jory's gray eyes darkened. "She's everybody's priority." He cleared his throat. "We'd like Madison alive."

Denver stilled. "Seriously."

"We talked about it on the way down. She has intel we want." Jory lifted his face to the wind and seemed to listen. "The storm is settling down. We need to move now." He took one step away, disappearing completely.

"That's a little freaky," Ryker muttered, inserting his earbud.

Denver secured the goggles on top of his head. His blood brother scar scratched against the inside of his glove, and he took a moment to feel it. "Guys."

Heath bumped him with a shoulder. "Got it and ditto. Let's do this."

Ryker settled his goggles over his eyes. "If anything happens to me, Zara—"

"Yeah," Denver said. He'd take care of Zara and Anya as if they were his own sisters, because basically they were. Ryker and Heath would protect Noni and the baby. "All around. We're covered."

Then he took a moment and dug deep. "If this is it, I don't regret a second. Not one moment of everything we've been through. We found one another."

Ryker's eyes darkened. His tone was hoarse. "Agreed."

Heath cleared his throat. He pressed a hand to his chest. "Thank you for being my brothers," he said, his voice rough too.

Denver's lungs filled. One of them had to make it just to remember, to pass that on. He shook his head to settle into the op. There wasn't anything else to say. He glanced at his watch. "Let's go."

Crouching low, they moved in formation toward the main building, keeping an eye out for scouts. With the storm so brutal, any guards were probably right inside the doors. Running around to the back of the building, they found the rear entrance that had been visible from the surveillance photographs. Ryker moved along the wall and found the right box, flipped it open, and went to work.

Nobody could fuck with a security system like Ryker. Nobody. Within a minute, he gave a short nod.

Good.

Denver moved to a window a few feet from the rear door. Using his goggles, he looked inside. Seemed like some sort of office or storage room based on the boxes piled in the corner. Giving a hand signal, he used his knife and edged the window up. His ribs protested when he slid over the sill, but he ignored them, landing silently.

Within seconds, his brothers had joined him. They moved through the room and out into a hallway with several doors. "We're in the office area," Denver whispered.

Ryker nodded. "You go to the second floor, I'll go down to the lab, and Heath will cover here."

Denver instantly pivoted and moved quietly down the hall, leaving wet boot prints on the wood floor. He reached a stairwell and started climbing. Hopefully Madison and the baby were upstairs. From the floor plans, it had looked like some bedrooms were up there. Madison wouldn't stay in the barracks.

He didn't encounter anybody, his sight strong with the goggles. Reaching a landing, he could see a small vestibule with four doors spaced a distance apart.

His heart beat rapidly, and he took several deep breaths to calm himself. Then he switched on the heat sensors and turned toward the nearest door. A small signature lit up yellow and red. Very small and not moving. Talia? He forced himself to scope out the other three rooms. No signatures. So he turned back to the one room and gently nudged open the door.

The room was small, with a worn dresser, changing table, and crib that had obviously been picked up quickly. The crib looked old and dented. No doubt unsafe. His breath hitched, and he moved forward to see the baby. She opened her eyes and gurgled. For a second, he was frozen. She was okay. His hands trembled.

She smiled, the sight trusting and innocent. Relief nearly took him to his knees. She was healthy and unharmed. Thank God. He reached for her, needing to hold her tight.

The cocking of a gun behind him stopped him cold. He slowly turned.

"Hello," Sheriff Elton Cobb said, lifting a flashlight to Denver's face.

The light exploded through the night-vision goggles, completely blinding Denver. Even so, he put himself between Cobb and the baby while ripping them off.

"Oh. This is gonna be fun," Cobb said with anticipation.

CHAPTER
35

Noni twisted the ring around her left ring finger while sitting at a long table made of what seemed to be redwood. The brownie in front of her looked good, but her stomach revolted. Zara sat across from her while Anya sat at the head to her right.

"We have to be able to do something," Noni muttered.

Zara leaned back and stretched out her arms. Her dark hair fell down around her shoulders. "I have bandages and antiseptic ready."

Anya nodded. Her red hair caught the light and shimmered while her green eyes were dark with worry. "I have blankets and more bandages ready."

"I already organized the thread in case we need to stitch anyone up," Noni murmured, caught by the sheer oddity of the entire conversation. "Life has gotten way too weird."

"Amen, sister," Anya said, her gaze catching on the sparkles. "Want to dish about the ring? That wasn't there yesterday."

Heat blasted into Noni's face, and she quickly put it on her other finger. "Denver gave it to me, put it on my right hand, and said it was a promise." He had not proposed marriage. She'd just wanted to see what it'd look like on her other finger. "It's my favorite stone."

"The diamonds are pretty, too." Zara pushed her uneaten brownie away. "This is excruciating. I can't even call in to Montana because they've gone all dark again since the raid started. My granny and her fiancé are there."

"Montana sounds nice," Noni said, wanting to talk about anything but the raid. How shocking to already trust these two women as much as she had anybody. They were truly bonded in what was happening.

Zara shrugged. "Sounds nice. Haven't been there." She looked at a pretty ring on her engagement finger. "Maybe we should all get hitched there. You know, have a triple wedding."

"I'm not engaged," Noni reminded her, trying really hard to ignore the pang in her heart from those words. "Not even close."

Anya shoved her hair away from her face. "A promise is a start. Zara got engaged twice to Ryker, right?"

Zara nodded. "Yeah. Well, he asked twice and I said yes twice, so it's all good. He really wanted to get it right." Love lit up her entire face.

Noni tried to not be a little jealous. Plus, it wasn't like she couldn't ask Denver if she was so inclined.

The lights went out.

Noni jumped up from the table, her gaze swinging around in the darkness. "What just happened?"

A chair scraped. "It's the storm," Zara said, her voice shaking a little.

Something rumbled, and the lights flickered and turned back on a bit dimmer than before.

Anya rushed over to the door leading to a wide deck and checked the monitor next to it. "The alarm is still activated." She turned and looked at them, her green eyes wide. "I think it's just the weather, and the backup generators kicked in. That makes sense, right?"

A chill slithered down Noni's spine. "Yes. That definitely makes sense." As if in agreement, the wind howled outside, scattering icy snow against the windows. "If the alarm is still blinking green, I think we're okay." She hoped.

Zara started to move toward the living room. "Let's bank the fire and get it roaring. Then we'll find some candles and flashlights in case the generator has problems." She kept walking toward the already roaring fire and pointed to the huge stack of logs next to it. "We're prepared for the entire night and just have to keep it stoked and loaded with wood."

Noni followed her. "I think we should all get our guns, too."

Zara pulled hers out from behind her back. "I have mine."

Anya looked at Noni. "Mine is in the bedroom."

"Mine too." Noni really hadn't been expecting trouble.

Anya reached her and slid an arm around her. "Let's go together." Good plan. Definitely a good plan.

* * *

Isobel Madison moved away from her lab samples to concentrate more fully on the monitor in the corner of her smallest lab, annoyed by the lights going out again. The weather in Boise wasn't supposed to be this extreme, and yet it was the third time in a month that her systems had been forced to switch to generators. It was fortuitous that the generators were top notch, because she held all of her important frozen genetic samples here. "Say that again."

Soldier Matthias leaned closer to the camera on his phone, his face larger on the monitor, his dark eyes serious. "I think I've found the Gray brothers, and I've just e-mailed you plans of the entire property in Montana." Snow swirled around him, the wind lifting his black hair.

She tapped her foot on the concrete floor, found the e-mail, and printed out the materials. Anticipation flowed through her veins, giving her a nice buzz. "Do you have a visual?"

"Negative," he said, his breath steaming in the air. "I scouted around the town all day today, and there's a new subdivision privately owned. I walked it, and they have impressive security even on the outer ridges."

Isobel enjoyed the heat that flushed through her. That was anticipation with maybe a hint of excitement. "So Montana it is." That silly Noni had given her the correct state, now, hadn't she? The Gray boys, those sweet soldiers she'd raised from birth, had sought refuge in the wilds of Montana. How adorable. To even think that she wouldn't find them was silly.

But she'd require the Lost boys—Ryker, Heath, and Denver—to bring them in. Then she'd need leverage. A lot of it. Maybe she could break Denver enough that he'd work with her. Want to be her son and help her to continue her work.

"Do you want me to infiltrate the property?" Matthias asked.

"Not yet. You'll require backup," she said. Probably more backup than she had available at the moment. She thought idly about calling in favors with the government, but that could get so sticky.

"There's more," Matthias said. "I saw a Blackhawk lift from the Montana property about three hours ago. Looked loaded for bear."

She paused. "Could you see who was in it?"

"I used binoculars and can't be sure. Best guess, I saw Nate Dean briefly, but I couldn't guarantee it." Matthias and every other solder in her employ had studied on a daily basis the pictures of the men she sought.

"Nathan," she breathed. If Nate had truly left Audrey to go on a mission, then it was crucial. Isobel looked around her quiet lab and the flickering lights from the generator. "Stay put. I'll be in touch." Disconnecting the call, she quickly typed on her keyboard, bringing up the security feeds. Nothing. If the storm had knocked out the power, this might be a coincidence.

She knew better. Grabbing her phone, she dialed Elton. The phone went to voice mail. He'd said he wanted to blow off steam and had headed to the gym on the second floor around eleven.

Her heart started to race out of pure instinct, and she eyed the wall at the end of the room. The one that looked like a bookshelf. Making up her mind, she quickly dialed her top soldier in the compound.

"Gleason," he answered.

"Where are you?" she asked, moving rapidly toward the bookshelf and pulling out the correct book. The wall slid open.

"Scouting to the north," he replied.

She stepped inside and closed the door. "Team of two?"

"Affirmative."

She kicked off her high heels and jumped into snow boots. "We're on red alert." If Denver and his brothers were there, it was too late to fight. "Execute Campaign Rabbit." Clicking off, she grabbed a semiautomatic Glock from the locker after throwing on a jacket and slinging her laptop bag over her shoulder. Pride filled her at how quickly her boys had found her when she'd tried to leave no trace. She knew they were here. She could *feel* them.

But now wasn't the time to take them in. She didn't have the resources to take on all three of them. All seven of them if the Blackhawk had arrived with the Gray brothers.

Hitching up her skirt, she climbed the stairs and pushed open the door at the top that couldn't be seen from outside. Gleason roared up in a Humvee a second later, and she jumped into the front seat, slamming her door. Another armed soldier was in the back.

She nodded. "I think—"

The world blew up. Fire shot high and fierce into the sky, and a barrel blew right into a tree. "Unbelievable," she muttered as her storage depot and the barracks went up in flames. Men started running from the barracks and from areas around the depot.

Gleason yanked the wheel and spun out, heading away from the demolished building.

Isobel turned around in time to see Heath barrel out of her hidden room. If she had to sacrifice him to teach his brothers a lesson, she'd do it. "Shoot him," she said evenly. How quickly had he found the room?

The soldier in back started to lean out the window, his gun already outside.

Her gaze met Heath's, and his hardened. Time seemed to slow. Did he know she'd made his eyes greenish brown on purpose? Did he know his ability to fight, his raw impressive intelligence, was all from her work? Did he want to know more about his genetics? He had to be at least a little grateful to her.

He lifted his arm and started firing at them.

Her soldier shot back.

She ducked down, panic heating her. "Go, go, go."

The heavy vehicle fishtailed, but Gleason punched the gas, speeding away from the melee. Bullets hit the back but didn't slow them. "What about Sheriff Cobb?" he asked.

Isobel sighed. "Either he'll survive or he won't." The man could fight, and he had no conscience. He had a good chance of making it through if he got the hell out of there.

Gleason's hands relaxed on the wheel as they put distance between them and the fight. "Destination?"

She pulled her laptop free and flipped it open, rapidly typing. "Just keep driving. I'll have a destination in about thirty minutes if my guess is correct." The two programs she'd need came up on a split screen, and her entire body settled.

Now was the moment.

This was the way.

She had to come at them from the side and not in a head-on fight. Oh, they'd hurried up her timeline, without question. But they were men of action, and she'd created them to be that way. In fact, she'd built them to be lone wolves and deadly soldiers. They seemed to misunderstand their purpose, their ultimate function, which did not, in any way, involve connections or familial bonds. It never had and it never would. To reach their full potential, to find the state she had created in them, they needed to be alone. To be singular in their pursuit of her agenda.

To make the ultimate soldier.

Her computer was just another extension of her brilliance. Her boys needed to come home and get back to work. For her.

Now it was time to teach them that lesson.

CHAPTER
36

Denver angled to the side, keeping Cobb's attention on him, not on the baby. Explosions rocked the world outside, and the floor shook.

Cobb stiffened. "Looks like you're not alone."

"I haven't been alone in years," Denver retorted, moving even farther from the crib. If Cobb fired, he would be aiming away from the baby. Far away from the baby. "Sounds like your depot just blew to hell."

"I'll get another one," Cobb retorted, taking a step toward him. "You wouldn't believe the money Isobel has accumulated through the years. We'll have fifty depots." His blue eyes blazed in the night and he again stepped forward, his hold steady on his weapon. "Last time we met, you confessed you killed my brother." His voice trembled with barely leashed fury.

"Yep." Denver kept his hands free, just waiting for the opportunity. The bastard wouldn't care if he shot the baby. Denver tensed to keep his body in the way.

Shouts echoed from down below.

"Sounds like a fight," Cobb said, his teeth gleaming, setting the flashlight down near the door. It was bright enough to illuminate the entire room.

Denver nodded. Gunfire ripped through the night, and the sound of a vehicle rushing away came clearly through the storm. "Is that Isobel? Did she just leave your ass?" God, hopefully the bitch was still on the property somewhere. Though it would be just like her to have an escape plan.

"If it is, I'll catch up with her soon." Cobb's shoulders squared. "I've been waiting a long time to pay you back for what you did. Maybe you'll live long enough to see one of your brothers die. Though I doubt it."

"I'd forgotten how much you like to talk," Denver said, flashing back to his childhood. "Yack, yack, yack. It's like you needed foreplay before getting to the hitting. We saw it as a weakness. Still do." The muscles in his legs bunched and prepared to launch. "I bet Isobel thinks you're weak, too. Has she gone looking for a younger version yet?"

Something flickered in Cobb's eyes.

Denver bit back a smile of satisfaction. The asshole had always been insecure. "Oh, she has gone a-lookin'. Rumor had it she used to bang some of her younger soldiers all the time." He gave a mock shudder. "There's no way you can keep up with a twenty-year-old highly trained killer, *Sheriff*." His sarcastic note on the word *sheriff* had gotten him punched more than once as a kid.

Apparently Cobb had learned some self-control. "She never tried with you."

Denver blinked. "You're kidding me. She never told you." Triumph, a dark one, roared through him. "She does like a good secret."

Cobb's chin lowered. "Told me what?"

The asshole had to ask. "She's my mum, Cobb. My mother. My mommy dearest." Denver barely kept himself from gagging on the last. So much for appearing stoic.

"Bullshit," Cobb growled.

"She told me." Denver lifted a shoulder, angling even more away from the baby. Tension pricked down his arms. "I wondered why she brought me presents as a kid. You know, I think I have her eyes." Fuck, he hated that.

Cobb drew back and visibly shook himself. "I think you're full of shit." His voice wavered.

"You know it's true."

That quickly, Cobb's vision cleared. "Then she'll have to forgive me for killing her son. If that's what you are. I'll give her another one."

Bile rose in Denver's throat at the thought of Madison and Cobb creating a kid. "Guess I'll have to kill you instead," he said in a low tone.

Cobb jerked his head. "How's your side? That knife wound had to hurt."

"Eh. I've had worse hangnails." Denver inched forward just a little.

"Stop moving, jackass." Cobb cocked his head to the side in the same way he'd done when Denver had been a helpless kid. As if he was studying a bug on a microscope slide, trying to figure out how to dissect it. "I've been waiting for revenge for so long that it hurts to end this."

"Revenge, huh? Did your oath as a cop ever mean anything?" Of course it hadn't. Good cops didn't hit kids. Malloy was a good cop, and he'd probably like to lock this jerk up. "You should want justice. Not revenge." If Denver could keep him talking, maybe Ryker or Heath would make it upstairs. Denver had to get the baby clear before any shots were fired. "Right?"

"Justice and revenge are the same thing." Cobb's chest puffed out. "Are you about done stalling?"

"I figured you needed time to catch your breath after running up the stairs." Another couple of feet, and Denver would be clear of the baby. "How about we take this outside?"

Cobb sighed and glanced toward the crib. "She's a pretty little thing."

The hair on the back of Denver's neck rose. "I'm glad I killed your brother." *Focus. Back. Here.*

Cobb swung his gaze.

Good.

"It hurts to lose something you love." His smile almost gleeful, Cobb turned slowly and pointed the gun at the crib. "Payback, loser."

Denver reacted instantly, throwing his body between the crib and Cobb. Three shots echoed in rapid succession, and pain bloomed across Denver's chest. The impacts threw him back against the crib, and he hit, falling to the floor.

Talia started to wail.

Denver choked out air, his body convulsing. Holy fucking shit. Pain overwhelmed his central nervous system, and he tried to roll over. God. He couldn't breathe.

Cobb grabbed him by the jacket and lifted him, shoving him into the dresser. The top drawer shattered. Denver's shoulders hit first, and his head flew forward and then back. The room went dark, and he shook his head, trying to stay conscious. He had to stay awake to protect Talia. Gravity grabbed him, and he slid down to land on his ass.

His body was one large pulsing nerve of raw pain.

Cobb was instantly in his face, crouching down, his hand around Denver's neck. "I've been waiting a long time for this."

Denver inhaled deeply and punched up, nailing the sheriff in the throat.

Cobb gasped and fell back, reaching for his trachea.

Denver tried to push himself to his feet, his legs unsteady. He used the dresser at his back and stood, wobbling slightly. The metallic taste of blood filled his mouth, and the scent wafted in the air around him. Definitely his blood.

Cobb released his neck and lifted his gun hand.

Denver kicked out, hitting Cobb's wrist and sending the gun clattering to the other side of the room. But Denver's balance was off, and he dropped to the floor on both knees.

"Oh, this is better." Cobb advanced, whipping a knife out from his back pocket. He grabbed Denver's hair and jerked his head back. "Much better."

Denver wheezed and forced a smile even as blood dribbled from his mouth. "You never won," he gasped, his chest shuddering. "You were bigger and stronger...and you never broke us." He let his head roll so he could look the asshole directly in his evil eyes. "Not once."

"Maybe not," Cobb snarled. "But I'm gonna kill you. It's a nice consolation prize."

Talia continued to scream, and Denver's body short-circuited. He couldn't leave that baby with this monster. Noni's face flashed across his vision. She trusted him. She needed him. They both did. "You just don't get it," Denver said softly, his entire being settling.

"What?" Cobb pressed the knife against Denver's jugular. "What don't I get?"

"You can't win. You can't beat us. Ever." With one smooth motion, Denver pulled his knife from his calf and shoved up, jumping from his knees to his feet and keeping going. The blade pierced beneath Cobb's chin and shoved right up into his skull. He fell back, and Denver fell with him, landing hard and sending the knife all the way home.

Cobb's eyes widened and then went blank.

Denver rolled off him, leaving the knife in place.

Talia kept crying.

"Just a minute, baby," he gasped, trying to roll onto his hands and knees. There wasn't anything he wouldn't do for that baby. Drawing on strength he had no clue he had, he made it to his feet and limped over to the crib, which was dented even more now. "I'm coming, sweetheart. Just a sec." Reaching down, he patted her belly. His vision wasn't clear enough for him to pick her up yet. "You're okay. I promise."

She kicked her legs out but stopped crying, as if she somehow knew she was safe.

Denver took several deep breaths and pushed the pain away, waiting until his body settled. Okay. There was some damage on his side, more than the knife wound. But his other side worked. So he gingerly leaned down and picked the baby up with his better arm, holding her to his chest. She snuggled her nose into his neck and sniffed around. "You're safe, sweetheart." He turned and looked at the dead man on the ground. The baby had her face against Denver's skin, so she couldn't see the mess. That was good.

Ryker was instantly in the doorway with Heath on his heels. They both paused, their gazes on the dead man with the knife hilt protruding from his chin.

Ryker swallowed. "You got him." He nudged Cobb with his boot.

Denver nodded. "Yeah."

Heath looked up and hurried toward him. "You're hurt."

"I'll live because of the bulletproof vest." Denver grabbed a blanket and wrapped it around the baby. "Let's get this girl to her mama."

Heath slid an arm around his waist and helped him toward the door, his other hand bracing the back of Talia against Denver. "We found the lab that still had our genetic samples. Then we set the explosives and should probably get a move on."

Denver looked at him. Seriously. "Okay. Run."

CHAPTER
37

Noni stood up again and looked out the window, her gun heavy in her hand. "I'm thinking it was just the storm."

"Agreed." Zara added a log to the fire and stoked it. "We're fine. It has been an hour, and if anybody wanted to make a move, they would have."

"Plus, there's no way anybody traced us," Anya said, relaxing in a chair with her gun on her legs. "It was just the wind, folks."

Something rumbled in the distance. Noni stilled and looked. "Is that a car?"

"Maybe." Anya leaped to her feet and ran to the front door. She looked out. "It's the SUV."

Noni hurried over, her heart nearly bursting through her chest. "Oh God. Are they all there? Can you see?"

"I can't see anything." Anya pulled the door open and walked out onto the porch.

The SUV pulled up with a lurch and slid a foot on the ice. A back door opened, and Denver shoved himself out, a green blanket in his arms.

Noni cried out and ran forward, reaching him at the edge of the front porch. "Talia," she breathed.

Denver turned the baby over to Noni, and she held her tight, tears filling her eyes. "You got her back." Turning, she hustled for the warmth of the house. Talia smelled like baby powder and Denver. The baby snuggled close, as if she knew she was home. Noni's hands shook, and she slowed. Tears slid down her face. "Let's look at you." Laying her on the sofa, Noni unwrapped her and checked her from head to toe. Relief made her sway.

She picked the baby up and turned to see Denver leaning against a wall, watching her. Her heart clenched tight. He'd saved Talia. She'd known he would. "Denver?"

Ryker moved in, setting a shoulder beneath Denver's arm and helping him into a chair. "Let's see how bad."

Noni gasped. He was hurt? Her head started to spin.

Heath was right behind them, his hands full of papers and his eyes full of concern. He had bruises down the right side of his face and what looked like burn marks across his neck. "I smell blood."

"It's mine," Denver said, grimacing as Ryker released the Velcro straps on the bulletproof vest.

Noni's stomach tensed. Holding the baby tight, she hurried over to Denver. "How bad?" God. He had to be all right.

"I'm fine," he said, his face pale beneath his five-o'clock shadow. "It's okay."

Ryker finished with the vest and lifted it over Denver's head. Blood soaked Denver's light gray T-shirt. Noni blinked several times as dizziness took her.

"Sit down, Non," Denver said. "I'm okay, but you need to sit down."

She looked frantically around, and Anya was instantly at her side with arms out.

"Thank you." Noni set the baby in Anya's arms and moved forward, dropping to her knees in front of Denver. He had to be okay. There was so much blood. Her ears started to ring. "We need scissors."

Zara ran in from the kitchen with a first-aid kit and scissors. She handed them over to Ryker, who quickly cut Denver's shirt away. His stitches had popped open, leaving red and jagged skin bleeding along his rib cage. And bruises, purple and dark red, covered his entire chest. His ribs were swollen and an even deeper purple—almost black.

"What in the world?" Noni breathed, studying the striations.

"Three bullets, but the vest took the impact, just leaving a few broken ribs," Denver said, looking down at his side. "No new bullet wounds?"

Ryker pulled him forward and ignored his groan as he looked down his back. "Doesn't look like it. Wait a minute." He lifted Denver's arm to show a huge gash. "Good news? The bullet just ripped through you. Bad news? More stitches."

Denver leaned his head back and groaned. "Wonderful." Then he opened his eyes. "Heath? Look through those papers while Ryker sews. There has to be something about a safe house for Madison in case her headquarters was infiltrated. You know she has one." Then he looked at his oldest brother. "Ryker? What's wrong with your left side?" He poked at Ryker's vest, lifting his head when Ryker hissed out breath. "Take it off."

Without waiting for Ryker to argue, Zara immediately went for his vest. Ryker let her with a long-suffering sigh, groaning when she yanked it over his head. "I'm fine. Got shot also…maybe a couple of broken ribs." He reached for the kit with his right hand, leaving his left arm against his body. "Unlike you, no blood."

"Fair enough." Denver leaned back again.

Noni reached for antiseptic. "I'm so sorry." She poured it on the wound.

Denver's eyes flared, but he didn't move a muscle. Man, he was tough. She gently wiped the blood away and then shifted to the side so Ryker could begin sewing him up again. After glancing back to reassure herself that Talia was sleeping peacefully in Anya's arms, she looked toward a wounded Denver. "Where are Jory and his brothers?"

"On the way to Montana," Heath said, tossing papers across the coffee table and kneeling to read them. "We found printouts and plans of their property up there in Madison's lab as well as a couple of pictures. So she knows where they are."

Noni swallowed. "She's still alive."

"Yeah," Denver said. "But not for long. Heath?"

"I'm looking," Heath said, scouring through papers.

Denver kept his gaze on Noni. "Is the baby okay?"

Noni nodded as Anya kept bouncing Talia, who was giving happy yips. "Yes. You saved her." How could she ever thank him? "What about Cobb?"

"Dead," Denver said, no inflection in his tone.

Ah. All right. Noni eyed him. "You okay?"

"Yeah." He said the word like he meant it. "I'm fine." He paled as Ryker drew the needle through his skin, but he didn't protest. "There's a tree down on the way into this property," he said. "Took out the electricity."

Anya slapped Noni gently on the arm. "Told you. Was just the storm."

Noni grinned. "You were the voice of reason."

Heath looked up. "Always." His gaze darkened. "You look good with a baby in your arms."

Anya blushed and then kept rocking. "I look good anyway." She rubbed her nose against Talia's forehead. "Such a sweet baby."

Noni's hands started shaking, so she clasped them together. What was happening? She cleared her throat.

Zara looked down at her with concern. "You okay?"

"Yes," she whispered.

Denver's gaze slashed to her. "Take deep breaths. You're coming down from the adrenaline." He smiled but still looked pained.

She levered up onto her knees to see Ryker put the needle in again. Her stomach lurched.

"All righty." Zara tucked her arms beneath Noni's arms and turned her around. "How about you don't look at the surgery." She clasped Noni's cheeks. "Better?" she asked gently.

Noni snorted and leaned back against Denver's knee, wanting to feel him close. She concentrated on Zara's stunning blue eyes. "Actually, that is better." So she didn't handle blood all that well. Who did? Besides everyone else in the room. Although Heath was lost in the papers, and Anya was having a good time playing smoochie kisses with the baby.

Denver's hand descended on Noni's hair, and he ran his palm down it in a soft caress. "We're almost finished," he said in a low rumble.

She tilted her head back to give him access, and he continued as if soothing himself as well.

Finally, Ryker leaned away. "We're all good. Stitched up and bandaged." He stood gingerly to his feet, still keeping his left side protected. "Let's find that bitch, go help in Montana, and then take a fuckin' vacation."

"Sounds good," Anya said in a singsong voice to the baby.

Talia giggled and planted her hand on Anya's nose.

"Let's get this done. Madison needs to die," Denver said.

"Copy that," Ryker said grimly. "If we don't kill her, she'll never stop coming for us. It has to happen."

"Well, now," said a cultured voice by the kitchen. "That's just not nice."

Noni gasped and swiveled around to see Isobel Madison come in from the other room, a gun in her hand and pointed at her. A soldier moved in from the bedrooms, and another came from the dining area. She hovered near Talia, not sure which intruder to shield her from.

They were surrounded.

CHAPTER
38

Denver stood and counted the positions and the angles of shots in a nanosecond, going into battle mode without moving an inch. Jesus. Three guns were trained on them, but there were six of them. If he charged, his brothers would follow, and somebody would get hit for sure. Maybe one of the women or even Talia.

"Dr. Madison," Ryker drawled, inching toward Zara. "What a surprise."

Madison gestured with her silver gun. "Stop moving or I'll shoot her in the head."

Ryker stopped moving.

Tension billowed through the room like the prelude to a tornado.

Noni moved close to Talia and Anya, obviously ready to throw her body over the baby if anybody started shooting. She looked wildly around. "How long have you been here?"

"Long enough," Madison said smoothly. "The storm has been quite handy."

Anya still held the baby. "Did you knock the lights out earlier?"

Madison's finely arched brows drew down. "Of course not. We've been here only an hour."

Denver loosened his arms. If the shooting started, he could get across the room and cover Noni and Talia as well as Anya, but they might get hit. There had to be a way out. He cocked his head. "How are you here?" he asked her. "You didn't follow us earlier. I know you didn't."

"No," she said, smiling broadly. "You're all too smart for that. But I don't need to follow you, do I, Denver?" Her voice lowered to a purr at the last.

Heath moved an inch toward the soldier by the dining area.

Denver kept her attention. "Apparently not, considering you found us here and at the hotel on the border." He narrowed his gaze. None of this made sense. He felt like puking. "How?"

Her cold blue eyes somehow sparkled. "I know you, my boy. Always have." She swept her gun out toward Ryker and Heath. "I know all of you. Don't you comprehend? You can't make any move I won't see coming."

"Life isn't a game of chess," Ryker burst out.

Denver slid closer to Noni, his mind spinning.

Heath coughed. "You've always been a crazy bitch."

Ryker moved still closer to Zara.

Madison sighed. "Would you all please remember your manners?"

God, Denver hated her calmness. There was no way she knew him this well. "How did you find us?"

She giggled. "Why won't you believe empirical evidence? I know how your minds work. I *created* you."

"You are psychotic," Noni spat, throwing her arms wide.

Denver took another step toward her. Smart woman, his girl. If they could keep Madison's attention moving, then they could keep moving into defensive positions. "I've always thought sociopathic," he said evenly. "But dishonesty is something new."

Madison sighed. "You're easy to trace. Period."

No, he wasn't. He let go of the fear and shame; he let go of any uncertainty. He was damn good at his job. So there had to be a way Madison had tracked him to the hotel the other night and then all of them to this place. Realization hit him so hard his ears rang. "You bitch."

Her eyes widened and then she giggled more. "Oh, Denver. You are too intelligent, aren't you?"

He could barely keep from lunging and taking her down to the ground. "You tagged *a baby*? You're that evil."

Noni gasped and turned to Talia. "Tagged? What does that mean?"

Denver cut a look at Ryker, who was trying to control his shock.

Ry shook his head. "Even for you, Madison. That's crazy. Beyond crazy. You definitely don't believe in an afterlife, but I do. You're going to burn in hell."

Noni took Talia from Anya's arms and held her close, turning to look at Denver. "What does that mean?"

"She's okay, Non." He kept his voice low and commanding. "It's just a small tracker beneath the skin so the person is findable. Madison has done it with soldiers before." But he still wasn't getting it. "All right, so that makes sense that you'd find us now. But not at the hotel near Montana last time, when you took Noni and Talia." He thought it out, clicking through facts.

She danced back in her boots. "You're getting it now."

Heat flushed through him. "You tagged the baby before we even won the auction. When the Kingdom Boys gang still had her." It was the only explanation.

Madison smiled. "Yes. Did you really think I missed the numerous sites that held your picture with that slut? Come on, boy. I contacted that little gang in the middle of your so-called auction. Paid them a nice amount to let me spend an hour with her. They didn't even ask why."

Noni rubbed Talia's back, her gaze still confused. Then ignoring everyone, she set her down and started feeling the baby's arms.

Madison sniffed. "The tracker is in her left heel. There's no need to search her."

"Noni," Denver said quietly, his mind reeling. How had he come from such a lunatic? "She's fine. Concentrate on the matter at hand."

Ryker took the opportunity and lunged at Madison. She fired, and he flew back into the wall.

"Ryker," Zara yelled, rushing for him.

"Stop," Madison ordered, "or I'll shoot again."

Zara hesitated, her gaze going from Madison to Ryker.

Ryker hissed and pushed himself into a sitting position, putting his back to the wall and grabbing his thigh. Blood welled between his fingertips.

"Ryker," Zara whispered, her voice tortured.

He gave her a lopsided smile. "It's just a scratch, Z. I'm fine. Just need a bandage." Sweat popped out along his forehead and dotted his upper lip.

"No more of that," Madison said coolly. She reached into her pocket and pulled out a blinking box. "We made good use of our time waiting for you."

Denver's blood chilled. "You planted explosives?" His voice had gone hoarse.

"Yes. Now we're going to have an honest discussion." Her voice, even while threatening mass murder, remained calm. "Where is Elton?"

"I killed him," Denver said instantly, looking her in the eye. "If you know me like you say, you can tell if I'm being honest."

She studied him, and her patrician nostrils flared. "You killed Elton." She tsked. "Denver. You'll be punished for that." Her chilling gaze moved to Noni. "I promise."

Noni straightened and put her body between Madison and the baby.

"Then we buried him where he'll never be found," Denver said easily. Oh, they'd left the soldiers with the burning buildings, but Cobb could be traced to them, so they'd actually broken into a crematorium and made sure he'd never be found. "I guess you did make us a little bad."

She sighed. "I suppose I did."

Heath barely moved closer to the soldier he was tracking. "We should also let you know that we destroyed your lab and the area where your samples were stored."

Her face flushed. "That was unkind of you."

Heath shrugged. "Yeah. Probably."

Everyone seemed to be holding their breath. Denver kept an eye on Ryker, who was getting pale.

Madison tapped her heeled boot. "I'll just have to obtain more samples, then."

Ryker grimaced. "We know you've found the Gray brothers. How many soldiers have you sent to Montana to fight them?"

She smiled. "Just one. I don't need to go to Montana. No. The Gray boys are going to come to me."

"By using us as bait," Heath ground out.

"Yes," she said, focusing on her two soldiers. "Do you have the dart guns?"

Both men whipped out dart guns, keeping their Sigs pointed at the room.

Denver's chest settled. If he and Heath were darted, she'd get them out of the house with Ryker. "We'll go with you without darts if we leave now."

She tilted her head and then shook it sadly. "I'm afraid that won't do."

God. She was going to blow the house with the women in it.

"You can't kill them all," Ryker snapped, his voice low with pain.

She sighed. "I have no other viable alternative."

"Now," Denver roared, hoping Noni would drop to the ground. He pivoted and went for the soldier nearest him while Heath did the same.

The soldier tackled him to the ground. Pain flared along his side, and his stitches popped open again. The agony burned.

Noni screamed.

Denver shoved away pain. He punched the guy hard beneath the jaw and rolled them both over, smashing his head into the ground and hearing it crack. The guy's head bounced twice, and he died instantly.

Grabbing the soldier's Sig, Denver leaped up and turned.

Madison stood next to Noni, her gun pointed at Noni's rib cage.

Noni had gone so pale her lips looked blue.

"You're okay," Denver said, pointing the Sig at Madison. Ryker lay panting on the floor while Heath had taken out the other soldier, who lay on the floor with his neck at an odd angle.

Heath moved easily toward Anya, covering both her and Zara.

Denver stared at Dr. Madison. He had to get her away from Noni. "I have your eyes," he whispered softly. Could he distract her?

Heath moved forward a couple of inches, keeping the women behind him.

Madison's chin lifted, and she angled slightly behind Noni. Those blue eyes sparkled, and her dark hair had escaped its clip. "Yes, you do. My father's eyes."

Denver took a step toward her, calculating the distance. "Your father. My grandfather."

She arched an eyebrow. "Yes. He was a soldier. One of the best."

Denver slid forward. About ten feet separated them. "Was?"

"Yes. Even though he was so strong, he still died." Fury darkened Madison's eyes.

"Is that why you create soldiers?" Denver asked, forcing himself to speak calmly when terror heated his chest. Madison's gun was angled so that a bullet would pierce Noni's heart. She'd die instantly if Madison fired. "Your experiments?"

Madison tracked his movement. "Stop. Or I'll shoot."

He stopped. "Is that why?"

"It's one of the reasons," she said, eyeing the door. "I'm gifted and was created to do something great. It's noble, and I'm changing the world one chromosome at a time. That matters, Denver."

He swallowed. "Okay. So let's get out of here. Just you and me. I'll help you."

She studied him. "I'm not stupid, boy. You can't love her and help me."

He stiffened, still pointing the Sig at her. She was taller than Noni and was still visible. "If you hurt her, I'll kill you."

Noni's eyes widened.

Madison stared at him, her gaze a little wild. "You're my son. You won't kill me."

"If it's you or them, you die." He'd given her the truth. Even though he'd planned to kill her, he was now hoping deep down she wouldn't force him into it. "Don't make me do this."

She smiled. "There's only one way for us to really be together." Her shoulders stiffened, and her grip on the gun tightened.

There was no choice.

Denver fired.

The bullet hit her in the center of the forehead. She jerked back, her body hitting the arm of the sofa and sliding down to the ground. Her gun clunked onto the floor a second later.

Denver gaped. His body went numb.

Noni turned and grabbed Talia before pivoting and running for him. He enfolded them, holding them tight, his gaze on Madison's wide eyes. God. He'd actually killed her.

Heath rushed forward and yanked the detonator out of her hand. "Holy shit. We have no idea how stable these explosives are. We have to run. Now."

* * *

Noni finished burping the baby after she'd had a bottle and then laid her in the portable crib. The small motel room outside of Boise was quaint but clean. Her mind still fuzzed, and her body still buzzed. After he'd killed Madison, Denver had spirited all of them out of the house and away to this motel, where he and Heath had quickly taken the bullet out of Ryker's leg.

Ryker knew some very interesting phrases.

Now Ryker and Zara were in the next room while Denver and Heath had gone back to the house to clean up. What did that mean? There were explosives in that damn house.

A knock sounded on the door, and she ran for it, yanking the door open. Denver stood in the snow, his eyes dark. She moved to let him in. "Is everything good?" she asked breathlessly.

He shut the door and leaned against it, his eyes weary. "Yes."

Oh, she needed more. "And?"

He removed his coat, scattering snow on the floor. "We took Madison's body and the bodies of the two soldiers to the compound near Boise to be found there. She has no connection to us."

Noni swallowed rapidly, trying to keep from going into a panic attack. "What about the explosives?"

He rubbed his shoulder. "We think we found most of them, but the Montana gang is sending experts over tomorrow to scan the entire property. We're out of it now."

She took several deep breaths. "What about any of Madison's soldiers from the compound who survived the attack earlier?"

"They're long gone," he said. "Probably on their way out of the country."

Relief made her knees wobble. She watched how slowly he was moving, and concern took her. "God. How are you?"

He shook his head. "Fine."

She studied him. Clear eyes, firm jaw, shoulders tense. "You shot her, Denver. Even though she was nuts and just an egg donor, she was biologically your mother."

"Fuck biology." His grin didn't reach his eyes, but the tension started to dissipate across his jaw. "My family is Ryker and Heath. The Gray brothers. And now you and Talia. That's family."

She gulped. Family? "You saved us. Protected us."

"That's my job, baby," he said softly, his gaze lightening. "I'm okay. Trust me."

She did. With everything she had. "How's your chest?"

"Good." He took off his shirt and kicked off his boots. "How's the baby?"

"She's fine," Noni said. Talia had no idea the night she'd just had. "We took the tracker out with tweezers and flushed it down the toilet." Ryker had instructed them, and it had been relatively easy. "I put a mermaid bandage on her." Why did she tell him that silly detail?

His grin did reach his eyes this time. "Mermaid?"

"Yeah." That was why she'd told him. They needed all the grins they could get, and if a mermaid did it, she'd run with that.

He moved to the bed and lay down, his chest a blend of different bruise colors. "You okay?"

"I'm not sure," she said, following him, her stomach kind of cramping. "I'm worried about you. About what you had to do."

He held out his good arm, and she stretched out next to him, her face on his biceps. His warmth and strength gathered around her, and she settled right into it, breathing deeply. "I warned her, and I had to protect you," he said, his voice rough. "I'm so sorry you had to see it all happen."

She flattened her hand over his heart, careful of his injuries. His skin was warm and his heartbeat steady. "She was threatening my baby and me. There wasn't a choice."

"No, there wasn't." He pressed a kiss to her forehead. "We're safe now, Noni."

She leaned into his touch. "Are we free? Finally?" Could it be possible that it was all over? That they were actually safe?

He rubbed down her arm. "Kind of."

"Meaning?" She lifted her head to see his eyes darken to a midnight blue.

"You'll never be free of me. I love you, Noni. You and Talia. I want us to be a family." He reached for her right hand. "I'll protect you both. Love you both. Be whatever you need me to be." Slowly, he slid the ring free.

Tears caught in her throat. It was all too much to be real. He was being so open and true, and she trusted him. She needed him. "I only need you to be you." He was more than she could've ever imagined she'd find. She wasn't sure she could hold on to so much happiness after such tragedy. But she had right now and right here and Denver. "I love you," she whispered.

"Marry me?" he asked softly, taking her left hand. "Move with me to the wilds of Montana and consider living with my overbearing, slightly crazy, definitely dangerous family, and I promise you'll never doubt for a second that you're loved and safe. So damn safe, Noni." He slid the ring onto her left ring finger, watching it sparkle. "Please."

"Yes," she breathed out, her life landing where she wanted. More than a year ago she'd given her heart to him, and she'd never gotten it back. He now held it even stronger than before, and she couldn't imagine her life without him. She and Talia could give him a family where he could just be himself. Where he could express himself without fear and be truly loved while keeping the crucial bonds of brotherhood he'd created and lived for his entire life. "I'll love you forever, Denver. I promise."

He smiled and kissed her so gently she could feel beyond him to what they could be. What they could have. The life they could live together filled with love and passion and security. "I love you, Noni. For eternity."

CHAPTER 39

Christmas Eve in Montana included a lot of colorful lights, snow fights, and spiked eggnog. Every color of light imaginable covered the tree, and festive music hummed from invisible speakers.

The place even smelled like pine.

Denver sat at a card table in the corner of the rec room, watching a pregnant Audrey Dean flip through a catalogue of baby clothes next to him. He had a sister. It was too amazing to think about, and he couldn't stop watching her.

She hummed happily. "If she has our eyes, we should buy this one." She tapped her finger on a very tiny blue dress with pink polka dots.

"I'll buy it," Denver said easily, studying this new sister of his. She had black hair and very blue eyes. But where their mother's eyes had been cold and calculating, Audrey's were all warmth.

She laughed. "You keep saying that."

His heart hurt from the enormity of it all. "I'm going to be an uncle. That matters." Holy shit, that mattered. His chest filled with heat. He had to get to know this amazing woman. Had to protect her.

She smiled and reached across to grab his hand. "We're going to have so much fun."

He exhaled. "I'm sorry. For what happened. What I did." He was still dealing with the fact that he'd killed his own mother, and it was going to take some time for him, but that was okay. He had time, and he'd do the same thing in the same situation, so that was that. "She was your mother, too."

Audrey tightened her hold, her gaze softening. "You had to save Talia and everyone else. Mother was a danger to all of us, and now we're safe." She sighed. "We'll handle it together."

Yeah. Together. They'd help each other deal with the fact that their biological mother didn't give a shit about them and had even forced him to shoot her. "You're going to be a great mom, Audrey," he murmured.

Her smile warmed him. "I know. And you're going to be an awesome uncle to her."

"Him," Nate Dean said as he passed through the room, grabbing an empty appetizer plate on his way.

Audrey laughed. "It's a girl."

"If you say so." Denver glanced at Nate's back as he moved into the massive kitchen area. "I'm not sure he's good enough for you," he teased.

Audrey snorted. "That's funny."

"Denver? Come talk to me," Matt Dean said from over by a long table.

Denver hesitated.

"I'll be fine, Den," Audrey said gently. "We have a date tomorrow to walk the property, remember?"

He nodded, fully prepared to make sure she didn't stumble. His heart was so full these days, and she definitely took up a big place in it. "Are you sure?"

"Yes." Her smile was sweet and accepting. "I'm glad you're my brother."

The words sank in and warmed him. "Me too." He patted her hand. God had given him so much. Keeping an eye on her, he moved toward Matt and Ryker by the table.

Matt was the oldest of the Dean brothers, also known as the Gray brothers. Denver had been on the property only for a day, and here he was, joining Matt in looking over maps of it, eggnog in his hand. Noni had gone to put Talia down for a nap in one of the main lodge's bedrooms.

"So, as you can see, we can build more houses over to the north." Matt pointed to a section near the other homes. "Every home is on a two-acre lot, so there's tons of room." He looked up, his gray eyes gleaming.

Denver couldn't help but smile. "None of us have agreed to move here." Though they were definitely all moving there. Might as well let Matt convince him. The guy seemed to like maneuvering everybody, so why not make him happy?

Matt shifted an impressive amount of muscle beneath his dark shirt. "Then build homes and then decide to stay for sure." He pointed to the existing houses. "This is where Laney and I live. She's a doctor, so you'll want to be close to us just for the baby's sake." Then he pointed to the other homes. "Nate and Audrey are here, Shane and Josie here, and Jory and Piper here." He grinned. "It's our own little subdivision."

Ryker leaned over and studied the plat map. "I like how the river runs behind them and they're all so nicely treed."

Denver barely kept from grinning. Ryker was so in. He loved this plan.

Mattie nodded. "Yeah. We could build your houses here."

Basically, just the next parcels in a huge roundabout with the main lodge in the middle. Denver sighed. "I take it Franny and Verna have already agreed?"

Matt's lips twitched. "Agreed? They've already found a house plan they love. And they insist on being right next to you and Noni—for the baby's sake."

Ryker laughed out loud. "Are they still calling him 'dickhead'?"

"They are," Matt confirmed, his eyes twinkling. "But they're saying it in softer tones, if that helps."

Denver frowned. "Where are the kids staying?" There were four teenage kids that had been saved from Madison, and one of them had stayed with Ryker for a little while.

Matt tapped the imprint of the main lodge. "We all wanted them to stay with us, but they elected to live in the main lodge with Grandpop Jim, Grams June, and Grandpa Earl." His voice lowered. "To be honest, June is the best cook in the entire state, so it wasn't a huge surprise. Plus, the kids keep the grandparents young, and the grandparents totally spoil the kids. Right now it's working well."

The place did seem like a perfect slice of country living.

Matt pulled out another sheet of drawings. "Here are the weapons systems, security measures, and escape plans if we ever need them."

Okay. Not completely country living. Denver whistled. "You have drones?"

Matt just smiled.

Ryker leaned closer. "Wow. Impressive." He looked over at Matt. "You still think there's danger?"

"No, but why not be prepared?" Matt asked easily. "If you guys stay, you can have a piece of any of our security businesses—national or international. Work or don't work. Up to you." He grinned as Heath approached. "So I'll leave you guys for a few moments to check on dinner. Laney always puts in too much salt." He loped gracefully from the room.

"Can you believe all of this?" Heath breathed. "This entire setup is awesome."

Denver took a sip of his eggnog and nearly coughed.

Ryker grinned. "Shane spiked that. Rumor has it don't drink anything that Shane has spiked."

"I like these guys," Denver said. "It feels like, I mean, that—"

"They're family." Heath sighed. "You know?"

"Yeah," Ryker agreed.

Denver looked closer at the map. "I, ah, don't want to go to work at their business." His stomach clenched.

Heath clapped him on the back. "Me either. It's a great offer, but Lost Bastards is our business."

"We could run it from here," Ryker said thoughtfully. "We've never had a main base."

"It's a nice place to live," Heath agreed. "But it's all of us or none of us. We stick together."

Denver hadn't realized how badly he'd needed to hear those words. They'd all moved on and found lives and women to love. But he needed his brothers. "I agree."

Ryker grinned. "I vote yes to staying here."

"Ditto," Heath said.

Denver nodded. "Then we move to Montana."

"I told you that would happen," Jory Dean said, coming into the room with Detective Malloy limping behind him on crutches. "Didn't I tell you that you'd end up here?"

Denver grinned at him. They'd get a chance to know each other now. "I believe you might have mentioned it."

Malloy rolled his eyes. "For pete's sake. You all are such girls sometimes."

Jory sighed. "The detective here has an early Christmas present for you guys."

Denver straightened. "What's that?"

Malloy's cheeks turned a little red. "Well. I used some contacts I had—totally illegally, by the way—and falsified evidence in the Ned Cobb killing. We pinned it on Daniel, the guy who was the Copper Killer. Your pictures are being taken down from any sites, the video has disappeared, and I'm sure cops all over the country are throwing printouts into the garbage. If they bothered to print them out in the first place."

Denver's breath caught. He didn't know what to say. "Malloy—"

The cop held up a hand. "Don't say anything. Just please stay the hell out of Snowville. All of you. Forever."

Jory cleared his throat.

"What?" Malloy groused.

"Uh, Tina has already chosen this lot to build your house," Jory said, pointing to one of the lots. "We've also started creating signs for your campaign to be sheriff this spring. The town needs a good sheriff."

Malloy's mouth gaped.

Denver tried incredibly hard not to laugh. The cop was family whether he liked it or not. Might as well give in now. "Uh, on that note, I want to check on Noni and the baby."

"Be in the main room in an hour for Christmas dinner," Jory said cheerfully.

Denver took another look at Ryker and Heath, who both gave him nods. They were together, and they were safe. He smiled and wound his way through the huge structure to a nice suite toward the back.

Noni was working on the computer, and the baby slept quietly in a crib in the corner. "Denver." Noni stood, looking uncertain.

That wouldn't do. He walked right to her and kissed her, hard.

She smiled, her eyes dazed. "Well, now."

He moved over and placed his hand across Talia's entire chest. The baby was sleeping on her back, her head turned to the side. Her small torso moved against his hand with each healthy breath, reassuring him. "How's our baby?" Releasing her, he turned toward the woman who held his heart.

Her smile widened. "Good. Laney looked at her ears, and she's fine. No damage, and she already has new antibiotics to take. Talia is fine."

His chest settled. "I want to be her dad. Your husband. I love you." Short words and sentences, but they came from the heart.

Her eyes softened into dark pools. "I love you, too. We'll have to finalize the paperwork in Alaska."

"Okay." He'd have Heath get reciprocity so they could get it taken care of quickly. "What do you think about staying here? Living and working here? Making a home?"

She laughed, the sound joyous. "I've already looked into moving our business here. We can build a nice structure over by the rock formation to the south."

He gaped. "We've only been here a day."

"Let's say I had some plans brought to my attention by my aunts." She slid her hands up his chest. "You're sure about this? About everything?"

He slowly nodded, his being full of her. She and that baby owned his heart, and he'd love them forever. "I'm sure." Then he kissed her, going deep and giving her everything he was or would ever be.

Finally. He had found peace.

Dear Reader,

We thought it'd be fun to include a bonus scene with the print edition of *Twisted Truths*, and I loved the idea of seeing Denver and Noni get married after the difficult time they had finding their way back to each other. I may someday write wedding scenes for the other brothers, and I definitely plan on writing the scene where Audrey has her baby, but this Denver and Noni moment wanted to find its way onto the page right here and now.

Plus, I love a winter wedding. Tony and I were married in the month of December, and we have such lovely pictures of us in the snow with the moody lake behind us. Everything was so festive with the Christmas decorations at the church and at the reception lodge that it really carried over into the celebration. And now every year during the holidays, I remember our wedding and get all nostalgic. I wanted that for Denver and Noni, too.

Happy reading!
XO

BONUS CHAPTER FOR
TWISTED TRUTHS
A WEDDING IN MONTANA

Denver strode around the fir tree, his tux askew and his adrenaline up. He and Ryker had checked out the river and outlying forest area. Nobody was after them any longer, but neither he nor his brothers had lost the need to secure any location they found themselves in. Even home.

"Noni doesn't want any guns at the ceremony. Period," Denver told his brother.

"I understand," Ryker said, positioning his Glock farther back in his waistband. With his tux overcoat, it didn't bulge. "See? It's invisible."

Denver rolled his eyes and stood next to the white arch thingy decorated with tons of wild pink roses that had been flown in for the occasion and the white flimsy stuff. The breeze picked up and made the flimsy stuff shimmer with sparkles. Pretty. "I don't have a gun," he said mildly.

Heath strode up with a tray of roses. "Liar," he said, frowning at the tray, his boots crunching the light snow.

Denver stiffened. Snow and the smell of pine wafted around. "An ankle gun doesn't count."

"Oh," Ryker said. "I guess that makes sense." He clapped a hand on Denver's back and looked at the rows of white chairs with an aisle down the middle. "You getting nervous yet?"

Denver took a deep breath, making sure the Montana sky was still nice and blue in an unexpected reprieve from the winter, and it was oddly warm for the day. Good. No clouds. "Not about marrying her. I'm a little nervous she'll come to her senses and make a run for it." At this point, he'd chase her down. She wasn't getting away from him.

"That'd be the smart thing to do," Malloy said, stomping out from behind a pine tree with a Bible in his hand and a heavy coat covering him. "This is crazy. How the hell I let you morons talk me into becoming a pastor online, I'll never know."

Denver grinned. "A sheriff and a pastor. Gun and Bible, buddy. There's power there."

Malloy's brown eyes gleamed. "I guess that's true. Let's just hope no one speaks up when I ask if anybody objects to the union, because I am packing heat."

They were all packing. Sure, they'd been safe in Montana for two months, but still.

Audrey bustled out of the side entrance to the lodge, her body wrapped in a bright red coat. She was due any day now and seemed to be sidling a little bit.

Denver moved down the aisle to her and grasped her biceps. Concern focused him. "Go back inside, Aud. The wedding isn't for another hour, and it's cold out here."

His sister shook her black hair. "I'm always hot, for goodness' sake." She motioned for Heath to come their way, and as soon as he arrived, she reached for the tray of roses in his hands. "Figured you'd need help with this so you didn't stab yourself." She expertly fastened the boutonniere on Denver's lapel. "There you go." Then she made quick work of Ryker's and Heath's.

The simple sweetness of the act took Denver by surprise. His chest filled.

Ryker and Heath moved away to mess with Malloy some more.

Audrey looked up at Denver, her blue eyes soft. "So. I was, you know, thinking."

He paused. During the last two months, as he'd gotten to know this sister of his, she'd never seemed hesitant. Not once. He looked around for any threat and, not seeing one, focused back on her. He'd fix whatever was bothering her. "What's going on?"

She shuffled her boots in the snow. "The weddings I've seen, I mean, the groom always walks down at the beginning with his parents, you know? So I was thinking that maybe I'd walk you down at first."

His heart warmed. "I think that'd be great." Ryker and Heath were his best men, and he thought they would all walk down together. The three of them would be able to make sure she didn't trip or anything. He'd noticed she'd gotten a little off balance as the pregnancy had progressed. "Thanks for offering." He leaned over and kissed her forehead. She had already tunneled right into his heart like a sister should. It was sometimes hard to believe he was this fortunate in life.

She smiled, her eyes twinkling. The wind picked up and dusted her with snow. "You couldn't wait until June for a summer wedding?" she asked, wiping her face off.

"No." He really couldn't wait until June. Talia's adoption papers were almost final, and he and Noni needed to be married for those. Plus, he didn't want to wait to make Noni his wife. He'd waited entirely too long. "Winter weddings are pretty." Or so Noni had said.

Audrey looked around. "They really are. The pictures will be gorgeous with the river behind you and the snow below you."

So long as Noni was in the photos, they'd be gorgeous. He smiled.

Franny and Verna moved out from the lodge, both with sprays of roses wound through their hair. He straightened and glanced at the walkway, making sure it was clear. The younger boys had done a good job of shoveling earlier.

Audrey bit back a smile. "Good luck," she whispered, heading back inside.

He waited until the women had made their way to him. Last week he'd tried to help Franny over some ice and she'd nearly taken his head off, saying she wasn't old enough to need help walking, damn it. He might be slow, but he eventually learned. "Morning, ladies."

Franny lifted an eyebrow. "Just because we gave you permission to marry her doesn't mean we're taken in by your obvious charm."

He leaned closer. The two women were among his favorite in life, and he'd make sure they were safe for the rest of theirs, whether they liked it or not. But he didn't have to tell them that. "Nobody in my entire life has called me charming."

Verna snorted. "I can believe that." She rubbed her gloves together. "Malloy still complaining about being a pastor?"

Denver nodded.

Franny rolled her eyes. "That's why he all but jumped at the chance to get ordained. The man couldn't be happier right now."

Verna's eyes brightened. "I heard from Sally Jones at the general store that he'd been ring shopping in Clerm's jewelry store last week. Rumor has it he bought a doozy of a diamond. Bet you didn't know that."

Actually, Denver had heard that from Ryker, who'd heard it from Mattie. The men were bigger gossips than the women around the ranch. "No," he lied. "That's good stuff."

Verna's eyes gleamed. "I know. Tina will be so surprised."

Considering the veterinarian had been in Clerm's the week before, pointing out to the store owner which ring she liked, probably not. But Denver smiled, enjoying Verna's delight.

Franny cleared her throat. "So. We just wanted to say welcome to the family."

The moment hit him in the gut. It was the first time she'd said that. They accepted him. Finally. His heart swelled, and his body settled. He breathed in. "I promise I'll take care of them both. Noni and Talia. Forever." And any other kids they may have.

Verna leaned up and kissed his chin. "That's what we're counting on." Her eyes teared, and she quickly turned and moved toward the door, pressing her arm through Franny's and helping her along. She leaned down. "We shouldn't call him 'dickhead' any longer," she whispered, her voice carrying easily.

Ryker and Heath approached again. "I hope they still call you 'dickhead,'" Ryker mused. "It's funny."

Heath nodded. "It fits."

Denver grinned, looking at his brothers in their black tuxes and white shirts. Even dressed like civilized people, they looked dangerous. Tall and broad and...family. He lifted his head. "I love you guys." That was all there was to it.

Heath sobered, his eyes darkening. "Yeah. Love you too."

Ryker cleared his throat. "Yeah. Me too."

Malloy stomped by behind them. "Girls. Fucking emotional teenaged girls," he muttered, scattering snow.

Ryker lifted an eyebrow. "You shouldn't swear with a Bible in your hand, Malloy."

"Geez, fuck. You're right." The cop disappeared inside the lodge.

Ryker clapped Denver on the back. "Time to get married, bro."

* * *

Just inside the lodge, Noni shook out the slight ruffle in her white dress. Sparkles adorned the form-fitting bodice that flared at the waist just a little bit. She wore white fur boots beneath the long skirt, but they couldn't be seen.

Franny and Verna fussed, fixing the dress, adding a few more roses to her hair. She'd worn her hair down and long with the pretty blooms winding throughout it. Denver liked her hair down and always had.

She was about to marry Denver. The badass PI who'd turned out to be even more dangerous than she'd initially thought.

Her protector and the man she loved.

The guitar chords played out the sweet song she'd chosen as Zara and Anya walked down the aisle.

"You ready?" Franny asked, messing with her hair. "We can still make a run for it."

Verna leaned closer. "I have the SUV gassed up and pointed toward town. You say the word, and we'll hit the road." She grinned.

Noni chuckled. "I think I'll stick this one out." She sobered, looking at the two women who'd taken her in years ago and made a life around her. "I think I should say something profound here." Tears pricked the backs of her eyes. "But all I've got is *thank you* and I love you. So much."

Franny's eyes swam with tears. "Oh, sweetheart. You made us a family. We love you."

Verna sniffed and smoothed a tear off Noni's face. "We're so happy for you. Denver is a great choice." She swept her hand around the lodge. "And we have such a fun and fulfilling life here. Who would've thought it?"

The music stopped, and the wedding march started. Greg, one of the younger boys, was a heck of a guitar player.

Noni drew in air and shook herself. "Okay. Time to go. You ready?"

The women nodded, each taking one of Noni's arms. They moved out into the bright day. The sun sparkled off a perfect blanket of snow on the ground, looking pristine and promising. She looked at the rows of white chairs.

The four Gray men, muscled and powerful, took up room next to the incredible women Noni had already become close with. Tina sat with the four teenaged boys, who were all serious for their ages but launched into fun more and more each day. Some people from town she'd befriended were in attendance as well as some friends from Alaska.

She was surrounded by people she cared about. How lucky could one woman be? More tears filled her eyes as her emotions overflowed.

She swallowed, walked to the start of the aisle, and paused.

Her heart stopped. Just completely stopped. Denver stood at the end, Talia in his arms, both waiting for her. His brothers were next to him, standing up with him, and Malloy stood in the center with a huge Bible in his hands.

The baby was in a pretty white dress decorated with pink flowers. She kicked out her white snow boots, watching her almost as intently as Denver was. Her family. Noni's heart hitched back into gear, beating fast, filling her with the need to run for them. To get there as soon as possible.

But she straightened her shoulders and let her aunts escort her down the aisle.

Denver's gaze caught hers and held. Blue and bold, intent and possessive, pleased and promising. His black hair ruffled in the wind, giving him the look of a rogue. Holding the baby, he looked strong and capable with just a hint of the danger she knew he held inside.

There was gentleness there as well. And love. A lot of love.

She reached him and her aunts peeled away to their chairs.

He took her hand and leaned down, so far down, to press a kiss to her mouth. She placed her other hand on his ripped chest, feeling the muscles beneath the suit.

"No kissing yet," Malloy muttered, standing in front of them.

Denver straightened. "You ready?" he whispered, his face chiseled and sure.

"I am," she said. "Yes." And she was. After the craziness of the last year, she was more than ready to start their life together in safe and a little wild Montana. "I'm gonna make you mine, Denver Jones."

He straightened, one hand on her and the other holding the baby safe. "You already did, sweetheart. More than a year ago."

Private investigator Ryker Jones has tried to outrun his past. But when he lets down his guard with a beautiful paralegal named Zara Remington, it becomes dangerously clear that his past is resurfacing. And it will use anything—and anyone—to get to him, including Zara...

AN EXCERPT FROM *DEADLY SILENCE* FOLLOWS.

PROLOGUE

Twenty years ago

Ryker never figured he'd find sunshine in hell. He looked up at the shining ball in the too-blue sky. How could it be warm and sunny here? At twelve years old, after spending most of his life in a series of orphanages with a few foster homes thrown in, he knew hell was more of an abstract idea than an actual place.

Some people just ended up there and stayed.

Sure, some of the foster homes had been nice, but he'd been ripped out of those quickly. He'd escaped from the other ones and ended up back in orphanages.

But this place. Oh, this place was something special. Whatever he'd done in a past life to deserve this must've been really bad. A dark need to fight back, to hurt the adults running his life, slithered inside him, and it wasn't the first time, so he probably deserved hell.

But something told him the younger kid fighting the three bullies on the edge of the dirt field didn't deserve this beat down. Or maybe Ryker was just tired of the wrong guys winning every time. North Carolina sun shone down, pretty but not strong, illuminating the scene as the new kid fought hard and fast. And dirty.

"It's time to step in," Heath said, picking a scab on his chin, his wiry body on full alert.

"He's giving a good fight, and those guys need to know he won't roll over if we're not around," Ryker said, his own hands clenching into fists. "We can't always cover his back."

The second Heath had caught sight of the little guy—another wounded animal for him to save—he'd tried to jump into the fray. Ryker had stopped him with a hand on his arm, promising to save the kid when it was time, trying to see the entire picture at once. His heart raced and the injustice of it all clawed through him, but he had to tamp down raw emotions to survive.

It was a lesson he'd learned early and Heath had yet to figure out.

Ryker and Heath had been best friends for the six months they'd spent in the boys home, facing off against too many bullies to count—kids and adults both. Ryker had been at the home for a month when Heath arrived. The kid instantly tried to save a lost kitten he'd found on the outskirts of the ranch. Seeing Heath take a beating for hiding the kitten made Ryker approach him the next day. He'd never approached anybody, but Heath had needed a friend. Maybe Ryker had, too.

Having Heath at his back kept him from going crazy, and he had to adapt and think things through for them both, so they didn't run on emotion and totally screw up. "Let the kid get in one more good shot."

The new kid—a gangly, dark-haired boy—bit into the neck of one of his older attackers, an asshole named Larry. Larry and his buddies were around sixteen and ruled the boys home when the jerk of an owner wasn't telling everyone what to do. They'd be kicked out soon to go be adults.

The kid dug in, slashing deep with his teeth.

"Jesus." Ryker ran forward and yanked the kid away from the bully. If the kid hurt anybody bad enough to need stitches, Ned Cobb, the owner of the boys home, would beat him to death. Stitches cost money.

Blood poured down Larry's cheek, and he slapped a hand to it. "You're gonna die for that, prick."

Ryker got into his face. Even though he was four years younger, they were the same height, and Ryker filled out his shirt better. Fury threatened to eat him whole. "Leave him alone."

Larry snarled. "You taking on another pet, shit-for-brains?"

Ryker stepped closer, and his hands closed into fists. In a couple of seconds, he wouldn't be able to control his temper, so he let it show in his bluish green eyes. "I really wanna hurt you, Larry."

Sometimes the truth just worked.

Larry blinked twice and then backed away. "You are *so* not worth my time." He turned and headed for the older kids dormitory, and his lackeys followed.

"Denver? You okay?" Ryker asked the kid, noting a bruised lip and swelling black eye. He tried to make his voice gentle, but he really didn't know how.

The kid pivoted and faced him squarely, his shoulders bunched.

Ryker held up a hand. "I don't want to hurt you." Too many people had clearly already hurt the boy, and his tortured eyes probably didn't give the whole story. A part of Ryker, the part he didn't like, wanted to walk away and not look back. Not take responsibility for one more person. Not care about one more person since their chances of surviving stunk. He could barely keep Heath from going off the deep end. What if he couldn't help both Heath and Denver? What if he wasn't smart enough or lost his own temper and things went to shit?

The kid whimpered, barely, and it was that sound that gave Ryker no choice.

Ryker straightened. Heath was right. This kid needed help. They could protect him in a way nobody had ever protected Ryker before he'd met Heath. "I broke into the main office and read your file after you got here yesterday." The kid had been abandoned in Denver as an infant and then had been claimed by a so-called uncle who had problems with booze and anger. However, considering the asshole hadn't even known Denver's real name, if he'd had one, there was some doubt there. That was how Denver earned his name, which seemed to fit him anyway. "Your life has sucked so far."

The boy drew back and then snorted.

Ryker grinned. "Your file says you don't really talk." The file didn't say why Denver didn't talk, and Ryker wasn't sure he wanted to know.

Denver didn't answer.

Fair enough. Talking just got kids hit, anyway. Ryker jerked his head toward their dorm. If they could get Denver there, he could take care of the cut bleeding down his chin. "It's gonna be okay. Oh, it's gonna suck for a while, and that's the truth. But in the end, I promise it'll be okay." He'd save this kid when he and Heath made a break for it. From day one, Ryker was all in or all out, and he didn't know how to be another way. If he gave Denver his friendship, his loyalty, it was forever. Heath had been Ryker's only friend, and if Heath needed to save this kid, then so did Ryker.

A car roared up the dirt driveway.

Ryker's gut clenched as he noticed it was the sheriff's dusty brown car.

"Shit," Heath muttered, kicking the dirt. He pushed back his dirty hair. "We don't have time to run."

"No." Ryker settled his stance, his knees wobbling. The owner of the boys home and the sheriff were brothers, which explained why they both liked to hit so much. "Denver? If the sheriff gets out and starts swinging, get behind me, okay?" The kid had already taken one beating, and the sheriff was known to use his nightstick on rib cages.

Denver didn't answer.

The car came to a stop, and Sheriff Cobb jumped out. The sheriff was in his midtwenties with way-too-light blond hair and blue eyes colder than a glacier. Probably. Ryker hadn't ever seen a glacier, but it was the coldest thing he could imagine.

The passenger door opened. "Dr. Daniels," Ryker said, watching the woman carefully, his sides cramping. The urge to run away was overwhelming, but he kept his body visually relaxed. "Here for more tests, ma'am?" He'd been impolite to her once by refusing to take one more damn written test after a long day, and the sheriff had made sure he couldn't walk for about a week without puking up blood. Ned Cobb had watched the beat down with a smile on his face, interjecting only once to remind his brother not to break anything because medical doctors kept records.

The woman stepped out, her fancy designer dress looking as out of place in the dismal home's terrain as a wild peacock would. She smoothed her long dark hair, and her bright red lips pursed. "Ryker. You've grown three inches, and it's been only a few months."

Her voice purred in a way that made him shuffle his feet. It was like she was seeing him differently somehow, and he didn't understand his reaction, but he knew he didn't like it.

Why was she always making Heath and him take written and physical tests? She paid no attention to the other kids at the home.

Then her gaze, a dark blue one, turned to Denver. "I'm here to welcome Denver to the boys home as well as study him a little. Denver, your file says you have a case of selective mutism."

Ah shit. Another test subject? Why them? Ryker glanced at the kid, who'd sidled closer to him. The kid had good instincts to be wary of the calculating woman. "What's that?" Ryker asked.

"He doesn't talk," Heath whispered.

Ryker bit his tongue. No shit. But they had to hide their brains around the lady who had them take so many tests. Why, he didn't know. But his instincts were usually good, too.

"I can make him talk," Sheriff Cobb said, striding around the car and flexing his chest muscles.

Denver swallowed audibly.

"Oh, Elton, that won't be necessary," Sylvia Daniels said, clasping her hands together. "I'm sure I can get Denver to speak. Right, boy?"

Ryker eyed the gun at the sheriff's hip.

Sheriff Cobb's lips peeled back. "Try it, kid. Please."

Ryker didn't answer, but he met the cop's stare evenly. Cobb was just another bully in a world full of them, and someday they were gonna meet on even ground.

When that day came, only one of them would walk away.

Ryker glanced at Heath and then at Denver. His chest heated and cooled. The only way they'd survive this was if he remained calm and used his head, never letting his temper take over. When he stopped thinking, he was as bad as the sheriff, and now with Heath and Denver counting on him, he had more to lose than Sheriff Cobb did. That had to count for something, right?

CHAPTER
1

Present day

Zara Remington brushed a stray tendril of her thick hair back from her face before checking on the lasagna. The cheese bubbled up through the noodles while the scent of the garlic bread in the oven warmer filled the country-style kitchen. Perfect. She shut the oven door and glanced at the clock. Five minutes.

He'd be there in *five minutes*.

It had been weeks since she'd seen him, and her body was ready and primed for a tussle. *Just a tussle.* Shaking herself, she repeated the mantra she'd coined since meeting him two months ago: Temporary. They were temporary and just for fun. This was her reward for working so hard: a walk on the wild side. Even if she was the type to settle down and devote herself to one man, it wouldn't be this one.

Ryker Jones kept one foot out the door, even while naked in her bed doing things to her that were illegal in the Southern states. Good damn thing she lived in Cisco. Wyoming didn't care what folks did behind closed doors. Thank God.

She hummed and eyed the red high heels waiting by the entry to the living room. They probably wouldn't last on her feet for long, but she'd greet him wearing them. While she still wore the black pencil skirt and gray silk shirt she'd donned for work, upon reading his text that he was back in town, she'd rushed to change into a scarlet bra and G-string set that matched the shoes before putting her clothes back into place.

If she was living out a fantasy, he should get one, too. The guy didn't have to know she'd worn granny-style Spanx panties and a thin cotton bra all day.

A roar of motorcycle pipes echoed down her quiet street. Tingles exploded in her abdomen. Hurrying for the shoes, she bit back a wince upon slipping her feet in. The little kitten heels she'd worn to work had been much more comfortable.

A minute passed and the pipes silenced.

She drew air in through her nose, counted to five, and exhaled. Calm down. Geez. She really needed to relax. The sharp rap on her front door sent her system into overdrive again.

Straightening her shoulders, she tried to balance in the heels as she passed her comfortable sofa set, the shoes clicking on the polished hardwood floor. She had to wipe her hands down her skirt before twisting the knob and opening the door. "Ryker," she breathed.

He didn't smile. Instead, his bluish green eyes darkened as his gaze raked her from head to toe…and back up. "I've missed you." The low rumble of his voice, just as dangerous as the motorcycle pipes, licked right where his gaze had been.

She nodded, her throat closing. He was every vision of a badass bad boy she'd ever fantasized about. His thick black hair curled over the collar of a battered leather jacket that covered a broad, well-muscled chest. Long legs, encased in faded jeans, led to motorcycle boots. His face had been shaped with strong lines and powerful strokes, and a shadow lined his cut jaw. But those eyes. Greenish blue and fierce, they changed shades with his mood.

As she watched, those odd eyes narrowed. "What the fuck?"

She self-consciously fingered the slash of a bruise across her right cheekbone. Cover-up had concealed it well enough all day, but leave it to Ryker to notice. He didn't miss anything. God, that intrigued her. His vision was oddly sharp, and once he'd mentioned hearing an argument several doors down. She hadn't heard a thing. "It's nothing." She stepped back to allow him entrance. "I have a lasagna cooking."

He moved into her, heat and his scent of forest and leather brushing across her skin. One knuckle gently ran across the bruise. "Who hit you?" The tone held an edge of something dark.

She shut the door and moved away from his touch. "What? Who says somebody hit me?" Turning on the heels and barely keeping from landing on her butt, she walked toward the kitchen, remembering to sway her hips before making it past the couch. "I have to get dinner out or it'll burn." She kept several frozen dishes ready to go, not knowing when he'd be back in town. The domestication worked well for them both, and she liked cooking for him. Enjoyed taking care of him like that... for this brief affair, or whatever it was. "I hope you haven't eaten."

"You know I haven't." He stopped inside the kitchen. "Zara."

She gave an involuntary shiver from his low tone and drew the lasagna from the oven and bread from the warmer before turning around to see him lounging against the doorjamb. "Isn't this when you pour wine?" Her heart fluttered at seeing the contrast between her pretty butter yellow cabinets and the deadly rebel calmly watching her. "I have the beer you like."

"You always have the beer I like." He didn't move a muscle, and this time a warning threaded through his words in a tone like gravel crumbling in a crusher. "I asked you a question."

She forced a smile and carried the dishes to the breakfast nook, which she'd already set with her favorite Apple-patterned dinner-ware and bright aqua linens. "And I asked you one." Trying to ignore the tension vibrating from him, she grasped a lighter for the candles.

A hand on her arm spun her around. She hadn't heard him move. How did he do that?

He leaned in. "Then I'll answer yours. I know what a woman looks like who's been hit. I know by the color and slant of that bruise how much force was used, how tall the guy was, and which hand he used. What I don't know … is the name of the fucker. Yet."

"How do you know all of that?" she whispered.

He lifted his head, withdrawing. "I just do."

There it was. He'd share his body and nothing else with her. She didn't even know where he lived when he wasn't on a case. From day one he'd been clear that this wasn't forever, that he wasn't interested in a future. Neither was she. He was her first purely physical affair, and that's why he could mind his own business. "Bully for you." She shoved past him for the wine waiting on the counter and twisted in the corkscrew with a little more force than was necessary. Why was he changing the game on her?

"Are you seeing somebody else?"

She stilled. Hurt, surprising in its sharpness, cut through her. "No." Yanking out the cork, she turned to face him. "We said we'd be exclusive for however long we, ah, saw each other."

He rubbed the scruff on his chin, studying her. "Part of exclusivity means nobody hurts what's mine."

She blinked twice at the possessive language. "I think we both know I'm not yours." What was going on with him? She studied him closer. Lines fanned out from his eyes, and a tenseness lived in his broad shoulders. "Are you okay?"

Without moving, he seemed to withdraw. "Yes. Been on a case."

"Is it finished?"

"No." A vein stood out along his tough-guy neck.

Ah. Ryker was a private detective who specialized in finding the hard to find. "Want to talk about it?"

"No."

Yeah, she'd figured. "Then let's relax." She poured two glasses of Cabernet and took a seat, carefully unfolding her napkin. Her toes ached in the sexy shoes, and for the first time, she wondered if all the effort was worth it. "We can have a nice dinner."

Slowly, he shrugged out of his jacket and draped it on his chair, drawing the chair out to sit, his movements controlled and with a hint of something... violent.

Her breath caught, and she filled their plates.

"I like your hair down," he rumbled, reaching for his napkin.

"Yet I kept it up," she said primly. They were on even footing. This was casual, and apparently they both needed a quick reminder. Sitting back, she took a deep drink of the potent brew, almost humming when it warmed her stomach.

He lifted his chin, amusement partially banishing the irritation in his eyes. "Have I done something to piss you off?"

Her gaze dropped to the food. "No." She wasn't being fair. Her law firm had hired him as a private investigator on a case, and one night after going through files together and drinking way too much beer, they'd ended up in bed for the most fantastic night of her life. He'd made it clear it was just temporary, *they* were just casual, and she'd agreed with her eyes wide open, meeting up whenever he was back in town. "You haven't done anything."

"Then why won't you tell me who hurt you?"

She sighed, her gaze meeting his. "Because that's not what we have."

"Oh?" One eyebrow drew up. "What do we have?"

She snorted and then caught herself, embarrassed. "We have this." She gestured toward the food. "And sex. That's all. Food and sex." He'd never proclaimed to be a knight in shining armor, especially hers, so why all the questions? "My everyday life doesn't include you. You're a fantasy who shows up periodically for fun, and then you're gone. Stop acting like you're more."

If the words affected him in any way, he didn't show it. Instead, he reached for his wine, his gaze holding hers like a lion watching a doe, and drank down the entire glass. Setting it aside, he tossed his napkin on the table. "Are you hungry?"

"Not even a little bit." She was more out of sorts than she'd thought.

"Good." He pushed back from the table, stood, and moved toward her. "This is a conversation better had where I can touch you." Dipping his shoulder, he lifted her in corded arms.

She yelped and grabbed his chest for balance. "What are you doing?" she whispered. How was he so strong? Even for a healthy guy who worked out, his strength was somehow beyond the norm. Fluid and natural.

He turned, grabbed his jacket, and strode for the living room, dropping onto her couch and setting those thick boots on her glass coffee table. The jacket had landed next to him. One arm remained beneath her knees and the other around her shoulders, easily cradling her against his rock-hard chest. His lips snapped over her jugular with just enough force to make her jump.

Then, clearly indulging himself, he tugged the clip from her hair, which cascaded down. Burying his face in the mass of dark curls, he breathed in. "I love your hair."

She tried to perch primly on his lap and not snuggle right into him. His strength was as much of a draw as his passion. "What conversation did you want to have?"

He leaned back and waited until she'd turned her head to face him. "We agreed to keep this casual."

"I know." She played with a loose thread on his dark T-shirt.

"Then you started cooking me dinner."

She blinked. "I like to cook."

"Then you started keeping my beer on hand and lighting candles with every meal."

She shrugged. "Candles create nice light that helps with digestion." Could she sound like any more of a dork?

"Right." He played idly with her hair, heat from his body keeping her toasty warm.

Flutters awakened again throughout her body, and her nipples hardened. Good thing the bright red bra had plenty of padding. She tried to shift her weight, not surprised when he kept her easily in place. "I have not asked you for anything," she murmured, panic beginning to take hold.

"I like that about you." He punctuated the words with a tug on her hair. "In fact, I like you."

"I like you, too." The words went unsaid, but that's all they had, and that's all they were. It was an adventure, and she was truly enjoying the ride. She knew where they stood. "Stop playing with me."

"I'm not playing." His gaze dropped to her lips right before he leaned in to rest his mouth over hers.

Liquid fire shot from her chest to her sex.

He nibbled on her bottom lip, kissed the corners of her mouth, lightly whispering against her. "This is playing." The hand in her hair twisted, drawing back her head and elongating her neck. "This is not." He swooped in, angled his mouth over hers, and took. Deep and hard, he kissed her, his mouth alone having enough power to drive her head back against his palm.

Hunger slammed through her, and she moaned low in her throat.

Pleasure swamped her, head to toe, vibrating in waves as she kissed him back. Her nails dug into his chest, and she tried to move closer into him. He controlled the kiss, taking her deeper, his erection easily discernible beneath her butt.

Finally, he lifted his head, his eyes the color of a rocky riverbed beneath a stormy sky. "Who hit you?"

The simple words struck like a splash of cold water in the face. Shock dropped her mouth open. Had he been trying to manipulate her by kissing her like that? Sure, he'd been passionate with her many times, but something felt different. A wildness she'd always sensed in him seemed to be breaking free. "Forget you." Slamming her hand against his chest, she shoved off his lap.

"Zara." One word, perfectly controlled. He held up a hand, showing a long scar across his love line. One that he'd never explained, even when she'd asked nicely.

Her knees shook, but she backed away until her shoulders hit the fireplace mantel. Anger and panic welled up in her, and she couldn't separate them and think, so she just spoke. "Unless we're eating or screwing, my life is none of your business." She was trying hard to keep her sanity and *so* did not need mixed signals from him. He didn't get to act like he really cared—not that way. "Got it?"

He stood, towering over her even from several feet away. "That may be true, but no way am I going to let anybody harm the woman I'm fuckin'."

Fuckin'. Yeah, that's exactly what they were doing. She was so out of her depth, she'd lost sight of the shore miles ago. "Stay in your own compartment, Ryker. My business is my own, and you're not to get involved."

For the first time, anger sizzled across his features. "Be careful what you say, little girl. I'll make you eat those words."

She blinked. Sure, he'd been commanding in bed...a lot. But

outside the bedroom, she'd never seen this side of him. "Don't threaten me."

"Then don't be obtuse. If you think I'm going to allow a man who hit you to keep walking, you've lost your damn mind." He put both hands on his fit hips, looking like a pissed-off warrior about to bellow a battle cry. "We may be casual, but even I have limits. A woman who cries on my shoulder after watching a stupid movie with dogs is someone who should never be harmed."

She gasped. "It wasn't stupid." It was sad when Juniper had died, darn it.

"Yeah. It was one of the dumbest movies ever made, and you turned into my shoulder to cry it out." He took a step toward her. "You don't want to mess with me on this. Trust me. Just give me the name, and tell me what's going on." Another step.

She couldn't back up any more or she'd be in the fireplace. So she held out a hand. Panic cramped her stomach, and she sucked in air and tried for anger. There it was. "I created a situation, there was an issue, and I've taken care of it." The truth would change his opinion of her, and she kind of enjoyed the view from the pedestal he temporarily had her on.

"No way did you create any situation that resulted in violence." The tone was almost mocking.

"That's it. You don't know me." Her chin lifted.

Something too dark to be amusement lifted his lips. "Oh, don't I?"

"No, you don't." Steam should be coming out of her ears. She reached down and plucked a high heel off. It was time to stop pretending to be somebody she just was *not*. "I don't like these, and I sure as shit don't walk around at work in them." Her tone was two octaves higher than normal, and she couldn't help it. Angling back, she threw the shoe at his head.

With lightning-quick reflexes, he grabbed the strap before the

shoe took out his eye. "Zara." The tone was low and controlled...
like always.

"You wouldn't like the real me." She kicked off the other shoe,
her mind buzzing and her temper flying free. Reaching under her
skirt, she yanked off the G-string underwear that had been shoved
up her butt, her legs wobbling when she pulled them down and over
her feet. "*Nobody* likes these." She flung it at his head. "I only wear
them for you."

He snatched the flimsy material with one finger, his cheek
creasing.

She fought the urge to stomp her foot and look like an idiot. He
wasn't getting it. "I don't even know where you live," she yelled.

His phone buzzed, and he held up a hand. "Put the tantrum on
hold, just for a second." Drawing the phone out, he read the screen.
Both his eyebrows drew down, and he lifted the phone to his ear.
"We've had movement?" Then he held still. His jaw hardened even
more. "Damn it. Okay, I'm going." He paused, and his eyes darkened. "Because you just got shot. It's my turn to go, and I'll be right
there." He shoved his phone back into his pocket.

Her breath heated. "Who got shot?"

"My brother."

Ryker had a brother?

He took several steps forward to grasp her neck.

She stilled. He'd never grabbed her neck before. Sure, his hold
was gentle, but his hand was *wrapped around her neck*. "What are you
doing?" she squeaked.

He leaned in, pressing just enough to show his strength. "I know
you don't wear shoes like that at work, and I know the underwear set
is just for me. I like that." He pressed a hard kiss to her mouth before
drawing away. "I have to go, or I'd stay until we reached an agreement tonight. That bruise on your face offends me, and I'm done

coddling you about it. You've got until tomorrow morning to give me the name of the guy who hit you, so I can have a conversation with him."

Ryker released her to grab his jacket and stride for the front door.

"Or what?" she asked, her voice trembling.

He opened the door and paused, looking back at her. "Or I'll find him myself and take him out for good." He yanked on his jacket, looking exactly like the badass rambling man he was. "And Zara? About where I live?"

"Yeah?"

"I moved permanently to Cisco a week ago."

Can't get enough of *New York Times* bestselling author
Rebecca Zanetti's Blood Brothers series?

SEE HOW IT ALL BEGAN...

DEADLY
SILENCE

LETHAL
LIES

'When it comes to high-octane thrillers, they don't get better than
Zanetti' *RT Book Reviews* on *Lethal Lies*

'Sexy and emotional, and filled with a rich look at love in all its
forms' *Washington Post* on *Deadly Silence*

Available from

HEADLINE
ETERNAL

CHECK OUT *NEW YORK TIMES* BESTSELLING
AUTHOR REBECCA ZANETTI'S SEXY
SIN BROTHERS SERIES.

FORGOTTEN SINS

SWEET REVENGE

BLIND FAITH

TOTAL SURRENDER

Available from

HEADLINE
ETERNAL

For thrilling passion played out against a dangerous
race for survival, look out for Rebecca Zanetti's
The Scorpius Syndrome series:

MERCURY STRIKING

SHADOW FALLING

JUSTICE ASCENDING

Available from

HEADLINE
ETERNAL